CAPTAIN CUTLASS

ALSO BY GORDON D. SHIRREFFS

CAPTAIN CUTLASS

GORDON D. SHIRREFFS

WOLFPACK
PUBLISHING
— EST 2013 —

Captain Cutlass
Paperback Edition
Copyright © 2024 (As Revised) Gordon D. Shirreffs

Wolfpack Publishing
701 S. Howard Ave. 106-324
Tampa, Florida 33609

wolfpackpublishing.com

Paperback ISBN 978-1-63977-302-2
eBook ISBN 978-1-63977-104-2

The master, the swabber, the boatswain, and I,
The gunner, and his mate,
Loved Mall, Meg, and Marian, and Margery,
But none of us cared for Kate.
For she had a tongue with a tang,
Would cry to a sailor "Go hang!"

— WILLIAM SHAKESPEARE, *THE*
TEMPEST

CAPTAIN CUTLASS

ONE

Hispaniola was a dark green mantle of vegetation rising from the sea off the port bow of the 42-gun privateer *Adventuress*. It was early dusk off Cabo Beata. The sea breeze had been fading steadily since sunset, and it was too early for the evening land breeze to spring up from the island.

Captain Alexander Campbell stood alone at the port rail on the quarterdeck of the slim and lovely Dutch-built frigate. He studied the distant shoreline through his long brass telescope, seeking the almost invisible entrance into the large landlocked bay that lay just behind the cape. Every officer of the privateer was on deck that dusk, looking at the cape. The entire crew, with the single exception of the man at the whipstaff helm, had their eyes on the lovely panorama of the island. Lushly beautiful as Hispaniola was, it always had an aura of mystery and danger about it. Every man jack aboard the *Adventuress* knew that if the frigate were trapped within the bay, were run aground, or were to split her hull on an uncharted rock, there would be no quarter shown to the crew by the Spanish garrison of Hispaniola or the powerful patrol ships of the *guarda-costa*.

"Captain Cutlass, sir!" Miles Yeoman, the frigate's sailing master, called boldly, out of sheer desperation. "The night is closing in too swiftly! Should we not lie off and on until dawn light, sir?"

Ian MacMillan, the Scots giant who was master gunner, gripped Miles Yeoman by an arm and shook his head. He did not speak, but his eyes and expression should be enough warning to Yeoman not to disturb Alec Campbell.

Alec turned slowly. The fitful sea breeze ruffled his long, sandy-colored hair. The twisted white scar that marred his left cheek, beginning from just beneath his left eye and traversing his cheek to vanish into his short reddish beard, stood out in vivid contrast to his mahogany-hued face skin. His light gray eyes thoughtfully studied the sailing master.

Yeoman walked forward. "I meant no disrespect, sir," he offered. "I was but concerned for the ship."

Alec shook his head. "None taken, Miles. Ye fear for the ship, and I do as well, but it's a risk we must take this evening if we are to rendezvous here with Kate Devon and Jacques Montbars."

Rais Gilles, Huguenot gentleman adventurer and captain of the afterguard, smiled easily. "We can't take chances with Jack Spaniard, sir. We might have been seen already by a *guarda-costa*. It wouldn't take a patrol ship of theirs long to reach their base at Bahia de Neiba to alert the squadron there."

Alec nodded. "True, but our business should be done here this night, Rais, providing Kate Devon and Montbars are in the rendezvous bay behind the cape. If they are, and we can conclude our agreement to attack the Spanish plate fleet together, we should be gone from Hispaniola with the dawn breeze."

Ian MacMillan spat over the lee rail. "I'd damned near rather trust Jack Spaniard than that bloody French devil Montbars, and I'm not too sure about Kate Devon either."

"Ye know we can't attack the treasure fleet without them, Ian. If we tried it alone, we'd be blown clear out of the water by their combined gunpower."

"We've always done well enough wi'out them!"

"True, laddie, but we've never had a crack at a sea monster of a plate ship like the *Nuestra Señora de la Candelaria*. Ye know she'll be herded along by a swarm of swift, heavily armed *naos* and *urcas*, those damnable fighting galleons, manned by crack crews, each of which easily carries as much metal as we do in the way of cannon. We couldn't get past them alone to attack the plate ship, and even if we did, we'd be half torn to pieces by the fighting galleons if we did defeat them."

Solemn Pieter Van Heydt, the boatswain, a bearded Hollander and a top-rated seaman and shipwright, spoke up: "Aye, skipper, and the *Nuestra Señora de la Candelaria* is said to fear nothing for herself but the land and fire. A mighty ship and perhaps the greatest of all the plate ships."

Surgeon Terence Shannon, North Irishman and once sawbones for the mighty Henry Morgan himself, nodded his head. "I saw her once, in Portugal, when I was there on a merchant ship. Before God, mates, she was as high as a sea cliff, with row after row of gunports wi' great cannon stickin' their ugly snouts out at ye like the jagged teeth of a flame-breathing dragon. When she fires a broadside, it's like an erupting volcano, so much that her crew call her the *Caca-fuego*—the *'Shitfire.'* It is said that she's sheathed with tough, resilient lanang wood from the Philippines, against which none but the heaviest shot will prevail. She's old now and very slow, but the *Adventuress* can't take her alone. We'll need the help of Kate Devon and Montbars."

Alec cupped his hands about his mouth. "Ahoy, mast-head! What do ye see?"

The lookout leaned over the rim of the crow's nest on the tall mainmast. "I think I can make out the topmasts of one ship within the bay, sir. A large ship, I think it is."

"Only one ship?"

"It's hard to tell against the trees and the dusk light, sir, but I think there is only one ship."

Alec Campbell rested his strong swordsman's hands on the teak rail and studied the shoreline. The decision was ulti-mately his, as it always was with any commander. This was the great loneliness of a leader of fighting men.

It was very quiet except for the soft thrumming of the wind through the myriad ropes and lines of the taut rigging and the muted chuckling of the water under the forefoot. Five bells rang out suddenly.

These were hostile waters and deadly to any nationality but Spaniards, as were most of the waters throughout the

Caribbean—the Spanish Lake. Most pirates, privateers, and buccaneers could command respect for their ships only as far as their largest cannon could carry. With the exceptions of bawdy, licentious Port Royal on Jamaica and Tortuga Island off the north coast of Haiti, there were few sanctuaries for the Brethren of the Coast, except for the open sea and a fair wind.

Alec raised his brass telescope and ran it out to its full length. The fine German lens picked out the three topmasts of what should be a rather large ship lying hidden within the landlocked bay. Was it the *Kate of Devon,* named after her beautiful red-headed mistress, or was it Jacques-Vincent Montbars' ship, the *Exterminator?* Or was it a Jack Spaniard, one of their powerful *guarda-costa naos,* carrying heavy metal and with her guns double-shotted and trained on the channel entrance into the bay, waiting for Captain Cutlass to poke the lovely nose of the *Adventuress* into the rendezvous? Whoever was in the bay would be well aware of the presence of the frigate by now.

Alec snapped shut the telescope. The decision had to be made *now.* There was little enough time and daylight left as it was. He turned and strode to the break of the quarterdeck. "Mister Yeoman!" he bellowed. "Get the courses and topgallants off her! Mister Heydt! Get a leadsman into the forechains! Mister MacMillan! Clear the main-deck guns for action!"

Calloused bare feet slapped the deck planking. Blocks creaked as the seamen under the verbal lashing of Sailing Master Yeoman and Boatswain Heydt furled the fore, main, and mizzen courses and got in the towering topgallant sails. *Adventuress* began slowly to close the land with only the topsails and the spritsail drawing wind.

The breech trappings of the bronze 18-pounder deck guns were cast loose and the tompions removed from their muzzles. Each gunner lighted his slow match. Powder monkeys came up from the powder magazine deep in the bowels of the ship, carrying cartridges and canvas bags of powder to the guns. Gunners, spongers, and rammers stood to at their respective guns.

Rais Gilles ordered his sharpshooters into the tops. They

climbed slowly up the ratlines carrying their arquebuses. Cutlasses and pistols were served out to the crew. The officers, with the lone exception of Cutlass, had armed themselves and put on their steel morion helmets.

"Any need for me to take me post of duty now, Cutlass?" Terence Shannon asked lazily.

Alec grinned. "I don't want ye to miss the evening breeze, cousin. It will be hot as the hinges of hell's own door down in the cockpit."

"Then you expect no action, eh, captain?" Rais Gilles queried.

Alec shrugged. "No, but it's better to be ready than to be sorry, Rais. We always sail the razor's edge in these waters."

"Main-deck guns cleared for action, sir!" Ian MacMillan bellowed.

"Fast time, Mister MacMillan!" Alec cried back.

The dusk light was almost completely gone. The frigate ghosted through the dimness under topsails alone.

"What depth do ye have in the chains?" Alec called out.

"No ground with this line, sir," the leadsman replied.

Miles Yeoman came aft. "It shoals fast before too long, captain, if I recall these waters." The Bristol seadog had a veritable chart of these dangerous waters in his head.

Alec looked toward the darkened land. They had not signaled as yet, if it was indeed either Kate Devon or Montbars, or perhaps both of them.

"What the hell is the matter with them!" Miles snapped. "Why don't they signal?"

Almost as though in answer to his question, a dim yellow light flashed out from the low, tree-covered headland on the starboard side of the channel. Then, one by one, three lights were hung in a vertical line.

"The agreed-upon signal!" Rais Gilles cried.

"By the deep fifteen!" the leadsman called out. "And a half fourteen! And a half fourteen! By the mark thirteen! And a half twelve! By the mark twelve! By the mark twelve!"

Alec glanced at Miles. "Shoaling fast, just as ye forecast."

The breeze had almost died away. The topsails fluttered as they began to lose wind.

"Hang three lighted lanterns in the fore rigging, Mister

Heydt, if ye will," Alec called out. "After three minutes, extinguish the first light, in another three minutes, the second light, and so on."

"You surely won't attempt the channel in the dark, eh, Cutlass?" the surgeon asked.

"No. There will be a gibbous moon later on, but I won't risk the ship in there even then. It would be like threading a needle. Miles, have the longboat readied."

"By the mark ten! And a half-nine! And a half-nine! By the mark eight! Quarter less eight! Quarter less eight!" the leadsman chanted monotonously.

Alec looked up at the sails. "Back the main topsail, Mister Yeoman."

The *Adventuress* slowly lost its way. The longboat was swung out overside and lowered into the water with a creaking and straining of tackle.

"I want picked men in her, Rais," Alec ordered.

The Frenchman nodded. He hesitated, looking closely at Alec.

"Including yourself, Rais," Alec added with a sly grin.

The mizzen and fore-topsails were backed, and the frigate drifted on the dark waters. The wind was almost completely gone.

"Mister Yeoman," Alec instructed the sailing master, "once I leave the ship, ye will take her offshore with what little wind we have left. Ye will lie off and on until dawn."

"Shall I bring her in then, sir?"

Alec shook his head. "Not until ye see my signal. I trust Montbars not at all and Kate Devon only when I see her standing in front of me."

Rais grinned evilly. "Or lying naked under you, and unarmed, eh, Cutlass?"

Alec shrugged. "Not even then, Rais. She can bite and scratch like a drunken wildcat if ye can't satisfy her."

"Has that ever happened to *ye*, Cutlass?" Terence asked slyly.

Alec walked to the break of the quarterdeck. "Tattoo! My broadsword, dirk, and pistols!" He turned. "Not yet, cousin," he added with supreme self-satisfaction. He half smiled reminiscently. "However, there have been a few times…"

Tattoo, the giant black, came noiselessly up the port ladder to the quarterdeck. His torso was wedge-shaped from his slender waist to his wide shoulders. His long arms and legs were corded with smooth, long muscles. The faint light from the binnacle lamp shone on his oiled skin and revealed his high cheekbones with the raised cicatrices of his tribal markings on them, for he was a Koromantyn, a Gold Coast slave of that type distinguished for activity, courage, and stubbornness. Years past, Alec Campbell had saved him from a *piragua* full of cannibal Carib Indians, who had been taking him to their island to castrate him so that he would fatten for a feast. He was devoted to Alec, with good reason.

Tattoo handed Alec his figured leather baldric, from which, depended his sheathed Highland broadsword. Alec hung it over his right shoulder so that the basket-hilted broadsword was at his left side. Tattoo ceremoniously handed Alec his famed Highland dirk, a mate to the ancient broadsword of Alec's ancestors. The dirk was figured with silver and had an immense cairngorm, or topaz, set in its head. On the side of the sheath in smaller sheaths were his knife and fork for dining. Both broadsword and dirk were heirlooms of Alec's family, the Campbells of Cawdor. The dirk hung at his right side.

Last, but not least, Tattoo handed Alec his *sqian-dubh*, or "black knife," the short-bladed, last-resort weapon without which no self-respecting Highlander would be seen in public. Alec slid the short weapon into a sheath on the top of his right seaboot.

Tattoo opened a polished teakwood case to reveal a pair of highly polished, brass-barreled, all-metal Highland flint-lock pistols with ram's horn butts made by Andrew Fletcher, that master of all Scottish gunsmiths. Alec slipped both pistols into loops on his baldric. Tattoo handed him a "mur-therer," a short, stubby, four-barreled, all-metal flintlock pistol with cannon-shaped barrels, which Alec slipped into the large righthand pocket of his full-skirted coat.

Alec grinned at the huge black. "Now we're all ready for the social graces of the evening, eh, Tattoo?"

Tattoo grinned back. "Yes, master. You can kill quick now."

Pieter Heydt had extinguished the three lanterns at three-minute intervals. The deck of the frigate was now dark except for the faint light from the binnacle lamp. The eyes of every man on deck were on the three vertically hung lanterns standing out sharp against the darkness of the low headland. One light blinked out. Every man began to count to himself. In three minutes, the second light went out. Three minutes later, the headland was as dark as it had been before the three lanterns had been hung there.

"It's them, all right," Miles Yeoman said.

Alec shrugged. "Maybe. Maybe not."

"Ye may be entering a trap, Cutlass," Terence Shannon warned.

"Who else would know our prearranged signal? Who else other than Kate Devon and Montbars? The Spaniards could hardly have learned them."

"Perhaps I wasn't thinking of Jack Spaniard, cousin."

Alec looked quickly at the Irishman. He had a gift of his Celtic blood, the "second sight." "What do ye mean?" he asked the surgeon.

Terence shrugged. "There is a high price on your head, Cutlass. The Spaniards would pay much to get ye into their hands again. No other *corsaire luterano* ever escaped their Inquisition as ye did five years past. Perhaps Montbars remembers that. Perhaps he might think it wiser to invest in turning ye over to the Spaniards for that reward, instead of working with us to take the Cacafuego."

Rais Gilles hung his baldric over his right shoulder. "Who knows that? Nothing ventured, nothing gained, good surgeon. You yourself said we can't take the Cacafuego alone."

"I wonder if even three ships such as ours could take her."

Rais smiled. He watched Alec Campbell descend the ladder to the main deck. "No, not three average ships, but what ships can compare with the *Adventuress* and the ships of Kate Devon and Montbars' *Exterminator?* Especially if they are to be led by Captain Cutlass himself?"

There was no rebuttal from the Irishman.

Miles Yeoman looked over the rail and down at Alec as he seated himself in the sternsheets of the longboat. "Captain Campbell, sir. If we don't hear from you by dawn, we'll come in to get you."

Alec looked up at the row of hard faces lining the railing. Most of them had been with him in the five years he had spent privateering in the *Adventuress*, and indeed, some of them had served with him along with Henry Morgan, the greatest buccaneer of them all. "Don't endanger the ship or your lives, mates. We'll be all right." He turned. "Fend off, coxswain. Give way together."

The longboat was pushed away from the looming black side of the frigate. The oars creaked in their tholepins as they dipped into the water. The longboat disappeared into the darkness and out of view of the crew of the frigate. The only signs of the longboat's passage were the little pools of phosphorescence that swirled about the oar blades.

The *Adventuress* drifted off into the thick premoon darkness, away from the shoal water and out of sight.

The shoreline was barely distinguishable except for the humped shape of the headland and the larger silhouette of the island behind it. It was very quiet except for the splashing sound of the oars dipping into the water and the chuckling of the parted water beneath the cutwater of the boat.

"It's like crossing the Styx in Charon's ferryboat," Rais muttered.

"Maybe it is, Rais. If those are Spaniards in there, we'll likely not get back."

"Damn you! Must you forecast so?"

Alec grinned. "Are ye nervous, Frenchman?"

"Damned if I am! You know me better than that, Scot!"

"I'll admit I'm nervous, Rais. It's only the unknown that frightens us in the Trade. We fear little else that we can see." Alec looked forward at Tattoo. The giant black stood in the bows of the longboat. His head was raised, and his eyes were half closed as though he was scenting and listening.

The coxswain touched Alec's sleeve. "We're in the

channel current now, sir. I can feel the tug of it. About three knots, I'd say."

The headlands on each side of the narrow channel seemed to close in on the boat. They were as black as pitch. One cannon shot, or perhaps a large rock dropped from either height, would hole the longboat and send her to the bottom.

"Tattoo!" Alec called softly. "Go in, if ye will."

The black stepped upon both of the gunwales of the bows. He withdrew his long-bladed sheath knife from his loincloth and placed it between his filed teeth. He arched cleanly into the dark waters and disappeared from sight.

Alec looked at the coxswain. "Way enough, Kelly."

"Oars," the coxswain commanded.

The blades were raised, dripping from the water.

The longboat drifted slowly into the inner channel on the current.

Half an hour passed.

There was a faint trace of moonlight in the eastern sky.

Something moved in the water behind the stern of the longboat.

Alec leaned over the transom. "Tattoo?"

The black head rose out of the water. Alec helped Tattoo into the boat. "Kate Devon? Montbars?" he asked.

Tattoo nodded. "Both ships, master."

Alec turned to the coxswain. "Take us in, Kelly."

The longboat moved quickly in, deep between the headlands, aided by the current. The channel was narrow and twisted to starboard so that the bay could not be seen from the sea. As the longboat rounded the starboard headland, stern lamp lights could be seen shimmering in reflection upon the calm waters of the bay.

The two ships swung at anchor—the *Kate of Devon,* a graceful 36-gun fighting *nao,* once a Spanish fighting ship, and the looming, slab-sided, 52-gun *Exterminator.*

Rais Gilles pointed at the *Exterminator.* "It was Montbars who did not house his topmasts so that they could not be seen from the sea, as you requested him to do."

Alec nodded. "No one can ever tell Montbars what to do, even if it's for his own good."

"If they had been seen by the Spaniards..." Rais' voice trailed off, "...they could have cut them off both by land and by sea, and we might have sailed into a trap."

"What boat is that?" the harsh voice of the officer of the deck bellowed from the sterncastle of the *Exterminator.*

"The *Adventuress!*" Kelly called out in approved "man-o'-war" style, giving the name of the ship whose captain was aboard the longboat.

"You mean the boat of Captain Cutlass?" the officer sneered. He did not like "man-o'-war" or privateer customs and manners in the least.

"He means the *Adventuress,* damn ye!" Alec snapped.

There was a moment's hesitation. "Captain Montbars is aboard the *Kate of Devon,* sir..." The "sir" seemed to be dragged reluctantly out of the man.

Alec spat over the side. "No damned discipline aboard those bloody pirates!" he growled.

The longboat came smartly alongside the *Kate of Devon.* Alec stepped easily from the longboat to ascend the Jacob's ladder to the deck of the *nao.*

"Captain Campell?" the officer of the deck queried. He knew who Alec was, of course, for few members of the Brethren of the Coast did not.

Alec smiled. He extended his right hand to grasp that of the officer. "How are ye, Macklin? It's been some time since we sailed together."

Ira Macklin was more than pleased at being recognized by Alec. "That was on the Campeche raid, eh, sir? Those were great times."

"There are greater times coming, Macklin. I want my boat's crew on board here tonight. Ye'll give them the best of your ship's comfort?"

"Have no fear. The very best. Captains Devon and Montbars are in the great cabin aft. They've been waiting for you."

A sentry stood at the break of the poop, guarding the doorway that led into the great stern cabin of the *nao.* "I'll let the captain know ye are here, sir," he said. He entered the great cabin.

Alec looked about the deck of the fighting ship. He knew

her well. Once, she had been an escort *nao* to the plate fleets which sailed the Windward Passage on their voyage to Spain, deep laden with the treasures of Peru, the Orient, and Mexico. She had been the *Invincible* then, captained by Don Rodrigo Alonzo de Mendez, a first-class fighting man, and had fallen back as a rearguard for the plate fleet with three other *naos*, to allow time for the treasure ships to beat their way northeast through the Windward Passage. Dogging the fleet had been a combined force of seven pirate and privateer vessels out of Port Royal on The Account. Among the hungry pack of freebooters had been Alec in his *Adventuress*, and Kate Devon had sailed her aged, worm-eaten hooker, the creaking, leaking *Swan of Bristol*, her first command.

In the close-in fighting to get past the four escort vessels, one of the Spanish ships had been blown up and another had drifted, flaming downwind. The *Swan of Bristol* had gone to the bottom; her worm-eaten timbers had given way under the crashing and shock of Kate's savage broadsides into another of the *naos*. Alec had picked up Kate's crew and herself, of course, and he had laid the *Invincible* board to board and then had taken her by the combined strength of the two crews. In the savage melee, Kate had suffered a pistol bullet in the creamy skin of her left shoulder, and Alec had had his face laid open by a sword stroke from none other than the doughty Don Mendez himself. Alec had given Kate the *Invincible* as a prize and then had freed Don Mendez in respect of his courage and fighting ability. Kate had always been grateful for the gift of the *Invincible*, but she had never forgiven Alec for freeing Don Mendez, for it had been he who had planted the bullet in Kate's shoulder and had spoiled forever an otherwise perfect and unblemished skin.

Rais looked up at the towering masts of the *nao*. "We should have kept her for ourselves, Cutlass. She would have made a fit running mate for the *Adventuress*."

Alec looked sideways at the Frenchman. "The ship or the woman, Rais?"

Rais grinned. "The ship could have been kept under

your control; the woman, never...you should know, if anyone does."

The sentry returned. He held the door open for them. "The captain will receive you, sir," he said.

Rais rolled his eyes upward. "I can't believe it," he murmured. "The Port Royal whore has taken on the airs of a duchess."

Alec nodded. "Times have changed, Rais. Well, to business with an ex-Port Royal whore and a shark in human form. God be with us, eh, Rais?"

Two

The great stern cabin of the *nao* was illuminated by thick candles of sweet-smelling Gedda wax from India, transported across the Pacific by the Manila Galleon, taken thence by muleback across Mexico to Vera Cruz to be transhipped on a treasure ship bound for Spain; the candles ultimately being destined for one of the great cathedrals of Spain. They were set in solid silver candelabra. Both the candles and the candelabra had been part of the spoils in the taking of the great *San Francisco de Campeche* in that same bloody action in the Windward Passage that had given Kate her own ship.

The deck was covered with a thick carpet. An immense carved mahogany sideboard glittered with a magnificent set of silver plates. The great table in the center of the cabin had been covered with a figured damask tablecloth thick enough to turn an arquebus bullet. The candlelight glittered and reflected from the finest of silverware on the cloth and from the immense silver punch bowl that dominated the center of the table. Many wine bottles were on the table amid a cluster of the finest crystal wineglasses.

Kate Devon sat at the head of the table with her back toward the opened stern windows of the cabin. She wore men's clothing: a coat of wine-colored velvet set with silver buttons made from Spanish *ocho reales* coins. There was a flowering of the finest Flemish lace at her smooth white throat and at her wrists. Her titian red hair flowed down to her slim shoulders in a mannish style. Her smooth white skin seemed almost transparent in the soft light of the many candles, and the many tropical suns under which she had served had dusted the bridge of her pert nose and cheek-bones with tiny freckles. Her nose was finely chiseled while her mouth was a sheer delight, full-lipped and luscious red parted moistly to reveal a set of pearl-like teeth. But it was the emerald green eyes of Kate Devon that could hold a man if he made the mistake of looking too deeply into them. In her time, before she had gone on The Account, she had been the queen of all the Port Royal whores, who could ask for her own price, and then only from the wealthiest of Jamaican planters and the richest sea rovers, and only those for whom she had a liking.

"Cutlass," Kate greeted Alec in that throaty, almost breathless manner of speaking she had, "you're late to the rendezvous."

Alec swept off his plumed hat, and at the same time, thrust out his right leg to sweep the squared toe of his seaboot with the plume of the hat. "Had I known ye were so eagerly waiting for me, your ladyship, I would have plunged over the side of my gallant ship to swim to your side!"

She grinned at him. "Stow that, Cutlass!" she said.

Jacques-Vincent Montbars was far better known throughout the Caribbean as Montbars the Exterminator because of his custom of leaving no survivors of any ship or town he captured. He had never sailed to an attack without showing the black flag of "No Quarter." Worse still, there never was a quick and merciful death for his captives, partic-ularly the women, for Montbars played with their bodies using fire and steel.

Montbars sat next to Kate Devon. His hooded eyes had a yellowish cast to them. They studied Alec from each side of a thin, bony nose, which always reminded Alec of the beak of a vulture. His thin mouth was virtually lipless. The man was an expert marksman and considered to be the finest swordsman among the Brethren of the Coast, with one exception—Alec Campbell. They had never tried each other's steel.

"Montbars," Alec greeted politely. He bowed his head a little. "We meet again. A pleasure, as always," he lied.

"Keep your damned courtly manners to yourself, Cutlass," Montbars snapped. "We're here for business."

"Sit down, Alec and Rais," Kate invited. Her great green eyes held those of Alec Campbell and an unspoken message traveled between them. They knew each other well.

Roche Brasiliano sat opposite Montbars and next to his mistress Kate Devon. He was a giant of a man, a Portuguese, or so some claimed, of Brazilian extraction. He was said to be a "mustee" or octoroon and likely had some Indian blood as well. He was Kate's righthand man and mate, and some claimed he was her regular stud when Alec Campbell or any of her other lovers was not handy.

Roche Brasiliano's dark, blood-tinted eyes held those of Alec Campbell for a fraction of a second, and then he turned them aside. If a magnetism always passed between Kate Devon and Alec Campbell when they met, nothing but pure hatred emanated from Roche Brasiliano when he was in Alec's presence.

The black Irishman, Patrick Quinlan, sat beside his master Montbars. Few men in the Brethren of the Coast could excel him in seamanship and battle, but those few, and Montbars and Alec Campbell for two of them, had a quality of leadership that the Irishman lacked. An excellent subordinate, he could never lead men on his own. He knew he would never likely rise to his own command, and the thought of it was venom in his system, for he believed that all he lacked was luck.

"Patience!" Kate bawled out. "Come and mix the punch, my pet!"

The slim Arawak girl, handmaiden to Kate Devon, came noiselessly from the small galley of the great cabin bearing a silver tray covered with bottles of spirits. She was naked from the waist up, wearing only a pleated kirtle to her knees and displaying a pair of immense breasts that were really all out of proportion to her slim body. Her skin was a soft and mellow coffee color. As she passed Rais Gilles, her bold, dark eyes slewed sideways to survey him speculatively.

"Before God," Rais breathed softly. He had never seen her before. He winced a little as the heel of one of Alec's seaboots came down hard on his right instep. The look in Alec's eyes warned the Frenchman not to make his interest too apparent. Rais glanced at Kate. He got the same message from her. The Arawak woman was not to be tampered with.

Kate leaned forward. "To business. Your plan, Cutlass. I want to get out of this trap of a bay by dawn light."

"Aye," Montbars growled. "If the *guarda-costa* find us..."

"They might have done so at that, Montbars," Alec said. "We saw your topmasts against the land while we were still well out at sea. I had suggested in my messages to both of ye that ye house your topmasts while in this bay."

"Who the hell are you to give me orders?" the Frenchman snarled.

"It was only to save your damned neck," Alec snapped back.

Montbars thrust out a long gaunt hand whose curved fingers were mantled in coarse black hair from knuckles to fingernails. His hooded eyes tried to bore into Alec's icy gray eyes to make them turn aside in fear. "I warn you, *Écossais!* I take no shit from you or any other man in these seas!"

Alec stood up. "Then there is no reason for this meeting, Frenchman!"

Kate Devon slapped a hand down so hard on the table that her wineglass leaped into the air and overturned. "God damn it!" she roared in her best quarterdeck voice.

"What the hell is the matter with you two fighting cocks? Save your fighting for Jack Spaniard! God knows we'll need it if we go after the *Cacafuego!* Now, if either or both of you can't see reason here this night, get the hell off my ship, and I'll sail after the *Cacafuego* myself!"

"And get your pretty arse shot off, Katie," Quintan murmured with a wide grin.

Kate threw back her head and laughed with the sound of tiny silver bells. "Trust a renegade Irishman to come up with a quip like that! Besides, when have you ever seen my pretty arse?" She turned up her wineglass and refilled it. "Come, *gentlemen*, if I may call *you two* that, let us to reason. The night wears on, and there is business to attend to." She looked up at Alec from under lowered brows.

The Arawak woman had been preparing the punch during the taut conversation, knowing full well that Rais Gilles' hot eyes were on her breasts as they swung back and forth over the bowel. She filled silver cups with the punch and passed them around, making sure she pressed a heavy breast hard against the shoulder of Rais Gilles as she came to him. Rais swallowed hard and kept his eyes on his brimming cup.

Patience placed silver bowls full of nuts, fruit, and sweetmeats on the table. She then served out long clay pipes to each of the guests and Kate after filling them with fragrant Sacerdote's tobacco.

Kate lighted her pipe with a spill ignited from a candle. She puffed it into aromatic life and then leaned back in her chair. "Well, Cutlass?" she queried.

Alec sipped the powerful punch. "As ye all know, one of my secret agents in Porto Bello brought me the news that the *Nuestra Señora de la Candelaria,* more commonly known as the *Cacafuego,* would not sail as usual to Vera Cruz with the rest of the plate ships this year. As ye know, the treasure ships from Cartagena and Porto Bello usually rendezvous with the *Flota* at Havana for the final leg of the journey to Spain. Instead, the *Cacafuego* will sail with two other plate ships to leave the Caribbean by way of the Mona Passage between Hispaniola and Puerto Rico, rather than by the Florida Straits. The *Cacafuego* and her two mates will be escorted by a powerful escort of two fighting *navios,* of perhaps seventy guns each, and a number of *naos,* the fighting galleons with which we are well acquainted. There will also be a number of smaller, swifter fighting ships, *pataches* and *zabras,* to scout for those of us who are on The Account."

"Why does the *Cacafuego* sail this different route?" Kate asked.

"You've heard of the ship *Navio del Oro* from Payta in Peru?"

Kate nodded. "Isn't she just a legend?"

"Part is legend, Katie, but still, she carries one of the richest cargoes of treasure from the mines at Payta. *That*, my lass, is true."

Roche Brasiliano nodded. "Yes," he agreed. "I have seen it. The richest cargo possible from Peru."

It was very quiet in the great cabin except for the gurgling of the water under the counter of the ship as she moved at anchor under the gentle force of the land breeze.

"Go on," Montbars urged as he leaned forward.

Alec drained his punch cup, and the Arawak woman quickly refilled it. Alec sipped at the brew. "The viceroy of Lima orders the Armada of the South Seas to sail each year from Callao in Peru, the port of Lima. The armada is instructed to touch at Payta to be joined by the *Navio del Oro*, loaded deep with gold and other precious treasures from the Province of Quito and adjacent districts. The armada then sails for Panama. There, the ships are unloaded, and the treasures are transported by muleback across the Isthmus of Panama to Porto Bello. There, it was always loaded on ships of the Galeones for transport to Vera Cruz, thence to Havana, and eventually to Spain."

"We know all that," Montbars said impatiently.

Alec nodded. "That ye do. Ye also must know that over the past twenty years, the plate ship carrying much of the treasure of the *Navio del Oro* was captured by buccaneers, and two of them were wrecked on the Florida coast because of the summer hurricanes. For a number of years now, no one has been sure just where and how the treasure of the *Navio del Oro* has been transported, if at all."

"That is so," Roche Brasiliano agreed.

Alec slowly shook his head. "Now, I have recently learned that every five years a great ship is still loaded with that incredible treasure beyond all dreams in value at Porto Bello and then she sails with two other plate ships and a powerful escort of fighting ships *to the Mono, Passage and thence to Spain…*"

"And this is the year," Kate breathed softly.

"The invincible and mighty *Cacafuego*," Quinlan added.

"Down to her marks in gold and other treasures," Rais put in. "A big, leaky, slow-moving tub." His eyes glittered.

Montbars drained his cup and wiped his mouth both ways with the back of a hairy hand. His yellowish eyes flicked back and forth like a snake getting ready to strike. He wet his thin lips with the tip of his long and narrow tongue.

Alec relighted his pipe. "Split three ways between the three ships, mates, every man jack aboard them from captain to the lowest powder monkey could retire forever."

"And will there also be ransom money?" Roche asked.

"Be satisfied with the treasure, Roche," Kate suggested.

Alec shrugged. "Who knows? I was informed that some of the finest young women of New Spain, the best of *gachupín* blood, might sail aboard the *Cacafuego* for Spain. That might include the daughter of the governor-general of Panama, but that is merely hearsay."

"There could be many thousands in ransom money in that case," Patrick Quinlan mused.

"What the hell difference does that make?" Kate snapped. "Why bother with a sobbing gaggle of females to hold for ransom when we can take the cargo?"

Montbars nodded absentmindedly. He smiled thoughtfully. He, himself, never collected ransom, no matter the status of his prisoners, especially young females. After having his way with them, he'd turn them over to his crew... he passed his tongue between his thin lips.

Alec looked up from his punch cup. "If there are such women aboard the *Cacafuego*, they will be held for ransom." His gray eyes looked directly into the cold yellowish orbs of Montbars.

Montbars laughed softly. "Quarter, eh, *Écossais?* You never did have the guts to fly the black flag of No Quarter."

It was suddenly very quiet. Alec stood up and placed his hands flat on the table. "What is that ye say, Frenchman? Who speaks of guts? Does it take guts to torture prisoners?"

"Damn you both to hell!" Kate shouted. "Can you not stay away from each other's throats? Are we not to sail together on this sea venture?"

Alec nodded, but he did not take his cold eyes from

Montbars. "Aye," he agreed slowly, "but only under the Articles."

"Agreed!" Kate cried. "I would not have it any other way." She looked at the surly Frenchman. "Montbars?" she queried.

"Is my word not good enough for you, woman?" he sneered.

She leaned forward. "My name is *Kate*, Frenchman. Kate Devon. *Captain* Kate Devon! You understand this? Ye'll treat me with respect, or by God, I'll challenge ye myself!"

Patrick Quinlan grinned. "Why not in bed, Katie?" he murmured slyly. "Ye'd be sure to win at *that*, lass."

Again, the witty Irishman broke the tension. Kate roared with quick laughter.

Montbars stood up. He looked down at Patrick Quinlan. "Call for my boat," he ordered stiffly.

The Irishman shook his head. "No, captain. This is not the way. Would ye let these two take the *Cacafuego* and deal ourselves out of such a treasure as no Brother of the Coast, including the great Henry Morgan, has ever known?"

"You disobey my order?" Montbars asked coldly.

Quinlan shook his head. "This is for your own good, captain. This might be the opportunity of a lifetime. Besides, if your crew ever finds out that we let these two go alone after the treasure of the *Cacafuego*, and *they got it*…"

Kate Devon smiled. "Drink up, damn ye all! Let's do business!"

Montbars grudgingly sat down. "Your plan, Écossais?" he asked in a surly tone.

"The chart, Rais," Alec asked.

The Frenchman took the chart from a coat pocket and pushed back the tableware so that he might spread it out.

Alec stood up. He placed a finger on the chart. "Here we are now, mates. Cabo Beata. Here, the Mona Passage—two hundred miles to the east, nor'east. Here is Isla Mona. We will rendezvous there after dusk in three days. Recognition signals will be arranged beforehand. The *Cacafuego* should reach the passage in four to five days, by my calculations. One of my agents from Porto Bello will meet us at Isla Mona with that information. The *Flota* will be facing a headwind at dusk and will shorten sail as they always do at night. There will be a new full moon later on that night, which should turn the Mona Passage into a situation almost like daylight. Therefore, between dusk and the rising of the moon, we must close in unseen on the convoy. Myself in the *Adventuress* and Captain Montbars in the *Exterminator* must close in under cover of darkness and surprise the larger of the fighting ships at the rear of the convoy. We must put them out of action immediately! I stress that, Captain Montbars."

Montbars waved a hairy hand in acquiescence.

"I suggest broadsides of solid shot to stagger them and sweep the decks. Then chain- and bar-shot to tear up their sails and rigging, followed by flaming spike-shot to set them afire."

"I know my business," Montbars growled.

Alec nodded. "I'm sure ye do. Once we put the rear guard out of action, Katie here must slip up on the Caca-fuego and open fire on her with bar- and chain-shot to destroy much of her rigging, but not all of it. Ye understand, Katie? She must be slowed down, but not made helpless, for we must cut her out of the convoy. It will take great skill in maneuvering for ye to do this."

Kate spat on the carpet and wiped her full lips on her sleeve. "Trust me, Cutlass."

"Let's hope so," Alec said dryly.

"We can hardly take the *Cacafuego* like that," Roche Brasiliano put in. "Besides, what of the big 70-gun *navios* you said would be with the convoy?"

"What can the *Cacafuego* do?" Alec asked rhetorically. "She will hardly be able to make her way through the passage against the headwind with half her sails gone. Mighty as she is, she can't escape from us. It will be up to Kate to herd her back through the passage while Montbars and I drop back to hold off the other Spanish fighting ships. We'll have the legs on them."

"And they'll have the weight of metal against us," Patrick murmured dryly.

Alec looked up at Kate. "Ye can harry the hell out of the

Cacafuego. They'll have to strike. With all those women on board, her commander would hardly fight to the death."

"Aye," Montbars agreed thoughtfully. He did not look up at Alec.

Alec looked about the table. "I call for a vote, mates."

"Madness," Patrick Quinlan said, "but I'm for it. Well thought out, Cutlass." He ignored the hard sideways glance he got from his own commander.

Roche Brasiliano nodded. "There will be losses, but one can't gamble like this without losses. I'm with you."

Rais Gilles blew a smoke ring. "What is life but one battle after another, from the day we poke our heads out of our mother's womb until the day we are wrapped in a shroud with a solid shot at our feet and popped over the side to the words of the Twenty-third Psalm? To go down in defeat in one final engagement, with cannon roaring and bright blades flashing. Aye! That's the ticket!"

"What the hell is this?" Montbars demanded. "Are you with us or against us, Huguenot?"

Rais blew a smoke ring toward Montbars. "There is no poetry in your soul, Montbars. You are a peasant with shit for blood, Catholic."

"Why, damn you!" Montbars roared. He dropped his hand to one of the pistols hanging from his baldric and then he saw the look in Alec Campbell's icy gray eyes. He shrugged and looked away.

"Well, Rais?" Alec asked with a grin.

"Count me in, Cutlass."

"Montbars?" Alec queried.

Montbars nodded shortly.

"You haven't asked me, Cutlass," Kate accused.

Alec looked at her. Their eyes met. "Do I have to, Katie?" he asked softly.

She smiled and stuck out the tip of her pink tongue.

"Your ships are well watered and provisioned?" Alec asked. "Have they recently been careened? Ye have sufficient powder and shot? Are your crews up to strength?"

Montbars drained his cup. "Are you in command then?"

Alec looked about the table. "I understood that was the

way it was to be. We can't act independently. Do ye think *ye* could command this expedition, Montbars?"

"Why not *me?*" Kate demanded. Her liquor was getting to her.

Rais Gilles refilled his punch cup. "If Cutlass does not command, leave me out."

Montbars looked quickly at Rais. "You are not the only one involved here."

Rais placed his cup on the table. He leaned forward and rested his elbows on the tabletop. "Let us reason together, brothers. We are of the Brethren of the Coast, are we not? Such matters as these are always settled by voting, and each man must have his vote, down to the lowliest powder monkey in the crew. Is that agreed?"

No one spoke. It was very quiet for a time.

Montbars looked about the table. "Vote then. I vote for myself."

"Roche?" Rais asked.

Roche looked down at Kate. "I vote with my captain."

"Kate?" the Frenchman queried.

Kate looked at Cutlass, in that certain way she always looked at him. "He's the best man among us."

Rais Gilles looked at Patrick Quinlan. "Ye've already got enough votes for Cutlass," the Irishman said.

"We go by the Articles, Quinlan," Rais reminded him. "All must vote. I vote for Cutlass."

Patrick Quinlan looked sideways at the glowering Montbars. "Kate is right, Jacques. He's the best man among us, at least for this task before us."

"Vote and be damned to you, Irishman!" Montbars snapped.

Kate leaned forward and fixed Montbars with those magnificent emeralds she had for eyes. She smiled. "Make it unanimous, Jacques," she pleaded sweetly, "for the good of us all."

Montbars nodded at last. "Have it your way," he said sourly.

"The Articles will now be read and voted on," Alec announced.

"Ye sound like a member of Parliament," Patrick said.

Rais Gilles took a large parchment roll from a coat pocket and unrolled it, weighing down the corners with table utensils and bowls. He looked about the table. "This copy has been signed or marked by every man aboard the *Adventuress*. We have used it while on The Account with Captain Campbell, and he is as much a party to its conditions as are all the rest of us."

Kate nodded. "They are much like mine," she added.

"Montbars?" Alec asked.

"What need for them? My word is my bond, or do you doubt that, Écossais?"

"I do not doubt your word, captain, but as elected commander of this venture, I insist that each ship's crew must be bound by these Articles."

Their eyes clashed again across the table.

"Well?" Alec asked.

"Read them then, and be damned to you!"

"The punch is getting to him," Rais murmured.

"I'll drink you under the table, Huguenot!" Montbars challenged.

Rais smiled easily. "Not tonight, Catholic, if that's what you call yourself now. But, *after* we take the *Cacafuego*, aye, *then* we'll see about that."

"Read the damned Articles!" Kate shouted.

Rais moved the candelabra closer to the parchment and began to read:

I. Every man shall obey civil command. Captain to have two full shares; master a share and a half; surgeon, mate, gunner, boatswain, one share and a quarter; all others one full share.

II. Every man has a vote on affairs of moment; equal title to fresh provisions or strong liquors at any time seized, and use of them at his pleasure unless a scarcity makes it necessary for the good of all to avoid a retrenchment.

III. He who takes up a weapon on board to strike another shall be punished as Captain and Company majority see fit.

IV. He who is proven coward shall be punished as in Article III.

V. He who runs away, or keeps any secret from the Company, shall be marooned with one bottle of powder, one bottle of water, one small arm, and shot.

VI. Every man to be called fairly in turn, by list, on board of prizes for his full fair share of the prize. He who steals anything from the Company, or holds back the smallest amount of treasure from them, shall be marooned or shot. If the robbery is only between one and another, the ears and nose of him that is guilty are to be split and he is to be set on shore, not in an uninhabited place, yet somewhere where he is sure to encounter hardships.

VII. He who strikes another while these Articles are in force shall receive Mose's Law, that is, forty stripes on the bare back with the cat-o'-nine-tails, less one.

VIII. That man who snaps his arms, that is, to pull the trigger of his gun and cause the hammer to hit the flintlock, setting off sparks, or smoke tabac in the hold without a cap to his pipe, or carry a lighted candle without it being held in a lantern, shall suffer Mose's Law.

IX. That man who does not keep his arms clean, or neglects his business, shall be cut off from his share, and suffer such punishment as the Captain and Company think fit.

X. To lose a joint in time of engagement, 400 pieces-of-eight. If a whole limb, 800 pieces-of-eight. He can remain with the Company as long as he sees fit.

XI. He that first sees the sail of a prize, shall have the best pistol or small arm aboard her.

XII. Good quarter to be given when called for.

XIII. If a prudent woman be captured, that man who offers to meddle with her without her consent shall suffer present death, at the hands of the man who apprehends him. All women of gentle birth are to be held for ransom, and the Company to share equally the amount of ransom payment.

Rais Gilles' voice died away. He looked up.
"Well?" Alec asked. "Commanders?"

"No objection here," Kate replied as she refilled her punch glass.

Montbars nodded.

"Give them their copies, Rais," Alec said. "Each member of their crews to sign or make his mark."

Rais gave Kate and Montbars their copies.

"They will be signed by ye here tonight, in the presence of these witnesses," Alec instructed.

"Pen and ink, Patience!" Kate bawled out.

The Arawak woman brought an ink bottle and pen to Kate. Kate boldly scrawled her signature below the Articles. "I say here, before all this company as witnesses, that each member of my crew will sign these Articles or make his mark before we sail tomorrow on this joint venture," she declared.

They all looked at Montbars. He shrugged and took pen in hand to sign his copy of the Articles. He shoved the parchment over to Patrick Quinlan and handed him the pen.

"Your declaration?" Rais asked.

Montbars stifled a yawn. "I say here, in the presence of this company, that each member of my crew will sign the Articles or make his mark upon them before we set sail on tomorrow's venture."

Quinlan signed the parchment and sanded the signatures. He rolled the parchment and placed it in one of his pockets. His eyes met those of Alec, and he nodded slightly as though to say without words that the crew of the *Exterminator* would sign the Articles.

Montbars stood up. "It grows late. Our business with each other is over then this night." He looked at Alec. "We sail with the dawn light, commander. I bid you goodnight." He bent his head slightly and strode from the cabin, followed by his mate.

"Well, I'll be God damned!" Kate exploded. "Meek as any kitten!"

Rais Gilles shrugged. "I trust him not," he murmured.

"Nor does any of us, good Rais," Kate agreed, "but we need his weight of gun metal to take the *Cacafuego*." She smiled. "Gentlemen, there is fine Madeira and Canary for your due consideration." Her eyes met those of Alec Campbell across the cluttered tabletop. He saw the warm invitation glowing within those incredible living emeralds she had for eyes.

Rais Gilles was no fool. He knew these two of old. He drained his punch cup and stood up. "I'll need some sleep this night if we are to sail at dawn. It will be a long day tomorrow, mates."

"There is a cabin at your disposal, Rais," Kate offered. She wanted to get him out of the great cabin as quickly as possible and would take any means to speed him on his way.

Rais looked sideways at Patience. "With a little Indian maid to tuck me in, eh, Kate?" He had been drinking too much, he realized suddenly.

Kate yawned a little and smiled slyly: "It was *her* cabin I offered you, silly."

Rais was astounded. He stood up. "You mean that, madam?"

"If she'll put up with you in her bed, mister. Look at her."

Rais looked, and understood immediately. He picked up a bottle of Madeira from the table and slid it into a coat pocket. He held out his arm to Patience. "Come, my dear, the cotillion starts within the hour." The door closed behind them.

Kate looked at Roche Brasiliano. "I'm afraid there won't be much sleep for you this night, Roche. Make sure all is ready for sea. Call me an hour before the dawn."

The door closed softly behind Roche Brasiliano.

Kate looked at Alec. "Will you sleep alone this night, you horny Scots bastard, or shall we have a drinking bout to see who ends up under the table?"

Alec looked idly at her. "Neither, lassie," he suggested. "I've not had quite enough to drink as yet. We haven't done much damage to your fine Madeira."

They sat there silently, each deep in thought. The night wind soughed gently through the open stern windows. Kate stood up and wet a thumb and forefinger with her pink tongue. She pinched out all the candles save one. She looked down at Alec. "Will you wait, pet?" she asked softly.

He shrugged carelessly. "What else is there to do?"

She bent and kissed him, pressing her full, soft mouth against his and then thrusting her tongue in and out between his parted lips and into his mouth. Then suddenly, she was gone into her sleeping cabin.

Alec filled a glass with the excellent Madeira. He looked at her closed cabin door and raised the glass in silent tribute to the delights, well known to him in past years, that she was preparing to reveal to him this night.

THREE

Alec filled his glass from the last of the punch and drained it. He shook his head a little at the powerful, warming impact deep in his gut. It was heady stuff. He stripped off his baldric and hung it over the back of a chair. He took off his coat and draped it over the baldric. He tiptoed to the door of the cabin and pressed his ear against it. He could hear the deep breathing of the sentry who was always posted outside her door when the captain was in her cabin. Alec slid the heavy bolt across to lock the door from within.

Alec walked back to the stern gallery and stepped out upon it. He could see the looming hulk of the *Exterminator.* The only light that showed from the ship was the high stern lantern casting a moving reflection on the water.

Alec returned to the cabin. He stopped short as he saw Kate standing in the open doorway of her sleeping cabin with her full shape outlined in silhouette from the dim lamp behind her. The soft light from the candle revealed the thin silk dress of emerald green she wore, a shade that matched her eyes with exactitude. The plunging bosom of the dress revealed at least the upper half of her creamy breasts, the proud nipples thrusting out just below the rim of the gown.

Alec rested his forearms on the back of Kate's chair and studied her. "By God, Katie," he breathed, "ye should wear gowns like that all the time. Ye do yourself no great justice in wearing men's clothing."

The scent of her exotic perfume drifted across the cabin to Alec, mingled with the fragrance of the candle wax and the pungent headiness of the punch bowl. Alec could feel his virility rising. "Madeira?" he asked casually.

"Of course."

She came to stand close beside him as he poured the wine. He held the glass to her full, moist lips. She drank greedily with her eyes probing deep into his. He slipped his free arm about her slender waist and then took the empty glass from her lips. He bent her backward and sought her mouth with his. She pressed her loins hard against his. She wore nothing beneath the sheer gown. She placed her smooth hands on each side of his face and kissed him with a half-open mouth while she thrust her loins spasmodically against his. Alec released her. There was plenty of time.

She sat down and rested her arms on the table while she studied him. "You still don't trust Montbars," she suggested.

Alec shook his head. "Do ye?"

"Only to the extent that he knows he can't take the *Caca-fuego* without our help.".

He shrugged. "That's something at least."

"Do you expect heavy losses?"

Alec refilled the glasses. "There will be no avoiding them, but then, the rewards will be immense."

"Enough to retire, eh, Cutlass?"

Alec nodded. "For all of us. Without question, Katie."

"And what then, my bold one?"

He sipped at the fine wine. A glow was working up within him. He looked at the deep cleft of her bosom and thought of the cherry-tipped nipples just below the rim of the gown.

"Alec?" she queried.

He looked up at her. "Who knows?"

"You can go back to Scotland and live like a laird. Or would it be France? You Scots are always welcome there, Alec. A horny Scot loaded with pieces-of-eight would be quite a hero in Paris."

Alec grinned. "'A fool and his money,' eh, lassie?"

She grinned back. "You'd drink and fuck yourself to death within ten years, my pet."

"A pleasant way to die, Katie. And what of ye? If we take the *Cacafuego*, what of Captain Kate Devon, the flower of the Spanish Main?"

She shrugged. The rich wine glistened on her full mouth. She licked it from her lips with the tip of her pink tongue. She lazily eyed Alec as though she was a surfeited cat. "Where could *I* go, Cutlass? You know, I was transported from England to Jamaica for stealing and whoring in Bristol when I was only fifteen years old. I can never return to England."

"There is always France."

She shook her head. "England is the only place for me. If I can't return there, I'll go nowhere else."

"Which leaves the Caribbean, and in the Caribbean, there are only two places ye might live—the Tortugas and Jamaica. Ye've been barred from Jamaica ever since ye went on The Account. That leaves Tortuga."

She spat on the carpet. "That den of thieves? There's nothing there for me, pet."

He looked about the great cabin. "This, then, would have to be your home." He shrugged. "But for how long, eh?"

Alec refilled the wineglasses and leaned toward her to brush her lips with his. She placed her arms about his neck and looked deep into his eyes. "I would go to Scotland or France with you if you would have me, Alec."

Alec drew back. "Ye know I am still outlawed in my own country. The Scots also know I took letters of marque from Charles II, king of England, to serve him as a privateer here in the Caribbean."

"But only as a convenience. It's simply licensed piracy in your case, Alec, and you know it!"

He shrugged. "It might save me from a rope about my neck if I'm ever caught, lassie."

"But you're on shares with English merchants!"

Alec grinned a little. "They'll have to catch me to make me pay up."

She leaned close to him and kissed him, then drew back.

"Damn you, Cutlass! Must you always play both ends against the middle?"

"It keeps me alive at least. But ye, once your days on The Account are over, what will happen to ye? Ye'll maybe end up as a drunken, broken-down old whore in some stinking tavern in Port Royal, pissing under the table and crying in her cups about the great old days when she was known as Mad Kate Devon, the Scourge of the Spanish Main."

She swung an open hand hard at his face, but he was too quick for her. He gripped her wrist and turned the blow aside. He stood up and forced her arm behind her back and then bent her over backward while he kissed her, hard. He thrust his free hand down inside her gown to feel and heft one of her fully rounded breasts. She struggled for a moment and then relaxed until she caught him off guard, when she brought a hard knee up into his groin. He cursed and released her.

Kate was beginning to feel the powerful effect of too much hot punch coupled with the Madeira wine. "Say that will not be so, Cutlass!" she cried. "You with your damned Scots second sight! Aye, we all know ye have it. Is that to be the future for me? Tell me that it will not be so!" The hidden melancholia of Kate Devon had crept out from behind the bold front she always wore. Her mood had swiftly changed, as it always did.

Alec studied her. "No one grows old on The Account, lassie. Their years are numbered for even the best of them— death in battle by land or sea. To be lost at sea in a hurricane, or by having their ship strike some uncharted reef. To have their crew or perhaps a trusted officer turn against them to depose them and perhaps to maroon or murder them as well. To die of the *vómito negro*, the black vomit of the scourge of Yellow Jack. Then there's always the Inquisition if Jack Spaniard catches ye and ye are not a Catholic. Have ye ever seen a heretic die under their metal pincers and fire, or by burning at the stake? I have, lassie…many of the Brethren have been lost or died in such ways as I have just described."

"So many," she murmured. "But, Alec, is this to be for us too?"

He drained his wineglass and refilled it. "I know naught of ye, Katie, but none of those fates will be for me."

"You're so damned sure of yourself!"

He grinned. "Why not? Come, lassie, I did not agree to stay here this night and talk of such disagreeable things. Drink up, Katie! The night moves on apace!"

"Tell me what you believe of me, damn you!"

He shoved back his chair. "Draw off my seaboots first, Katie, like the good lass ye are."

She got to her feet and turned around, kilting up her silk gown so that she could get his left leg between her rounded thighs. She gripped the boot. Alec planted his right foot on her rather narrow rump; it was her one great failing in his estimation, for she was built like a boy in that respect. But it was a little enough failing in view of her other attributes and was easily overlooked in view of her inordinate skill in bed combat. She pulled on the boot as he shoved on her rump, and the boot came free. She kilted up the gown again as she turned. He viewed her long, creamy white legs and her extraordinarily tiny feet in their high-heeled satin slippers, emerald like her eyes and her gown.

"Jesus God, Katie," Alec breathed heavily, "ye've stems on ye, lovelier than any long-stalked lily."

"All the better to stalk you with them, you horny bastard!" she crowed.

Her mood had switched again. She turned and spread her legs to allow him to thrust his right leg between her thighs. Alec reached forward and flipped her gown up onto her back when she bent over to withdraw the boot. He placed his left foot on the bare, smooth skin and shoved hard. The boot came loose, and as it did so, the *sqian-dubh* fell free from its scabbard.

Kate snatched up the deadly little knife and whirled to face Alec. The candlelight glittered on the polished steel. She stood poised there, bent slightly forward so that one of her breasts, sweat-dewed with tiny little drops, swung free from its flimsy confinement. The candle light shone on her glorious hair and on her full, moist lips.

"Gad, what a picture, Kate!" Alec exclaimed.

She was drunker than he thought she was. "Defend yourself, ye Scot's bastard!" she cried.

Alec roared with laughter. He slammed a hand down hard on the table so that the wineglasses jumped and fell over to spill their contents like bloodstains onto the fine damask. Suddenly, Alec stopped laughing.

Kate moved catlike toward Alec with the deadly, glittering blade extended toward him and her left hand upraised for balance. Her great eyes were fixed on his.

"Kate," Alec murmured. "Now, Kate..." He raised a placating hand.

She did not speak; nothing but the slow, silent approach.

Kate lunged toward Alec's face. Alec rolled out of the chair, and the knife tip struck the back of the chair where he had been seated a fraction of a second before.

Alec rounded the table with his eyes fixed on the woman.

She stalked him like a great green cat.

Alec moved away from her approach. He held out his hands. "What's got into ye, pet?" he demanded.

Her very silence made the scene all the more deadly.

Alec darted past the chair where his baldric and coat hung. He ripped the dirk free from its scabbard and jumped back as his own *sqian-dubh* passed through the very air where he had been standing.

Alec backed away from the silent woman. He held the dirk with the blade protruding between his thumb and first finger. The damnable, unpredictable she-cat kept on coming.

"Stinking Scots coward!" she spat out at him.

"English whore!" he snapped back.

"Stand and fight, ye skulkin' bastard!"

"Dinna challenge a Scots gentleman so carelessly, ye damned Sassenach bitch!" he roared.

Alec waited for her now, lightly poised on the balls of his feet, blade extended, and icy gray eyes fixed on her eyes.

She slashed hard. He parried and turned the *sqian-dubh* aside. She was far stronger in the wrist than she looked.

The bright blades flickered back and forth. Her blade

cut through the French lace at his throat. He slid his razor-sharp steel under her right shoulder strap and flicked it upward to sever the strap. Her right breast swung free.

Alec retreated while rounding the table. He ripped away his throat lace and tore off his sweat-soaked shirt to cast it to one side. The candlelight shone glistening on his sweating, muscular torso with its manifold scars and a few puckered bullet holes.

The next clash traced a thin line of red beads of blood across his chest while his blade cut through her left shoulder strap.

Her sweat-damp breasts swung back and forth with her quick, catlike movements. She was a master knife-fighter, a product of her early days as a street urchin and young whore in the streets and alleys of Bristol Town. She had earned a reputation with her knife during her days in Port Royal. Some said she had three kills to her tally from those days before she had gone on The Account. She had killed a half-blood PPortuguesemustee woman who had fancied herself as the queen of the Port Royal whores. She had killed a Dutch trader who had thought she was helpless drunk and had tried to sodomize her. Her last tally had been a Jamaican planter who had drunkenly challenged her for a twenty-pound wager, with first blood drawn to win the wager. He had made the mistake of first losing the wager and then trying to kill her. That was why Kate Devon had left Port Royal and Jamaica in such a hurry to become a sea artist.

Alec rounded the table. He snatched up a bottle of Madeira and drank deeply, but kept his eyes on her all the time he was drinking.

"A truce," she suggested cunningly. "I need a drink."

"Come and get it!" he challenged.

She ran at him, but he was gone. She paused at the head of the table, watching him from under lowered brows.

Alec undid the ties of his breeches with his free hand and then stepped out of them, always watching her. She did not move. Slowly she reached out for a bottle and then drank deeply with her smooth white throat working convulsively until the bottle was half-empty. She placed the bottle back on the table and slowly wiped her mouth with the back of her free hand.

Alec stripped the socks from his feet and stood up, naked except for his fine linen underdrawers. They eyed each other, knowing they would fornicate, but not without a struggle first.

There came a gust of the night wind. One of the stern windows banged against its frame. Kate whirled in surprise.

Alec launched himself clear across the table, scattering wine bottles, glasses and the punchbowl. Kate turned to face him. His left hand caught at the thin silk about her slim waist so that it ripped freely from her body as she jumped back. She ran toward the front of the cabin and turned to face him, naked except for her tiny silver-buckled shoes. Tiny beads of sweat glistened on her torso. The red patch at her crotch stood out sharply against her creamy skin.

Alec grinned. "Ye're beginning to look more interestin' now, lass." He began to stalk her around the table.

Kate wanted a drink badly enough to risk reaching for a bottle. Alec moved so quickly that she could not get out of the way. He deftly twisted the *sqian-dubh* out of her grasp and flung it across the cabin where it stuck quivering in the ornately carved mahogany sideboard. She went battling to the carpeted deck with him on top of her. She clawed at his face with her long nails until blood and sweat dripped from it and splashed on her face and breasts. He gripped her wrists in a steel-like grasp and thrust his taut face close to hers.

"Damn ye, ye drunken bitch," Alec growled. "Will ye not stop this madness?"

She smiled irritatingly up into his face. Her lips parted. She stuck out her pink tongue and then slowly withdrew it. "Kiss me, ye great Scots booby," she murmured. "I have need of ye." She pushed her loins up against his.

They clung together, working their mouths together, and thrusting hard against each other. She slid her hands down to his waist and tore at his underdrawers until they came free from his body. She cast them to one side and then wrapped her arms about his neck to draw him close to herself.

Alec, at last, stood up. He shook his head. "Whew! Damn ye, Kate, ye bled me." He wiped the clotted blood from his face and chest.

"Not for the first time, Alec." She laughed musically.

Alec drank deeply. He looked down at her where she lay quietly with her hands locked together at the nape of her neck so that her fine breasts were thrust upward. He kneeled beside her and cradled her in his arms. He picked her up. There was no resistance from her now. She slid her left arm about his neck and pressed her face against his. Alec kissed her as he carried her into her lamplit sleeping cabin. He placed her on the scented silken sheets. She flung her arms and long legs out sideways and smiled languorously up at him.

She drew close to him and placed a leg over his uppermost hip when he lay down beside her. Alec slowly passed a hand down her face. She lay back from him. He passed the hand over her smoothly rounded throat and then down to her breasts to tease the nipples into erect-ness. He kissed the nipples while he passed his exploratory hand down her smoothly rounded belly to the meeting of her thighs. They lay face to face with their mouths and tongues working together.

Alec worked his hand in between her sweat-slick thighs. She moaned softly and rolled back and forth. "Oh, Alec," she murmured. "It's been *so* long."

"Don't try to tell me there haven't been others, Katie."

"Of course there have been, but none like my good Scots stud, Alec, pet."

"Like Roche Brasiliano?"

She stiffened, and her fingernails began to dig into his back. "Damn you," she whispered. "Sometimes he *is* better than you are."

"Does he still beat ye into submission before he rogers ye?"

She raised her head. "How did you know that?" she demanded.

"No man can get into your drawers, Katie, unless he defeats ye first."

She tried to sit up, but he forced her back and gripped

her wrists to hold her hands above her head and pinned down to the bed. "Can't ye ever act like a lady in your love-making, lass?" he asked.

"I never knew it any other way until I went out onto the streets of Bristol at the age of fifteen to turn professional. I thought I might as well get paid for it. If I give it away, a man must fight for it."

He shook his head. He released her and passed his hands down her smooth, sweating body to her thighs. She opened them like an unfolding flower.

Alec awoke once during the quiet night. It was still dark. The wind had shifted, and the *nao* had swung at her anchor to head into it.

Kate murmured sleepily. Alec took her up into his arms and kissed her. "Oh God, Alec," she murmured, "not *again!*"

Alec savaged her again until she was a moaning, sobbing creature who went limp in his arms and then slept.

Alec awoke with a start. The faintest of light showed through the window port. He arose and padded about the main cabin with his pistol and dirk in his hands. He stepped out on the stern gallery to feel the cool, soft breeze on his sweating flesh. No light showed from the dark bulk of the *Exterminator.* The dawn wind was stirring the treetops. A faint trace of pewter-colored light showed in the eastern sky.

Alec dressed quickly and slung his baldric over his right shoulder. He sheathed his dirk and *sqian-dubh* and then emptied the last of the Madeira down his gullet for a morning starter.

He tiptoed to the door of the sleeping cabin. Faint light shone through the window port onto the bed. She lay sprawled on the sweat-damp silken sheets with one arm outflung and the other lying across her breasts. Her lips were slightly parted, and she was breathing softly.

Alec looked down upon her. She was lovely and a real woman. At any other time or place...the thought died aborning. What was to be the destiny of Kate Devon? His own words came back to haunt him: *No one grows old on The Account, lassie. Their years are numbered for even the best of them.*

Alec bent over and touched her soft mouth with his. She

murmured sleepily and slid her arms up about his neck to draw him close. "Stay, Alec," she whispered throatily.

Alec gently withdrew her arms and then straightened up. "No, lass, for the dawn wind commands me away." For a moment he paused, and then he gently touched her flushed face with a hand. He turned quickly and left the cabin.

Alec tapped on the door of the Arawak woman's cabin. "Rais?" he called softly. "It's dawn."

The boat's crew was ready at the side of the *nao* when Alec and Rais stepped out upon the deck. They clambered down into the longboat. Alec looked up. The dark and impassive face of Roche Brasiliano looked down at him.

"Ye sail at dawn, Brasiliano," Alec reminded the mustee.

Roche Brasiliano nodded.

They cast loose from the *nao* and moved slowly across the calm waters of the bay, now ruffled here and there by gentle cat's paws. The oars creaked in the tholepins and echoed from the dark shore.

There was movement on the *Exterminator.* Bare feet slapped the deck. The capstan pawls clicked as the ship was brought up short over her anchor preparatory to catting it.

Montbars looked over the quarterdeck railing and down at the longboat as it passed the stern of his ship. Alec raised his head to Montbars. Montbars nodded.

"The Scots stud is right on time," Patrick Quinlan said from behind Montbars.

Montbars nodded. "I've often wondered if he's as good at fighting as he is at fornicating."

The mate shrugged. "We've seen him fight, sir. We have only his word on the fornicating, and if he can satisfy that red-headed whore over there, he must be quite the stud."

The longboat passed through the channel and onto the slow, uneasy surge of the open sea.

Tattoo stood in the bows of the longboat. He turned to look at Alec and then pointed out to sea.

The *Adventuress* was slowly approaching the land under topsails only.

"Give the signal, Tattoo," Alec ordered.

The giant black struck flint and steel and lighted a small ship's lantern. He raised and lowered it three times.

A light showed on the foredeck of the frigate. It was raised and lowered three times.

"Ho for the Mona Passage!" Rais Gilles cried out.

The oarsmen grinned as they stroked steadily toward the approaching *Adventuress*. For them it would be wealth such as they could hardly realize, or sudden death on the seas. There could be no other alternative when on The Account with Captain Cutlass and the *Adventuress*.

FOUR

Alec Campbell slammed shut his long brass telescope. "It's the plate convoy," he announced. The late afternoon view from the rocky heights of Isla Mona had revealed the ships of the Spanish convoy heading in toward the Mona Passage. "Three plate ships," Alec added. "One of them must undoubtedly be the *Cacafuego*. I know of no other ships of her size and tonnage in these waters. There are two other fairly large ships other than the plate ships. They must be *navios*, the big fighting galleons. There are three smaller galleons, also fighters, or I miss my guess. There are two fast *pataches* scouting ahead and one each out on the far flanks of the convoy. Maybe they're looking for us." He grinned.

Kate Devon and Jacques Montbars looked at each other surreptitiously behind Alec's back. Montbars nodded in satisfaction.

The *Adventuress*, the *Kate of Devon*, and the big *Exterminator* were huddled together in the lee of the island and out of sight of the approaching convoy.

"I'll leave a man up here to keep an eye on the Spaniards," Alec continued. "The convoy should be abreast of the island about dusk. My man will then signal to us. By the time we up anchor and hoist our sails, we can slip out into the passage under cover of the dusk to tail the convoy."

Montbars nodded shortly.

Kate Devon smiled quickly. "Aye, Cutlass!"

They walked in single file down the steep pathway to the beach. Montbars led the way with Alec bringing up the rear while watching the fascinating rump action of Kate Devon as she strode after the Frenchman, wearing her man's clothing and square-toed seaboots of finest red leather.

The sea breeze had died out at sunset, but now, with the coming of dusk, it was picking up again, giving a headwind directly into the Mona Passage against the slowly moving ships of the Spanish convoy. As the dusk crept over the sea, all eyes on the three corsair ships were on the darkening heights of the small island.

A light, shielded from being viewed from the passage, flicked on, flicked out, and flicked on again.

Alec Campbell turned from the stern railing of his quarterdeck. "Mister Yeoman, sir! Up anchor! Prepare to make sail!" he shouted.

"Hands to the capstan and halyards!" Yeoman bellowed.

The sounds of command came drifting across the waters from the *Kate of Devon* and the *Exterminator*.

"They will be racing us to see who sets sail first, Mister Yeoman!" Alec reminded the sailing master.

Miles Yeoman grinned. "No chance of them beating *us,* sir!" He cupped his hands about his mouth and spat out his commands: "All hands up anchor! Ready there forward! Heave away! Keep step—stamp and go, God damn ye all for a pack of lubbers!"

Little wizened Paddy Cavanaugh, the fiddler, leaped atop the turning capstan and tucked his battered fiddle under his chin. The wheezy, scratching notes of "The Hunt Is Up" squeaked out above the stamping of calloused bare feet on the deck planking and the steady clicking of the capstan pawls.

"Anchor's apeak!" Bosun Heydt shouted.

The topmen had already scampered up the shrouds to the yards to take the stops off the topsails.

"Let fall!" Yeoman commanded.

The topsails fell instantly and caught the rising wind to fill out their classic curves.

"Sheet home! Hoist away! Brace up forward!"

"Hoist the mains'l!"

Halyards ran through the squealing blocks.

"Hoist the fore stays'l. Let fall the sprits'l. Sheet home!"

"Anchor at the cathead, sir!" Heydt bellowed.

The *Adventuress* heeled slightly as the rising wind filled her sails with the sound of low thunder. The frigate began to draw away from the island.

Alec looked across at the *Kate of Devon* as the *Adventuress* drew abreast of her. He heard Kate cursing at her crew: "Damn ye for a set of plowboys! Get your fat arses in motion, or by God, I'll clap the lot of ye in the bilboes, ye lazy scum!"

Rais Gilles grinned. "Always the lady, eh, Cutlass?"

Alec looked at the helmsman. "Course nor'east by east, helmsman."

"Aye, sir, course nor'east by east!"

The *Adventuress* heeled to the swell of the sea and the thrust of the freshening wind. She rounded the island into the passage covered by the darkness. She steadied on her course up the Mona Passage. The *Kate of Devon* and the *Exterminator* showed dimly in the darkness astern of the frigate.

"Mister MacMillan!" Alec called out.

"Aye, sir!" the master gunner responded smartly.

"Ye'll need flaming spike-shot for this night's action, master gunner."

"We've twenty rounds ready at the bow chasers, sir!"

"Good! Then clear for action, mister!"

The frigate's crew broke out into a swarming beehive of ordered activity. The boatswain and his mates secured the lower yards by reeving chains to sling them, then doubled the important sheets, ropes, and braces. Netswere spread under the masts and across the upper deck to catch any wreckage that might fall from aloft. The carpenters got out spare parts to repair the chain pumps in case of damage, as well as shot plugs, mauls, plugs of oakum, and sheets of lead for shot damage.

Surgeon Shannon and his mates spread old sails on the deck of the cockpit situated on the orlop deck. The medicine chests were opened. Lanterns were lighted. Fresh water was poured into tubs. Basins, tourniquets, ligatures, linens, powders, forceps, saws, bullet extractors, tapes, and tow were set out for instant use. Two large vessels were filled with water, one in which to wash the bloody instruments and the other to hold amputated limbs until such time as they could be thrown overboard. Basins were readied for mixing restrictives. Pannikins were set out for warming oils. Cordial bottles were placed near at hand to revive men when they fainted.

Sand was scattered on the decks so that men might not slip on the blood. Spongers and rammers were hooked to the beams above the main battery of 24-pounders on the gun deck. Spare matches freshly soaked in saltpeter were coiled in small tubs next to each cannon. Heavy shot was placed in the shot racks beside each gun on the main and gun decks. Powder monkeys came hurrying up from the powder magazine deep in the bowels of the frigate carrying powder and cartridges in leather-covered "budge" barrels to stow them amidships away from the cannon to prevent premature explosion. Tubs of water and soaked blankets were placed between each gun. Other tubs were filled with a mixture of vinegar, water, and urine for sponging the guns after every fourth or fifth shot. The main powder magazine doors far below decks were hung with wet blankets against sparks. Lead plates were removed from cannon breeches, and the breech trappings were cast off.

"Cast loose and provide!" Ian MacMillan commanded.

The training tackles were strained at to haul the ponderous guns back for loading. The tompions were jerked from the muzzles. Powder bags were rammed home into the breeches, followed by a solid shot. The touch holes were filled with fine-corned priming powder, and each gunner laid a fine train of powder from the touchhole to the base ring of the piece. The gunports were opened to the squealing accompaniment of the tackles. The lashings of the guns were cast loose, and the trucks rumbled and squealed as the guns were run forward until their grim snouts peered through the open gunports.

Rais Gilles ordered his sharpshooters and grenadiers into the fighting tops of the masts where they had a clear field of fire for their arquebuses and grenades. He had cutlasses, pistols, pikes, and boarding axes issued to the rest of the crew. Tattoo brought the weapons and morion helmets of the afterguard to the officers.

"Ship cleared for action, sir!" Miles Yeoman reported.

"Fast time, Cutlass," Rais Gilles observed.

Alec nodded. "As good as the Royal Navy, Rais."

"Mister MacMillan!" Alec called out. "Report to the quarterdeck."

The Scots giant came up the quarterdeck ladder. "Aye, sir?"

"If we get the weather gauge on the starboard fighting galleon, we'll open fire with a surprise broadside or two with a solid shot to stagger them. If the opportunity arises thereafter, we'll fire bar-shot and chain-shot from the deck guns into their rigging to cut it down. Meanwhile, the main battery must hammer them with a solid shot. Once they are partially disabled and cannot maneuver, we'll fire flaming spike-shot from the bow chasers to set them afire. Meanwhile, Montbars will do the same with the port fighting galleon to keep them out of the way while Kate Devon closes in on the Cacafuego to maneuver her away from the convoy."

Ian smiled. "Auld Clootie is doin' your thinking this night, sir."

"Get to your post then, Mac. Ye'll have hot work this night."

Rais Gilles put on his morion helmet. He looked at Alec. "Auld Clootie?" he asked.

"Scots for the devil, Rais."

The three darkened ships sailed close together and within hailing range, with the *Adventuress* ahead of the other two ships, a trio of deadly seagoing predators after a prize that could stagger the imagination of any man.

"Tattoo. Up into the maintop," Alec ordered. The black had eyes like a cat.

Tattoo sped swiftly up the rigging into the maintop.

Minutes ticked past. An hour was spent.

"Tattoo?" Alec hailed through cupped hands.

"Just within sight, master! Two fighting galleons. They've shortened sail."

Alec turned to Rais. "The signal."

Alec looked forward. He could just make out the dim stern lamps of the convoy ahead of them, by means of which the Spaniards could follow each other through the passage.

Rais lighted a bull's-eye lantern. He faced the stern of the frigate. He rapidly raised and lowered the lamp shutter to send out a series of long and short flashes. There would be no response, for the Spaniards could easily see such a light and know that none of their ships were that far behind the convoy.

"Message sent," Rais reported.

Alec nodded. "Have our stern lantern lighted, Mister Gilles, and see that it is shielded from the front and both sides so that it shows only astern."

The *Adventuress* moved swiftly through the water on a port tack under the impulse of the freshening breeze off the land. She was under all plain sail, but the cautious Spaniards had already shortened sail for the night.

Slowly and steadily, the frigate closed the gap between herself and the two Spanish ships ahead of her.

"The deck!" Tattoo hailed.

"Aye!" Alec responded.

"There is a great ship that has fallen behind the other ships who are ahead of the two ships just ahead of us. She is larger than the other big ships."

Alec looked at Rais. "The *Cacafuego?* Here's luck, Frenchman!" He strode to the break of the quarterdeck. "Get down your topgallant sails, Mister Yeoman!" He looked astern. "Why does Montbars lag? He should be abreast of us by now and following the port galleon."

The *Adventuress* had slowed down with the furling of the topgallant sails, but still, she was footing faster through the water than the two Spanish ships just ahead of her and Montbars' *Exterminator* as well.

Rais opened out the long brass telescope and studied the dark silhouettes of the two ships ahead of them and then looked farther ahead to the rest of the convoy. "These two last are likely fighting *naos*, Cutlass," he reported. "There is a great ship ahead of them, and sailing alone. Beyond her are two other large ships, but they do not seem to be as large as she is. There are several stern lights to be seen ahead of the other large ships."

"Likely the third of the fighting galleons and the big *navios*," Alec mused. "Scouting ahead toward the Atlantic." He smiled. "Instead of dropping back here to see what is going to go on." Alec eyed the two stern lights just ahead of them. "We're closing in. They're about five hundred yards apart. About two hundred and fifty yards for each broadside."

Rais almost dropped the telescope. "What the hell do you mean?" he demanded. "Sir," he added hastily.

"Montbars won't catch up in time. We can't wait for him. I'll take the *Adventuress* in between the two *naos* and fire both broadsides, one for each of them."

"At two hundred and fifty-yards' range? My God, Cutlass, if they suspect who we are and are ready for us, we'll be blown out of the water without so much as a chance to make our peace with God!"

Alec shook his head. "Knowing Jack Spaniard as we do, ye can almost be sure that even if their guns are loaded and ready for action, they won't have time to fire them before we get in a few killing broadsides. It's got to be the shake of the dice, Rais."

"We can *almost* be sure," Rais commented dryly.

Alec took the telescope and drew it out to its full length. He studied the huge silhouette of the great ship ahead of the two fighting galleons. "Send for Mister Shannon, with my compliments, Mister Gilles," he said.

The surgeon reported to the quarterdeck. "Aye, sorr?"

"Take this telescope into the maintop. Take a sight on that big ship ahead of the two *naos*. Tell me if you can recognize the *Cacafuego*."

The surgeon went aloft to the maintop.

"How big is she?" Rais asked.

"At least two thousand tons and with sixty or more guns. She is said to be the largest ship of her kind in the world."

Rais whistled softly. "And full of treasure for the taking."

"It's not quite as easy as that." Alec looked astern. "Damn Montbars! He will not catch up in time now. We needed his metal against those two *naos.* "

Terence Shannon came down the main shrouds to the deck and came aft to report. "It's her, all right, Cutlass," he said quietly. "No mistake."

It was quiet aboard the *Adventuress* except for the thrumming of the wind through the myriad ropes and lines of her towering rigging, the muted creaking and groaning of the hull as it worked in the slow surge of the sea, and the chuckling of the water under her forefoot and about her rudder as she forged ahead in the darkness, as though drawn to those two bobbing stern lanterns like a moth drawn to a flame.

Would the *Adventuress* be challenged by those two Spanish ships before she was in firing position between them? That thought was paramount in the minds of every man aboard the frigate. If that happened, and the two *naos* opened fire first on the frigate, or even simultaneously…

The *naos Rosario* and *Cazador* rolled lazily in the slow surge of the sea. Blocks clattered as they swung together. The steady clanking of a chain pump came from the deck of the *Cazador* asthe watch lowered the water in the well. The maintop lookout on the *Cazador* was looking ahead toward the dim, huge bulk of the lumbering *Cacafuego* as she pitched and rolled heavily. Soon, the *Cazador* and the *Rosario* would have to shorten sail to keep their station as the rearguard of the convoy. The maintop lookout on the *Rosario* was sound asleep.

Foot by foot and yard by yard, the *Adventuress* closed the gap between herself and the two unsuspecting Spanish ships.

"Light your matches, gunners," Ian MacMillan ordered tersely. "Pass the word there!"

The muted hail came from the quarterdeck of the *Cazador* off the port bow of the *Adventuress.* "What ship is that?"

There was no answer from the frigate as she gained headway to forge in between the two galleons.

"Run up the Red Jack, Mister Yeoman," Alec ordered.

The sailing master ran up the privateer's flag with his own hands.

The hail came again, this time much sharper. "What ship is that? Identify yourself!"

"Have each gun fire as it bears, Mister MacMillan," Alec ordered. "I'll give the command to open fire."

"What ship is that?" The faint hail came from the *Rosario* off the starboard bow of the frigate.

A drum began to beat to quarters on the *Cazador*.

Alec raised his brass-speaking trumpet to give the classic reply of the sea rovers: *"From the sea!"* He turned and spoke again through the trumpet. "You may fire at will, Mister MacMillan!"

The gunners of the first broadside guns in both the 18-pounder main-deck and 24-pounder gun-deck batteries applied the slow matches to the touchholes of their respective guns. All four guns blasted flame and smoke almost simultaneously. A roaring ripple of gunfire seemed to race along both sides of the frigate as she forged abreast of the two fighting galleons. Nine 18-pounder and ten 24-pounder solid shot from each broadside smashed into the *Rosario* and the *Cazador*. Stinking smoke blew back along the upper deck of the frigate and swirled about the quarterdeck. The heavy guns slammed back into their breechings.

"Stop your vents!" Ian MacMillan shouted.

The gunners pressed their leather thumbstals down on the touchholes to prevent the rush of eroding gases through the vents. Sponge staffs were dipped into water tubs and then rammed down the bores to swab out any sparks that might remain. The sponge staffs were withdrawn, and powder cartridges were thrust into the smoking muzzles and rammed home to be followed by the solid shot. Gun trucks rumbled over the deck planking as the gun crews strained at the tackles to run out the guns. As soon as the guns were fully extended, they were fired.

The galleons seemed to stagger as solid shot after solid shot slammed into their hulls or whined over their gunwales. The foremast of the *Cazador* was snapped off even with her gunwales. It swayed aft, helped by the freshening wind, and crashed down on the starboard side gun battery, killing or crushing the excited gunners who were trying to get their guns into action.

The *Adventuress* passed ahead of the two *naos*. "Wear ship, Mister Yeoman!" Alec commanded. "I want to rake that starboard Spaniard, sir! Run up your topgallants'!"

"Aye, sir! Hands to the braces! Hard astarboard!"

Men jumped to the windward sheets which controlled the big spritsail whose powerful draw could swing the ship in either direction. Sheet ropes were released. The canvas fluttered and spilled the wind as the leeward sheet was let go. The helm had been put down. The big heavy yards of the courses and topsails came around, and the bosun had his men haul on the trimming braces. The topgallant sails were let fall and sheeted home to add their power to the ship. The maincourse at last went over and filled with a rumble of low thunder. The capstan pawls clicked rapidly as the maincourse braces were hauled tight. The *Adventuress* began to stand off on the new tack. Gear slammed. The sheaves in the blocks rumbled and squealed. The canvas of the sails snapped, jerked, and murmured and then began to fill. As each sail filled fully into its classic curve, the frigate set off on its new course diagonally across the bows of the oncoming *Rosario*.

"Rake the bastard as each gun bears!" Ian MacMillan shouted above the din of the slatting sails.

It was an unnecessary command for the frigate's gunners knew their business. The first two guns of the starboard batteries crashed out, long, leaping tongues of orange-red flame and billowing smoke. As the *Adventuress* heeled to the power of the freshening wind, each gun in the starboard batteries raked the helpless Spaniard from bowsprit to quarterdeck. Mingled 18- and 24-pounder solid shot swept across her decks, hurling the gunners from their posts at their silent guns, ripping into the foremast to weaken it dangerously, and snapping the bowsprit so that it let the spritsail fall into the sea to lie athwart the bows of the *nao*. The *Rosario* lost steerage way with the loss of the spritsail.

The *Adventuress* had crossed athwart the Spaniard's bows as the starboard batteries emptied their guns. The frigate's smoking starboard guns were being reloaded.

"Wear ship!" Alec ordered.

Again, the swiftly moving frigate turned and swept back across the bows of the almost motionless *Rosario*. The frigate's port batteries flamed in a rippling of gunfire to rake the Spaniard again from stem to stern, turning her decks into an abattoir. Her foremast fell sideways into the sea, and the drag of it turned the *Rosario* off course. Blood began to trickle from her scuppers into the dark sea. The big main-yard broke loose and crashed down on her deck, killing and crushing the crews of four main deck guns.

"Where the hell is Montbars?" Alec yelled above the crashing of the guns.

Rais pointed off the starboard bow. "There! By God, Cutlass, he's closing in on the *Cacafuego* with the *Kate of Devon!* He's left us alone to handle these two *naos!*"

Through the stinking clouds of smoke could be seen the two ships sailing under all plain sail and passing to the east of the *Adventuress* and her two opponents.

"Shall we follow them?" Rais asked.

Alec's face was grim. "Not yet. We've work to be finished here. But then ..." His voice trailed off bitterly.

The *Adventuress* wore ship and then sailed in between the two *naos*. As each broadside gun bore the 24-pounder solid shot from the gun deck, the battery smashed into the hull while screaming, whining bar-shot and chain-shot were fired from the elevated upper-deck battery to rip and tear the rigging and sails of the two Spaniards into shreds and tatters. The decks were covered with falling gear and tangles of rope. The mizzenmast of the *Cazador* went by the boards, and she lay dead in the water.

The *Adventuress* was now astern of the *Cazador* and the *Rosario*. Her stern chasers situated in the great cabin below the quarterdeck flamed and roared, sending burning spike-shot into the *Cazador* at two hundred yards' range. The spikes stuck in the transom of the Spaniard and the burning oakum with which they had been wrapped set fire to the dry wood. Another fire had started from somewhere within her hold, and the thick smoke rose from the main hatchway to form a pillar high above the doomed ship.

"Rockets, sir," Rais Gilles reported. He pointed to the east.

Red and yellow fire arched up into the dark sky and burst high above the big fighting *navios* in the van of the convoy.

"They'll be coming after us with a stern wind," Rais said gloomily.

"There's not much time then, is there?" Alec asked. He did not expect a reply.

The *Rosario* opened a sporadic fire on the *Adventuress* from her stern chasers.

"Wear ship, Mister Yeoman!" Alec commanded. "I want to put the quietus on that last Spaniard as we pass her to go after the *Cacafuego* before those *navios* get back to her." Alec strode to the break of the quarterdeck. "Load with spike-shot, Mac! I want to torch this last Spaniard."

The *Adventuress* wore ship and turned to beat upwind past the *Rosario*. The frigate's 18-pounder guns were all being loaded with spike-shot. The 24-pounders had already been loaded with solid shot for a last killing broadside.

The upper deck of the *Rosario* was a bloody shambles cluttered with the dead, the wounded, and the dying. Not one gun crew remained on their feet. Below, in the gun-deck battery, only one man stood to his gun, a massive bronze 36-pounder. He was Bartolome Mendez, sixty-five years old and blind in one eye. Now, he stood stiffly at attention behind his gun. The gun was loaded and primed, and Bartolome Mendez had his burning, slow match in his hand. He could just see the bowsprit of the *corsairo luterano* poking its way past the *Rosario*, at two hundred yards' range.

It was a time for any prudent man to run for what little shelter he could find in the doomed ship, but Bartolome Mendez was a loyal seaman of His Most Catholic Majesty, and had been in His Excellency's service for fifty-two years.

Bartolome could see the guns of the frigate bearing on his ship. As her broadside flamed, he touched off his gun. The big 36-pounder slammed back in its breechings. A moment later, a 24-pounder solid shot came in through the opened gun port and neatly decapitated Bartolome Mendez at his last post of duty.

A 36-pound solid shot came low over the starboard gunwale of the *Adventuress* and struck the foremast to make a great crack that reached from the deck to her lower cross-trees.

"Get the sails off the foremast!" Miles shouted. "Else, she might go by the boards!"

As the foremast sails were furled, the frigate lost speed while sailing under her main and mizzen sails alone.

"Get that foremast fished, Yeoman!" Alec commanded. "We're going to need that sail power before this night is over!"

Miles Yeoman and Bosun Heydt saw to it that extra spars were lashed about the lower mainmast to support it.

Alec looked aft. As he did so, the *Cazador* exploded in a tremendous volcano of smoke, flame, and gases to illuminate the Mona Passage.

The drifting *Rosario* was aflame in scores of places where the flaming spike-shot had struck into her hull or masts. Not a soul moved on her brightly lighted deck.

Gunfire flashed as the *Kate of Devon* and the *Exterminator* fired chain-shot and bar-shot into the rigging of the lumbering *Cacafuego* to slow her down so that she might be turned back and herded into the Caribbean.

"There goes her main topmast!" Rais yelled.

"Good shooting," Ian MacMillan said.

Rockets soared up from the two big *navios* and the last of the three fighting *naos* as they dropped back with a good stern wind to take up a position between the corsairs and the remaining two plate ships.

"Watch Kate," Rais said in admiration. "How she handles that ship of hers, like a terrier after an elephant!"

Kate was maneuvering her ship in front of the *Cacafuego*, so close that it seemed as though the towering bowsprit would touch her masts and yards. A few random shots from the huge galleon's bow chasers popped off, but by that time, Kate was gone and was already wearing ship to return across the bluff bows of the *Cacafuego*.

Montbars was between the *Cacafuego* and the other two plate ships. He sailed slowly back and forth like a patrolling sentry.

"Ye notice that he has not yet endangered his ship," Alec observed. "The damned double-crosser!"

Rais shrugged. "He's only doing what he was told to do, Alec."

"He was told to help us fight the *two naos* back there, wasn't he?" Alec snapped. "We could have taken them in minutes instead of us having to waste all that time and get a damned lucky shot in return that cracked our foremast!"

The *Cacafuego*, with the loss of her topgallant and top sails had fallen off the wind. Her huge spritsail fluttered and then began to draw, bringing her head around to port, so that she now lay athwart her previous course.

"Kate is making her turn," Rais said. "The wind and the current are against the *Cacafuego*. She'll never be able to catch up with the convoy now, even if Kate wasn't in her way."

The flaming *Rosario* was drifting helplessly with the wind and current. Her sails and rigging were like flaring torches that cast an eerie light on the dark waters.

The two Spanish *navios* had turned in their course to take up position behind the two remaining plate ships, but the third of the *naos* that had been with the convoy still sailed steadily with a stern wind toward Montbars' ship, which stood between the oncoming Spanish fighting ship and the *Cacafuego* as well as Kate's *Kate of Devon*.

The last of the Spanish *naos* was the swift and powerful *frigata La Victoria*, manned by a crack crew and commanded by Don Rodrigo Alonzo de Mendez, once commander of the *Invincible*, which had been captured by Alec Campbell and Kate Devon in the Windward Passage. Don Mendez knew there were three powerful *corsairo luterano* ships attacking the *Nuestra Señora de la Candelaria*, but this meant nothing to him; his duty meant all to Don Mendez. And further, his fiancée, Rafaela Maria Espinosa de Vasquez, only child of Don Pedro de Vasquez, governor-general of Panama, was aboard the *Nuestra Señora de la Candelaria* as a passenger to Spain, where she was to marry Don Rodrigo himself.

Alec Campbell climbed partway up the mizzen shrouds, the better to see the oncoming Spanish ship.

"Whoever that Spaniard is, he's got his share of fighting guts."

"He's bluffed Montbars," Rais said. "See, the damned shark is turning away from him."

"If that Spaniard gets close enough to Kate, he'll likely put her out of action."

"Why doesn't Montbars attack him?"

A powerful explosion drew their attention astern in time to see the *Rosario* blow up in a soaring column of smoke, flame, and gases in which could be seen fragments of the ship and bodies being hurtled high in the air. Then, the remains of the *nao* went hissing under the waves, and it was dark again, in that intense darkness just before the rising of the tropical moon.

Miles Yeoman and his crew had lashed spare spars about the lower part of the cracked foremast to strengthen it. Bosun Heydt was already preparing to hoist the forecourse at a command from Alec Campbell. The *Adventuress* would soon be ready to maneuver in the forthcoming clash between herself and the lone Spanish fighting ship.

The three ships were but dark and tenuous shapes to each other. In the far distance to the east could be seen the faint stern lights of the fleeing convoy, while toward the west, and getting farther away from the scene of action, were the *Cacafuego* and the *Kate of Devon*.

The *Adventuress* was beating into the headwind. The Spanish ship had the weather gauge on the frigate. Montbars seemed unable to make up his mind. Now, he had worn ship and was slowly crossing the passage toward the *Adventuress* and across the course of *La Victoria*.

"Damn!" Alec exploded. "It's like maneuvering in a pot of ink! Why doesn't Montbars give us a recognition signal? We can't distinguish him from that damned Spaniard."

"The gun flashes will light them up," Rais said.

"When it might be too late, Rais."

"Wear ship!" Alec shouted.

The *Adventuress* slowly came about and slanted back across the passage toward the two dark shapes of the other ships. One of the other ships had come about and was sailing toward the *Adventuress*.

"Ready to open fire, sir!" Ian MacMillan called out.

"Hold your fire until we can see who the hell that is coming down on us!" Alec shouted.

"It's the *Exterminator!*" Rais cried.

"Are ye sure?" Alec asked.'

Rais shrugged. "I'm almost sure." He grinned. "We could make a mistake and open fire on him, eh, Cutlass? A great loss, of course…"

Alec snatched up his speaking trumpet. "Montbars!" he roared. "I've been damaged and am making repairs! Get between me and that Spaniard! It's up to ye now, Frenchman!"

There was no reply from the oncoming ship.

"What the hell is the matter with him?" Miles Yeoman shouted.

The *Exterminator* was moving faster than the *Adventuress* and had the weather gauge as well.

Alec had a terrible premonition. "Miles!" he yelled. "Wear ship, for the love of God! He means to run us down! Hands to the braces!" He whirled on the helmsman. "Hard astarboard!"

The *Adventuress* started to come slowly around. She heeled with the strong pressure of the wind abeam. Her sails fluttered and cracked sharply like many whips being snapped.

The *Exterminator* neared the *Adventuress* while the frigate was still turning. "Fire as your guns bear!" Jacques Montbars commanded from his quarterdeck.

Rais Gilles clasped his hands and bent his head. "For what we are about to receive, Dear Lord…" His voice trailed off.

The guns of the Frenchman roared and spat long tongues of flame and smoke. The solid shot smashed into the sides and gunwales of the *Adventuress*. Great splinters flew from the woodwork of the frigate. A seaman was skewered by a piece of wood four feet long and as ragged as the bill of a sawfish. He lay shrieking on the deck until one of his shipmates mercifully put a pistol bullet between his eyes.

"Fire!" Alec shouted desperately.

It was too late. The *Exterminator* had already passed the

frigate. Montbars wore his ship and came about, to pass astern of the *Adventuress.* His broadside guns roared and flashed again, and the shot ripped into the stern of the frigate, damaging her rudder, smashing in the rear of the stern cabin, and killing the crews of the two 12-pounder stern chasers before they could open fire.

Alec leaped up on the railing of the quarterdeck. "Damn ye, Montbars!" he yelled futilely.

"My apologies, Écossais*!,*" Montbars yelled back. "I thought you were a Spaniard coming up on me through the darkness!" He laughed uproariously as the *Exterminator* sailed off toward the distant Cacafuego and the *Kate of Devon.*

There was no time to curse. The Spanish *frigata* was bearing down on them. The litter of splinters and cordage was cleared from the main-deck guns. The dead, the dying, and the wounded were dragged aside.

"Doubleshot your broadside guns, Mac!" Alec commanded. "Load your bow chasers with bar- and chainshot! Jump and make it so! We'll likely have only one chance with this Spaniard!"

It was very quiet on the blood-stained deck of the frigate as the Spaniard bore down on them under full sail and with a ghostly white bone in her teeth. Behind her, to the east, far across the Atlantic, there was a faint wash of moonlight against the dark sky.

"Why doesn't she maneuver?" Rais asked. "She's got the weather gauge."

"What's wrong with him?" Miles Yeoman demanded.

Alec narrowed his eyes. "It can't be possible."

Rais Gilles nodded. "Before God," he murmured, "he thinks we're one of his own people…"

"Point-blank, Mister MacMillan!" Alec called out. "We'll only have the one chance. If we miss, or he opens fire first, that'll be the end of us, for he'll give us no quarter."

The hail came drifting across from the *La Victoria.* "What ship is that?"

Alec raised his speaking trumpet and garbled some Spanish through it, clearly repeating the word "disabled" twice.

"Do you need assistance?" came the query.

"No! Get after the *Cacafuego!* We'll be all right!" Alec replied in his excellent Spanish.

The *La Victoria* was within two hundred yards of the *Adventuress* now. The men on the frigate could hear the strident commands on the Spaniard's quarterdeck preparatory to tacking on a course for the Cacafuego.

The Spanish ship swung broadside to the *Adventuress* and was less than one hundred and fifty yards away from her.

"Now!" Alec roared.

"Fire at will!" Ian MacMillan commanded.

The entire port broadside of the frigate blasted forth a solid shot that slammed into the *La Victoria* with stunning force.

"Wear ship!" Alec ordered. "Hands to the braces! Hardalee!"

As the frigate slowly swung away from the *La Victoria*, the two 12-pounder bow chasers fired simultaneously, hurling bar-shot into the rigging of the Spaniard, and before the *Adventuress* had turned much farther away from the *La Victoria*, the two bow chasers were reloaded with bar-shot and fired. The bar-shot tore through the rigging and braces of the mizzenmast and brought it down in a tangle and clutter onto the quarterdeck.

The *Adventuress* was turned and then bore back toward the Spaniard. A few of the *La Victoria's* guns flamed in the darkness, but the aim was bad and only one shot struck the frigate. The starboard battery of the frigate roared as she passed the *La Victoria*. The Spaniard's mainmast came down in a horrendous tangle of spars and cordage which showered down on the living, the dead, and the dying.

The moon came up as the *Adventuress* tacked away from the disabled Spaniard. The soft light revealed the *Cacafuego*, now seemingly sailing in convoy with the *Exterminator* and the *Kate of Devon*.

The gunners of the frigate had reloaded their guns. They stood to their weapons and looked expectantly aft toward the quarterdeck, waiting for the command that would put an end to this Spaniard like the two other *naos* the *Adventuress* had defeated. To defeat three Spaniard fighting ships, each of which had equal gun power, or perhaps better than the *Adventuress*, would be a feat that would make the name of Captain Cutlass and the *Adventuress* ring throughout the Caribbean.

"We've got her cold, by God!" Ian MacMillan exclaimed.

Rais Gilles nodded. "She hasn't a chance."

The moonlight fully revealed the two ships now standing within five hundred yards of each other. Alec raised his telescope and focused it on the Spaniard. He could see the main-deck gunners standing to their guns. The moonlight shone on the polished morion helmets and breastplates of the Spanish officers on her decks. Axes rose and fell as the crew cut away the fallen mizzenmast and its wreckage to clear the helm and the quarterdeck.

"We've not got complete rudder control, sir," the helmsman reported.

Alec nodded. "That damned Frenchman's broadside into our stern took care of that."

"As well as the interior of your cabin and the crews of both stern chasers," Rais added.

The frigate was closing in on the *La Victoria*.

Alec studied the drifting Spanish ship. One face he remembered well seemed to swim into focus. "Don Rodrigo Alonzo de Mendez," Alec said quietly, almost as though to himself.

Rais looked quickly at him. "Him that you freed after we took the *Invincible?*"

Alec nodded. He lowered the telescope. "Helmsman," he said, "steer for our other ships."

Every man on the main deck of the *Adventuress* looked at Alec Campbell in disbelief. He was letting a sure thing slip right out of his hands.

Alec walked to the break of the poop. "We gain nothing by sinking yon Spaniard, men. We'll be risking further damage, too, if we close on him."

As the *Adventuress* passed the *La Victoria* within hailing distance, and without firing, the waiting Spaniards could not believe their eyes.

"Will you not fight, sir?" Don Rodrigo shouted in English.

"Ye've had your fight, sir! Be satisfied!" Alec called back. "What ship is that?"

"The *Adventuress,* sir! *From the sea!*"

Don Rodrigo looked down at his main-deck guns. The frigate was within good range. There might be a chance of disabling her yet.

"Open fire, sir," Carlos Morelos, the captain of the after-guard, pleaded.

Don Rodrigo shook his head. "He could have had us at his mercy. This is not the first time he has given me quarter."

"They are *corsairos luteranos!* Heretic devils!"

"Damn you, Morelos! They could sink us with one broadside! This way, we'll live to fight him another day! I am not through with him yet! One day, we'll face each other in single combat, and then I shall kill him!"

Carlos Morelos looked astern. The three ships, one of which was the mighty *Cacafuego,* were almost hull down on the moon-lighted sea. "But, *mi capitán,* your fiancée, Rafaela de Vasquez, is aboard the *Cacafuego.*"

Don Rodrigo nodded. "That is why I am not going to fight this Captain Cutlass to my death here in the Mona Passage. The man is a cutthroat and a thief, but he has honor, of a sort. My fiancée will not be harmed as long as he is her captor."

The *Adventuress* bore away toward the distant *Cacafuego* and her attendant ships, the *Exterminator* and the *Kate of Devon.*

Alec strode to the break of the quarterdeck. "Mister Yeoman! I want the topsail and the topgallant sail set on the foremast. We've got a fine fresh wind astern. Can we not set up studding sails as well?"

Miles Yeoman came aft. "Captain, sir, we can't even safely carry the press of sail we have on her now. I was going to ask you if we could take down the forecourse to ease the mast. The bowsprit took a solid shot and is cracked as well. We've at least a dozen 24-pound and 36-pound shot between wind and water. There is four feet of water in the well, and it's rising fast. I'm starting the pumps, but we'll have to fother the largest of the leaks, or the pumps won't be able to keep up with them. If we don't take the time to do it now, sir, the *guarda-costa* from Hispaniola will have us by dawn light."

"And the rudder has been damaged," Rais Gilles added.

"Always the bringer of good news, eh, Rais?" Alec asked sarcastically.

Rais shrugged. "It's a fact, Cutlass. There will be no chasing after Montbars this night."

Alec smashed a fist down on the shot-splintered railing of the quarterdeck. "Gulled, by God! Gulled by a double-crossing Frenchman and an English whore!"

"You think Kate was in on this?"Rais asked.

Alec turned on the Frenchman in a fury. "Damn ye! Ye *know* she must have been! They worked it out to a nicety!"

The Frenchman shrugged and held out his hands, palms upward. "We win one, we lose one. Alec, there will be other prizes."

"Not like the *Cacafuego!*"

Rais shook his head as he studied Alec. "It's really not that at all, my friend. It's being gulled by those two, especially the woman, that won't set in your craw. Look about you, Cutlass! We're lucky to be afloat! By the time we get this ship ready to sail after them, they will have been gone for weeks. It's a hopeless cause, Alec. For your own good, see it that way. Besides, this ship and her crew are your first concern, are they not?"

Rais was right. Alec nodded in agreement. "Always the man of logic, eh, Rais?"

Rais smiled. "I do my feeble best, Cutlass."

Alec walked to the break of the quarterdeck. "Miles!" he called out.

The sailing master hurried aft. "Aye, sir?"

"What's the butcher's bill?"

"Twenty-one dead. Seven mortally wounded. Eighteen others wounded."

Alec passed a hand across his eyes. "Christ's wounds," he murmured. He turned away and walked to stand silently at the taffrail.

Every man and officer aboard the *Adventuress,* even those slightly wounded, worked to their utmost capacity that moonlit night off the Mona Passage. They knew what would happen to them if the *guarda-costa* caught them by dawn light.

The fishing on the cracked foremast was redone and strengthened. Cut and torn lines and ropes were replaced. Buckets of seawater were sloshed over the decks to wash the sand and blood from them. The pumps never stopped their monotonous clanking. Old sails were fothered over the leaks at the waterline and just below it. The gunners sponged out their guns with vinegar water mixed with urine. Surgeon Terence Shannon was still carving and cutting away down in the gloomy, blood-spattered cockpit. A neat row of shrouded dead lay on the main hatch, with solid shot attached to their feet to make them sink to the bottom of the Mona Passage come dawn light.

By the time the first pewter traces of dawn light showed over the Atlantic, the *Adventuress* was under all plain sail on a course to the south, southwest, with her pumps never ceasing.

FIVE

They sighted the great dismasted hulk in the late afternoon, four days after they had sailed from the Mona Passage. The huge vessel rolled sluggishly on the slow sea surge. She was low in the water and had a list to port.

Alec Campbell closed up his telescope and turned to his officers. "It's the *Cacafuego*, all right. No doubt about it."

"Any signs of life aboard her?" Rais Gilles asked.

Alec shook his head. "None that I could see."

They all looked at each other.

"Then Montbars and Kate must have stripped her of her treasure and taken her passengers and crew with them as prisoners," Terence Shannon suggested.

"Let us *hope* they have taken prisoners," Alec said quietly. "Ye all know Montbars."

The wind was fitful and light, dying away only to return with renewed vigor as the frigate neared the huge plate ship.

"Fire a gun across her bows to wake them up, Mister MacMillan," Alec ordered.

One of the bow chasers was fired. The echo rolled along the sea. A feathery plume of spray arose just ahead of the bows of the derelict.

Minutes ticked past. There was no response from the *Cacafuego*.

"Lower the longboat, bosun," Alec ordered. "Serve out

sidearms to the boat crew. I'm going aboard. Mister Gilles, ye will accompany me."

The entire ship's crew of the frigate lined the rails watching the longboat crawling over the smooth sea like a large water beetle. There was something ominous about that huge hulk of a vessel rising and falling heavily in the sea surge.

The great size of the plate ship became more apparent as the longboat neared her.

Rais Gilles whistled softly. "Two thousand if she's a ton, eh, Cutlass?"

Alec nodded. "At least that."

The drab yellowish side of the ship towered above them, studded with closed gunports and with lines and ropes hanging from the decks like the dry, stringy hair of a long-dead corpse.

Rais narrowed his eyes. "Are those stripes of red paint below her scuppers?" he asked quietly. He knew better.

Alec shook his head. "Dried blood, Rais."

A faint and sickening odor drifted from the ship as the longboat came close to the side.

No one spoke as the longboat bumped against the side of the ship and was fended off. Alec stepped easily from the sternsheets to grasp the Jacob's ladder that still depended from the starboard gunwale high overhead. He looked down into the boat. "Kelly," he said to the coxswain, "leave two men in the boat. Lead the rest up to the deck after Mister Gilles."

"Thanks," Rais said dryly.

Alec smiled sweetly. "No bother, Rais."

Alec climbed slowly until he reached the thick, wide gunwale railing. He looked downward. Rais was climbing just below Alec, and Kelly was leading his men from the boat. Alec drew his dirk from its sheath and thrust it between his teeth in approved buccaneer fashion. He climbed quickly and rolled over the high gunwale to land light-footed and spraddle-legged on the deck with his dirk outheld in his right hand.

Alec did not move. He slowly lowered his right hand. "Mother of God," he murmured in Spanish.

The sickening odor he had noticed down in the boat was now a veritable stench that seemed to fill the waist of the ship. Corpses grotesquely swollen after several days under the burning tropical sun littered the deck by the dozens. Many of them were headless. Even as Alec stared incredulously at the scene of carnage, one of the corpses moved and emitted foul gas as the body cooled now that the sun was gone.

Rais Gilles poked his head above the gunwale. He immediately withdrew his perfumed handkerchief from within his left coat cuff and pressed it against his nose and mouth.

The thick deck planking was covered with great gouts of dried blood, while the rolling of the ship had caused little rivulets of blood to flow back and forth in intricate patterns until they had finally coagulated and then dried under the sun.

"An abattoir," Rais mumbled through his handkerchief.

"Montbars, *his mark...*" Alec said quietly.

The men of the boat's crew were sickened as they reached the deck of the *Cacafuego*. They were used to blood and sudden death in their dangerous calling, but none of them, even the most experienced, had ever seen anything like this.

"Shall we look for treasure, sir?" Kelly asked foolishly. He realized what he had said right away. Jacques Montbars and Kate Devon would have stripped the plate ship of anything of value before abandoning her. They had chopped through the masts and had dropped them over the port side of the ship, probably out of sheer wanton destruction.

"Why didn't they blow her up or sink her at least?" Rais asked. "Why leave this charnel house to float on the clean sea and pollute the air?"

Alec turned to look at the Frenchman. "Montbars." It was all he had to say. That one name explained everything of horror that had happened on the doomed *Nuestra Señora de la Candelaria.*

It was twilight now. The old ship creaked and groaned as she rolled listlessly. Alec sheathed his dirk and drew one of his pistols. He turned. "Kelly, search the forecastle. Sims, ye and Gentry search the gun deck. Penfield, Morrow, and MacIver look down in the holds."

"What are we lookin' for, sorr?" MacIver asked.

"Anyone still alive."

MacIver rolled his eyes. "On *this* death ship, sorr?" He shook his head.

Rais followed Alec aft to the great sterncastle. They mounted the ladder to the quarterdeck. A door suddenly banged in the motion of the ship as she lifted to a large surge and then dipped heavily again.

"They will have taken the women and the gentry with them," Rais suggested hopefully.

"According to the Articles, Rais." Alec turned. "He broke the Articles when he opened fire on us. For that, he'll pay…"

Alec opened the door of the great cabin. It was dark inside. Faint light shone through the broken stern windows. Alec groped around until he found a candle. He struck flint and steel and lighted the candle. He placed it on a sideboard.

"For the love of God," Rais breathed.

Alec turned quickly.

A gray-haired man sat in a high-backed chair at the head of the large table that dominated the wide cabin. His thin, white hands rested on the tabletop in front of him. He was dressed in funereal black with a touch of white lace at his throat.

"Is he alive?" Rais whispered.

Alec held the candle out toward the old man. Trickles of dried blood that had run from his eyes were on his thin cheeks. He had been blinded.

The old man was motionless. He must have died sitting in that position.

Alec turned to look into the sleeping cabins.

"Have you returned for more slaughter?" the thin, reedy voice said in Spanish from behind Alec and Rais.

They looked quickly at each other and then turned slowly.

"Perhaps you have come back to murder me too?" the

old man asked. "You should have had the mercy to kill me before you left my ship. But, to leave an old man alive and blinded aboard this ship whose only cargo now is death, that is inhuman."

"Who are you, sir?" Alec asked in Spanish.

"You don't know? You who looted my ship of the king's treasure and took away the young women, the finest blood of New Spain, for your own brutal purposes? You ask me who I am?"

"We were not with the others," Alec explained.

"Who are you then? From the Royal Navy? The *guarda-costa?* If so, you are far too late."

"No. We are privateers, sir."

"Ah! That is more like it! *Corsairos luteranos!* Kill me, then! There is nothing more to be taken from my ship. Even now, she dies slowly and alone on these waters."

"We know," Alec agreed sympathetically. "Is there anyone else alive on this ship?"

"Only the great rats in the lower hold."

"And the treasure?"

"They worked for two days taking it into their ships. I showed them where everything was and had my crew help them place it on their ships. They had given their word that if we did so, they would not harm any of us and let us alone."

"And you believed them?" Rais asked.

The old man raised his thin hands. "What else could we do? We were helpless before them. Ah, that devil of a Frenchman and that red-haired harpy of a woman! Hell will receive their souls!"

"Who are you?" Alec repeated.

He drew himself up erect. "Don Bartolome Jaime Raphael de Varga y Arriola, captain of His Most Catholic Majesty's ship *Nuestra Señora de la Candelaria!*"

"What happened here, sir?" Alec asked.

Don Bartolome bent his head. "They took the young women with them first. One of them is Rafaela Maria Espinosa de Vasquez, the only child of Don Pedro de Vasquez, governor-general of Panama."

"Who slaughtered your crew?" Rais asked quietly.

"It was the Frenchman! That grinning devil. He ordered the crew down into the hold and had them come up one by one while he stood at the hatch with his sword in his hand, lopping off heads while he roared with laughter…"

"*Jesus,*" Alec murmured.

"When he tired of his bloody sport, he turned his crew loose on the remainder of my men. When I protested, Montbars, that soulless savage, personally put out my eyes and locked me here in my great cabin. I have been here ever since they left."

"The red-headed woman," Alec asked, "was she here when your crew was being slaughtered?"

Don Bartolome shook his head. "She had already left, that scarlet whore!"

"He's right there," Rais murmured.

Alec walked toward the table. "Come then, old man, we'll take you to our ship and see that you are sent ashore on a Spanish possession."

"No, I cannot report to my king that I lost his great ship without firing a shot."

"You can't stay here," Rais protested. He came forward. "Here," he offered, "take one of my pistols, then."

"I am a Catholic, señor. I would be eternally damned if I took my own life."

Rais looked at Alec. He shrugged.

They walked to the door together. Alec turned. "I mean to destroy your ship, Don Bartolome."

The Spaniard nodded. "That is as it should be."

"You won't come with us?"

"No."

"*Vaya con Dios,* then, Don Bartolome."

Don Bartolome waved a thin hand.

Alec closed the door behind himself.

The boat's crew waited on the deck. "Not a sign of life anywhere, sir," Kelly reported.

Alec nodded. "Return to the boat, Kelly."

Alec and Rais stood alone on the darkened deck. Alec looked sideways at Rais. "Ye too, Rais."

"I'll wait with you, Alec."

Alec shook his head. "I can handle it alone."

When Rais was gone, Alec found a lantern and lighted it. He descended the blood-splattered ladder down into the main hatchway and then down through the dark gun deck and the pitch-black orlop deck to the huge powder magazine. He placed the lantern on the deck, all the time fully aware of the reflection of the light on the tiny reddish eyes watching him from the darkness beyond the pool of lantern light. There was a rustling and squeaking among the great ship's rats. They were suspicious.

He laid a powder train from the magazine to the foot of the ladder. He struck flint and steel and lighted the end of the powder train and then leaped for the ladder an instant ahead of a rush of the huge rats.

Alec climbed, almost in a panic, for he knew they would be swarming up the ladders after him to abandon the ship as he planned to do. He reached the upper deck and ran for the side of the ship just as the first of them appeared at the top of the ladder. Alec swung himself over the gunwale and dropped down the Jacob's ladder, missing every second or third step in his mad haste to outrun the panicking horde.

"Shove off!" Alec yelled as he dropped into the boat.

The first rats began to drop over the side of the ship. Some of them landed in the sea while others dropped atop the men in the boat. The men cursed and yelled, striking out at the desperate creatures.

Rais and Alec drew their swords and spitted rats to flip them over the side. "Row, God damn ye, row!" Alec yelled at the boat's crew.

They thrust out the oars and began to pull with all their strength away from the towering side of the *Cacafuego*. Some of the rats clung to the oars until spitted by Rais or Alec.

They swung in alongside the *Adventuress*. "Let's get to hell out of here!" Alec yelled hoarsely.

The frigate was drawing slowly away from the *Cacafuego* under all plain sail when the plate ship blew up in a thunderous explosion, showering burning debris high into the night air. Burning fragments pattered on the decks of the frigate, and a huge block struck the ship's bell as though impelling it to ring a knell for the end of the greatest plate ship of them all—the *Nuestra Señora de la Candelaria*.

Six

The island lay humped like a great sea turtle mantled in dark forest green. The wide bay lay protected within a far-flung coral reef like the necklace of a savage. Some of the coral heads thrust up out of the sea, revealing themselves by the white scarf of foam washing about them, while those hidden beneath the water gave themselves away by mysterious swirlings on the surface as the underwater currents worked around them. Two ships were anchored within the bay. Beyond the ships were the red dots of campfires glowing in the dusk like rubies placed against dark green velvet.

The onshore wind had eased with the arrival of dusk. The heavy pinnace had cautiously approached the island under oars with the cover of darkness and now pitched and surged in a low ground swell just beyond the reef.

Alec Campbell lowered his telescope. "It's the *Exterminator* and the *Kate of Devon,* all right, Rais."

Rais shrugged. "Now that we've found them at last, Cutlass, what are we going to do about it? We don't know the passage through the reef, and even if we did, you know damned well that Montbars and Kate must have emplaced shore batteries to cover the channel. If we poked our nose into that bay under the coming moonlight, we'd likely get an 18-pounder shot right up our bungholes. No, Cutlass, there will be no going in there tonight in this pisspot of a pinnace with that 3-pounder brass swivel gun we've got for armament. I still think we should have waited until the *Adventuress* was repaired and ready for sea again."

"Ye sound like a damned sea lawyer! If we had waited for the *Adventuress* to be careened, it would have taken weeks. By that time, Montbars and Kate would have been long gone from here."

"So, we didn't wait! So we sailed over a hundred miles in an open boat on the edge of a hurricane, and now we're here. Do we wait for moonlight and run up a flag of truce? Montbars pretended he mistook us for a Spaniard back there in the Motna Passage and damned near put us out of business. He won't take chances with us now."

"The irrefutable logic of a Frenchman." Alec grinned. He looked at the coxswain of the pinnace. "It's dark enough now to hoist our sails, Cutting. Bring her about and sail her back along the coast to find a likely landing spot. Besides, we need fresh water. That's reason enough to land, isn't it, Rais?"

They raised the two stubby masts and hoisted the standing lug sails. Cutting steered a course east along the shoreline until the firelight on the beaches could not be seen. Two miles from the Great Bay, they found a place where the coral reef did not guard the shore. They took the heavy pinnace in under oars toward a mangrove-bordered beach and ran her up a shallow freshwater stream until she was fully concealed by the thick foliage.

Alec fitted his baldric over his shoulder and slid broadsword and dirk into their frogs. He removed the charges from all three of his pistols and reloaded them with fresh charges. The crew buckled on their leather belts, heavy with cutlasses, pistols, and long knives. They withdrew the loads from their pistols and calivers, the short-barreled and deadly arquebuses with big bores, and reloaded them.

"Two men to stay here with the boat, Cutting," Alec instructed.

Rais nodded. "Good thinking! That will leave us eight men besides yourself, me, and Tattoo. Surely enough to face down Montbars and Kate Devon and their five hundred or so men."

Alec shook his head. "I'll enter the camp alone, except for Tattoo."

"You're mad!"

Alec smiled. "Do ye think having nine men with me would make any difference, Rais?"

"Montbars will have you killed on sight!"

Alec shrugged. "Perhaps, but then again, if I can appeal to Kate and the two ships' crews that Montbars voided the Articles, it might swing them my way."

"Now, who's a sea lawyer? Besides, I think Kate was in on the deal with Montbars. It all worked out too smoothly, Cutlass. At that, it was a beautifully planned piece of work."

"If Kate was in on the deal, she voided the Articles too. If I can convince both crews of that, they might rise and depose both her and Montbars."

"A slender reed upon which to lean."

"It's all I have, Rais. Come, we've got a short walk ahead of us this evening."

Alec and Rais led the way down the yellow beach, ghostly pale in the dimness. The beach was bordered by coconut palms which overhung it, while beyond the fringe of palms was a dense jungle through which the muted sound of nocturnal creatures and insects carried to the silent men.

"Wait," Alec said.

They stopped. The onshore wind had died away. The air was quiet before the rising of the moon. The faint sound of the beach camps came to them.

Alec turned. "Tattoo!"

The giant black vanished instantly into the tropical forest as silently as the movement of one of the shadows of the night.

"There is hell being raised in those camps," Rais suggested. He grinned. "And here we stand on a wet beach with sand in our boots, sober and without women. And, by tomorrow? Perhaps we'll all be dead at the hands of Montbars the Exterminator."

Alec shrugged. "Ye did not have to come with me, Rais. Ye could have sat on your arse back at the hideout while the rest of the crew sweated, careening the frigate."

"How could I resist? To see a mad Scot walk alone into

such a hell's brew as we can hear along the bay, to beard Montbars in his den. Aye, and the Lord will not be there to protect you in *that* lion's den as he did Daniel."

Alec nodded thoughtfully. "We'll put it to the test, though." He rested his left hand on the basket hilt of his broadsword. "The Lord and my guid steel blade, perhaps, eh?"

Tattoo came back through the dark jungle. "Guards along beach, mebbe tree hunnert yards, master. Shore battery beyond guards. Two guns. Big. Maybe 24-pounders." He held up two hands with outspread fingers. "That many men with guns." He pointed back toward the jungle. "Path dere. No one guards. I follow. See into camp, but they not see me." Tattoo grinned to reveal his filed teeth.

"Montbars?"

Tattoo nodded. "And Kate too."

"What else did you see?"

"White women in pen like cattle. Young. Dark hair. Spanish maybe. I see two of them escape. But guards see. Men follow them into jungle. Many pipes of rum and wine on beach. Men all gettin' drunk."

"Did the guards catch the women who escaped?"

"I didn't see."

"But they're still in the jungle?"

Tattoo nodded. "They catch when moon comes up." He pointed toward the east. A faint wash of moonlight stained the sky.

"Show me where these women are, Tattoo. Rais, get under cover until I send Tattoo for ye."

"And, if you don't send him?"

"Then the *Adventuress* is yours and the other officers'."

"This is madness!"

Alec grinned. He pointed toward the rising moon as Tattoo had done. "I always get this way with the coming of the full moon." He followed Tattoo into the jungle.

As the moon arose, pale shafts of its light came down from openings in the jungle cover to form faint pools on the jungle floor.

Tattoo halted. He turned and placed a finger to his lips. He pointed up and then around to indicate that the night creatures and insects were silent now, as though something had disturbed them.

A grunting sound came to them, like a hog rooting in the soft soil. A woman cried out suddenly.

Alec and Tattoo catfooted forward to look into a moon-lighted clearing. A man's back was toward them. His thick legs were straddled outward, and his hands were cupped under the knee joints of a pair of outspread naked legs. A pair of badly worn shoes and another pair of man's legs showed between the erect man's legs, and they moved with a convulsive rhythm.

Alec moved sideways. A plump woman, stripped to the skin, lay under the man on the ground. It was her legs that were held far outward by the man who stood.

"Drive it home, Walt!" the standing man cried hoarsely. "Hurry up! I'm liable to come while standin' here watchin' ye fumblin' around."

"It's the rum slowin' me down, Charley," Walt complained over his right shoulder.

"Then get off and let *me* have a crack at her!" He dropped the woman's legs and stood off to one side while he fumbled with the front of his breeches.

The woman's mouth was open and contorted, but she made no sound other than a stifled gagging noise. Her round face was marked with livid welts, and a thin trickle of blood ran from the corner of her mouth.

Charley never knew what killed him as the broadsword drove into his back and pierced his heart. He fell sideways without a murmur while still holding his erect cock in his right hand.

The woman's dark eyes opened as she saw the tall, scar-faced man standing to one side and looking down at the man who was raping her.

Walt must have felt something boring into the back of his head, for he slowly turned it to look up into a pair of icy gray eyes he had known all too well in his spotted past. He opened his mouth to speak, but no word came to his dry lips.

"Get up, ye filthy bastard," Alec ordered.

Walt got up. He hastily stuffed his cock back into his

filthy breeches. "For God's sake, Captain Cutlass! Montbars canceled the Articles this day! Me and Charley there had a right to this."

Alec slowly shook his head. "No man has a right to take a woman prisoner wi'out her consent, dog, Articles or no Articles."

"Not so on Montbars' ship!"

"Ye are not on Montbars' ship now."

Walt spread out his dirty hands. "Give me a chance, Cutlass!"

Alec smiled thinly. "How do ye want your chance now, scum? Wi' sword or dagger? Fists and boots?"

Walt looked down at the blood-stained double-edged blade of the broadsword and then at the mate to it, the ancient silver-mounted dirk held in the left hand of Cutlass. "I've no chance wi' ye and that damned murderous broadsword. Knives, then."

"Knives it is." Alec stepped back and thrust the tip of the broadsword into the soft ground and then stepped away from it while he transferred the dirk from his left hand to his right hand. The broadsword swayed back and forth like a thing alive.

Walt ripped his dagger loose from its belt sheath and charged desperately, throwing caution to the winds, hoping to get in the first killing thrust.

Alec stepped quickly to one side. His dirk blade met that of Walt's dagger, and they clicked together to rise up to eye level. Walt raised a knee to smash it into Alec's crotch, but a hard left fist smashed into the pit of his belly, and he gasped for breath and bent forward. Alec dragged back on his dirk while it was still locked with that of his opponent. He pulled Walt to one side and thrust out his right leg. Walt fell sprawling over Alec's thigh. Alec disengaged his dirk. Walt stumbled forward, half bent over. The dirk plunged deep into his back, and he fell heavily. He was dead before he hit the ground.

Alec stepped back. He carefully wiped the dirk blade clean on the dead man's sweat-soaked shirt.

The woman was sobbing as though her heart would

break. She had sat up and let her long dark hair fall forward to cover as much of her nakedness as it could.

Alec found the woman's torn petticoat and black dress where they had been ripped from her body. He dropped them beside her and then turned his back on her. "There, there, señora," he soothed in Spanish. "They haven't hurt you that much, have they?"

"It was the shame, señor, not the act itself. To be serviced like a broodmare, flat on my back in the dirt, is not the way I like it."

"How are you called, señora?" Alec asked.

"Teresa Gomez. I am maidservant to Señorita Rafaela Maria Espinosa de Vasquez, daughter to His Excellency Governor-General Don Pedro de Vasquez of Panama."

Alec whistled softly. "I've heard of her, the loveliest flower of New Spain." He narrowed his eyes. "Was she not a passenger aboard the *Nuestra Señora de la Candelaria?*"

Teresa nodded her head. "She was, *señor.*"

"And where is she now?" Alec demanded.

A woman's thin scream echoed through the jungle.

"That could be her now!" Teresa cried. "We escaped from the prison pen at the beach! I stayed behind to fight off these two rutting pigs to allow her to escape!" Her voice died away as she saw Alec and Tattoo running lightly through the jungle toward the place from which the scream had seemed to emanate. Teresa snatched up Walt's dagger and waddled off after the two men as fast as she could go.

The jungle was dark and quiet again. Faint moonlight filtered down from up above the overhanging treetops. Two shadowy figures moved noiselessly through the undergrowth.

Something crashed through the jungle. A man laughed.

Then it was deathly still again. There was a little savannah of tall grass in the distance. It was ringed around with the thickset trees and creepers of the jungle. The moonlight shone down on the dry yellowish grass.

A young woman, naked except for a silver chain and crucifix about her neck, broke into the savannah. Her fair white skin was scratched and bleeding. She ran wearily out into the center of the savannah. Muted sobs broke from her as she ran. She turned and looked back toward the jungle from where she had come. Her lustrous black hair hung over her face and shoulders. Her breasts were full and proud, brown-budded with outthrust nipples. Her legs were long and slim and beautifully shaped. She couldn't be more than seventeen or eighteen years old, but she was a grown woman, at least in figure.

The woman did not see the two motionless men standing within the shadowed shelter of the jungle just behind her. Instead, she looked back to the far side of the savannah.

There were five of them, reeling and swaying from drink, who burst out of the green tangle and stopped at the edge of the jungle. They wore ragged finery, stained with food grease, dirt, and liquor slops. The moonlight shone on the gold earrings dependent from their hairy ears. One of them had stripped to the waist with his great hairy belly bulging over his low-slung breeches.

Big Belly peered wearily across the savannah. "There's the naked little jaybird! Stay, *señorita! Párate!* Halt, I say!"

They spread out into a slowly moving crescent and walked, swaying and lurching through the tall grass. One of them drank from a jug and then passed it on to the next man.

She ran wearily toward the forest and then turned at bay with her back against a tree and her arms behind her back and about the tree trunk. Sweat ran down her fair skin. Her dark hair hung before her oval face.

"A fair piece, I say!" one of the men yelled. "Who'll be first to pluck her cherry?"

Big Belly turned his head. "Me," he replied truculently. "Who denies my right?"

"There are four of us, Ned."

Ned grinned, revealing crooked yellow teeth. "Ye challenge me, eh, Jimbo?"

"There are always the dice," another man suggested as he lowered the rum jug from his mouth and wiped his lips both ways with the back of a hairy hand.

Ned shook his head. He stopped walking and whipped out his heavy brass-guarded cutlass. The moonlight glittered on the wide blade. "This is *my* cast of the dice, Ben. A winning cast, say ye?"

No one challenged Ned.

Ned turned toward the girl and held out a greasy hand while he sheathed his cutlass. "Come, love, make it easy on yereself. We go by the rules on Montbars' ship. No woman is to be bothered except by the man who champions her. Otherwise, lass, these four horny fuckers will be on ye like dogs on a bitch hound in heat. Ye understand? Come to Ned, eh?"

"For the love of God, *señores,*" the girl pleaded in Spanish, "I am a virgin, betrothed to Don Bartolome de Mendez. I was on my way to Spain to marry him at the court of His Majesty."

Ned stared at her. "What gibberish is this? If ye don't play nice with old Ned here, I'll bite off them rosy nipples of yours." He laughed uproariously.

Ned began to stalk toward her with his head bent low.

Alec Campbell stepped out of the shadows into the full moonlight, claret-colored full coat, wide-brimmed plumed hat, silver pistols, silver-mounted dirk, and broadsword, along with a cold smile on his scarred face. "The young lady says she is a virgin, betrothed to Don Bartolome de Mendez, and was on her way to Spain to marry Don Bartolome at the court of His Majesty," Alec translated.

Ned stopped short. His piggish eyes surveyed Alec. "Cutlass," he said quietly. "They said ye were dead, sunk sixty fathoms in the Mona Passage."

"Perhaps I *am* dead, Big Belly."

It was suddenly very quiet except for the faint sounds from the encampment on the beach.

"He's lying!" Jimbo cried. "That's Cutlass, sure enough! I once sailed along with him and Henry Morgan!"

"And ye sat in the bilboes aboard the *Adventuress* for two days for stealing from your shipmates," Alec added.

Their eyes flicked back and forth, trying to see if Cutlass was alone. They could not see the immobile black Tattoo standing in the deep shadows, holding his hand over the mouth of fat Teresa to keep her quiet.

Alec stood just in front of the space between two thick-boled trees with his left hand resting lightly on the basket hilt of his broadsword. Rafaela stood in front of the tree to his right.

"He's alone," Jimbo said out of the side of his mouth.

Ned grinned. "Easy pickings. I'll take the weapons, the coat and hat. The rest of ye can fight over what's left."

"Ye're a fine one, Ned," Ben murmured.

Alec smiled. "How do ye want it, scum? All together or one at a time?"

Teresa tried to scream. Tattoo placed powerful fingers at the side of her neck and pressed firmly. The woman sank to the ground unconscious. Tattoo dragged her into the under-growth and then returned to stand unseen behind one of the trees beside Alec. He withdrew a razor-sharp cutlass from its sheath.

"I'm waiting," Alec said patiently.

Ned roared with laughter. "Listen to the cocky Scots bastard! Why, ye cockerel! I'll split your brisket from throat to navel in one blow!"

Alec reached out with his right hand and gripped the left arm of the trembling girl. Ned saw his chance. He rushed forward, ripping his cutlass out of its sheath as he did so. Alec shoved the girl behind himself and whipped out his broadsword with his right hand while he drew his dirk with his left hand. The moonlight flashed from both blades as Alec leaped forward to meet Ned's attack. The broadsword went up high to parry the cutlass blow, and the dirk flicked in to pink the underside of Ned's right forearm. Blood spurted. Ned staggered back, cursing luridly. He charged again. This time, the dirk parried the cutlass, and the broadsword came down in a Highlander's drawing slash that split Ned's face open from the bridge of his nose to the point of his jaw. Ned dropped his cutlass and staggered backward, clasping both hands to his slashed face.

Ben had cut sideways while Alec was occupied with Ned. He jumped into the shadows to the left of Alec to work his way in behind him. Ben didn't see, among the shadows, the tall black shadow that was Tattoo. The cutlass rose and fell with killing force as though Tattoo was split-ting a coconut. Ben's head dropped to the ground. For a fraction of a second, the headless body still stood, spouting blood from the great ragged hole of the throat, and then the body fell headlong. Rafaela screamed in terror at the sight.

Jimbo led the attack on Alec. Broadsword rang against cutlass. The point of the broadsword was dropped and lunged for the throat. The blade transfixed Jimbo's throat, and an inch of it protruded through the back of the neck while the dirk came up from underneath and ripped into Jimbo's guts. Jimbo fell and Alec leaped over his body to charge the other two combatants.

"*Cruachan!*"Alec screamed hoarsely. He had on him the battle madness of the wild Celts.

The last two men on their feet stared incredulously at Alec. "I've always said he wasn't human, Sam," one of them said to the other out of the side of his mouth.

Sam held out his left hand toward Alec. "Cutlass, me and Jack here wanted no part of this. Let us go, and we won't try to harm ye anymore."

Ned had crawled to one side, thinking he was out of Alec's view. He slowly drew his pistol from his belt and cocked it. He raised it to fire. Alec turned sideways and hurled his bloody dirk at Ned. The point struck Ned in the throat, and he fell backward while raising his pistol. Reflex finger action pressed the trigger, and the pistol flamed. The ball sang thinly off into the treetops.

Jack looked back over his shoulder.

"Ye violated the Articles," Alec said quietly. "Run or stand. Either way ye die here."

Jack ran. Sam stood his ground.

"Tattoo!" Alec called.

Tattoo streaked from the woods like a great black panther with bloody upraised cutlass. Jack looked back over his shoulder. He screamed once. The cutlass rose and fell.

Sam charged, driving Alec back momentarily. Their blades clashed and rang together. Alec threw Sam back when they locked swords at chest height. Sam saw the killing look in Alec's eyes. He broke free and turned to run. Tattoo was walking quickly toward him with a glistening upraised blade. Sam whirled. He thrust hard at Alec. Alec parried the thrust. His broadsword point drove a hand's span into Sam's chest, and the pirate dropped lifeless at Alec's feet.

Alec drew his dirk from Ned's throat. He wiped dirk and broadsword on Sam's breeches and then stripped the shirt from the corpse.

"Get rid of these human vermin, Tattoo," Alec ordered. "Hide them deep in the jungle."

Alec walked to the edge of the trees. "*Señorita!*" he called out in Spanish. "You are safe here now. Here, put this on. It's all I have to give you. It's not in the latest fashion, but it will cover you exceeding well." He tossed the shirt into the shadows.

Rafaela came slowly from the woods, enveloped in the large shirt which came down almost to her shapely knees.

Alec could not help but smile.

"Do not laugh at me, *caballero,*" she pleaded.

He placed a hand under her chin and raised her head a little. He smiled winningly. "I do not laugh at you, little one. I just thank God we came here in time."

Teresa crept from the woods and stood behind her mistress. Her eyes were wide in her head as she watched Tattoo dragging a corpse into the woods.

"You are Señorita Rafaela Maria Espinosa de Vasquez, daughter to His Excellency Governor-General Don Pedro de Vasquez of Panama, are you not?" Alec asked Rafaela.

She nodded. "That is true, but how did you know, sir?"

"Teresa told me, but I had previous knowledge that you would be aboard the *Nuestra Señora de la Candelaria.*"

She narrowed her lovely dark eyes. "How did you know that? Who are you, *señor?*"

Alec swept off his plumed hat and bowed, sweeping the plume across the toe of his outthrust right boot. "Captain Alexander Duncan Campbell, of the Campbells of Cawdor, at your service, seño*rita.*"

Rafaela paled a little. One of her fine-boned hands crept up to her smooth throat. "But, you are known otherwise here in the Caribbean, are you not?"

He smiled. "Some call me the Mad Scot, but I think you must mean the nickname I earned while sailing with Sir Henry Morgan. I earned the name Captain Cutlass during the sacking of Cartagena. That name was given to me by my enemies, your people, *señorita*, but as you can see, it is a misnomer, for I carry the broadsword and dirk of my great-grandfather, Sir Duncan Campbell, second son of Argyll and once thane of Cawdor."

"Captain Cutlass," she murmured. "It is said that you are the Scourge of the Spanish Main, Captain Campbell."

"Merely one of many, señor*ita*. There are many competitors for that title, I am afraid." He looked back over his shoulder in the direction of the beach encampment of Kate Devon and Jacques Montbars.

"What will you do with us, captain?" she asked quietly.

He turned and looked at her. "Back from whence you came."

"For the love of God! No! No! No! It is a madness they have in them there. They drink and openly fornicate with whores on the beach sands and in the jungles. Some of the gentlewomen who were captured with us on the *Nuestra Señora de la Candelaria* have already been raped and beaten by those devils. I was told I was to be next. I escaped with the help of one of them by promising I would wait for him in the jungle to satisfy his lust."

"That was foolhardy, *señorita.*"

"What else could I do?"

"There are said to be Caribs living on the north shore of this island. Do you know of the Caribs?"

She shook her head.

"They are cannibals, lassie."

"Mother of God!" Teresa cried.

"Ye would not have lasted two days in that jungle," Alec continued. "If the poisonous fer-de-lance snakes did not bite you, the Caribs would have caught you."

Rafaela closed her eyes and quickly turned her head aside.

"I do not tell ye this, señor*ita*, to frighten you. When I said I would take ye back from whence ye had come, I did not mean the camp of Montbars and Kate Devon, although we must go there first, but rather back to Porto Bello."

She turned her head slowly. "To free us, *señor?* I don't understand."

He smiled. "For ransom. As the daughter of the governor-general, you should bring a pretty price, but only if you are unharmed."

"But, that was not the intention of that French monster and that red-headed whore!" Rafaela cried.

Alec shook his head. "They broke the Articles, not only in your case, but also in mine. I mean to bring them to account."

She looked back over a shoulder. "Where are your men?"

"I am alone, except for Tattoo."

She turned quickly. "You'll go in there alone?"

Alec nodded.

"This is a madness! There are hundreds of armed men in that camp. What chance would you have, *señor?*"

He half smiled. "It is a question of honor."

It was her turn to smile, half whimsically. "Among thieves?" she asked dryly.

He raised his eyebrows. "I am not a thief! I bear letters of marque as a privateersman from King Charles of England."

"That is said to be merely licensed piracy," she accused.

"But only by you Spaniards," he countered.

She tilted her lovely head to one side. "I don't understand."

"You Spaniards deem any other nation than your own as pirates or buccaneers in this so-called Spanish Lake, as you call the Caribbean."

She was puzzled. "But the Treaty of Tordesillas between Spain and Portugal established the spheres of influence in the New World, thus giving Spain the right to the Caribbean Sea and the lands adjacent thereto."

"By a papal bull of 1493 that defined that right," Alec added dryly. "Issued by a Spanish pope."

"So?" she demanded angrily.

"So, your pope and the Catholic Church gave this half of the known world to the Spanish and the Portuguese, without ever considering the rights of the English, Scots, Hollanders, and the French, as well as all the other

European nations. Were they ever consulted about the matter?"

"But the treasure of the New World does belong to Spain and Portugal!" she cried.

"By what right? The right of conquest! Did Columbus, or Cortez, or Pizarro ever think to ask an Arawak, a Carib, a Toltec, an Aztec, or an Inca for permission to land in their countries in order to rape the land of its treasures? To enslave their peoples? To slaughter them like sheep? To take hundreds of shiploads of the greatest treasure the world has ever seen back to Spain?"

"But your people are *corsairos luteranos!* You do not believe in the True Church!"

Alec nodded. "And you do?" He shrugged. "I can see there is no use in furthering this rather interesting discussion."

Tattoo came noiselessly from the jungle. He nodded to Alec.

The wind had come up and had shifted so that the sounds of revelry from the camp came to them through the jungle tangle, mingled with the odors of woodsmoke and roasting meat.

"Come, ladies," Alec invited.

"Can't we be taken to your ship?" Rafaela asked.

Alec shook his head. "You are still Company property."

"Then why did you save us from dishonor and death only to turn us over to those white savages there on the beach?" she demanded.

"Because of the Articles signed by every man aboard those two ships in the bay and my own ship, which the Company swears to stand by. Jacques Montbars and Kate Devon broke those Articles. They betrayed me and my shipmates. They nearly cost me my ship. Therefore, I mean to bring them to account. If I were to send you to my ship, instead of returning you to their camp, I too would be guilty of breaking the Articles and would have to stand punishment for it."

She studied him curiously for a moment. "You are indeed a strange man, *señor.* You slew the men who attacked

Teresa and myself, and yet you would turn us over to their kind on the strength of your so-called Articles."

"I gave the word of a Scottish gentleman and a member of the Brethren of the Coast when I signed the Articles. If I must stand alone this night in bringing those others to account, *señorita, then that is what I will do.*"

"Then you are a stupid fool, with all your shabby airs of a gentleman!" she snapped. "Alexander Duncan Campbell, of the Campbells of Cawdor! You make it sound so grand! Is it because you mean nothing yourself that you must take on the pompous airs of a grandee of Spain?"

It was as though she had struck him across the face with a mailed fist. Tight lines formed at the corners of his mouth. A film of ice seemed to form over his gray eyes. He turned on a heel and strode out across the savannah.

Tattoo shook his head. "No, missee," he said in guttural Spanish. "Not do that again. If you were a man, you would be crossing blades with him by now."

Rafaela touched her fingers to her mouth. "I did not know," she breathed.

"Come, we follow him to the camp," Tattoo said.

They caught up with Alec, who was standing just within the edge of the jungle beyond which was the yellow beach and the sprawling encampment.

Alec turned. "If I do not return, Tattoo, ye must take these ladies back to the pinnace. Tell Mister Gilles that Lady Rafaela is to be held for ransom. Further, if she is touched or harmed by any man aboard the *Adventuress*, I'll rise from me damned grave and haunt him to cut off his damned bollacks at the roots!"

SEVEN

The moonlight was almost as bright as day. The encampment of the buccaneer rendezvous sprawled along the forest edge of the wide yellow beach and partway into the jungle clearings. There were many *ajoupas*, or Arawak palm-thatched huts, and structures of old sails spread across poles. There were booths set up by merchants and traders who had come to the rendezvous from Port Royal on Jamaica to deal with the buccaneers for the rarities and treasures they had stripped from the great *Nuestra Señora de la Candelaria*. There were many booths where liquor and food were sold or traded for loot, and the liquor booths far outnumbered those that sold food. Drunken men lined up before flimsy shelters where aged, raddled whores plied their profession at prices a hundredfold greater than they could have got in Port Royal.

Pig and cattle carcasses slowly turned on spits over glowing beds of embers. Heaped on old sails and expensive carpets stripped from the *Cacafuego* were bags of *ocho reales*, the famed pieces-of-eight of the Spanish Main; piles of silver bars; chunky kegs filled with wedge-shaped pieces of silver molded into shapes like the cuts of a pie; containers of pearls from the Isle of Margarita off the Venezuelan coast. There were heaps of fine clothing stripped from the murdered passengers of the plate ship and taken from their luggage. Piles of silver plates reflected the light of the moon, and there were many bags of gold pistareens and double pistareens. Cases of finely polished wood were filled to the top with gold and silver ornaments and jewelry mingled with precious stones, both cut and uncut. Pistols, firelocks, cutlasses, swords, and daggers were piled up like cordwood.

Jacques Montbars and Kate Devon sat on chairs behind an immense table loaded with piles of coins and other valuables. Standing beside Montbars and Kate were the boatswains of their ships, for, by the rules of the Articles, it was the boatswain who saw to it that the proper shares were doled out to those men who had participated in the taking of a prize.

Drunken crewmen staggered from the table, clutching their shares, be they coins, jewelry, weapons, or clothing. They headed with an unerring instinct toward the broached pipes of rum and wine or toward the improvised canvas whorehouses set up just within the shelter of the jungle where it encroached on the sands.

To one side of the camp was a crude fenced-in area like a cattle or pig pen, and within it were kept the score or more of women prisoners taken from the Cacafuego. They were all comparatively young, for the older women and all the men passengers had been murdered and their corpses left aboard the doomed plate ship.

Kate Devon sprawled in her chair with her long, sea-booted legs thrust out in front of her and with one arm dangling negligently over the back of the chair. She was wearing a fine suit and breeches of black velvet, once the property of a young man of substance aboard the *Cacafuego*. A froth of the finest lace showed at her throat and wrists. The firelight reflected from the silver buttons of her coat. A slim-necked bottle of fine wine was on the table and close at hand. She was already half drunk.

Jacques Montbars slumped in his chair with his hands resting on the table before him, but his hooded eyes were not on the immense wealth spread out before him. Now and again, he would look surreptitiously toward the pen that held the Spanish women prisoners, with the moonlight and firelight soft on their white shoulders.

At first, no one noticed the tall figure of a man who had

stepped from the edge of the jungle to stand plainly in view on the yellow sand of the beach with his left hand touching negligently the basket hilt of a magnificent broadsword and his right hand resting easily on his hip with elbow akimbo.

A drunken seaman from the *Exterminator* had traded in all his loot for a large crock of kill-devil rum and the services of a blowzy whore for the rest of the night. He was staggering toward the jungle with the whore in tow when he stopped short and stared at the man standing coolly at the edge of the trees.

The hundreds of men and the dozens of women on the beach heard the startled cry of one of their comrades. The men's hands dropped to the hilts of cutlasses and daggers, or to the butts of pistols.

Alec Campbell walked slowly forward across the smooth sand. The firelight glittered on the squared Gaelic silver buttons of his fine broadcloth coat and on the immense cairngorm stone inset into the hilt top of his dirk.

"Christ!" Kate Devon spat out. "It's Cutlass or his damned ghost!" She jumped to her feet and turned sideways to look down at Montbars with a look of fury on her beautiful face. "Damn you to hell, Montbars! I said you could not kill him!"

Montbars slowly turned his head. He stood up. "Quinlan! De Rosiers! Villiers! Yarrow! Onstad! To me!"

The five officers of the *Exterminator* came to stand beside their commander.

"It's his ghost!" a seaman cried.

"Ghost be damned!" Montbars spat out. "It's *him* all right!"

Kate Devon picked up her wine bottle and drank deeply. She placed it back on the table so hard that a dollop of the spirits slopped up out of the neck of it. She slowly wiped her full mouth with the back of a hand and then rested the hand on the hilt of her sword.

It was very quiet now except for the crackling of the fires and the distant booming of the surf on the reef at the mouth of the bay.

Slowly, the men of both ships came to form a great semicircle about the table and the piles of loot, almost as though they feared what this lone man might do to them, for such was his great reputation throughout the Caribbean.

"What do you want here, Écossais?" Montbars demanded.

Alec halted twenty feet away from the table. He slowly surveyed Montbars and then Kate Devon. "I mean to call ye to account for breaking those Articles by which we bound ourselves to the venture whereby ye attained this loot and those women prisoners!" Alec called out in a clear, strong voice.

Montbars smiled thinly. He looked about himself and then at his men and finally toward the two ships anchored in the bay. "I do not see your famed crew, Cutlass, or your ship in the offing."

"I came alone to confront ye. I charge ye, Montbars, with attempting to destroy my ship and crew in the Mona Passage."

Montbars slowly raised his eyebrows. "Is that so?" he drawled. "Well, Écossais, you will have to forgive me for that. In the darkness and the heat of battle, we mistook you for one of the Spanish ships. An easy mistake to make. I…" His voice trailed off as he saw the icy look on Alec's face.

Alec looked at Kate. "And ye, Kate?" he asked quietly. "What of ye?"

She looked away from him.

"I am standing *here*, mistress! Look not elsewhere! Look at me and swear that ye had nothing to do with this Frenchman's treachery."

She turned quickly to face Alec. "Why, damn you, Cutlass! I don't fear you!"

"That is not the point. Did ye, or did ye not, plot with Montbars to put me and my ship out of the way so that the two of ye might share the treasure that rightfully belongs to us all?"

"I don't have to answer that, you Scots bastard!" she yelled.

Alec nodded. "Ye have just given me your answer, Katie."

There weren't too many friendly faces among the hundreds of men watching the tense drama being played in front of them. Some of these men had previously sailed with Alec. Some of them he had dismissed from his ship because they had not come up to his strict code of conduct, and others because he had never trusted them. The least friendly-looking men were those officers of Montbars who now sided him with their hands upon their weapons. Each of them was a skilled professional and a killer by nature or they would not be serving under the greatest killer of them all—Montbars, the Exterminator.

Montbars smiled thinly. "Perhaps you *have* proven a point, Écossais. If so, what does it merit you? One word from me and you'll die upon these very sands and my officers can shake dice over who will get the famed weapons you claim you inherited from your ragtag Scots ancestors." The Frenchman laughed. "The Campbells of Cawdor! You cry out that obscure family name as though you were referring to the highest nobility of all Europe instead of a pack of penniless mountain peasants running around in women's dress!"

"You damned idiot," Kate murmured out of the side of her mouth. "You've done it now. Sweet Jesus! You've signed your own death warrant…"

Alec's face had gone taut. Little lines worked at the corners of his mouth. He looked slowly about himself at the hundreds of men watching him. "Ye men! Ye signed the Articles, or made your mark upon them in agreement to stand by them as do all true Brethren of the Coast! None of ye is above those Articles once he signs his name to them or makes his mark! Even your officers and commanders must be held to those Articles! Is that not true?"

The men looked uneasily at each other. Some of them muttered out of the sides of their mouths.

"Pay no attention to this madman!" Montbars shouted.

Kate Devon looked back over her shoulder. Her crew was smaller in numbers than that of Montbars, although no less tough and intensely loyal to her. Her great green eyes met those of her officers. Every one of them nodded as though to say: "Cutlass is right. He stands on good ground here."

Montbars turned to his officers. "Take him," he ordered.

Alec Campbell rested his left hand on the hilt of his broadsword. His eyes held those of the Frenchman. "Jacques Montbars! I charge ye with breaking the Articles which ye signed for this recent venture in the taking of the *Nuestra Señora de la Candelaria!* Specifically, by attacking my ship, the *Adventuress*, in the Mona Passage the night of the attack on the Spanish convoy. I further charge ye with abandoning my ship and crew to the mercy of the Spaniards while ye escaped from the scene with the prize for which we went on the venture. I further charge ye with murdering the crew and many of the passengers of the plate ship *Nuestra Señora de la Candelaria.* I also charge ye with taking prisoners, the young gentlewomen who were passengers on that same ship, not for the purposes of ransom as specified in the Articles, but for immoral purposes of your own. I further charge ye with dividing the treasure of the prize here among the officers and crew of your ship and that of Captain Kate Devon, without consideration of the officers and crew of my ship, who should equally share in that same treasure, according to the Articles you signed." Alec's voice rang out, clearly carrying to those men who were farthest from him. Some of the men began to talk in asides to each other.

Montbars looked back over a shoulder. He could sense the uncertainty working through the two crews. He looked sideways at Kate Devon. She shrugged. He knew then that he could not be sure that Kate and her crew would back him in his stand against Cutlass.

Montbars turned and placed his hands on his hips. He looked from one to the other of his own crewmen. "Who listens to this Scots braggart? He's alone. His ship may have foundered, and all of his crew might have been lost, save himself. Who is he then? Nothing! A commander without a ship or a crew. He is nothing, I say!"

A bearded Englishman, a master gunner of Montbars' crew, stepped forward. He had once served with the great Henry Morgan and later with Alec Campbell, so he knew him well. "Captain Montbars, sir," he called out respectfully, "if any of us who are standing here this night ever attempt to sign on another ship of the Brethren, and this tale gets out, we will be refused service with them, and with good reason. For, by God, most of us stand by the Articles, which are for our own safeguard. All of us signed the Articles before we left on this last venture. We must stand by them. Further, if any harm comes to Captain Campbell in this encampment, it will be the worse for you and for us, for then you will have turned against your own kind, and henceforth would be known as a sea artist who preys upon his own brethren—a 'mad dog'!"

"Hear! Hear!" the cry went up from different areas of the massed crews and gained in strength until it seemed as though at least three-quarters of the men of both crews were in favor of the speaker's viewpoint.

Montbars looked coldly at Kate. "Well, woman?" he asked. "How do *you* stand?"

She casually filled her wineglass. "There's only one way out of this for you, Frenchman. You know the rules."

Montbars nodded. He had supreme confidence in himself as a polished killer of men. He looked at Alec.

Alec walked forward. "Will ye depose yourself, Captain Montbars?" he asked formally.

"Do you challenge me, Captain Campbell?"

Alec smiled. He bowed a little. "If ye wish, sir."

A shout went up from the mingled crews.

Montbars pointed toward the sea. "There is a naked sandbar athwart the mouth of the channel. Tomorrow? At dawn?"

"Agreed. The choice of weapons is yours by right."

"Swords and daggers, then." Montbars smiled. He was a skilled swordsman, at one time considered to be the best in France, until he had been driven from his native land on a charge of the cold-blooded murder of a young aristocrat.

Alec nodded. "So be it." He walked to the table and helped himself to a cup of wine from Kate's private bottle. He drained the cup and turned to look at the watching crews. "On the basis of what has just happened, shipmates, there will be no further division of loot this night. Further, there will not be any division of loot until my ship arrives here, perhaps in another week or so."

"You're damned sure of yourself, Cutlass," Kate murmured.

He looked into those incredible green eyes of hers. "Maybe it should be ye as well as Montbars meeting me on that naked sandbar tomorrow at dawn."

She did not look away. "You believe that of me?" she asked softly.

"Yes," he replied, "unless ye can prove otherwise to my satisfaction."

"Why, damn you!" She raised a hand to strike him.

He caught her by the wrist and twisted it hard and savagely, drawing her close to himself. "If I ever find out," he grated between set teeth, "I'll cut your lovely throat as though ye were a sow for slaughter!" He released her. There was a furious hell in her green eyes, but she turned aside without a word.

Alec walked toward the jungle. He waved. Tattoo and the two Spanish women came from the forest. Alec turned. "I want these two women kept in your *ajoupa*, Kate, as my guests, until such time as they can be returned to their people for ransom."

"You've got no right to do that," Montbars growled.

Alec looked at the Frenchman. "I have until dawn tomorrow," he reminded Montbars.

Alec turned to Kate. "See that they have the best of care and some of their clothing from the loot. They will likely be able to identify it."

Kate smiled winningly. "Of course, dear. And you? Where will you spend this night?"

"As far away from ye as possible, Katie."

"Tattoo," Alec said to the black, "get Rais Gilles and the others. I'll need a second for tomorrow morning."

Tattoo grinned. "Master fights? Who?"

Alec nodded. He pointed to Montbars.

Tattoo nodded. "Master wins."

"And if he does not?" Kate asked.

Tattoo placed a hand on the hilt of his cutlass. "Then Frenchman dies too, somewhere, someplace mebbe, *but he will die...*" Tattoo turned and loped off toward the jungle.

EIGHT

The first cerise flush of dawn light showed in the eastern sky. Fires had been lighted on the beach in front of the sailcloth tents and the *ajoupas*. Shadowy figures passed back and forth as the buccaneers aroused their shipmates from their drunken sleep. No one wanted to miss the classic duel between Jacques Montbars, rightly nicknamed the Exterminator, and Alec Campbell, the legendary Captain Cutlass.

The naked sand cay was barely above water level in the channel entrance to the wide bay. Some underwater obstruction of many years past had caused the tides to pile up sand atop the obstruction. The great shadowy shapes of the *Kate of Devon* and the *Exterminator* showed, one at each end of the sand cay and within the arms of the bay just short of the channel. Before dawn light, the small boats of both vessels had been busy plying back and forth to bring their crews out to their respective ships, as well as the many whores from the beach encampment. Both ships would provide ideal grandstands for the forthcoming duel.

Alec Campbell sat in the sternsheets of the wherry that was taking him out to the cay. Rais Gilles sat next to him. "Alec," Rais murmured, "you did a foolish thing to challenge Montbars in front of the crews of his ship and that of Kate."

Alec spat over the side. "What else could I do? The situation was tense and on a delicate balance. If I had not swayed the mob…"

"The man is skilled and dangerous and easily your equal in swordsmanship."

"I asked him to depose himself. He could have done so."

"Never! He knew that if he had done so, he would have lost all respect from the Brethren of the Coast. Never again would he have been able to raise a crew for another venture, and even if he could, no other commanders would work with him. He had no choice. This duel will surely be the end for one of you."

Alec looked at Rais. "Was there any other way? If I had not challenged him, I would have lost the day then and there."

"The crews might have seen to it that you could have left the camp in safety, despite Montbars."

"To what end? By the time we got the *Adventuress* here, both ships would have been gone with the loot." Alec looked back toward the small boat that was bringing Jacques Montbars from the shore to the cay. "Besides," he added quietly, "I could not let him escape me."

Rais felt a cold chill work its way down his spine at the tone of Alec's voice.

The wherry grounded just offshore. The crew went over the side and ran the boat further up onto the beach so that Alec and Rais could step dryshod onto the sands.

"Look!" Rais exclaimed. He pointed toward the channel entrance. Black fins, like so many small lateen sails, were cutting swiftly through the water into the bay.

The wherry's coxswain nodded his head. "They come like this every morning, sir, to feed on the offal from the shore and that which is dumped over from the ships. It's worth a man's life to swim in these waters."

The sand cay was perhaps twenty-five yards long and about fifteen yards wide at the widest part. It was entirely bare of vegetation, and the bottom on all sides shelved abruptly into deeper water.

Montbars' boat grounded at the opposite side of the cay, and he stepped ashore, followed by Patrick Quinlan. Montbars stood there unconcernedly while Quinlan approached

Alec and Rais. Rais lifted his plumed hat in salute to the Irishman, who returned the compliment. Rais and Patrick walked together to the center of the cay. "The principals have agreed on swords and daggers," Rais said. "Is that correct, sir?"

Montbars was studying Alec from under lowered brows. The dawn light coming from behind the Frenchman made him seem larger than he really was, and the black silhouette of the man had a forbidding appearance.

"How shall this be decided, gentlemen?" Quinlan called out. "Shall ye call it quits after the first bloodletting? Or perhaps if one of ye suffers a disabling wound?"

Montbars shook his head. "To the death, gentlemen." Rais narrowed his eyes. "That is not necessary." He looked back at Alec. "How do you choose, captain?" he asked.

"Captain Montbars knows there will be no going back for either of us," Alec replied. "Only one of us can leave this cay alive."

Rais looked at Patrick Quinlan. Quinlan nodded. "Let it be so, gentlemen," the Irishman announced. "To the death."

Both combatants stripped to the waist. They unsheathed their swords, while Alec withdrew his dirk and Montbars unsheathed a fine Spanish *main-gauche* dagger with an intricate cross hilt.

Rais drew a line on the sand in the middle of the cay and at right angles to the length of it. "When you are ready, gentlemen," he said. Both he and Quinlan returned to their boats, which were shoved off and allowed to drift fifty feet offshore, held in position by an occasional stroking of the oars.

Rais Gilles stood up in the sternsheets of his boat, holding a lace handkerchief in his right hand. "Ready, gentlemen?" he called out. Both combatants nodded. Rais raised his hand and dropped the handkerchief.

Montbars was larger and thicker through the body than Alec. His muscles were more solid and heavy. His thick chest was covered with short, wiry hair as were his forearms. There was an air of confidence about him. Many men had died under his blades in hand-to-hand combat, in duels and when they were defenseless prisoners. He had

had plenty of practice in bloodletting and in dealing out death.

Montbars raised his sword. Alec tapped it with his broadsword. A low murmur arose from the people watching from the ships. The blades struck against each other with a musical sound from the finely tempered steel.

They circled slowly. The sun was beginning to show itself. Alec tried to work Montbars around so that the rising sun would shine in his face, but the Frenchman was far quicker in his reactions than Alec had anticipated. Time and time again, Montbars drove in at Alec with a stamping, thrusting attack in the Italian style. His blade rang musically against Alec's sword in a flurry of hard-striking blows like a smith striking an anvil. His continuous attack drove Alec back and still farther back until he stood ankle-deep in the water, which slowed down his footwork.

Montbars pressed his attack, stamping hard with his right foot as he thrust with powerful force, but his every thrust and stroke was deftly turned aside by the ever-present parrying broadsword. The blades rang and chimed together. Montbars lost his temper and attacked so viciously and wildly that he lost his footing and staggered sideways. Alec leaped from the water and brought down a slashing, drawing cut that smashed aside Montbars' parrying dagger and traced a red line across the Frenchman's hairy chest. A thin trickling of blood ran down his taut belly.

They circled on the damp sand. Alec was much the more agile. He began to notice that when he struck from right to left toward Montbars' left side, the Frenchman's reactions were slower, as though his vision on that side was not quite right.

Montbars attacked again, using his superior weight and strength to his advantage. They locked blades, sword against sword and dagger against dirk at chest height. They glared into each other's eyes until Montbars spat fully into Alec's face and then threw him back. Alec staggered, half-blinded by the spittle. Montbars pressed his advantage, slashing and thrusting to drive Alec farther and farther along the cay until, at last, his heels were again sinking in the wet sand.

Montbars lunged. Alec stepped deftly aside to Montbars'

left, and as he did so, he backthrust with his dirk. The dirk struck Montbars' left bicep and was withdrawn, leaving a thin trickling of blood running down the arm. Alec retreated. An instant later, Montbars whirled and thrust with his sword. The point pinked Alec in the left shoulder. The Frenchman's dagger grated hard against Alec's dirk, slipped sideways, and was dragged back, tracing a red, beaded line across Alec's muscular belly.

They circled slowly with their breathing coming harsh and irregular from their throats. The stinging sweat ran down their faces and bodies.

Montbars grinned, showing his teeth, but there was no mirth in the forced grimace. "You're doomed, Écossais," he grated.

"Fight, don't talk, Frenchman," Alec returned.

They flung each other back after locking blades at chest height. They faced each other warily, circling slowly. The sun was now fully up, a bright and silent explosion of golden color that instantly brought with it a forecasting of the heat of the day.

"Do you want time, gentlemen?" Rais Gilles called out.

Montbars slewed his eyes sideways. Alec shook his head. He saw his chance when Montbars looked away, which he should never have done. The broadsword flicked out and slashed across Montbars' left bicep, almost where Alec's dirk earlier had pinked the flesh.

Alec retreated, followed by a dogged, angry Montbars. Montbars attacked, but his wounded left arm had begun to sag so that it was getting more difficult for him to keep his dagger in the guard position. A touch of panic showed on the Frenchman's sweating face. He drove into a wild and furious attack. Alec kept falling back, weaving a curious Maltese-cross pattern with the tip of his sword in the High-land fashion, to flick aside each thrust of the Frenchman's blade. No matter how hard Montbars tried, he could not get past that skillfully executed defense.

"Stand and fight, damn you!" Montbars shouted angrily.

Alec grinned. "Like this?" he asked. He stood still with both blades outthrust and with his eyes on those of Mont-bars. Montbars thought he saw his chance. He charged into the attack, but his blades either clashed against the parrying blades of Alec or met thin air. Once, he struck so hard with his sword that he missed Alec's sword altogether and staggered sideways to drop to one knee, almost defenseless against Alec. He looked up desperately into the sweating face of the man he knew wanted to kill him.

"There's your chance, Cutlass!" Rais cried. "Kill the sonofabitch!"

Alec stepped back and moved quickly to one side so that Montbars would face the bright sun when he arose. He rested his sword tip on the sand and watched Montbars.

Montbars got slowly to his feet. Blood was trickling down his hairy chest and belly into his breeches and his crotch. The front of his breeches was soaked in mingled blood and sweat. The bright red dripped from Alex's left shoulder and belly. He could feel the blood running down his crotch and legs.

"There is yet time for one of you to withdraw, gentlemen!" Patrick Quinlan called out.

They both shook their heads.

"You will die, Écossais," Montbars growled.

Alec smiled wearily. "Let's have at it again, Frenchman, and we'll soon see who is going to die and who is not."

The fighting was slower now and less skilled, more of a slow hammering attack and a sluggish defense, but Alec always managed to keep Montbars facing into the sun. Time and time again, he tried to get around Alec, but it was no use. The stubborn, skillfully fighting Scot was always in his way. At last, Montbars stood with his heels at the water's edge.

Alec smiled, but there was ice in his gray eyes. "Do ye remember the bloody shambles ye left on the deck of the *Nuestra Señora de la Candelaria?*" he asked softly. He thrust in hard. Montbars parried slowly and stepped back. The water washed about his ankles. A second and a third driving thrust were parried, but Montbars was forced back again until, at last, he stood knee-deep in the water on the steeply shelving bottom.

No matter how hard Montbars tried to regain the land, he was met always by the skilled defense of Alec, and with the sun in his eyes, he saw not much more than the dark outline of his opponent and the sun reflecting from glistening broadsword and dirk.

"Do ye remember the old man Don Bartolome Arriola whom ye left blinded on his own ship to die slowly and alone?" Alec asked grimly. The tip of the broadsword was thrust into Montbars' left forearm. The backslash of the sword caught Montbars' sword at the guard and tore it loose from his weakening grasp. The sword glittered as it spun through the air to disappear into the sea. Montbars cursed savagely as he switched his dagger from his left hand to his right. The water lapped about his thighs.

Alec stood knee-deep in the water. The broadsword flicked out and neatly took off Montbars' left ear. He clapped his left hand to the wound. "For the love of God, Écossais!" he shrieked. "Spare me!"

"What mercy did ye ever have for any of your slaughtered victims and for the men of my crew you killed?" Alec asked.

The sharks had sensed the smell and taste of blood in the water. The black fins began to converge on the end of the sand cay and behind Montbars.

Alec lunged with the tip of his sword pointed directly at Montbars' eyes. Montbars staggered backward into waist-deep water. He could feel his heels settling in the sand and sliding slowly backward on the steeply shelving bottom.

"Coward!" Montbars screamed. "I have lost my sword!"

Alec turned and cast his broadsword toward the cay so that it struck and quivered in the sand. He turned again and shifted his dirk from his left hand to his right. He waded toward Montbars.

They met waist-deep in the blood-tinted water. Montbars clawed at Alec's face with his left hand and got a knee in the crotch for his pains. He gasped and bent forward. Alec backed up a little, and then he felt the agonizing, almost paralyzing dagger thrust low into his left side. He grunted in savage pain, and as Montbars straightened up, Alec struck at him with all his remaining strength. The thrust went too high. The point pierced Montbars' left eye. He screamed in animal-like agony and clasped his hands to his face. Alec shoved him backward into the water just as a covey of fins closed in at incredible speed.

Alec staggered backward. There was a wild flurry in the water ahead of him. Spouts of spray mingled with a tinting of blood appeared on the surface. Once Montbars' left arm rose above the surface as though he was supplicating a God whom he had forsworn long past, and then he disappeared forever in a frenzied flurry of sleek, spindle-shaped bodies whipped into a maddening and ravenous hunger for his body.

Alec stood reeling in the waist-deep water. A shark drove in at him in a mad frenzy. It snapped its double row of razor-sharp teeth at Alec just before his blade came down in a slashing blow that drove into the shark's skull.

Rais Gilles leaped from the wherry and ran to Alec with a drawn sword. He splashed into the water and dragged Alec back to the shore. He plucked the *main-gauche* dagger from Alec's side and staunched the instant flow of blood with his handkerchief.

"Madman!" Rais Gilles cried. There was great pride in his voice.

It was the last word Alec Campbell heard before he seemed to sink into a bottomless pit of whirling, swirling darkness.

NINE

The burning fever came upon Alec Campbell after his duel to the death with Jacques Montbars. At first, they thought it was the dreaded *vómito negro,* the scourge of Yellow Jack, but the symptoms, although much like yellow fever, were not quite the same. When neither surgeon of the two ships in the bay could diagnose the fever nor its treatment, it was Teresa Gomez, maidservant to Rafaela de Vasquez, who realized what it was. Before Teresa had gone into the service of the de Vasquez family in Porto Bello, she had been a nurse in the convent hospital of Saint Catherine.

"Poison," Teresa said quietly after her first examination of Alec Campbell. She looked up at the others who stood beyond the couch whereon Alec Campbell sweated and tossed and spoke in delirium.

"What the hell do you mean?" Kate Devon demanded.

Patrick Quinlan nodded. "She's right, Kate. I've known Montbars to poison his dagger."

Kate paled. "Did you know that beforehand, you Irish blackguard?" she demanded. "If so, by God, I'll…" Patrick Quinlan shook his head. "Ye know me better than that, Kate."

"You swear to that? You were his second!" Quinlan drew his sword and held it up before her with its wide cross hilt. "I swear on the True Cross, Kate."

"Papist nonsense!" she snapped. Still, she believed him. Rais Gilles looked down upon the drawn, sweating face of Alec Campbell. "I'm leaving today to return to the *Adventuress*," he said. "Our surgeon, Terence Shannon, might be able to cope with this. We'll sail back here as soon as the frigate is ready."

Kate shook her head. "That will be weeks." Rafaela stood in the background. Her face was pale, and her great eyes filled with tears as she looked down upon the heretic man who had saved her virginity and her life, as well as sparing her a possible terrible fate in the encampment.

Kate turned on Rafaela in contempt. "Is that all you can do?" she demanded in her execrable Spanish. "Before God, I think he might have come back into the camp for your sake alone and might have met his death for that reason!"

Rais Gilles shook his head. "He would have returned here in any case, Kate. This bickering does Cutlass no good."

Patience, the Arawak woman, came silently into the room. She approached the couch and placed one of her slim and lovely hands on the forehead of Alec Campbell. Kate narrowed her eyes. "Patience? Can you help?" Patience turned. "Caribs and Tainos use poison on arrows. Men rot and die in tree day." She nodded her head toward Alec. "Like this on first and second day. Third day, they rot. In five days, dead." Rafaela stifled a sob.

Kate paled. "Is there nothing that can be done?" Teresa nodded. "The Indian woman is right. I have seen this type of poisoning before. But there are jungle plants and herbs that can be made into a potion that can arrest the poison." She quickly crossed herself. "With the help of the good God and a lot of luck."

"You know these plants and herbs?" Rais Gilles asked.

Teresa looked at Patience. "She does. They might be found on this very island."

"Patience?" Kate asked.

"Yes, mistress. I know."

Kate, always the woman of action, wasted no time. She formed a strong escort party led by no less a person than Roche Brasiliano to guard Teresa and Patience while they hunted for the healing plants and herbs. Then Rais Gilles left immediately to return to the *Adventuress* to bring her to the island rendezvous. Kate Devon turned to liquor and within two hours was dead drunk in her room in the sprawling habitation she had ordered to be built for herself, a mingled shebang of *ajoupa* and sailcloth tent like the pavilion of an Arabian chief.

When all had become quiet again, it was Rafaela de Vasquez who crept back into the room where Alec Campbell lay in delirium to bathe his face and naked torso with cool water from the bubbling spring of clear, cold water that lay a short distance behind the habitation. She had remained beside his couch all that long night and well into the next day until Teresa and Patience returned with the necessary plants and herbs.

In the long, lazy days that followed Alec's poisoning and his slow recuperation, either Rafaela, Teresa, or Patience was always by his side. Throughout the day and night one of them would always be within call, but it was principally Rafaela who took care of him. She learned quickly from both Teresa and Patience so that, in time, she was as skilled in her care of him as either of them had been.

Kate Devon had her habitation set at quite a distance from those of her officers and the officers of the *Exterminator*. In turn, their quarters were somewhat apart from the miscellaneous shelters both crews had built for themselves of old sailcloth or palm branches. Many of the crewmen simply slept off their drinking in the open or in the green glades that dotted the dense jungle where it lay back from the wide yellow beach. Now and again, one or more crewmen would be missed. The dense, brooding jungle was no place for a lone man, loaded to the marks with rum-fustian or kill-devil, to wander. There were eight-foot alligators guarding the many streams, capable enough of dragging a man to his death. The deadly fer-de-lance and coral snakes were rarely seen before they struck, and death from their bites was almost instantaneous. Then, there was the persistent rumor that man-hunting cannibal Caribs had been seen deep in the jungle.

The *Kate of Devon* was brought in close to the shore at

high tide for careening, and when the tide receded, her bottom had been scraped and burned free of barnacles and weed growths. Once the *Kate of Devon* was ready for sea again, the *Exterminator* was careened. There was a constant undercurrent of activity about the two ships and the encampment as though something big was in the offing. Coopers repaired kegs and barrels and made new ones for the freshwater supply of the ships. Sailmakers spread their canvas on the smooth yellow sand and made new suits of sails for the vessels. New rigging was set up and the old repaired. Several times a week the gunners would practice on kegs cast adrift on the wide bay. Armorers set up shop on the beach and repaired and refurbished cutlasses, daggers, boarding axes, pikes, pistols, arquebuses, and calivers. One day a supply ship from Port Royal showed up at the rendezvous loaded to the marks with large stores of food, gunpowder, rum, canvas, and cordage, as well as small arms and other weapons. When she sailed for Port Royal, she took with her the traders who had been at the rendezvous since the two ships had returned with the fabulous loot of the *Nuestra Señora de la Candelaria*. The raddled whores left on the same ship as well, pale but proud with their new wealth.

The room, if it could be called that, which had been partitioned off for Alec Campbell in Kate Devon's pavilion, overlooked the jungle glade wherein bubbled a freshwater spring which filled a deep pool of clearest crystal water. A small stream meandered through the glade from the overflow of the pool. Its banks were mantled in emerald green growths, almost the same color as Kate Devon's fabulous eyes. The clearing was overhung by tall trees from which depended lianas strung with magnificent blossoms of tropical flowers. The interior of the habitation had been divided into various rooms by hanging materials from the rich loot of the plate ship—silks and satins, damasks and carpetings. These hangings could be rolled up or parted so that the pavilion became one large room through which the sea breeze blew by day, and the land breeze blew by night. Kate had her furniture from the *Kate of Devon* brought ashore, along with some of the fine furniture of the plate ship, to furnish her habitation.

The day that Alec returned from the limbo of fever and poison, he opened his eyes to look up into the great dark eyes of Rafaela de Vasquez. She was passing her small, smooth hands, cooled with fresh spring water, across his naked chest and belly.

Alec smiled wanly. "Where am I?" he croaked. "In the Paradise of the Mohammedans being nursed by an houri whose beauty would relaunch the thousand ships of the Greek heroes to return to take the Troy of legend?"

Rafaela blushed. She instantly withdrew her hands. Alec reached out and gripped her small wrists. "Did I frighten you? Please continue. I'm sure that is what has saved my life, *señorita.*"

"Teresa!" Rafaela called. "He has awakened!"

Plump Teresa waddled into the room with enormous breasts heaving and swaying. "Blessed Jesus!" she cried. "He has heard my prayers!"

"Another houri," Alec croaked with a half grin on his pale, gaunt face. "Larger, but still a houri."

Teresa hurried to get a cooling drink. She sat down on the couch and cradled Alec's head against her enormous bosom. There were tears in her soft, dark eyes.

"You've saved my life, ladies," Alec said. *"Gracias, mil gracias."*

Rafaela smiled. "It was Teresa and Patience, the Arawak woman, who knew how to treat you. The surgeons of both ships could do nothing, and your own surgeon, who might have helped you, was far away."

"I seem to recall vaguely many nights when you alone were with me, Rafaela."

Teresa slewed her eyes sideways to look up at Rafaela. There was a knowing look on her round face.

"Did you not save my life and that of Teresa?" Rafaela asked.

He waved a thin hand. *"Por nada, señorita,"* he murmured.

"But, it was *not* for nothing! Are we of such little importance to you that you say it was for nothing?" Rafaela stamped a little foot on the thick carpeting. "I thought better of you, Captain Campbell!"

He smiled. "My given name is Alexander. Alec for short."

She was not to be mollified so easily. "A strange, outlandish name."

Alec shrugged. "Scots," he explained. "After a great hero, of course. We have other names that are far more outlandish than Alexander."

"I meant no offense, Alexander."

He shrugged. "None taken. We Scots are devilish proud of our outlandish names."

"And many other things as well," she suggested slyly.

"You watched the duel?" he asked. He grinned. "Am I not a pretty fighter?"

"I did not watch the duel, but I did see you fighting in the jungle to save my life and that of Teresa. I saw no fear on your face then, but only a great pride in yourself and in those magnificent weapons of yours."

"And you Spaniards are a people without such pride? I know differently, *señorita.*"

She smiled a little self-consciously. "That is true. Please call me Rafaela if I am to call you Alexander."

"A pretty scene," Kate Devon said dryly as she entered the room. She jerked her head at Rafaela and Teresa. "You can leave now," she added tartly.

She was wearing her fine men's clothing, but now the material was stained with food and drink. The lace at her throat was bedraggled and dirty. There were lines at the corners of her eyes and mouth. Her eyes were dull and bloodshot.

Kate dropped into a chair. "So, you've come back to life, eh, Cutlass?"

"So it seems. How long has it been?"

"More than a week. Ten days, to be exact. You knew little of what has been going on?"

He shrugged. "I knew, Katie. But everything was vague and unreal as though it were a dream."

"But you knew the Spanish woman was always in here, or hovering about outside."

He nodded. "Of course I did."

Kate studied him. "She's in love with you, Alec."

He stared at her. "Ye talk foolishness, lassie."

She shook her head. "A woman *knows*, Alec."

She came to the side of the couch and bent over him. Her breath was fruity and sour as though she had been long at the bottle. She passed a slim hand alongside his gaunt face. She bent and kissed his cracked lips. "Oh, God, Alec. I thought I had lost you forever!"

Her breath and appearance sickened him a little. "Ye've been long at the rum jug, eh, lass?" he asked quietly.

She straightened up and swayed a little to regain her balance. "I said I thought I had lost you forever. What more do you want out of me?"

He eyed her. *"When* did ye think ye had lost me forever? After Montbars slammed that murderous broadside into my ship, or when he stuck his poisoned dagger into my guts?"

She turned away from him. "You still think I was in on the plot with Montbars to get rid of you in the Mona Passage?"

"Ye must have known my ship was badly damaged. We hadn't a chance! Even if ye weren't in on the plot with Montbars to sink my ship, if he could, why didn't ye turn back and see if I needed help? Montbars could have handled the Cacafuego alone."

She whirled angrily. "And let that French sonofabitch get away with all that loot?" she demanded. Her face changed as she realized what she had said. "Oh, Alec! It's the drink talking! Forgive me!"

Alec looked into her eyes. "I'll likely never know if ye were in on the plot with Montbars before we attacked the convoy, but if I ever find out..."

She laughed. "What could you do? Look at yourself! Weak from your wounds and fever! Alone on this island where I, Kate Devon, am in full command! Why, one word from me, Cutlass, and you'd be taken out and executed."

Alec studied her. Her tongue was liquor-loose this night. "So? What has happened to Montbars' ship and his crew?"

Kate walked to a table and filled two wineglasses with good Canary. She handed one of the glasses to Alec. "Patrick Quinlan was elected commander of the *Exterminator* by his officers and crew. He knows he can handle one ship in action, but he's no leader of a sea venture and he knows it. He's asked to serve along with me and the *Kate of Devon*. I'll be full commander. There will be equal shares between the crews."

"Ye think ye can command two such ships, Kate?" Alec asked dryly.

"You're God damned right I can!" she snapped. "I've already made my plans for the next venture." Her voice died away. She was talking far too much.

Alec sipped at the wine. "Does that equal-share agreement include the loot and prisoners from the *Cacafuego?*"

"Of course! It's already been parceled out."

"And what of my share and that of my officers and crew?"

She sat down in a chair and thrust her long legs out in front of her. "After all, it was Montbars and myself who herded the *Cacafuego* away from the convoy and brought the loot and prisoners here without you, Cutlass."

"Leaving me with a badly holed ship, which would have gone to the bottom if the *guarda-costa* or bad weather had turned up."

She grinned wickedly. "You've always preached that in this deadly game, we play with Jack Spaniard—one either wins or loses, and there is no halfway point."

"But my loss was not of my choosing *or* that of Jack Spaniard."

"Why not admit that Montbars outfoxed you, pet?"

He nodded. "Ye have me there, but only for a time, woman. Ye know where Montbars is now. His bones are mingled with the beef and pig bones dumped overboard from the ships in the bay to feed the sharks, the blood brothers of Montbars himself."

Kate refilled the glasses. "Tell me, Alec," she said thoughtfully, "did you plan to kill him that way?"

"It was an afterthought," he admitted. "There was a time or two there when I thought he had me."

"Why was it an afterthought?"

He looked quickly at her. "I saw twenty-one of my crew torn to pieces by his solid shot. I saw the deck of the *Caca-*

fuego after he was done with the passengers and crew. Were ye in on that bloodbath?"

Her eyes narrowed. "What the hell are you talking about?" she demanded. It was obvious that she was not covering up. "I left the *Cacafuego* with about half of the loot and all of the women prisoners." She leaned forward. "Alec, for God's sake, *what are you talking about?*"

Alec quietly told her of the horrifying and grisly scenes he had found aboard the derelict plate ship and of the old man, her commander, sitting quietly in his cabin, blinded and waiting for the end aboard the ship he refused to leave.

Kate jumped to her feet. She ran from the room and Alec could hear her retching and gasping just outside the pavilion.

Alec nodded to himself. Kate was a drunkard and a wanton and not above killing in a fit of temper, but she was no murderess or a butcher of helpless prisoners. Alec sat up on the edge of the couch and reached for the bottle of Canary. He raised the bottle to his lips and took a good slug. The fine wine seemed to course through his body to give him added strength, but he knew full well that he was in no shape to take care of himself, at least for quite some time.

Alec heard the splashing of water and looked through the open rear of his room to where Kate was kneeling beside the pool and laving water over her face.

"She drink alia time, master," Tattoo said quietly from behind Alec. "Drunk alia time now."

Alec turned. "Damn ye, Tattoo!" he snapped. "Do ye have to come up on a man like a damned hunting cat?"

Tattoo smiled. He held out his hands and palms upward.

"Red-headed mistress doan like Tattoo around here. Men doan want me around, neider." He grinned widely. "They afeared of Tattoo. Tattoo kill too quick and too quiet. They tink me black devil."

Alec nodded. "I'll agree with them on that. Where have ye been?"

Tattoo jerked his head. "In jungle. Never very far. Mistah Gilles, he say before he leave: Tattoo, you stay with master always. No trust these people. If anything happen to master while me gone, I'll cut off your bollacks at roots!"

Alec grinned. "If he could ever catch ye, that is."

"I doan like this place. Doan like these people. Dey gets ready for something big. Big!"

"Like what, Tattoo?"

Tattoo shrugged. "Two big black ship offshore. Dese people, dey send out pilot to bring dem into harbor past reef."

"Ye recognized the ships?"

"One look like *Sea Venture.*"

"Joshua Swan's ship? Ye're *sure*, Tattoo?"

"I know it well, master."

"And the other ship?"

"Not sure. Might be a Sea Beggar."

"A Dutch ship?"

"Like our ship, but much bigger, more guns."

"Patience!" Kate Devon roared from the spring. "Bring me towels and fresh clothing! *Women's* clothing!"

Tattoo turned suddenly and looked toward the front of the pavilion. He turned again to Alec. "Someone come. Tattoo leave. Not far away. If ye need me, call me loud." Tattoo vanished behind a hanging and was gone as noiselessly as he had arrived.

Alec stood up. He walked unsteadily to where his weapons lay on a small table. They were all there, broadsword, dirk, the matched pair of metal Highland pistols, and the deadly four-barreled "murtherer." He took the dirk and the four-barreled pistol and placed them beneath his pillow. Something "big" was going on in the camp of the buccaneers, and now two other buccaneer ships were in the offing. Joshua Swane was not the man to join forces with any others of the Brethren of the Coast until it *was* something big, as Tattoo had suggested.

Roche Brasiliano came into the room. He nodded to Alec, but his eyes were on Kate Devon as she stripped herself to the buff and then plunged into the pool.

Alec refilled his wineglass with the good Canary. He looked up at the mustee. "What beings ye here into the Temple of Venus, eh, Brasiliano?" he asked. "I know ye did not come here to inquire about my health."

Roche took his eyes away from Kate Devon who was

now frolicking in the pool, splashing the clear water about, and now and again surface diving so that her white rump rose up above the level of the pool before she plumbed the depths.

Alec gestured to the wine bottle. "Have a drink, Roche. It might loosen that tight tongue of yours."

The mustee took the bottle and raised it to his thick lips. He drank deeply and then wiped his mouth both ways with the back of a hand, but his blood-flecked eyes did not leave Alec. "I thought to see you dead, Cutlass," he said quietly. "Puffed up and putrifying after a few days with that poison in your guts."

Alec tilted his head to one side and studied Brasiliano. "Ye *knew* about that?" he asked softly.

Brasiliano shrugged. "Montbars was known to use a poisoned dagger before. That is all."

"And how would that have set wi' ye?"

Roche narrowed his eyes. "What the hell do you mean?"

"It seems to me that your mistress out there splashin' around in yon pool was in on that deal with Montbars to take the treasure and prisoners of the *Cacafuego* for your own."

The mustee placed his hand on the hilt of his dagger. "Be careful, Scotsman! You're in no condition and in the right place to make accusations such as that. I can kill you before you could raise a hand."

Alec slowly shook his head. "No, Brasiliano. If ye tried to kill me, ye'd have to answer to Katie out there. Ye know that. Further, before ye could strike with that dagger, I'd have a bullet or two in yere belly. Mark that, mustee!"

There was pure, unadulterated hatred in the brooding eyes of Roche Brasiliano. He knew the Scotsman was right. If anything happened to Alec Campbell, with the responsibility being that of Roche, Kate Devon would have Roche killed on the spot, if she didn't kill him herself. Further, Alec Campbell never made idle threats.

Kate Devon came from the pool and stood mother-naked on the green mantle of verdure bordering the pool. Patience handed her a huge towel and helped her to dry herself. The Arawak dried and brushed Kate's red hair.

Kate slipped into a sheer white gown and came toward the pavilion. She was a little startled to see Roche Brasiliano in Alec's room.

"The *Sea Venture* and the *Lion* have arrived offshore, captain," Roche reported. "They are being piloted into the harbor now."

The *Lion,* Alec thought quickly—by God, that is Jan Van Schouten's ship! Van Schouten, the Dutch Sea Beggar, who had taken the fabulous plate ship *San Juan Batista* just off Havana, having cut her right out from under the protection of her escort, without the loss of a man. He had raided Port of Spain on Trinidad and had been in on the great Campeche raid along with Kate Devon, Montbars, Alec, and others, buccaneers of the first water, the best of the sea artists.

"Patience!" Kate bawled. "Wine!"

"Haven't you had enough, captain?" Roche asked hesitantly. "You've got to meet with Captains Swan and Van Schouten this night. You should have your wits about you."

Kate lowered her red head. Her eyes looked at Roche Brasiliano from beneath her brows. "You're saying I can't hold my spirits?" she demanded. "You mustee bastard!"

Roche smiled, an effort for him, and then he smiled only with his mouth and cheeks, a muscular contraction rather than a spontaneous lighting of his dark face. "I meant no disrespect," he said sourly.

"I can handle me liquor, and don't you forget it! Now, get to hell out of here with that ugly face of yours, and don't come back until I send for you!" Kate shouted.

Roche Brasiliano left the pavilion, muttering to himself beneath his breath. Someday…

"Ye've a great way about ye wi' handling men, Katie darlin'," Alec murmured.

She turned on him. "Do you want some of it?" she demanded hotly.

Alec shook his head. "Not this night, lassie. I'm in no condition to fight ye or fornicate wi' ye, though I'd take a stab at the last on a chance I *might* be able to make it, being as how ye look like a damned angel in that white dress."

Kate stared at him and then threw back her head to laugh. "You damned lecherous Scot! I believe you would!"

Alec hitched himself up so that he sat on the couch. "Still, the mustee might be right at that, Katie."

Her face changed. "What do you mean?"

"Ye've got a big meeting this night, lassie." Alec reminded her. He eyed her speculatively.

Kate filled the wineglasses and handed one to Alec. "I can handle those two," she said.

Alec raised his eyebrows. "Swan and Van Schouten? Ye'll do yourself proud in that respect, Katie."

She sat down and thrust her long legs out in front of her. "It's about a plan Montbars and I had before you killed the sonofabitch."

"So? Was I to be left out of it?"

"You weren't here, were you?" she demanded.

"Through no fault of my own. I wonder how long ye would have lasted with Montbars if he had killed me instead of me feeding his carcass to the sharks?"

There was a quick look of horror on her face. "God forbid!"

He nodded. "That too. Once he was through using ye as he used ye in the taking of the Cacafuego, he would have disposed of ye like an empty rum jug."

"He wouldn't have dared!" she snapped.

"The more fool ye to believe that, Katie. But, no matter, there's still the matter of the division of the spoils of the Cacafuego that is yet to be settled."

She draped an arm negligently over the back of her chair and twirled the wine about in her glass, but she did not look at Alec.

"Ye hear me, Kate?" he asked. "The night I challenged Montbars, I set down that rule, according to the Articles, and stated that there would be no further division of loot until my ship and crew arrived here."

"That's so," she agreed, pleasantly enough. She slanted her great eyes at Alec. "But where is your ship and crew *now,* Captain Campbell?"

He stared incredulously at her. "Ye mean ye have no intention of dividing the spoils according to the Articles?"

She shook her head. "The loot has already been divided between my crew and that of Montbars. There can be no redivision of that now. Can you imagine what would happen if I even suggested such a thing?"

"But the Articles!"

She spat inelegantly on the carpet. "Piss on your damned Articles! You've nothing to back yourself with now, Cutlass. I've got two fine ships under my command, either one of which could easily be a match for your *Adventuress*, besides which, two more ships are entering the channel this very minute—Van Schouten's *Lion* and Swan's *Sea Venture*. Why, you stupid Scot, if you attempted to force a redivision of the spoils, you'd be blown sky high out of the water!"

There could be no arguing with her now. Kate Devon held all the aces. "What about the women prisoners?" Alec asked.

She studied him. "Which of them?" she asked slyly. "The quiet Rafaela, that Spanish milksop?"

"I mean all of them, Kate."

She shrugged. "They are no longer any concern of yours."

"Then ye've divided them among the crews as well as the loot? Ye've broken every other rule of the Articles, so ye might as well break that one, too."

She refilled the wineglasses. She was beginning to get a glow on again. "No harm will come to them," she promised.

"What do ye intend to do with them?" Alec asked. A sudden thought raced through his mind. "Have they anything to do with Van Schouten and Swan showing up here? Ye'll have a big force at yere command then, lassie, providing Swan and Van Schouten let ye rule the roost. Somehow, I can't see ye ordering those two bullies about."

She smiled secretively. "I have the means to that, Cutlass."

"Such as?" Alec eyed her. "Ye mean to take the Spanish women back to Porto Bello for ransom? Ye'd hardly get enough ransom money for one ship's crew out of the Spaniards, according to custom, without splitting it up between four ships' crews..." His voice died away as an ugly thought came into his mind. "Surely, ye don't intend to…" His voice died away again.

She nodded. "Hostages, Cutlass. Hostages to force the surrender of Porto Bello without our firing a shot. I've always wanted to raid that damned treasure house, but I knew the force required would have to be a huge one, and one I could not raise. By God, if Drake and Morgan could raid Porto Bello, Kate Devon can do the same!"

"Ye're drunk," he said scornfully. "A drunken, stinking bitch!"

She hurled her wineglass at him. He fended it off with a forearm. She jumped to her feet and looked about for a weapon. She darted toward the table where his broadsword and highland pistols lay. She ripped the broadsword from its sheath and whirled.

Alec cocked the four-barreled pistol and raised it to point it at her flushed face. "One step toward me, lassie," he warned coldly, "and I'll blow that lovely face of yours into a red jelly."

She wanted to strike him! *God, how she wanted to strike!*

He moved his head a little. "Put my sword back into its sheath, Kate. Come now, like a good wee lassie."

She looked into those four deadly barrels and then into his icy eyes, and she knew damned well he meant what he said. Slowly, she backed away, keeping her eyes on him until she reached the table. She placed the broadsword on the table.

"Into the sheath, Kate," Alec ordered.

She did as she was bid to do.

Alec smiled. "Now fill the wineglasses, lassie, and let's have no more of this damned temper of yours."

She filled the wineglasses and returned to her seat. Soft dusk light now filled the air. They sat silently in the dimness.

"Ye'll no reconsider then?" Alec asked.

She shook her head. "I can't, Alec. I've already committed myself to this venture with Quinlan, Van Schouten, and Swan. They'll be ashore this night for a conference. You know I can't back out of it now."

"Ye said ye could command them," he reminded her. "Or, is it that ye don't want to reconsider the matter?"

"I've agreed to sign the Articles for this venture!" she cried.

Alec shrugged. "Oh, in *that* case, there's nae going back for ye, is there?" He smiled a little. "Ye've *always* kept by the Articles, have ye not?"

There was no reply from Kate. She stood up and quickly left the room.

Alec drained his glass. He let down the hammer of his pistol and replaced it under his pillow.

Rafaela came quietly into the room. She lighted a candle. "Are you ready for your dinner, Alexander?" she asked.

He looked up at her. He nodded. "But only if you'll dine with me, Rafaela."

She looked over her shoulder. "Captain Devon may not like that," she suggested.

"To hell with Captain Devon!" he snapped.

She turned and studied him. "You're upset."

He nodded. "That woman is powermad."

"What has happened? We saw two great ships come into the harbor. They are *corsairos luteranos?*"

"Yes. Two of the best, or worst, depending upon how ye view them."

"Are we women still being held for ransom?" she asked.

He looked away from her.

"Tell me," she insisted.

Alec told her, holding nothing back.

She clasped her fine hands on each side of her lovely oval face. "Mother of God! Is there nothing that can be done?"

He shook his head. "I don't know. My own ship is far from here. Even then, my ship and crew would be outnumbered four to one. Besides, we Brethren of the Coast cannot turn one against another, else we are called mad dogs by the Brethren and are outlawed by our own kind."

"So there is honor, of a kind, even among thieves."

He nodded. "Since you put it that way—yes."

"I'll have Teresa bring the dinner," she said. She came close to him and placed a cool hand on his forehead. He looked up into her lovely face and those immense doelike eyes of hers. He slid an arm about her slim waist. She drew back a little and then impulsively bent to his lips. He drew her down across his lap, and for several long moments, they remained that way, until at last she straightened up and turned her face away from him.

"It's all right, my dear," he murmured.

She shook her head. "I am betrothed," she murmured.

"It's harmless," he assured her. He was lying in his teeth.

She stepped back and looked into his eyes. "No, Alec, it's *not* harmless. You know that as well as I do. Please, not again!" She turned on a heel and ran from the room.

"She's in love with you, Alec," Kate Devon had told him. "A woman *knows*…"

TEN

Captain Joshua Swan of the *Sea Venture* was a tall, spare man, with a ruff of iron-gray hair about his bald, freckled scalp. Despite his years in the tropics, his color still had a false ruddiness about it, while beneath the taut skin was a grayish pallor. His face was gaunt, hollow-cheeked, and lined, with almost a death's-head appearance. But it was the eyes of Joshua Swan that caught one's attention: They were an icy gray-green almost like a pair of marbles, and with as much feeling in them. Few people could ever look long into Joshua Swan's eyes, for there was an impenetrable quality about them that forbade such a long scrutiny. Despite his rather spare frame, he was one of those said to be constructed of "rawhide and gun metal." He was a Massachusetts Bay Colony man.

Captain Jan Cornelius Van Schouten was built as solidly as one of the windmills of his own country. He was seemingly square in appearance, with immensely broad shoulders and a deep chest coupled with rather short but powerful arms and legs. His fair complexion had turned to a ruddy mahogany hue from the suns of the East and the West Indies, both areas in which he had spent a great deal of his mature life and with which he was thoroughly familiar. His small eyes were of a guileless blue in hue, but when the light of battle shone in them, Jan Van Schouten was a man to be feared and respected. If a set pattern for a Dutch *zee rover* were to be fashioned, Jan Van Schouten would have been the perfect model.

The "council of state" set up for the proposed sea venture had been arranged by Kate Devon. Somehow, she had sobered up enough by the time her three guests arrived, Patrick Quinlan of the *Exterminator* being the third of them. She had wisely, and partly on the suggestion of Roche Brasiliano, changed from the sheer and diaphanous white gown she had worn when she had last met with Alec Campbell into her more usual men's attire. Women pirates were few in number, and of buccaneers, the elite of the Brethren of the Coast, there were none at all. Even Kate Devon, for all her experience at sea had never ventured on a land raid of the stature of those carried out by such as Drake, Morgan, and L'Ollonois. Both Captains Swan and Van Schouten had had the experience at least several times. These two worthies were leaders, not followers, and in a joint venture with other sea artists, they were usually the commanders. This was something new to both of them— Kate Devon, of whom neither had a high opinion, at least as a leader of a sea venture, would have to give a worthy and convincing argument indeed—especially since she was a woman. Still, along with Montbars, she *had* taken the mighty *Cacafuego.* That fact was indisputable. It was the only reason for both of them to bring their ships to the island rendezvous.

The four captains dined sumptuously in Kate's pavilion, and when the table had been cleared and the great silver punch bowl, for which Kate Devon was justly renowned, had been filled to its marks with potent ingredients—the finest of French brandy and wine from the Canaries, much sugar, and a bowlful of egg yolks, fresh from the chicken coops of the *Kate of Devon*—they settled down to the business at hand.

"How many of these Spanish women of quality do ye have?" Joshua Swan asked Kate.

"There are twelve of them, along with a number of common folk, maids and so forth, who were traveling with them to Spain."

"Young women?" Swan asked. He touched his thin lips with the tip of a tongue.

"Aye," Alec Campbell replied as he entered the room, "and not to be tampered with, Joshua, else they will be damaged goods to be returned to their people."

They all looked at Alec. He had lost weight during his illness, and his face was pale and drawn.

"Ye look like ye was dragged through a knothole, Cutlass," Swan said. He grinned like a death's head.

"What the hell are you doing here, Cutlass?" Kate demanded.

Alec sat down and filled a silver cup from the punch bowl. "I will have a say in the disposition of the female prisoners, Kate, or will ye dispute that here in the presence of these gentlemen?"

Jan Van Schouten looked quickly at Kate. "What is this?" he demanded. "The prisoners are yours, are they not? What is this Cutlass says?"

Patrick Quinlan looked up from his punch. He had come to the meeting loaded partway down to his marks with kill-devil rum, and the hot punch was adding fuel to the gently roaring fire in his gut. "Ye'd better leave, Cutlass," he suggested. "This meeting is not for ye, friend."

Alec held the Irishman with a cold glance. "Are ye making the rules then, *friend?* Since when?"

Patrick Quinlan tried to hold Alec's eyes, but then he looked away. He wanted no part of a feisty Alec Campbell, even if the Scot was still weak and feverish from his wounds.

"Cutlass has nothing to say here," Kate put in. "Unless, of course, he wants to join us in this venture."

Van Schouten nodded. "A welcome addition on my part, Katie. Porto Bello is well fortified and has a large garrison of excellent troops. Besides, there is the jungle and the swamp with which we must deal if the Spaniards will not meet our terms."

Swan nodded. "I agree. What say ye, Cutlass? Ye'll join us?"

Alec shook his head. "The Articles that were signed before Kate here, Montbars, and myself took our ships to the Mona Passage to take the Cacafuego, prohibit the usage of women prisoners as hostages. Article XIII, to be exact."

"It merely states that they are to be held for ransom!" Kate snapped.

"Exactly," Alec agreed. "Further, that ransom is to be shared equally among the Company."

"Article XIII again," Quinlan said dryly.

"I say here and now," Alec continued, "that Kate Devon and Jacques Montbars violated those Articles in the taking of the Cacafuego, for by God, my officers and crew were left out of their division of the treasure."

Jan Van Schouten was puzzled. "How is this, then, Katie? Your message to Captain Swan and myself mentioned nothing of this."

Alec leaned back in his chair. "For the simple reason she knew she would have a difficult time in finding men such as yourselves to join in a venture if they knew she had broken the Articles."

Jan Van Schouten looked dubiously at Kate. Joshua Swan rubbed his leathery face. "There's a technicality here, mates. The way I see it, although all three captains and their crews did sign the Articles, the Cacafuego was actually taken by the *Kate of Devon* and the *Exterminator.*"

"Ye talk like a damned sea lawyer!" Alec roared.

The New Englander looked casually at Alec. His eyes were like rime ice. "Where was the *Adventuress* when the Cacafuego was taken?" he asked quietly.

"Why," Alec began, "we were back fighting the *naos.*"

"Who saw ye fighting the *naos?*"

"Kate here and Montbars."

"Montbars is dead," Quinlan reminded Alec. "By your own hand, too, Cutlass. He's not here to defend himself."

"Kate?" Alec asked.

She shrugged.

"But it was Montbars who fired into my ship and partially disabled it," Alec said hotly. "Ye were there, Quinlan. Ye saw that."

Quinlan fiddled with his punch cup. He looked up at Alec. "All I know is that we fired on some ship in the darkness."

It became very quiet in the room. A breeze blew through the pavilion and flickered the candles. Alec looked from one to the other of them. There was no warmth toward him shown on any of those faces.

"There was enough loot taken from the *Cacafuego* to make all three crews rich men," Alec continued quietly. "Even without the female prisoners' ransom money. Montbars and Kate could have spared the passengers and crew of the *Cacafuego* and let her go on her way in peace."

"It was none of my doing!" Kate shouted. "It was Montbars who slaughtered the passengers and crew! You told me that yourself!"

Alec nodded. "But, as Captain Quinlan here has already stated—he's not here to defend himself..."

"We waste time here with this man," Joshua Swan argued. "Cutlass, either agree to go with us on this venture and forget what happened with the *Cacafuego*, or get to hell out of here and let us about our business."

Alec shook his head. "No. Ye cannot use those women prisoners as hostages."

"They will not be harmed!" Kate spat out.

Alec looked at the death's-head face of Joshua Swan and into the guileless blue eyes of Jan Van Schouten. "Katie," he suggested quietly, "supposin' ye land your forces before Porto Bello and blockade it by sea. Supposin' ye state your terms to the Spanish commander: The hostages for your freedom to pillage the city. Supposin', just supposin' now, the Spaniards refuse to accept your terms?"

"Then we'll take it by storm!" Kate cried.

The hot punch was getting to her.

Alec shook his head. "Ye've not the skill or experience to undertake such a venture." He looked at the three other captains. "Neither has Quinlan here. But Swan and Van Schouten have that skill and experience, and they would not attack as soon as their terms were refused."

"They would if they were under my command," Kate insisted.

Alec smiled a little half-smile. "Foolish female," he murmured. "Once ye are in the field before Porto Bello do ye think these two bully boys would let ye keep command?

To lead their buckos in a bloody attack on a fortified city defended by a *tercio* of tough Spanish troops serving under excellent commanders? The Spaniards may not be the greatest of sea fighters, lassie, but Spanish infantry has dominated Europe and the New World for a hundred years. Well-trained, experienced troops against a ragtag and bobtail mob of buccaneers fighting out of their element—the sea. No, lassie, it canna be, but I will tell ye what will happen, and mark this well: Hostages have been used before in this business of ours, by other commanders, including both Swan and Van Schouten. They know the rules, lassie. If their first demand is not met, the head of one of their hostages will be thrown into the city. If that doesn't work, each day another head will be thrown after the first head, and so on, lassie, *until the demands are met...*"

Kate paled. She looked from Swan to Van Schouten. "Is this true?" she asked.

Swan shrugged. "It's better than losing good men."

"It always works," Van Schouten added. He smiled grimly. "One time, we used nuns ahead of our advancing lines. The nuns carried the scaling ladders. We thought the Spaniards would not fire on them. Well, they had a tough and obstinate commander there that day."

Kate stared at him. "You mean..."

The Hollander nodded. "We finally had to run up our own scaling ladders. Cost us a lot of men, but we had run out of nuns by that time. Hawwww!" He slapped his hands down on the table so hard that the bottles, glasses, and utensils flew up into the air.

"You didn't tell me of this before," Kate accused both Swan and Van Schouten.

Joshua Swan fixed her with those gray-green stones he had for eyes. "Ye didn't ask us, Kate."

"But..." Kate's voice faltered and died.

Swan leaned toward her. "Listen to me, woman. Ye invited me and Van Schouten here to come to a rendezvous for a proposed sea venture. We lost valuable time to do this. There were other ventures we had in mind, ye understand? Now, it seems to me, ye are sitting on the queen's throne after your taking of the *Cacafuego*, so why ye'd want to risk taking Porto Bello is your own business. But, Van Schouten and me here have been having hard times. Now, we came here like I said, on your invitation, based on our use of the hostages ye took from the *Cacafuego*. There is no going back from this now, ye understand?"

"I do what I will!" Kate cried.

Swan slewed his marble eyes to look into the blue eyes of the Dutchman. Van Schouten nodded. Swan looked again at Kate Devon. "Ye are dealing with men this night, woman. Now, if ye have a change of mind about this venture and will not go, ye must recompense me and Van here for our loss of time."

She stared at him. "The treasure?"

He shook his head. "We are not 'mad dogs,' Kate. No, the treasure of the *Cacafuego* is rightfully yours and that of Quinlan and his crew. However…"

"Go on," Quinlan urged. He leaned forward.

Joshua Swan sipped at his punch and then cleared his throat. During this time his eyes never left those of Kate Devon. "As payment, we want those female prisoners."

"For the ransom money?" Kate asked.

Swan shook his head. "As hostages. For, woman, with ye or without ye, me and Van here are going to take Porto Bello."

Kate looked at Patrick Quinlan. "Quinlan?" she asked quietly.

Quinlan emptied his punch cup. "They're right. I'll throw in my half of the women prisoners to be used as hostages."

Alec's strategy was failing. He had though to turn them one against the other, but Joshua Swan had outsmarted him and Kate as well.

"Now, woman," Swan continued, "do ye throw in with us and to hell with this damned Scotsman here, or do we take the women with us when we leave?"

Kate looked at Alec. "Alec?" she asked.

He shrugged. "What do you want of me?"

"Throw in with me, and I'll go along with them!" she cried. "Think of it! Porto Bello, the treasure house of the Spanish Main!"

"Ye've a fortune now, Kate, what wi' your own shares from the *Cacafuego* and half of that which was due the *Adventuress*. What need do ye have for more?"

Kate stood up. "Gentlemen: Will you give me twenty-four hours to give you my decision?"

"Why?" Swan asked.

"Perhaps I can persuade Captain Campbell to throw in with us."

Swan cast a knowing look at Alec. "Do ye think he's up to such persuasion? He looks hardly fit for anything but a game of dice wi' ye. Hawww!"

Most other men than Joshua Swan would have seen the warning signals in Kate's green eyes. Patrick Quinlan saw them. "Come, Josh, and ye too, Van. I've got some excellent French brandy in me tent. We can talk over plans for the Porto Bello venture there."

Swan nodded. He stood up. He looked at Alec Campbell. "Cutlass, think it over well. There ain't a better commander than ye in the Brethren of the Coast. Ye've shown the Brotherhood that time and time again. By God, Cutlass! *I'll* serve under ye if ye change your mind!"

Jan Van Schouten emptied his glass and stood up. "I'll agree to that, Cutlass. With Quinlan here, and Kate Devon, if she has a mind, the four of us could easily get several others of the Brotherhood to join us."

Alec looked at Patrick Quinlan. The Irishman nodded slightly. He did not look at Kate Devon.

"What the hell is this?" Kate demanded. "It was *me* that thought this venture up! *I've* got the women prisoners! Without them, you have nothing!"

Alec yawned a little. "Ye've already been told by Josh Swan here that they mean to take the women prisoners wi' them as recompense for coming here."

"But I wanted to lead the venture!" she cried.

"Why?" Alec asked lazily. "To prove ye are as good as any man? Ye've never served on a land expedition, lassie. Ye'd be leadin' some of the roughest, toughest fighting men on the face of the earth. Ye've got to hold them in the palm of your hand, and ye canna make mistakes, not for one second!"

Kate reached for a bottle.

Alec stood up. "If ye mean to drink, go ahead. If ye think to throw it at me, I'll break the damned bottle in midair wi' a bullet, and the next bullet will be for ye!" he warned her.

Patrick Quinlan looked at Swan and Van Schouten. "The preliminaries are beginning. We gave her twenty-four hours. Let her have them." He left the pavilion, followed by Swan and Van Schouten.

Quinlan turned to look back at the habitation. "One of these times, it will end up wi' one of them killing the other one. In this case, if it happens, I hope to God it isn't Cutlass. We have need of him."

Swan nodded. "The woman is nothing." He looked sideways at Quinlan. "Ye think he'll be persuaded?"

Quinlan shrugged. "She's good at that, at least."

"In bed?" Swan leered.

"I wouldn't know, but Cutlass is too canny, as the Scots say, to be bribed into anything for just a tumble in bed wi' a woman—*any* woman."

"Can he be trusted?" Van Schouten asked.

Quinlan smiled a little. "Trust not the Scot," he murmured, "for he can touch pot and flagon wi' ye and be hail-fellow-well-met, until some dark night, when ye least suspect, he'll pay off some old, half-forgotten debt wi' the point of his dirk."

ELEVEN

It was getting late. The subdued murmuring of voices from the men on the beach had been dying out for some time as the crewmen sought their pallets. The crescent moon hung in a clear sky, shedding a pale, translucent light down upon the island. There was no wind. The night was almost deathly quiet.

There was only one light on in the sprawling habitation of Kate Devon, tucked away on the border of the jungle. It was a guttering candle on the cluttered table in Kate's portion of the habitation. Alec Campbell sat alone at the table, as he had the last time he had been with Kate, waiting for her to change into something more tempting with which to work her wiles on him.

Alec had already begun to feel his strength returning to him after his week-long bout with fever and poison. Maybe it was the effect of the fine wine mingled with the hot punch. Oddly enough, he was in one of those stages where the spirits seemed to have little effect on him, except that his perceptions and senses seemed more acute rather than dulled as they should rightly have been from the drinking he had been doing.

"Alec?" she said softly from behind him.

He turned slowly. She stood in the opening between her bedroom and the dining area. She wore a thin, strapless dress of black silk, which accentuated the creamy white skin of her shoulders and arms. She had piled her red hair atop her shapely head. It was obvious that she was wearing nothing beneath the gown.

"When shall we two meet again?" Alec asked dryly.

She came toward the table. "What is that supposed to mean, Alec?" she asked curiously. "Is it that damned Scots 'second sight' of yours again?"

He leaned back in his chair. "A premonition perhaps, lassie. The line is frae the Bard, wi' a minor changing of mine. Macbeth it is, lassie. My ancestor is mentioned therein —Thane of Cawdor," he said thoughtfully. "The Campbells of Cawdor." He rolled the clan name from his lips as though savoring something of which she had no knowledge and would never know.

"You and your damned ancestors!" she snapped. "That Scots pride of yours!"

Alec filled her wineglass. "I'm sorry, Katie. I had no intentioning of lordin' it ower ye."

She sat down across from him and rested her elbows on the table. "I don't believe you. You can't help lording it over us 'common' people, Alec. Admit it!"

He looked at her over the rim of his glass. His eyes drifted down to her deep cleavage. Damn her! She could arouse him as few other women had ever been able to do.

"Alec?" she queried.

He looked up and into her great green eyes. "Aye, then," he agreed quietly. "It's so. I was born wi' it. A failin' of the Scots."

"Damn you! You don't think of it as a failing at all!"

He grinned irritatingly. "Then have it your way!"

She sipped at her wine. "Will you come in with us, then?" she asked.

"As leader?"

She smashed the wineglass so hard down on the table that the thin stem snapped. "I'm to be leader!" she shouted.

Alec shook his head. "No, lassie. I told ye what that would entail. Further, if ye fail those men in your leader-ship, providin' they *let* ye lead them, which is out of the question, ye'll get a bullet in your pretty back when ye least expect it, and Swan or Van Schouten will take ower. They have no intention of lettin' ye lead them on this impossible venture."

She studied him. "Impossible? That's not so and you know it! It could be done! We've got the ships and the men. We can get more of the Brethren of the Coast on the strength of you joining us with the *Adventuress* as leader. We've got the Spanish women as hostages."

"I told you what would happen to them."

"So?" she demanded. "This is war, isn't it? You've always said that. War between Spain and the rest of Europe over control of the Caribbean. You've said that control of the Caribbean would be control of Mexico, the Isthmus of Panama, and the northern coast of South America." She leaned forward. "Aye! And for that matter, if that control is gained, that could lead to control of the Pacific coast and the vast riches of Peru and the Orient, brought to Mexico by the Manila Galleon. I've heard you talk about that time and time again, Cutlass. Could not this venture be a foothold for that dream of yours?"

He looked up at her from perusing the wine in his glass. "Dream?" he asked softly. "What dream?"

She smiled a little. "I've just told you that dream, Alec. Don't deny it. It fits your character like your skin. That's the only reason you got letters of marque from the English—the bloody Sassenach, you call them when you're drunk. By God, Cutlass, you want to be the conqueror in these waters. Admiral Alexander Duncan Campbell of the Campbells of Cawdor! That's it, isn't it? A Scots admiral?" She roared with laughter, a dangerous thing to do, but Kate Devon was now beyond a state of caution. "A Scots admiral!" she repeated scornfully. "They haven't even got a navy!"

He looked steadily at her. He would not let her prick his great pride. "They had one once," he said quietly.

The look in his eyes sobered her. This was not why she had asked to be alone with him.

Alec refilled their wineglasses. "Ye really want me to go wi' ye on this madness?" he asked. He did not wait for an answer. "But what's in it for ye? Ye've got great wealth now, what with the taking of the *Cacafuego* and the rightful share of myself and my crew. But, ye need *more*, do ye not? Ye speak of my dream, but what of yours, Kate?" He leaned forward a little. "Shall I tell ye?"

She looked away from him. She feared his second sight.

"Dinna look away, Kate. Ye want wealth and more wealth, the wealth of a Croesus or a Midas, for one reason alone—ye want to return to England, for ye know that money such as ye might accumulate will open many doors. Ye will not be satisfied with living your life out aboard yon ship in the harbor, in the company of those animals who just left here. Ye know what your fate will be. I told ye of that when we were at the rendezvous."

She winced a little and thrust out the palm of a hand toward him as though to prevent him from repeating the forecast he had made of her future.

Alec nodded. "Ye know…"

She turned and looked at him. The truth was plain on her lovely face.

"Then ye shall have that dream, lassie," Alec promised. "For I'll go wi' ye, but, although I agree the Spanish women prisoners can be used as hostages, there will be no killing of them to force the Spaniards to surrender."

She eyed him suspiciously. "Why this sudden change of heart?" she demanded. "Is it because of that milk-faced Rafaela? She's in love with you, Cutlass. Perhaps you're in love with her as well! By God! Is *that* it, you conniving Scots bastard?"

Alec half smiled. "I can't believe that ye think that of me. Ye know me better than that. Love? Tell me the meaning of the word, Kate, if ye can." His voice died away. It was easy to gull Kate when she was drinking.

"Then you'll go with us?"

He nodded. "As leader or not at all."

She hesitated.

"Think, lassie," Alec urged in a low voice. "Your chances of leading are nonexistent. If Swan and Van Schouten lead, ye'll likely be thrust into the background if they don't see that ye are shot in the back in the first exchange of musketry. Ye know my record. Ye know ye and Montbars would never hae taken the *Cacafuego* wi'-out my plan and leadership. Come! Admit it!"

She nodded at last. "You're right, Cutlass. Damn you! You're *always* right in such matters, at least."

He nodded wisely. "And many other matters, tae numerous tae mention wi'out me making myself look too pridefu'."

She grinned and then shook her head. "Alec," she murmured. "You're the one, you're the *only* one…"

A faint cool breeze soughed through the quiet jungle. The hangings moved sinuously in the draft. The candle flame wavered. Alec stood up. He leaned over the table and blew out the candle. She met him at the end of the table and clasped her hands against his drawn face. She kissed his fever-cracked lips as though she could not get enough of them.

Alec reached up and hooked his fingers at the low neck-line of her gown. He pulled the thin material down about her waist to let those gorgeous breasts of hers swing free. She tore at his loose shirt and stripped it away from him. The buttons pattered on the thick carpet beneath their feet.

The faint light from the crescent moon shone down into the glade where the spring bubbled gently to the surface of the pool. The moonlight turned the pool into a silver mirror. A night bird called suddenly from the deep jungle.

Kate kicked off her tiny shoes and turned away from Alec. She ran out onto the green mantle of verdure that bordered the pool and looked back over a creamy bare shoulder at him.

"Sweet Jesus," Alec murmured. He took off his low shoes, snatched a bottle of wine from the table, felt within his pants pocket for his chunky four-barreled pistol and then followed her out into the jungle glade. The soft moonlight made her look like a sylvan goddess out of some ancient Greek tale.

"Aphrodite," Alec murmured.

"One of your other whores?" Kate asked.

"In a way," Alec replied dryly.

She sat down at the edge of the pool and then lay back, hooking her hands at the base of her neck so that her proud breasts were outthrust. Alec sat down beside her. He rested on one elbow and played with her breasts. She closed her eyes. He bent his head and kissed her, then passed a hand down over her breasts and flat belly to slip it under her gown.

She put her arms about his neck and drew him to her so that they could mold their lips together. She opened her eyes. "Thank God you're coming with us, Alec," she murmured. He did not look into her eyes. He slid an arm under her neck as he lay down beside her. The faint cool breeze drifted over them.

Alec suddenly raised his head. Some sixth sense, honed by years of living on the very razor's edge of danger, had alerted him. He looked toward the pavilion. It was in darkness. Nothing moved except the draperies activated by the breeze.

"What is it?" she whispered into his ear.

He shook his head. He stood up and withdrew his pistol from a pocket. He stole toward the pavilion and into it. It was deathly quiet. He peered into the compartment shared by Rafaela and Teresa. He saw their dim forms on their low couches and heard faint breathing as though both of them were asleep. Alec padded to the front of the pavilion. He could see the moon-lighted beach through the thin screen of trees between the pavilion and the sands. There was no one on the sands. Someone was singing softly near the men's quarters. A man laughed. The four ships lay quietly to their anchors, heading into the land breeze. Only their faint riding lights shone through the soft moonlight.

Alec walked noiselessly through the pavilion. He looked into the tiny compartment where Patience slept. She wasn't there. Alec grinned. The Arawak woman was like a bitch dog in heat at night—*any* night.

Alec paused at the rear side of the pavilion. Kate still lay there, naked to the waist, with her eyes closed.

Alec stood over her. He bent and placed his pistol close at hand. Her eyes were closed. He pulled the black silk gown down over her hips and off her long, lovely legs. He cast the gown aside and looked down at the almost-perfect contours of her body.

She sat up suddenly. She gripped the top of his loose seaman's pants and tore them down about his ankles. He wore nothing beneath them. She passed her hands down his lean belly and teased his privates. She looked up into his eyes with a she-demon look on her oval face. Then she jumped to her feet and ran toward the jungle, only to turn and skirt the rim of the pool, looking back over a milky white shoulder as she did so.

Alec started to run after her.

"Be careful you don't trip, Cutlass!" she called back, "or you'll pitchfork yourself into the pool!"

She paused on the far side of the pool and watched him as he stopped and eyed her. Slowly, she let herself down into the water so that it rose to just beneath her breasts. Then she let herself fully down into the water and shoved off to swim underwater toward the center of the pool.

Alec dived cleanly into the pool. He sank deep and then curved upward so that he came face to face with her underwater. They clasped their arms about each other and sank together to the firm, clean white sand of the bottom where the tiny, jewel-like bubbles of the spring prickled over their bodies.

Kate lay back and spread herself out for Alec. He moved into the cleft between her legs and seated himself firmly there. Together, they rose to the top of the pool to gasp for air before they sank again to the bottom, where she lay beneath him with her long legs wrapped about his slim waist.

They rose to the surface again and somehow worked their way, joined together, to the shallow water where she rested her head against the bank while the lower part of her body was still underwater.

"Would you drown me for lust, Alec?" she murmured into his ear.

"Try me," he gasped. The fever had taken more out of him than he had realized.

"If you must," she added, "do so, for I can't think of a better way of dying together."

He looked into her great eyes, and somehow, he knew that she meant it. But, thanks to the unseen help of Aphrodite, or perhaps it was Bacchus—that trenchant thought was Alec's as he and Kate strove together—they both made it at last. Alec crawled weakly from the pool and lay exhausted, face downward on the bank. She crawled on her hands and knees and lay down beside him, resting her cheek on a crooked arm so that her face was but inches from his. She reached out with her other hand and passed it along his face.

They lay side by side for a long time. The moonlight was waning. Shadows moved across the pool. Suddenly, the faint sound of nocturnal birds and insects in the jungle ceased abruptly.

Alec raised his head. He got to his knees.

"What is it?" Kate asked quickly.

He stood up. "Sweet Jesus," he murmured.

"Alec?" she queried as she sat up.

He turned aside from her and plunged into the pool. He crossed it with five quick strokes and hauled himself out on the far bank. He ran to his pistol and snatched it up.

"Alec!" Kate cried. "What is it?"

He turned as he ran toward the pavilion. "*Caribs!* Get to hell away from there!"

"For God's sake, Alec!" she screamed. "Don't leave me!"

Alec crashed into a woman standing just within the shadow of the pavilion. It was Rafaela in her nightdress. Alec hurled her back into the pavilion. "Run!" he snapped. "Caribs! Run to the beach!"

Rafaela fainted dead away.

Alec whirled. Seven of them emerged from the jungle, lean, bronzed figures with long dark hair hanging across their red-painted faces. They raised no weapons. They were on a meat-hunting raid.

Alec raised the pistol and fired the two upper barrels simultaneously. The lead Carib dropped and rolled sideways into the pool as the shot echoes rang through the jungle. The white powder smoke drifted like a screen between Alec and the other Caribs. He undid the barrel latch of the pistol and turned the two bottom barrels into the uppermost position and then cocked the pistol.

Kate screamed as she went down under two clawing Caribs. The other four warriors ran toward the pavilion. Alec picked up Rafaela and half dragged and half carried her out to the beach. He whirled as the four warriors burst from the pavilion.

Men shouted along the beach. Someone fired a gun. The heavy shot echo reverberated along the thick border of trees to die away along the beach.

Alec raised his pistol as the Caribs closed in on him. He fired at ten-foot range. The lead warrior went down as though poleaxed, and one of his mates fell over him. The remaining two warriors turned and fled back into the pavilion as Roche Brasiliano burst from his tent with a naked sword and ran toward Alec. One stroke of the sword decapitated the warrior who had fallen over his dead mate.

"Where's Kate?" Roche screamed hoarsely.

"At the pool!" Alec yelled.

Together, they ran through the dark pavilion just in time to see the two warriors plunge into the jungle as though diving into a deep green pool. Kate and the two warriors who had grappled with her were gone. Her clothing and that of Alec still lay on the bank of the pool. The dead Carib lay on the white sand bottom of the pool with his long dark hair floating about his face. His eyes stared upward. The water about him was tinted with blood. The bottom part of his face was a red jelly.

Roche Brasiliano plunged toward the jungle.

"For Christ's sake, Roche!" Alec yelled. "Ye'll ne'er catch them in there! Ye'll only meet your death!"

Roche turned and pointed his reddened blade at Alec. "She was with you, you bastard!" he yelled. "Why didn't you stay and fight for her?" He whirled and tore into the thickness of the jungle. As he did so, a faint woman's scream came back to them.

Tattoo catfooted to one side and just ahead of the four Caribs and the screaming, struggling Kate. He stepped behind a huge boled tree and let the first three of them and Kate pass. The last Carib never knew what hit him. Tattoo closed in on the next warrior. The cutlass rose and fell. A long-haired head fell sideways into the brush, followed by the headless body, aided by a quick push from Tattoo.

One of the last two Caribs looked back over a shoulder. That was a fatal mistake. He did see the dark, shadowy form behind him. He did not see the stroke that killed him. The last Carib turned at bay. He shoved the woman behind him and raised a long-bladed knife in his right hand. The cutlass swung to the left and severed the hand at the wrist, and the reverse stroke cut his throat from ear to ear.

Tattoo stepped over the dead Carib. Kate had fainted dead away. Tattoo had eyes like a cat. He surveyed the lush white nakedness of the woman and whistled softly. "¡Ay de mí!" he murmured in his guttural Spanish. He looked back over his shoulder toward the encampment. If he had time... then he heard someone crashing noisily through the jungle.

"Kate! Kate! Kate!" Roche Brasiliano screamed hoarsely, half-insane with the loss of her.

Tattoo slipped into the blackness of the jungle and became part of it, but he did not sheath his bloody weapon.

Roche stumbled over a dead Carib. Then he saw Kate. He dropped his sword and then dropped to his knees beside her. He cradled her in his powerful arms, and great tears flowed down his dark face.

Tattoo looked speculatively at the nape of Roche Brasiliano's thick neck. He wet his lips and ran a thumb along the razor edge of his cutlass. Before God! One good stroke... then he thought of something. He had seen the lovemaking and aquatic fornication between his master and the red-headed whore. He knew also that the young Spanish woman, Rafaela, had been watching them as well from the shadows of the pavilion. Then he had seen his master rush away from Kate, with whom he had just fornicated, to save the Spanish woman. Tattoo shook his head. Why his master would want to save that Spanish woman, hardly more than a girl, when he had something like Kate Devon with which to play and fuck, was beyond his understanding. But, there was one thing he did understand: When Kate Devon returned to her camp, knowing that Alec had left her to the Caribs while he rushed into the pavilion to save the Spanish girl, there would be hell to pay.

Tattoo vanished into the darkness, almost like a disembodied spirit. Someone moved at the edge of the jungle. Tattoo went to ground. "Master?" he called out softly, ready to move instantly if it was not Alec.

"Tattoo?"

Tattoo came swiftly to Alec. Alec was dressed. He carried his naked sword in his right hand and his four-barreled pistol in the other.

"The woman is safe, master," Tattoo reported. He grinned, showing his filed teeth. "Four Carib. All dead."

"Where is she?" Alec asked.

"With that damned mustee. He cry over her like baby."

Alec nodded. "Show me," he said.

Tattoo shook his head.

"What the hell is the matter with you?" Alec demanded.

Tattoo told him.

Alec rubbed a hand across his lean face. "Sweet Jesus," he murmured. "I never thought of that."

"Best we get out of here, master. Now!"

Alec shook his head. "I can't leave the Spanish woman."

"Can't do her no good now. Come! Tattoo stole small boat one night when everyone drunk. Sail it to dat place where we hid pinnace. Got food with it. Water. Sails. Compass. We sail it to meet *Adventuress*. Master, we got to get to hell out'a dis place, or you die suddenly."

Alec grinned wryly. "And ye, Tattoo, can ye not die suddenly too?"

Tattoo shook his head. "Not time for me; not time for you. You ready?"

"Let me get the rest of my weapons."

They faded into the jungle as silently as two night-hunting cats.

Roche Brasiliano met the rescue party, blundering their way through the jungle with torches held up high. "Get back," he ordered. "I killed four Caribs to save her," he boasted. "Find that Scots bastard Alec Campbell! I want him!"

They all crashed back through the jungle.

Roche Brasiliano carried the naked woman to her room in the pavilion. He lighted a candle and looked down at her. There were livid bruises and red scratches on the pure whiteness of her lush body. Roche wet his thick lips. He reached down with a calloused hand and hefted one of her rounded, red-budded tits.

"Mister Brasiliano!" Ira Macklin cried from the front of the pavilion. "We can't find Campbell!"

Roche walked heavily to the front of the pavilion. "Keep searching," he ordered. "I want him—dead or alive. Where are the two Spanish women who stayed here?"

"Under guard on the beach."

"Good! Then put them with the others in the prisoner pen."

Macklin looked beyond the big mustee. "Captain Devon? She's all right?"

Roche nodded. "I'll stay with her to see that she's all right."

Their eyes locked and then Macklin looked away. He knew…

Roche Brasiliano watched Macklin lead his men across the darkened beach. He turned on a heel and walked back into the pavilion. He walked through all the rooms. There was no one there. Patience was likely out in the camp fornicating. The Arawak bitch never seemed to get enough. Roche should know.

Roche returned through the dining room. He picked up a full bottle of Canary and drained half of it. He slowly wiped his mouth with the back of a hand, then stalked toward Kate's room.

She was awake. Her face was pale, and she looked sick.

Roche held out the bottle to her. "Drink this," he said.

She shook her head. "Not now, Roche."

"Drink," he insisted.

"Who the hell do you think you're talking to?" she demanded.

"You, you whore," he said in a low voice.

"Macklin!" she cried.

He smiled thinly. "He ain't here."

"Patience!" she called out.

He grinned. "She's out fucking somewhere."

They eyed each other.

"Drink," Roche said again.

She shook her head.

He moved so fast she could not resist. He twisted her left arm up behind her back and forced the mouth of the bottle against her lips and into her mouth. He tilted it up so that the wine ran freely down into her throat and flowed out of the corners of her mouth. She gagged and drew back. He withdrew the bottle.

Kate passed a hand across her eyes. "I'll have you locked in the bilboes," she threatened. "I'll have your bollacks cut off and shoved down your throat. I'll..."

"You'll shit," he sneered. "Drink, damn you!"

She drank and drank until she could hold no more. She fell sideways weakly and heaved out the wine. She raised her head. "For God's sake, Roche!" she gasped. "What is it you want of me?"

He stepped back and stripped himself to the skin. He moved toward her again. "This," he said.

"What the hell do you mean?"

"You know, you bitch! Fucking with that damned Scotsman! Only time you need Roche is when you're in trouble."

She stared at him. "What do you mean?"

He bent his head and looked into her eyes. "You know what everyone thinks? Even Cutlass? They think I service you all the time when no one else is around. You know that?"

She made the mistake of laughing in his face. He caught her open-handed alongside the head and knocked her sprawling on the bed. She shielded her head with crossed arms, but he pulled her up again.

Roche emptied the wine bottle. He threw it to one side. "You ready now?" he demanded.

She shook her head. He hit her so hard that she went sprawling off the couch and onto the floor. He kicked her in the side, and she cringed and drew herself up into a protective ball. Two more kicks, and she raised her head to look piteously up into his dark, contorted face. He straddled her while standing upright, crooked a finger at her, and then smiled. He patted his stiff erection.

She pushed herself up from the floor to meet his demand. The last thing she remembered for a time was that when she had finished the job, he hit her alongside the head to drive her to the floor again.

Roche staggered into the dining area. He lighted a

candle and helped himself to the residue of the punch bowl. He drained another wine bottle. An hour later, he heard her cry out softly.

Roche lurched to his feet. He blew out the candle. He swayed perilously as he felt his way to the bedroom.

Kate cried out protestingly. The sound of hard blows followed her protests. Then, it was quiet for a little while. Kate screamed thinly, like a wounded mare, and then it was quiet for the rest of the night.

TWELVE

I t was the dark of the moon. The *Adventuress* ghosted along with only her topsails set. The island was a dark, humped shape, like a colossal turtle asleep on the gently heaving sea.

A faint speck of yellow light blinked on, then off, then on again; there was a pause and then the light blinked twice again.

"The signal," Alec Campbell called back over his shoulder. "Back the main tops'l, Mister Yeoman."

The *Adventuress* was heaved to. She rolled slightly in the scend of the slow ground swell.

"Mister MacMillan!" Alec cried out. "Clear your guns for action! We don't know for sure who might be flashing that light."

Surgeon Terence Shannon nodded. "It had better be Rais Gilles, Cutlass. He owes me five English pounds from our last dice game."

The rumbling sound of the guns being run out died away. The hull creaked and groaned gently in the movement of the sea. The steady offshore breeze thrummed through the rigging.

The pinnace came footing through the dimness with her lugsails drawing full and a bone in her teeth.

"What boat is that?" Boatswain Heckart hailed.

"Rais Gilles!" the Frenchman called out.

The pinnace came alongside, and her sails were dropped. Boat hooks held her fast to the rising and falling side of the frigate, and Rais stepped easily from the stern-sheets to meet the Jacob's ladder that had been flung, clattering over the side.

Rais came quickly aft to the quarterdeck. "Cutlass, all four ships are still there in the anchorage," he reported.

"Any of them being careened?"

Rais shook his head.

Alec nodded. "We've made it, then," he murmured. "All officers to the quarterdeck!" It was a useless command. They had already anticipated it.

"I'll take a landing party ashore immediately," Alec said. "Heckart, get the longboat over the side. I'll need both the longboat and the pinnace to bring back the Spanish women." Alec looked at Rais. "We'll land at the same place we did before, Rais."

"Lovely place," Rais murmured. "I missed it."

Alec shook his head. "Ye'll not be going, lad. We've at least eight to nine hours of darkness. When we leave the ship, ye'll sail it to the harbor, but stay well offshore at first. Give us two hours, then open fire on the ships. For God's sake, Mac, dinna overshoot and hit the encampment, for the women will still be there."

Ian MacMillan nodded. "Never fear, Cutlass."

"Once the bombardment starts, I'll move in on the camp, hoping that everyone's attention will be on the bombardment."

Ian grinned. "It will be, no fear o' that, Cutlass. I'll use flaming spike-shot to occupy their attention."

"When we're well clear of the camp, I'll fire a green rocket," Alec continued. "Then ye can open fire on the beach area. When we reach the boats and are heading out to sea, I'll fire a red rocket. Meanwhile, Rais, after bombarding yon beach, ye can sail back along the coast tae pick us up."

"As easy as that," Rais suggested dryly.

"How many men will you need?" Miles Yeoman asked.

"Twenty, no more. All volunteers. Each man to carry a cutlass, a dagger, and a brace of pistols. No calivers or arquebuses. We'll have to move fast. I'll command the pinnace; Bosun's Mate Heckart will handle the longboat."

"Twenty men?" Rais asked incredulously. "For a landing party?"

"Ye've forgotten we'll have at least a score of women coming back with us," Alec reminded him. "I don't want to overload the boats. Besides, not all of us may be coming back."

Rais studied Alec. "You really believe you're going to bring *all* of the women back?" he asked skeptically.

Alec smiled. "Of course!" He walked to the break of the quarterdeck. "Tattoo! Bring my pistols, a dirk, and a cutlass. I'm feared my lang broadsword would only be a disadvantage in yon jungle."

Alec stripped off his clothing and dressed himself in loose, cut-off canvas trousers that reached below the knee. They had been heavily coated with pitch, the buccaneer's defense against sword and cutlass slashes. He put on a loose linen shirt and bound a bandanna about his head. He buckled on a thick belt and thrust the sheathed cutlass through the leather frog at the left side of it.

Bosun's Mate Heckart was tolling off the names of the volunteers to Jonas Pitts, the ship's clerk, as they went over the side: "Owen, Cutting, Davis, Wheeler, Burdick, Johnson, Dahlman, Hamilton, Cole, Murino, Riley, Coombs, Mullner, Casper, Valois, Palfrey, Horn, Dow, Ely, and Dodd." The men tumbled into the two boats. They raised the masts in the longboat.

Alec walked to the Jacob's ladder followed by Tattoo, who was like a black shadow behind his master. Alec looked over the railing at the dim faces upturned to look at him from the two boats. "Ye ken," he said, "that if any of ye, including myself, are too badly wounded to keep on, we canna bring them along wi' us." He could see the heads bob as the men agreed. "Further," he continued, "if we do leave such a man behind, the Caribs will hear the shooting and will likely find him… it's up tae his mate to see that they do not find him alive. Ye ken?" Again, the heads bobbed. Alec nodded. "If any one of ye have changed your mind about volunteering, he can return to the ship, and no ill will be thought of him, but he must sing out now." No one spoke.

Alec went down the ladder, followed by Tattoo. Alec got into the pinnace. "Shove off," he ordered. He took the tiller. "Up sail!" The lugsails were hauled up and immediately caught the breeze. Alec made a long tack in toward the shore against the wind. The longboat's sails we're a ghostly blur in the darkness behind the pinnace. The commands came across the water from the *Adventuress* as the frigate was turned and began to sail back along the dark coastline toward the encampment.

Tattoo went forward in the pinnace to find the entrance through the coral reef. Alec ordered the sails dropped, and the pinnace went in under oars, closely followed by the longboat. The men went over the sides of the two boats and worked them up into the freshwater stream that meandered through the mangroves. Tattoo led the raiding party through the mangrove swamp to the hard, yellow beach.

They could see the faint pinpoints of light from the sprawling encampment and the four ships in the bay two miles up the beach. The wind brought the faint odor of woodsmoke to them.

Bosun's Mate Heckart passed around a pot full of soot garnered from the frigate's galley stove. The men rubbed it on their faces. Heckart looked at the big black. "Tattoo?" he asked, as he held out the pot. He grinned.

Tattoo led the way with unerring instinct into the thick jungle. They crossed the savannah where Alec had rescued Rafaela. As Alec crossed it, he had a quick mental picture of Rafaela as she had been that moonlit night, naked except for a silver chain and crucifix about her shapely neck, with her fair white skin and lustrous black hair and those full and proud breasts with outthrust brown nipples. He recalled in exact detail those long, slim, beautifully shaped legs of hers. He remembered all too well the night she had come to him in the pavilion and had kissed him, pressing her full breasts hard against him. "Sweet Jesus," Alec murmured in Spanish.

Bosun's Mate Heckart looked quickly at Alec. "Yes?" he queried.

Alec shook his head. "Nothing, boatswain."

But there was more—the memory of his lovemaking with Kate in the cool waters of the pool behind the pavilion and of how Alec, running naked with pistol in hand to save Rafaela from the Caribs, had stumbled into her standing just within the pavilion in her nightdress. It hadn't occurred to him then, but it had come to him later that she must have viewed the whole torrid act of fornication he had performed with Kate Devon.

They went to ground a hundred yards from the edge of the encampment while Tattoo vanished into the darkness.

Tattoo came back to the waiting raiders. He crouched beside Alec. "All de women in the pen. Guards outside dere. Big fires along beach. Men eating now."

"Rafaela?" Alec asked.

Tattoo nodded. "And fat lady Teresa."

The sound of nocturnal creatures came to the raiders—chirpings, buzzings, clickings, and hummings, with now and then, a raucous bird cry breaking up the monotony.

"It's like the raid on Cartagena," Heckart reminisced. He grunted in satisfaction. "Great days then, captain."

Alec nodded. He had a puckered bullet hole scar in his left arm as a souvenir of that raid. "We were younger then, Davie man."

They were silent again, each occupied with his own thoughts.

The *Adventuress* wore ship and tacked back toward the distant bay. Rais Gilles stood on the foredeck with Alec's long brass telescope, studying the faint specks of light. "How much closer, Mac?" he asked back over his shoulder.

"Two miles, Rais," the master gunner replied.

"There will likely be time for at least two broadsides from each battery before they can open fire with their shore batteries," Rais said. "They've got heavy metal in them— 36-pounders. And, if the ships can get their batteries quickly into action…

"We can do our damage with two broadsides," Mac promised.

Rais turned. "Mister Yeoman!" he called. "We'll go in under the courses alone, to get as close as possible before we are seen. Once we open fire, they will have no doubt as to how close we are. Then get your tops'ls and top-gallants'ls up with all speed, for we'll need them to outrun their shot."

"Aye, aye, sir," Yeoman responded. "Hands are already at the sheets and braces."

Minute after minute ticked past.

The lights seemed to grow larger on the beach.

The large, shadowy silhouettes of the anchored ships could now be seen.

The main-deck gunners and seamen began to look over their shoulders at the imperturbable Frenchman. If the shore batteries were alerted…

"You may open fire, Mister MacMillan," Rais said calmly.

"Fire!" Ian MacMillan roared.

The starboard main-deck 18-pounders and gun-deck 24-pounders lashed out leaping tongues of orange flame and white smoke. The thunderous crash of the broadside carried along the water and reverberated from the shore.

"Down helm!" Miles Yeoman bellowed. "Wear ship!"

The raiders saw the flashing of the guns through the thin screen of foliage between them and the encampment. The gun echoes seemed to slam against the thick wall of the jungle.

Alec got to his feet. "Ready," he said over his shoulder.

They could hear yelling and screaming from the ships in the bay as the solid shot smashed into them. Men ran about the beach shouting at each other. The Spanish women in the prison pen began to scream.

The offshore frigate was dark now as she wore ship. Then, the port broadside bellowed out across the sea.

"Now!" Alec snapped.

Tattoo led the way, running lightly with his naked cutlass swinging from his right hand.

They could see the dim lines of the prison pen just ahead of them. Men were running toward the shore batteries. The sea was dark again as the *Adventuress* turned to swing back to repeat her starboard broadside.

Bald and one-eyed Henry Williams was old for a buccaneer, and his luck had always been bad, for he had shared in few prizes. This was to be his last sea venture, and then he hoped to return to England with his share of the loot to live in comfort for the rest of his days. They had given him an easy task; that of guarding the Spanish women prisoners. Besides, Henry was old and hardly fit to bother the females. But his age had brought on something else—weak bowels from too many years at sea eating poor food and from the racking fever he had gained at Maracaibo. He had left his lonely post of duty at the rear of the pen to enter the edge of the jungle. He had dropped his trousers and was squatting in the shadows with his head bent over.

Tattoo loped easily along. He did not see Henry Williams. The giant black went sprawling over Henry. Henry stood up with his loose trousers about his ankles. Henry was old, but his lungs were still strong. Henry shrieked twice, a piercing warning to the other guards at the prison pen, before Dave Heckart's cutlass dropped him into his own pile of feces.

Three guards came running to the sound. One of them raised a caliver and fired at the shadowy knot of running men. Charley Coombs went down with a .74-caliber soft-lead bullet in his head. A pistol bullet fired by Alec dropped the musketeer in his tracks. Another guard raised his caliver, but Dave Heckart closed in on him. One cutlass swipe drove the barrel downward so that the weapon was fired harmlessly into the ground, and the next cutlass swipe half decapitated the musketeer. The third guard spun on a heel, hurled away his caliver, and sprinted down toward the encampment, shrieking the alarm.

The starboard battery of the *Adventuress* bellowed and spat out flaming spike-shot like a miniature volcano. The deadly flaming projectiles arched through the air, trailing sparks to strike into the hulls and masts of the four ships in the bay, or hissed out in the firelit waters.

The first shot roared out from one of the shore batteries. The heavy 36-pound shot raised a ghostly plume of spray just ahead of the *Adventuress* as she wore ship.

"Get the women out of the pen!" Alec shouted.

The shrieking guard had kept his head. He had raced to the headquarters section of the encampment to alert Roche Brasiliano. Roche, always the man of action, rallied a score of men and led them back along the beach toward the prison pen.

Cutlasses slashed through the wooden railings of the pen. The women were screaming in unison. They turned away from their would-be black-faced rescuers and huddled in a far corner of the pen.

Alec placed a hand on the front railing of the pen and vaulted into the enclosure. "Rafaela!" he called out.

"Who are you?" Rafaela cried. "Devils from hell!"

"It's Alec Campbell! For God's sake, tell these women who we are! We haven't any time to lose!"

A buccaneer thrust a caliver between two of the rails and aimed it at Alec. Alec's pistol cracked, and the buccaneer fell backward. Alec caught the muzzle end of the short musket and dragged it into the enclosure.

The raiders were darting about within the enclosure and then dragging the women to the place where they had cut through the railings on the jungle side. Fat Teresa was a paragon of strength and courage, kicking and slapping the screaming women to drive them through the opening into the nearby jungle.

Half a dozen men ran toward the prison pen with drawn cutlasses and pistols.

"Fire!" Heckart roared.

Seven of the raiders thrust pistols between the front railings of the enclosure and fired in unison. Four of the men went down. One turned and ran. The sixth man stood his ground, facing two of the raiders charging him. He didn't see Tattoo close in from behind.

"Get those pistols! Gather up those calivers! Get the powder and shot!" Alec shouted. "Fall back to cover the women!"

The port broadside of the *Adventuress* flashed flame and smoke, this time from a much closer range. Nineteen flaming spike-shot soared through the smoky air to strike havoc in among the anchored ships. A thin pillar of flame was already rising from Joshua Swan's *Sea Venture*.

Roche Brasiliano led his party toward the empty enclosure. He saw the bodies of some of his men sprawled on the beach. He waved his sword in the direction of the jungle.

"They're Caribs!" a man shouted. "Didn't ye see their painted faces? We'll never catch them now! If ye go into that jungle, ye'll ne'er come out alive!"

The rest of the men hesitated. They turned to look at their panic-stricken mate. They wanted no part of the Caribs.

Roche turned in a fury. He swung his sword across the open mouth of the shouting man. He glared at the rest of his men. "Come on, God damn you all!" he roared. "That's the damned Scot Campbell in the jungle! He's got the Spanish women! They can be worth a fortune to us, mates! Come on!" He ran toward the jungle.

Just as Roche and the first of his men reached the edge of the forest, pistols and calivers flamed from the cover of the foliage. Five men went down, but the big mustee was unscathed. He charged through the swirling powder smoke, followed by his surviving men.

Ira Macklin led the second party after Roche. They could see the powder smoke from the shooting but nothing else except the empty prison pen, the scattered bodies of the dead and wounded, and the now silent jungle.

A rocket soared up from within the jungle. It burst with a faint plop high in the air and showered out green fire.

The shore batteries had begun to open fire. All they could see of the frigate was her topgallant sails being hoisted as she swung in closer to the land. Then, the frigate opened fire on the beach immediately after the green rocket exploded high overhead. Solid shot plowed into the shore batteries or rebounded from the hard-packed sand of the beach to knock men right and left. The frigate wore ship and returned to flash out a second broadside at the beach. She wore ship again and bore away from the land at ever-increasing speed with white feathery plumes of spray rising in her wake from the shore batteries' shooting.

The fire on the *Sea Venture* had been put out. The *Lion's* anchor was being hoisted. Her courses were rising and flapping in the breeze from the land. The *Exterminator* was being readied for the forthcoming sea chase. They had no doubt in their minds but that the attacking ship was Captain

Cutlass' *Adventuress*. They had seen the lovely outline of her hull and her towering masts in the light from her flaming guns.

"Anchor's apeak!" the boatswain of the *Lion* shouted.

Jan Van Schouten had his ship turned toward the channel. The offshore breeze had increased to fill the courses, and the topsails were being sheeted home while the topgallant sails were being dropped from their yards and were already filling with the wind.

"We can't find the channel in the darkness!" Van Schouten's sailing master shouted at his commander.

"God dammit!" the raging Dutchman roared. "We *make* a channel!"

At that instant, the *Lion* scraped her bottom and a moment later ran full aground on the sand spit where Alec Campbell had fed Jacques Montbars to the sharks. The wind still filled the sails, and the power of it turned the *Lion* sideways across the channel to block it effectively.

* * *

Alec Campbell catfooted behind Tattoo through the tangled jungle growths, followed by Davis, Murino, Dahlman, Palfrey, and Casper, who were each carrying captured calivers. To their right, beyond a thick screen of foliage and creepers, Roche Brasiliano was making slow progress in his pursuit of the raiders and the women.

Tattoo held up an arm. The raiders crouched behind him. There was a small savannah to their right. The last group of Brasiliano's party were crossing it to follow the main party into the jungle.

"Thirty yards," Alec whispered over a shoulder. "Volley-fire with the calivers at my command, then discharge both your pistols and follow me in a charge."

They raised the stubby, big-bored muskets. They sighted on their pursuers. Alec raised both his pistols and aimed them.

"Fire!" Alec shouted.

The weapons belched flame and smoke. A moment later, each musketeer raised a brace of pistols, one in each hand,

and fired through the swirling gunsmoke in the direction of the buccaneers.

Alec thrust his smoking pistols under his broad belt and whipped out his cutlass. *"Cruachan!"* he roared. He leaped out onto the savannah, closely followed by his shouting men.

Seven of their opponents had been downed by the volley fire. The rest of the group turned to face the raiders. Cutlass grated and clanged against cutlass. Casper went down with a pistol bullet in his chest. Davis staggered backward with a deep cutlass slash across his left shoulder. His shirt front was drenched with blood.

Alec thrust under an opponent's guard and sank the tip of the cutlass a hand's span into his brisket. Alec withdrew, whirled, came down in an overhand slash, and cut halfway through the neck of a man who had downed the wounded Davis and was preparing to finish him off.

Men shouted in the jungle. A weapon cracked.

"Retreat!" Alec commanded.

"Captain!" Casper cried. "Don't leave me!"

"Dahlman! Murino!" Alec barked. "Bring him along!"

They dragged the wounded man back into the cover of the jungle just as Ira Macklin led the second party of buccaneers out onto the savannah. A caliver spat fire. The wounded Davis, staggering along behind his mates, caught the bullet in the middle of his back. He pitched forward onto his face and lay still.

"Master?" Tattoo cried. He pointed with his bloody cutlass at the fallen Davis.

Alec turned. There was no time to make a decision. "Finish him off!" he snapped. He turned and followed the rest of his men as the cutlass rose and fell.

Bullets tore through the jungle as Alec retreated, paralleling the advance party of buccaneers led by Roche Brasiliano, who had halted and looked back at the sound of heavy firing and combat from their rear. The raiders passed ahead of them and headed for the mangrove swamp.

Then it became very quiet. All the clickings, buzzings, hummings, and chirpings of the night creatures had died away at the first sound of firing. The only sounds were the squelching of shoes in the soft, wet ground and the dragging of branches and creepers across the bodies of the swiftly moving men.

"For God's sake!" Casper cried. "I can't go on!"

They halted. Dahlman and Murino lowered the coughing Casper to the ground. They all stood there looking down at the agonized face of the wounded man. The only sounds were the heavy breathing of the men and the dreadful bubbling sound that came from Casper's throat.

"Can you try to go on, Casper?" Alec asked at last. He knew it was hopeless.

Casper's eyes were wide in his head. He gripped Alec about one of his ankles. "For God's sake," he pleaded. "Don't leave me!"

They all looked at each other. They remembered what Alec had told them while they waited in their boats at the side of the ship: *"Ye ken that if any of ye, including myself, are too badly wounded to keep on, we canna bring them along wi' us. Further, if we do leave such a man behind, the Caribs will hear the shooting and will likely find him... it's up tae his mate to see that they do not find him alive. Ye ken?"*

Tattoo raised his head. He pointed silently back to the way by which they had come.

"We have no time left, Casper," Alec said quietly.

"They come fast!" Tattoo said.

Alec looked about at his men. "Who's his mate?" he asked. He knew. They all knew. It was Murino, a gunner and the only Italian in the frigate's crew. Murino's eyes widened. He shook his head.

"Would ye leave him tae the Caribs?" Alec asked.

Alec thrust an arm out in the direction they had been heading. "Move out!" he ordered. He strode off into the jungle, closely followed by Tattoo and the rest of his party, with the exception of Murino and Casper.

Murino looked down at his shipmate.

"It's the only way, mate," Casper gasped. He turned his head to one side.

Murino drew one of his pistols. He cocked it. He crossed himself, pressed the muzzle of the pistol against the nape of Casper's neck, and squeezed the trigger.

Alec turned a little as he heard the muffled report.

"I never thought he'd do it," Dahlman murmured.

"It was that or the Caribs," Alec reminded him.

Murino caught up with them. They plunged on into the jungle.

The women prisoners had been making slow and unsteady progress. Some of them staggered and fell but were instantly hauled to their feet by the softly cursing raiders and driven on through the thickening muck of the mangrove swamp.

Now and again, the sound of firing came from the jungle. Bosun's Mate Heckart turned. "Where the hell is Cutlass?" he demanded. He expected no answer.

"Should we go back and look for him?" Burdick asked.

Heckart wanted to go back. God, how he wanted to go back!

"Our orders were to get the women to the boats," Rob Johnson reminded them.

Heckart nodded, but he did not move.

"By God, Dave," Burdick said, "if we do go back and Cutlass is all right, he'll clap us all in the bilboes on bread and water for disobeying orders."

A musket cracked flatly somewhere in the darkness. It was closer than the last sound of firing had been.

"It could be them," Johnson warned the boatswain. His meaning was clear enough. "Besides, the Caribs will be out there in the darkness. I'd hate like hell to run into them. They know these jungles and swamps like the palms of their hands. We don't."

They slogged on after the women.

Alec and his little party splashed into the edge of the mangrove swamp. Alec looked back. The jungle was quiet.

"Maybe they've turned back," Dahlman suggested.

Alec shook his head. "Not if Roche Brasiliano is leading them."

Tattoo caught up with them. He had gone back to see how close their pursuers were. He held up two hands with fingers outspread.

"Ten of them," Alec said. He turned. "Spread out on both sides of the trail. Give them one volley with the calivers. Then it's each man for himself."

It became very quiet except for the slow, insistent dripping of water from somewhere and the humming of mosquitoes. Nothing moved. The faint light of the crescent moon filtered down into the swamp.

A man appeared on the trail. He looked to the right and then to the left. He walked forward ankle-deep in the squelching muck. His white face shone palely in the dimness. Then, fifty feet behind him, three other men appeared, walking slowly, turning their heads to left and right to peer into the dim recesses of the swamp.

Roche Brasiliano appeared leading the main party. His naked sword shone dully.

"Now?" Murino whispered to Alec.

Alec shook his head. He slowly raised his caliver as Roche Brasiliano closed in on the three men ahead of him.

A rocket hissed up into the air from somewhere at the sea edge of the mangrove swamp. It burst into a red flower of flame. Heckart and his men had reached the boats with the women prisoners.

"Now!" Alec shouted.

The calivers roared. Four men went down, but Roche Brasiliano, with some devil's luck of his own, was untouched.

Alec dropped his caliver and ran toward the sea edge of the swamp, followed closely by Murino and Tattoo.

Firearms flamed behind the fugitives. Murino staggered in his stride, shook his head, then kept on.

They broke out onto the beach two hundred yards from the two boats. Heckart had taken no chances. The heavy pinnace was already fifty yards offshore, loaded down with most of the women prisoners. The longboat, with the rest of the women, was being run out of the shallow stream. Even as Alec, Murino, and Tattoo slogged down the beach, the longboat was floated free and the men clambered over the sides to shove out the oars.

A musket cracked, and then another. Bullets hummed past Alec and his two men. Alec looked back over his shoulder. A dark knot of Brasiliano's men had reached the beach. Gunfire sparkled from them, and the shot echoes ran along the edge of the jungle.

"Swim, goddamn you! *Swim!*" Heckart roared.

They cast off their shoes and threw aside their weapons to splash into the shallow water with bullets kicking up little spurts of water all about them.

"Wait for me!" Big Wally Dahlman shouted as he burst from the swamp, crossed the beach, and plunged into the water.

They opened a covering fire from the boats to disconcert Brasiliano's men. Tattoo reached the longboat first and turned to see where Alec was. He grinned as Alec's head bobbed up in front of him. They clambered into the longboat and hauled a puffing Murino in after them.

"Thank the good God," a woman murmured behind Alec.

He turned to look into the eyes of Rafaela.

Dahlman reached the longboat and was hauled over the side.

"Where's Palfrey?" Alec asked.

Dahlman shrugged. "I never saw him again after we opened fire."

The longboat dipped to the incoming waves. The lug sails were raised to aid the power of the oars. The last bullets from the beach made a *pict-pict-pict* sound as they ricocheted over the water.

Ralph Burdick was pulling the port stroke oar. He looked sideways at Murino. "Did you have a good shore leave, Richie?"

Murino nodded. He held his right hand over a bullet furrow on his left shoulder. "Passable, Ralph, passable," he murmured.

Burdick grinned. "Where's your shipmate Bill Casper?"

Murino looked away from Burdick. His eyes glistened.

Alec looked past Murino at Burdick and shook his head. He pointed back to the jungle. Burdick nodded in understanding.

They saw the ghostly-looking topgallant sails of the frigate two miles offshore. A light blinked out from the pinnace. An answering signal came from the *Adventuress*.

The two boats bumped alongside the frigate. They were

quickly unloaded and then hoisted aboard with a great creaking and straining of tackle gear.

"Quarter the women in the great cabin and the officer's quarters," Alec ordered.

Rais Gilles came to Alec. "Where away, Cutlass?"

"Porto Bello," Alec replied quietly.

"One of their ships tried to get through the channel to chase us. I think she might have gone aground. There was another ship behind her. They'll waste no time in pursuing us, Alec."

"They'll not catch us if we have a fair wind astern," Alec claimed. He turned to Miles Yeoman. "Fly your studding sails, Mister Yeoman. We'll need to put as many sea miles behind us the rest of this night as we can."

"They'll know we will be sailing for Porto Bello, Cutlass," Rais warned.

Alec shrugged. "A stern chase is a long chase. Thank God the *Adventuress* has recently been careened."

"So have *Kate of Devon* and probably *Exterminator,*" Rais reminded Alec.

"I don't fear being caught by Swan's *Sea Venture,* Van Schouten's *Lion,* or Quinlan's *Exterminator.* We've got the heels on them, Rais!" Alec boasted.

"Aye, but you didn't mention Kate Devon's *nao.*"

There was no answer from Alec. The *Kate of Devon* was almost as fast as the *Adventuress.*

The studding sails were flown, and the frigate heeled to the strong offshore wind with a ghostly white bone in her teeth. It was eight hundred sea miles to Porto Bello on the Isthmus of Panama. Porto Bello—the Treasure House of the Spanish Main.

THIRTEEN

The breeze died away at sunrise on the third day at sea. The sails of the *Adventuress* hung slack from their yards. By noon, the sea was glassy calm. The frigate drifted aimlessly.

"Sail ho!" The mainmast lookout shouted down to the deck.

"Where away?" Miles Yeoman bellowed.

"Dead astern, sir."

"Can you make her out?"

"Not yet, sir. I can only see her topgallants'ls."

"Send him up my telescope, Miles," Alec told the sailing master.

Rais Gilles looked at Alec. "Guess who?" he murmured dryly.

"It could be someone else. A trader, perhaps?"

"Alone? In these waters? Not a chance."

Alec nodded. "Wishful thinking on my part, Rais."

They rigged an awning from an old forecourse over the quarterdeck and allowed the Spanish women up on deck. They were a bedraggled-looking lot, with torn and dirty clothing and unkempt hair. Presently, with buckets of sea water and the help of Sailmaker Jem Cartwright and his needles, they managed to make themselves look more presentable.

In the middle of the torrid afternoon under a pitiless sun

blazing down from a cloudless sky upon the flat, glassy sea, the hail came again from the maintop. "Sail ho!" the lookout shouted.

"Where away?" Rais called back.

"Dead astern, sir!"

"The same ship, you muttonhead?" Miles Yeoman roared.

"No, sir! I can still see that one too. This is another ship. They are close together."

"How can that be?" Rais asked. "There's no wind."

Yeoman nodded. *"Here,* Rais, but they might have some, where they are. Enough to move closer to us, at any rate."

An hour later, the hail came again. "Sail ho!"

"Where away?" Rais cried out.

"Dead astern, sir! There are *three* ships astern of us now."

"Get Captain Campbell up here," Rais ordered.

Alec came quickly to the quarterdeck. "Aye?" he asked.

Rais pointed aft. Three white dots showed close together. "They've likely got some wind, Cutlass," Rais suggested.

"Or they're being towed by their own boats. Maybe a combination of both."

They looked at each other. "Our recent friends?" Rais queried. "Or maybe Jack Spaniard?"

"Either way, we can lose, Rais."

Alec turned. "Boatswain!" he called out.

Pieter Heydt came aft. "Aye, sir?"

"Have the cutter and the longboat launched. We'll try towing her to the wind if the wind won't come to us."

"It will be murder rowing under this sun, sir," Heydt suggested.

"It will likely be murder if those three ships catch up wi' us, Pieter, man. Ye ken?"

Heydt smiled grimly. "I ken, sir."

For hours, the steady thumping of the oars in the tholepins came back to the slowly moving ship as the two boats towed her across the flat surface of the water. Men passed out at the oars. Finally, they had to be relieved every half hour.

An hour before dusk, it was plainly apparent to everyone

aboard the frigate that there were four ships now astern of her and evidently moving a little faster than she was.

When darkness came at last, there was still no wind. Men fell exhausted in the bottoms of the towing boats. Sea water was dashed over them and they were sat up at their oars again. Nothing could be seen astern. There would be a first-quarter moon that night.

A faint breeze began to blow just before the rising of the moon—a paradox, for an old seaman's saying was: "The moon swallows the wind."

There was a wash of pewter light against the eastern sky. The wind began to pick up. The sails of the frigate fluttered. Then, the wind died away again.

The moon filled the eastern sky with light and shone down upon the calm waters.

"Before God!" Rais cried.

One of the four ships was now no more than two miles astern of the *Adventuress.*

"Maintop!" Alec shouted. "How does she sail?"

"She's got a good wind, sir. Full and by!"

"She's brought it with her, then," Miles Yeoman grumbled.

"Deck!" the lookout shouted. "I can see the other three ships in line ahead, dead astern of the first one!"

Alec scratched his beard. He could hear the ragged rhythm of the oars in the pulling boats. If the wind astern held out, those four ships would soon be within extreme cannon range. With a little luck they might disable the *Adventuress,* and then it would be all over, for she would not be able to outrun them or maneuver to defend herself in a gun battle.

The wind came swiftly across the calm sea and instantly filled the slack sails of the frigate. She began to forge ahead close behind the towing boats.

"Bring the boats alongside!" Alec ordered.

The longboat and cutter bumped alongside. Some of the exhausted men climbed weakly up the Jacob's ladder, but many of them had to be hoisted aboard with a whip sling from the main yard. The boats were lifted, dripping from the water and stowed in their cradles on deck.

"That first craft is moving faster than we are," Rais reported.

Alec spat over the lee side. "If those ships are who I think they are, we've got the heels on all of them."

"That first one is moving fast, Cutlass. Besides, 'they've had the wind far longer than we've had it."

The Frenchman was right. The first ship had moved closer.

"Can you make out what that ship is?" Alec shouted to the main top.

There was a moment's hesitation. "Aye, sir! I sailed on her once, afore I joined the *Adventuress*. She's a Spanish ship, sir! I know her by the cut of her sails!"

"Sweet Jesus," Alec murmured.

"But she ain't Spanish no more, sir," the lookout added. "It's the *Kate of Devon!*"

Alec looked up at the maintop. "I should kick your arse for that, ye muttonhead!"

Rais shrugged. "What difference does it make who they are, Cutlass? If that's Kate Devon instead of a Spaniard, then it stands to reason those other three ships are those of Joshua Swan, Jan Van Schouten, and Patrick Quinlan."

"Aye," Alec murmured, "and we'd get nae mair mercy frae those buckos than we'd get from Jack Spaniard."

"Less," Rais corrected. "For perhaps, if they were Spaniards, we could deal with them in exchange for the women prisoners."

The moon was fully up. *Kate of Devon* had closed the gap between them, for she was sailing with a speed Alec had never thought possible from the ex-Spanish *nao*.

Miles Yeoman studied the pursuing ship through the telescope. "She's got a new suit of sails, Cutlass."

Alec nodded. "And she was careened at their rendezvous."

"Still, we should have the heels on her."

Alec smiled grimly. "I think it's the spirit of two people aboard her that's driving her on."

Miles lowered the telescope and turned to look sideways at Alec. "So?" he asked curiously.

"Kate Devon and Roche Brasiliano, Miles. They're both

thirsting for my blood."

There was a puff of white smoke from the foredeck of the *Kate of Devon*. The flat sound of the cannon shot echoed across the water. A feathery plume of spray rose two hundred yards behind the *Adventuress*.

"Good shooting that, for the range, and by moonlight at that," Rais said quietly.

"Mister MacMillan!" Alec shouted.

The big Scots master gunner came running aft. "Aye, sir!"

"Try your hand wi' a stern chaser at yon ship, Mac."

The master gunner hesitated. "Well, sir…"

"What is it?" Alec demanded.

The Scot grinned. "Ye know the stern chasers are in your great cabin, Cutlass."

"So?"

"The cabin is full tae the ceiling beams wi' wimmen! We'd no be able tae work the guns."

"Run 'em out," Alec ordered. He grinned. "They won't mind. They know what would be in store for them if yon bastards catch up wi' us."

The sleepy women were sent out to the deck. The gunners of the two 12-pounder stern chasers loaded their charges. The *Kate of Devon* had gained a little, but now it seemed as though the *Adventuress* was holding her own.

The bow chasers of the *Kate of Devon* were fired again. One 12-pound solid shot plunged into the sea on the port side of the frigate, even with the quarterdeck. The other shot hummed directly over the ship and parted a forebrace before plowing through the forecourse.

"Prime shooting," Alec admitted. "That one shot could have taken out our mizzenmast wi' a wee bit o' luck."

"Or our heads," Rais added dryly.

Alec went below to the great cabin. Some of the Spanish women were crowded in the companionway while others were in the small officer's cabins which were just off the companionway. Rafaela smiled as she saw Alec.

Alec paused. She was extraordinarily attractive in the dim lantern light of the narrow companionway. "Are ye all right?" Alec asked her.

Rafaela nodded. "As well as can be expected, Alec."

A solid shot struck on the quarterdeck above them. Wood splintered, and a man cried out. Calloused bare feet slapped on the quarterdeck.

"They're gaining on us," Alec murmured, almost as though to himself. He looked down at Rafaela. "You and the other ladies had best get down to the cable tier. It's a dark, wet, and dirty hole, but it's about the safest place for you."

As Alec spoke, the two stern chasers opened fire through the gunports at the after end of the great cabin. The women began to cough. One of them screamed hysterically.

"Get to the cable tier!" Alec ordered. He ran out onto the deck.

A cannonball hummed through the air and struck the mizzenmast just above the doublings. The mizzen topmast, with the pull of the topsail, snapped off and fell in a clutter of cordage down onto the quarterdeck, missing Alec by a yard. The helmsman was killed instantly. He let go of the whipstaff, and the frigate fell off by the head. Her sails fluttered as they lost the wind.

"By God!" Rais Gilles shouted. "That was no 12-pound bow chaser ball! That was a 24-pounder!"

Bosun's Mate Heckart led a detail of men armed with boarding axes to cut through the tangle of rigging to free the topsail and its yard from the helm.

The two stern chasers roared from the great cabin. Alec whirled and looked toward the *Kate of Devon*. There were two splashes a hundred yards ahead of her. She was still just out of range of the *Adventuress'* 12-pounders.

Two guns flashed on the foredeck of the pursuing ship. The humming sound of the solid shot came just before the sound of the detonations. One shot passed clean through the lateen sail on the mizzenmast of the frigate, about ten feet over the heads of the men working to free the whipstaff. The other shot whipped through the main course and carried on through the forecourse and then landed in the sea a hundred yards ahead of the frigate.

"They've got our range and to spare," Alec commented dryly.

"Can we not get one of our 24-pounders into the great

cabin?" Terence Shannon asked as he kneeled beside the uncovered helmsman.

"It would take too much time," Alec replied. "Besides, we'd have to get one of the 12-pounders out of the way first. By the time we did that and got the 24-pounder in there, we'd be disabled and maybe cut to pieces by those 24-pounders firing at us."

They dragged the dead helmsman from the quarterdeck. Another crewman took his place. The frigate steadied on her course.

Alec walked aft to the taffrail. The two guns on the *nao* flashed again.

Rais Gilles closed his eyes and bent his head. "Dear Lord," he murmured. "For what we are about to receive, we are truly grateful." Alec was thrown violently backward as several solid shot slammed into the great cabin below the deck where he stood. He regained his balance and ran to the break of the quarterdeck and plunged down the ladder to the main deck. He worked his way through the smoke-filled companionway. He could hear some of the gun crews of the stern chasers screaming and shouting. He found himself in the smoke-filled great cabin and instantly slipped on a great pool of blood on the deck to come down hard on his side and found himself looking into the staring eyes of a head lying by itself on the blood-drenched deck.

The whole after end of the cabin had been smashed into kindling wood and splinters. One of the 12-pounder guns lay on its side with part of the muzzle missing. There were only four men of the two gun crews still standing on their feet, shaken and dazed from the impact of the heavy shot.

Ian MacMillan wiped the blood from his face. He turned to look dazedly at Alec. "Twa shot right in our bloody faces, Cutlass. Twenty-four-pounders, no less! One struck fair on the muzzle of that capsized gun there." He looked about himself. "Aye, and a dommed mess they've made o' your cabin, Alec." He grinned wryly.

"Get back into action," Alec ordered.

The master gunner nodded. It was the best thing to do under the circumstances. "We'll hae only the one gun, though."

"Start shooting it!" Alec snapped.

Two spouts of water soared into the air fifty yards astern of the frigate. Alec looked about himself. Half a dozen more shots like the ones that severed the mizzen topmast and the ones that blasted into the great cabin, and the *Adventuress* might be disabled enough so that she could be overtaken by all four of the pursuing ships. Once the Spanish women were taken from the frigate, Alec had little doubt about what would happen to himself and those of his crew who might refuse to join the proposed Porto Bello venture.

Alec went up on deck. He looked aft. The *Kate of Devon* was closing the gap. He looked at the sky. The crescent moon seemed to be sailing swiftly into a dense cloud bank that hung low over the sea as far as the naked eye could see.

A solid shot hummed through the air and plunged into the main deck of the frigate, scattering huge splinters which flew through the air to transfix those crewmen closest to it. Another solid shot plunged into the sea but inches from the port side of the quarterdeck.

"We can't take much more of this, Cutlass," Rais warned.

Alec nodded. "Yeoman!" he shouted.

The sailing master came aft. "Aye, Cutlass?"

"Get a jury topmast up on the mizzen. Work as though the devil himself was at your heels. We need that topsail!"

The lone 12-pounder crashed out from the great cabin.

"Look!" Rais cried.

The bowsprit of the *Kate of Devon* slowly fell to one side and dropped into the sea to entangle its sails and rigging across the bows and foredeck of the *nao*, covering up her bow chasers.

Alec thrust a fist upward. *"Cruachan!"* he cried. "That will hold the bitch back a while!"

The moon sailed over the miles-long cloud bank, and the sea was almost instantly darkened.

The crewmen of the *Adventuress* did work as "though the devil was at their heels." The splintered butt of the mizzen topmast was sawed off. The topmast was stripped of sail and rigging and then hoisted up to its former position and made fast. New topmast shrouds and stays were set up.

Ian MacMillan had stopped firing. The *Kate of Devon* had slowed down with the encumbrance of the bowsprit spritsail and spritsail topsail dragging in the sea across her cutwater. She was slowly losing ground to the *Adventuress,* besides which the stem chaser gun flashes would give away the frigate's position.

Hours went by, and the moon did not reappear from behind the cloud bank. The main topmast lookout had Alec's excellent German telescope with which he kept a constant watch on the dark sea astern of the frigate.

"I hope to God we've lost her," Rais muttered.

"Sail ho! Dead astern!" the lookout shouted. "I can just make her out!"

"How close is she?" Alec shouted.

"Not more than half a mile, sir!"

"Sweet Jesus," Alec murmured. "Once daylight comes, they'll pound us to pieces with those bow chasers."

"Kate's hanging on like a bulldog," Rais added. He grinned wryly. "She's after your blood, lad."

Alec nodded. "Like a vampire."

"What's to do?" Miles Yeoman asked. "We're carrying every yard of canvas we can hang. Even if we gained on her, she'd still be in sight by dawn light."

"And maybe in gun range," Ian MacMillan put in.

Alec cupped his hands about his mouth. "Can ye see any of the other ships?"

"No, sir. They've fallen away behind." Rais shrugged. "That's not much consolation. If Kate is close enough to open fire by daylight and can disable us, there's no question but that those other buckos will be close behind her."

Alec walked aft to the taffrail. "There's one thing left to do, lads," he murmured, almost as though he was talking to himself.

"Turn and fight her?" Ian MacMillan asked.

"It's likely our only chance," Miles Yeoman agreed.

Alec turned. "There's one other."

Rais stared at him. "Such as?"

"Board her, mates."

None of them spoke.

Alec looked aft again. "We can load the pinnace with

good lads and stay in the *nao's* course. We can toss grapnels at her as she passes and get alongside. Then, board her up the sterncastle after disabling her rudder, enter the great cabin, and capture the officers. Get control of the quarter-deck. Batten the hatches to keep the mass of the crew below. Spike her deck guns. Cut up her rigging. In general, disable her."

Rais shrugged. "Just like that."

Alec nodded.

"And how do you propose getting the boarders off the *Kate of Devon* after they've done all this, providing they're still alive?" Miles Yeoman asked dryly.

"We'll signal to ye. We'll cast the pinnace loose once ye are close enough and get aboard. Then ho for Porto Bello!"

"You're mad," Rais murmured.

"Can ye think of a better plan, any of ye?" Alec asked.

There were no answers.

"Who'll lead this forlorn hope?" Terence Shannon asked.

Alec stared at him. "Why, *me*, of course."

"Why ye?" Ian MacMillan asked. "Why not me?"

"Ye're needed to handle the guns, Mac."

"Or me?" Rais asked.

Alec shook his head. "I need ye here to command the *Adventuress*." He grinned. "Besides, I wouldn't want tae lose any of ye, lads."

"What about ye?" Ian demanded.

"Who else of ye are mad enough to try such a damned-fool stunt and get away wi' it?" Alec demanded.

Alec won that point, too.

"Tattoo!" Alec called. "My weapons!"

"How many men will you take?" Rais asked.

"Twenty," Alec replied. "With cutlasses, pikes, boarding axes, and a brace of pistols each."

"Twenty?" Rais exclaimed. "To take a ship like that? She has over two hundred and fifty men aboard her."

Alec shrugged. "So, if we can't take her with twenty—thirty, forty, or fifty of us won't make any difference. Besides, we can't overload the pinnace."

"Scots' logic." Rais grinned.

"We'll need spikes and mauls to spike the deck guns and wooden wedges to jamb her rudder," Alec added.

"Combustion materials?" Rais asked.

Alec hesitated. "No," he answered at last. "If we can disable her, that should be enough."

Rais studied Alec. "It would be easy enough to fire her. That way, she'd be eliminated altogether."

Alec shook his head.

"The crew could be picked up by the other ships," Rais added.

Alec turned on the Frenchman. "God dammit! No! It will be enough to disable her! We'll be at Porto Bello long before they can get there." He strode to the break of the quarterdeck and went down the ladder to the main deck. There, he met Tattoo, who handed him his weapons.

"Ye were treading on dangerous ground there, Rais," Ian MacMillan said in a low voice.

Rais looked at him. "You think…" His voice trailed off.

The Scot shook his head. "I don't know. He loved her once, ye ken."

"Years ago."

"There's still something left, Rais. An old love, ye know…"

Rais nodded. "I know," he agreed. He wasn't thinking of Kate Devon and Alec Campbell then. There had been a lost love in Scotland…

They lowered the pinnace into the sea and towed her alongside while the men slid down ropes into it. The pinnace could easily carry thirty men, but she would be lower in the sea and slower to handle at crucial moments.

They cast the pinnace loose, and the frigate moved on into the thick darkness. They put out the oars and turned the boat so that she would head into the oncoming *Kate of Devon.*

Boatswain's Mate Hal Hamilton checked the grapnels and lines. Much would depend upon them when the *Kate of Devon* came down on the pinnace.

The sea was dark. Nothing could be seen of the *Kate of Devon.* If they missed her in the darkness…

FOURTEEN

One moment there was nothing to be seen but the velvety darkness and then the faint loom of the sails showed through the gloom. The pinnace was directly on the *nao's* course.

Bosun's Mate Dave Heckart had the tiller of the pinnace. "There she is!" he called out.

Four men, led by Gunner's Mate Wally Dahlman, were to try and leap up into the bowsprit rigging so as to take the foredeck lookout by surprise and then spike the two bow chasers, once the main deck was under control.

Dahlman stood up in the bows of the pitching pinnace with a coiled line in his left hand and the sharp-tined grapnel iron in the other. His four men crowded up close behind him. Two other men stood on the starboard side of the pinnace with similar grapnels in their hands.

"Pull hard port!" Heckart commanded. He stood up in the sternsheets of the boat while gauging the speed of the oncoming ship. If he miscalculated, the pinnace would either be run down, or the ship would pass them and leave the pinnace bobbing futilely in her wake. In either case, it would be all over for the boat and her crew.

"Pull easy, starboard!" Heckart barked.

"Sweet Jesus," Alec murmured. "How damned big she looks from down here."

The *nao* loomed high overhead. Dahlman cast the

grapnel upward. It caught on the bowsprit, and in that instant, the gunner's mate went hand over hand up the line as the pinnace bumped hard against the starboard side of the bow. Two men leaped upward and caught hold of the maze of bowsprit rigging. Another man missed and fell into the sea to be run down by the cutwater. The fourth man caught the trailing line and went into the sea. Dahlman began to haul him up.

The pinnace bumped against the side of the ship and was fended off. As the boat swept along, one grapnel was cast into the lower part of the main shrouds, and the line was allowed to run free from its coil within the bottom of the pinnace. The third grapnel was cast into the mizzen shrouds and held fast. The pinnace swept back toward the stern of the *nao* until both grapnel lines were snubbed to bring the boat up short, just even with the stern of the ship.

Boathooks were caught in the fancy aftercastle molding to hold the pinnace close under the stern right next to the rudder. Alec Campbell stepped barefooted from the stern sheets, caught hold of a molding, and scrabbled with his toes for a hold on the carved scrollwork of the *nao*. Tattoo gave Alec a shove upward. He passed close alongside the high, ponderous rudder and gripped the rudder chains to pull himself up under the gallery that was just outside the great cabin. Tattoo climbed up beside Alec and handed him a coil of line. Alec made a noose and slipped it over the carved head of a gargoyle and then dropped the line down to the pinnace. Several men had already made their way up the carved work and were clinging to it like lizards against a sunny wall.

A bag of wedges was hauled up, and one of the men braced himself and set a wide wedge in between the rudder and the rudder post. He tapped it in tight with strokes of a big maul.

Alec reached up and caught hold of two supports of the gallery railing. He let his body swing free and then pulled himself up and over the railing at the starboard end of the gallery and just beyond the last window of the great stern cabin. He pulled Tattoo up beside himself. Together, the two of them helped ten men, one after the other, up onto the gallery and then gave them a boost to climb up the stern to reach the upper deck of the sterncastle. They were led by Dave Heckart, whose task it would be to gain control of the quarterdeck and then to turn the small falconet swivel guns down toward the main deck to cover the men whose task it would be to kill or capture anyone on the main deck of the *nao*, then to batten down the hatches to keep the mass of the crewmen below.

The foredeck lookout had heard the pinnace bump against the starboard bow of the ship. He was still looking over the gunwale when a pistol butt caught him behind the left ear, and he was heaved over the side. Wally Dahlman looked about himself. Four men lay asleep on the foredeck beside one of the two 18-pounder bow chasers. One of them stirred in his sleep. Dahlman jerked his head at Morgan. Morgan clamped a hand over the restless sleeper's mouth and then drove a dagger into his back. The body splashed into the sea. It was but a few minutes' work to dispose of the other sleepers.

Dave Heckart poked his head over the taffrail of the sterncastle. He whistled softly. "All clear, Captain," he called down. "We've got control of the helm and quarterdeck."

Alec flattened his back against the rear of the great cabin and looked over his right shoulder through the end window. The cabin was empty of life. A dim lantern hung from an overhead beam and moved with the easy motion of the ship, alternately lighting various areas of the cabin or casting them back into shadow.

There were three men crammed into the end of the gallery, besides Alec and Tattoo—Horn, Van Decker, and Mitchell. Two more men were still working to disable the rudder.

Alec drew two pistols and cocked them. He tiptoed to the gallery doorway of the great cabin. It swung open easily to his touch. He walked softly into the cabin. Something alerted him—that sixth sense he had acquired through a life of danger. He stepped quickly to one side to look beyond the shifting pool of lantern light. Horn and Van Decker came into the cabin, followed by Tattoo.

Four pistols spat flame and smoke from the deeply shadowed forward end of the cabin near the door to Kate Devon's sleeping chamber. Horn and Van Decker went down instantly. Tattoo staggered as a bullet creased his scalp. He fell backward through the doorway and bumped into Mitchell, driving him back over the railing into the sea. There was a thin cry from Mitchell before he struck the water and went under in the wake of the *nao*.

Swirling, stinking smoke filled the cabin. Alec discharged both his pistols through the smoke in the general direction of where he had seen the gun flashes. The bullets thudded into the woodwork.

Roche Brasiliano charged through the smoke. He was on Alec before Alec had time to draw his sword and take guard. Roche's sword flashed down toward Alec's head. Alec jumped sideways. The heavy blade bit into the back of a heavy chair, and a chip flew from it. Roche whirled. Alec whipped out his sword just in time to parry a second powerful downward blow. The blades rang together. Alec darted around the table.

"Stand still and fight!" Roche shouted.

They met on one side of the table in the narrow way between the table and the heavy mahogany sideboard. Roche was no skilled fencer, but he had great strength and stamina. His blade flashed constantly in thrusts and slashes so that Alec was hard put to keep the big mustee back. Sweat flew from their faces. Roche drove Alec back and further back until Alec's back was to the gallery doorway.

Roche thrust in hard for Alec's vitals and took a sword slash against his left bicep for his effort. Alec jumped back onto the gallery. He turned to one side and jumped back over Tattoo's body. Roche charged through the doorway into the darkness of the gallery. He did not see Tattoo's body, but he did see the dim figure of Alec Campbell at the end of the gallery with his back against the railing.

Roche charged again. He fell forward over the unconscious Tattoo. Alec pressed himself hard against the rear of the cabin to allow Roche to fall with his belly across the railing. Alec dropped his sword. He gripped the mustee by his ankles and uplifted them so that Roche fell overboard. He crashed down into the bottom of the pinnace and lay still.

"Is he still alive, Cutlass?" Kate Devon asked from behind Alec. "If he is, you should have killed him before you threw him overboard."

Alec turned quickly. He reached for his sword.

She stood beside the doorway with the faint lantern light shining on her. She had a brace of cocked pistols in her slim hands. She smiled sweetly. "Let your great-grandfather's sword lie, pet, or I'll put two bullet holes into your belly."

Then Alec remembered, to his sorrow, that there had been *four* pistol shots within the great cabin. She had been hiding in the cabin during the time Alec had fought with Roche. Why hadn't she killed Alec then?

Alec smiled ingratiatingly. "My men have control of your helm and quarterdeck, lassie. Your rudder has been disabled. Some of my men have boarded ye at the bows and taken over there. By this time, your hatches have been battened down with most of your crew below decks."

She nodded calmly. "I expected as much."

Alec smiled again. He held out his hands. "See then? You're helpless, Katie. Be a good lass and put up yon pistols."

She shook her head. "Your men may have control of my ship, Cutlass, but *I* have control of you."

Alec shrugged. "Foolish woman," he said sadly.

"Now, you'll come with me to the main deck and order your men to lay down their arms."

Alec shook his head.

"Do you want to die, then?" she demanded fiercely.

"Ye won't kill me, Kate. I mean too much tae ye."

She spat at him. "Damn you! You tricked me into believing you'd throw in with us on the venture to Porto Bello! Then you made love to me!"

Alec shrugged. "I see nothing wrong wi' that. When did we ever have to have a reason tae make love, Katie?" He knew right away his reply had not gone over with Kate. She was damned, outright venomously angry with him.

She shook her head. "It wasn't that so much. It was when you left me defenseless, naked and alone to those bloody Caribs! You bastard! You ran to save that Spanish bitch!" Her voice rose high and shook in her intense anger with him.

Ben Thomas had been disabling the rudder. He had completed the job when he heard Roche Brasiliano fall into the pinnace. Then he heard the voices coming from the gallery just above his head. He recognized those voices. He thrust his dagger between his teeth and gripped the railing supports. He drew himself up slowly to one side and behind Kate. He gripped his dagger with one hand and raised it to strike into Kate's back.

"Kate!" Alec cried. "Behind ye!"

She laughed. "You can't fool me with that old chestnut, Cutlass." Then she saw the look on his face. She turned and fired one of her pistols point-blank into Thomas' face. The seaman fell from the gallery into the wake of the ship.

Kate turned quickly. The smoke from the discharged pistol wreathed about her face. She jerked her head. "Get into the cabin!" she snapped.

Alec raised his hands. He stepped over the body of Tattoo and walked into the cabin. Kate came in close behind him.

Alec turned. He saw then the old bruises on her lovely face. "What happened to ye, lassie?" he asked in genuine pity.

"Never mind!"

He narrowed his eyes. "The Caribs?" he asked.

She shook her head.

He noticed then the sadness in her great emerald-hued eyes. "Roche Brasiliano?" he guessed.

She didn't reply. She didn't have to. The answer was plainly on her face.

"I should have made sure of him," Alec said.

"He's been more loyal to me than you have."

"Do *I* owe ye loyalty?" he demanded hotly. "I owe *nae* one loyalty!"

Kate nodded. "Only yourself, Cutlass. Can you deny it?"

He opened his mouth to speak and then he closed it before he uttered a word. Nothing he could say would convince her otherwise.

"Get out onto the deck," she ordered. "I'll be right

behind you. One wrong move and you die! By God, Alec! I *mean* it!"

His broadsword lay just at his feet. Could he reach it and strike to disable her before she put a bullet into him?

"Get out onto the deck!" she repeated.

"I told ye my men control the ship."

"Will they save your life by giving me back my ship? Or do they have little or no loyalty to you, Cutlass?"

Tattoo had opened his eyes at the sound of the pistol shot. He lay just behind the doorway on the gallery. He crawled slowly so that he could see Kate's back.

"Move, damn you!" Kate shouted.

Tattoo reached out and gripped Kate by an ankle. He jerked the leg back toward him. Kate leveled her pistol as she fell forward. The pistol flashed. The bullet struck Alec in the right bicep. He clasped his left hand to the wound and whirled about, dropping to his knees.

Kate kicked back with her free leg, and the heel of her shoe caught Tattoo right between the eyes. He released his grip on her ankle. She darted toward the forward cabin door, then whirled and ripped her sword from its scabbard.

Alec picked up his broadsword with his left hand. There was pure icy hell in his gray eyes. "Ye bitch!" he grated between set teeth.

She laughed at him. "You were only pinked!" she scoffed.

He shook his head. "Ye meant to kill me and have done wi' it, Kate."

The blood ran down his arm, soaking his shirt sleeve, and then dripped from the ends of his fingers. He did not take his eyes off her. Slowly, he placed the broadsword on the table. He reached for a bottle of wine and pulled the cork out with his teeth. He spat out the cork and then drank deeply, but he kept his eyes on Kate. He placed the bottle back on the table and slowly wiped his mouth with the back of his left hand.

Alec picked up his broadsword. "Will ye hae a drink wi' me, lassie?" he asked coldly.

She looked quickly back over her shoulder.

Alec shook his head. "Ye can't escape that way."

They eyed each other.

"You can still throw in with us, Cutlass," she suggested.

Alec shook his head. "And trust ye and your three partners? I told ye what would happen."

She lunged at him with sword point outthrust. He parried it, then struck her blade aside and pointed his own sword tip at her lovely green eyes. Slowly, ever so slowly, he moved toward her. She retreated. She thrust again. Again the thrust was parried, so hard that her hand tingled with the shock of blade against blade. She thrust, recovered swiftly, and then thrust again. The tip of the blade traced a thin red line along Alec's right shoulder.

She stepped back on the defensive, but he did not counterthrust. She grinned. "You're a wee bit slow with that left arm of yours, you Scots bastard!"

He shook his head. "But quick enough tae kill ye at will, ye Sassenach bitch."

"Captain Campbell!" a seaman called from the stern gallery. "Where are you? We've got control of the ship. It's only a matter of time before the crew breaks loose from below."

Alec inadvertently turned his head.

Kate ran quickly through the companionway toward the main deck.

Burdick came into the stern cabin. "Jesus," he murmured as he saw the blood-soaked right shirt sleeve. "Do you want me to chase that red-headed devil, sir?"

Alec shook his head. "She can't get far."

Burdick took a napkin from a drawer of the sideboard. He bound the bullet wound. Alec took another drink from the wine bottle and then handed the bottle to the seaman. "How bad is it?" he asked.

"It's not good. They've got boarding axes below and are chopping up through four different hatches. We may get quite a few of them if they do break through, but they'll overpower us in the end, captain."

Alec nodded. "Are the guns being spiked?"

"Yes, sir."

Alec picked up his broadsword. He walked slowly to the companionway. He passed through the dimness of it and saw the dull yellow light of lanterns on the main deck. He walked to the doorway and looked out upon the deck. He could hear the chinking of metal against metal as the spikes were being driven into the touch holes of the 18-pounder broadside battery guns.

Kate Devon stood with her back to the mainmast and with her naked blade in her right hand. Her eyes were on Alec.

Burdick came up behind Alec. He held up a pistol. "I can drop her neatly from this range, sir," he suggested.

Alec shook his head.

"I'll only wound her, captain."

Alec turned a little. "God dammit! No! This is something I must settle for myself."

Alec walked forward. His men looked back over their shoulders from their various tasks at disabling the guns and the rigging of the ship.

"Throw down your sword, Kate," Alec called out.

"Come and make me, you Scots bastard!" Kate cried. She looked about herself. "See your brave Captain Cutlass," she jeered. "Afraid of a frail woman!"

"Frail like a 24-pounder gun," Burdick said dryly.

Alec could hear the thudding of the boarding axes from below the main deck as the confined crewmen chopped their way up through the hatches. There were hundreds of them below decks. There were stands of arms for their use. Alec's boarding crew had lost at least a quarter of their strength and probably more. Some of his men stood at the hatches with ready pistols and cutlasses to hold back the forthcoming rush of maddened men from below. As Burdick had said: "We may get quite a few of them if they do break through, but they'll overpower us in the end, captain."

The *Kate of Devon*, without the use of her rudder, had fallen off the wind. Her sails fluttered and snapped and the yards creaked. She was making little way through the water. It would only be a matter of time before three consorts would show up through the darkness, and they would know at once something was wrong with the *nao*.

Dave Heckart came aft to where Alec stood. "We're

ready to chop away at the stays and braces when you give us the word, sir."

There was no reply from Alec.

Heckart looked at the trapped woman. "Kill her or take her with us, sir, but we've got little enough time left."

Kate laughed. "He doesn't dare! My men will soon enough be up on this deck, and we'll sweep the lot of you scum overboard."

"They're breaking through the forehatch, captain!" Wally Dahlman yelled. A pistol cracked.

"Signal the *Adventuress*, Heckart," Alec ordered. Kate grinned. "Worried, you Scots bastard?" she jeered. Heckart took one of the lanterns from the lower rigging and hurried forward to the foredeck. He swung the lantern back and forth in the prearranged signal.

"Start cutting the rigging, Burdick," Alec ordered. They chopped away at braces, sheets and stays with keen-edged boarding axes. Some of the sails streamed out straight in the wind as the sheets were severed. The *nao* lost more way and then turned slowly to lie across the wind. She began to wallow in the waves.

Heckart hurried aft. He looked aloft. "Those topmasts may come down, sir, what with the stays cut loose," he warned.

Blades clashed just at the break of the foredeck. Pistols flashed. The ship's men imprisoned in the forecastle had broken free. Wally Dahlman and his men dropped back aft, holding off the determined rush of a dozen crewmen. Byrne and Harper went down from cutlass slashes. Dahlman fired a brace of pistols and then charged with a naked cutlass, followed by three of his men.

They killed and wounded most of the crewmen and drove the others back into the forecastle.

A bright axe blade shone in the lamplight as it broke through the main hatch. Someone poked a pistol through the hole and fired at random. The slug whined thinly just over Alec's head.

Alec turned to Heckart. "We'll leave now, bosun."

Heckart shouted to the rest of the boarding party. "Rally! Aft here! Let's go, you bastards!"

There were only eight of them left, including Heckart, and there might be one or two more in or on the sterncastle. They ran for the ladders that led up to the quarterdeck. Wood splintered at the main hatch, and a man poked his head through it. He fired a pistol. Callahan went down with a bullet through his right shoulder, but Dahlman and Ward dragged him to his feet and pulled him up the steep ladder leading up to the poop deck. Heckart and some of the others on the quarterdeck fired their pistols down into the waist to slow down the rush of armed men toward Alec Campbell.

"Run!" Kate jeered at Alec.

He retreated slowly with broadsword extended toward one of the quarterdeck ladders. Ira Macklin raised a pair of pistols and aimed them at Alec. Kate reached out with her sword and slapped them down. "No!" she cried. "He's mine!"

Alec grinned crookedly. "Ye take a lot on yourself, lassie."

The waist was crowded with the crewman of the *nao*. One pistol shot from them would easily take care of Alec, but Kate Devon's word was law on her ship.

"He'll kill you," Ira Macklin said in an aside to Kate.

She shook her head. She advanced on Alec. Their blades clashed and rang together. Alec parried her thrust and then drove her back. They circled on the deck with their blades flickering in and out, tapping lightly or striking hard.

Alec's men lined the forward railing of the high poop deck, watching the duel between the two accomplished sword-fighters. Wally Dahlman loaded and primed one of his pistols. "I can drop her from here, Dave," he murmured to Heckart.

The bosun shook his head. "You'd kill Cutlass too, as well, you damned fool! The instant she'd go down, they'd fill him with a bucketful of slugs."

Kate came in hard. Alec was tiring. He had lost far more blood from his bullet wound than he realized. He retreated slowly toward one of the quarterdeck ladders until he felt his heels against the bottom of it. He lunged and twisted his sword sharply so that Kate's sword flew from her hand and struck point down in the deck where it quivered, swaying back and forth.

Alec turned and gripped his sword between his teeth while he went up the ladder with the aid of his left arm only. He turned at the top of the ladder to look down into the contorted face of Kate as she slashed at the rungs of the ladder just below his feet. Chips flew to right and left. Alec reached the quarterdeck and took his sword back into his left hand just as Kate's head appeared level with the quarterdeck.

"You've got her now!" Heckart roared.

"Off with her damned red head!" Burdick shouted.

Alec shook his head. He retreated toward the poop-deck ladders. Kate advanced quickly. Their blades crossed, rang together and then parted. Blood trickled down from a scratch on Alec's left shoulder. Sweat dripped from their faces. Alec looked into her great green eyes. She meant to kill him. He was positive of it.

Heckart looked forward. A light flashed ahead of the *nao*. "Time to leave, Captain Cutlass!" he shouted.

Alec nodded. "Go, then!" he yelled.

"Not without you, sir!"

"Do as you're told, damn you!" Alec roared.

One by one the boarders went down the after end of the stemcastle. They slid down lines to the pinnace. Only Heckart and Dahlman remained on the poop deck.

Ira Macklin led half a dozen men up the quarterdeck ladders. Alec was fighting on the defensive now with his back against a poop-deck ladder. He drove Kate back and looked up at Heckart and Dahlman. "Now!" he shouted.

The two seamen fired two pistols each over Alec's head into the crewmen on the quarterdeck. At the same time, Alec parried a hard thrust and lunged, full force, straight and true, to drive the point of his broadsword into Kate's right bicep so that the tip of the blade came through on the back of the arm after gazing the bone. Kate dropped her sword and staggered back. Her face went white. She gripped the wound with her left hand and gasped in shock and pain.

Alec went up the poop-deck ladder, partially concealed by the swirling powder smoke from the discharged pistols.

He saw Heckart standing there reloading a pistol. Dahlman had already slid down a line to the waiting pinnace. Feet thudded on the quarterdeck as Ira Macklin led a charge toward the poop-deck ladders.

"Go!" Alec shouted over his shoulder at Heckart.

The bosun handed Alec the loaded pistol and then vaulted over the railing to drop into the sea below.

Alec slashed at the first two men to appear at the top of the ladders. Ira Macklin fell down with his face laid open from right temple to left cheekbone.

"Don't kill him!" Kate shrieked. "I want him for myself!"

"Too late, lassie!" Alec cried. He turned and jumped up onto the taffrail of the poop deck. He balanced there for a moment. "Cast loose, you there in the pinnace!" he yelled down to his men in the boat.

They rushed Alec. He fired the pistol into the face of a man and then hurled the empty weapon into the face of another. He drove his swordpoint a hand's span into the chest of another man, withdrew the bloody blade, and slashed sideways to cut halfway through the neck of the next man eager to die suddenly.

The *nao* lurched broadside to a big wave. Alec thrust his broadsword between his teeth and dived into the sea, followed by half a dozen pistol shots.

Alec's head bobbed up fifty feet from the pinnace. They cut loose the grapnel lines and drifted toward Alec. They dragged him up over the side and dropped him atop Tattoo and Roche Brasiliano, who lay in the bottom of the boat.

Pistols flashed and detonated from the after end of the high poop deck and from the stern gallery of the great cabin. Seaman Dodd took a bullet through the head. Walker got his through the left shoulder. Then, the pinnace vanished into the darkness.

"What do we do with that damned mustee?" Dave Heckart asked as he bandaged Walker's wound.

Alec looked down into the baleful eyes of the trussed-up Roche Brasiliano. "Can ye swim, mustee?" he asked.

Roche nodded. "Well enough to live and kill you someday."

Alec looked at his bloody broadsword. "I could kill ye

now, mustee." He shook his head. "I'd rather wait until that 'someday' comes, so I can kill ye in fair combat." Alec looked at Dahlman. "Over the side with the bastard," he ordered.

Roche splashed into the sea. He drifted astern. "Your day will come, you Scots bastard!" he shrieked.

Alec looked aft. "I'll be waiting, mustee," he promised. "You'd better save your breath for swimming, Brasiliano!" He laughed as he turned away.

The *Adventuress* came ghosting through the darkness in response to the signal lamp flashed from the pinnace. The crew was taken aboard, and the pinnace was hoisted from the water.

"Where away?" Rais Gilles cried.

"Porto Bello," Alec replied.

The *Adventuress* wore ship and set off on a long tack through the darkness with every possible sail flying and drawing well.

FIFTEEN

"**B**ack the main topsail, Mister Yeoman," Alec Campbell commanded.

The bright late-morning sun glinted on the clear blue sea from a cloudless sky. Porto Bello was in the offing. The sunlight shone on the whitewashed buildings and the red tile roofs. It shone on the fortresses of San Juan and El Castillo which guarded the channel entrance into the harbor. It reflected from the white sails of three Spanish ships that were sailing from the port to meet the frigate.

Rais Gilles lowered Alec's brass telescope. "Those are fine, tall fighting ships, Cutlass. They carry heavy metal. Any one of them could be a good match for us even if they are sailed by Spaniards."

Alec nodded. "Still, they won't open fire on us, Rais, once they find out what precious cargo we carry aboard." He looked across the quarterdeck to where the Spanish gentlewomen were clustered while their serving wenches were on the main deck. Alec was not looking at the young gentlewomen as a group. It was Rafaela de Vasquez upon whom he was intent. She turned her head slowly as though she felt his hot eyes upon her back. She smiled a little, almost shyly, and then turned away again. There had been moonlit nights on the stern gallery of the frigate which Alec would never forget as long as he lived. Still, although they had kissed passionately and he had been allowed to fondle her somewhat, that had been as far as he had gone, but he had not stopped his lovemaking because of her rather weak protests. It had been because he had not wanted to take her virginity in that manner. He was sure she would not have protested too vigorously if he had carried her into his sleeping cabin and stripped her to that lovely ivory-skinned body he had seen that moonlit night in the jungle.

"Shall we prepare for action, sir?" Rais Gilles asked.

Alec's thoughts were near and yet so far away. It was almost as though he could see right through the black satin dress she wore and see that smoothly rounded rump of hers. He shook his head at the memory. "Sweet Jesus," he murmured.

"You don't *want* to run out the guns, Cutlass?" Rais asked. He looked narrowly at Alec. "What are you thinking about, my secretive friend? Is it the Spanish gentlewoman again?"

Alec was a little startled. Had his thoughts been so apparent on his face? He looked quickly at Rais Gilles.

Rais nodded. "It's obvious, Alec. It's been obvious ever since the night you returned from the *Kate of Devon*. Aye, and the interest is returned from her. That, too, is obvious to anyone with half an eye."

"She's in love with you, Alec," Kate Devon had once told him. "A woman *knows…*"

"Captain Campbell, sir!" Master Gunner MacMillan called from the main deck. "Can I not clear for action?" There was an anxious tone to his voice.

Alec nodded to the master gunner. "Clear for action, Mister MacMillan. Mister Gilles, have a flag of truce run up under our colors. I do not want Jack Spaniard to get close enough to heave a surprise broadside or two into us."

The white flag was run up under the colors at the same time the gunports were triced up and the guns run out, ready for action. It would be a foolhardy Spaniard indeed who'd sail close enough for a surprise broadside with nine-teen shotted guns staring him in the face.

Upon seeing the flag of truce run up, the three Spanish ships immediately backed their main topsails and lay heaved to. A trumpet and a dram sounded from the quarterdeck of the nearest Spanish ship.

"Request for parley," Rais said.

Alec nodded. "Have our trumpeter and drummer reply."

The brazen trumpet notes and the steady rumbling of the big drum carried across the water to the Spaniard. A longboat was swung outboard and lowered into the water.

"Lower the longboat, Mister Heckart, if ye will!" Alec requested.

The bright sun reflected from polished half armor and steel helmet as the Spanish parley officer descended the side of his ship into the longboat. A white flag was run up on the short jackstaff of the longboat.

"Tattoo!" Alec called out. "My best coat and hat!"

Tattoo brought up Alec's claret-colored coat and plumed hat to match. "Weapons, sir?" he asked.

Alec shook his head as he shrugged into his coat.

Rais Gilles lowered the telescope. "The Spaniard is armed, Cutlass. Besides, you know what ship that is?"

Alec clapped his hat onto his head. "She has a familiar look," he replied.

"She should. That's the last *frigata* we shot the hell out of in the Mona Passage."

Alec turned slowly. "Don Rodrigo de Mendez's command?" he asked quietly.

Rais nodded. "That's him in the longboat, Cutlass."

"Get my weapons, Tattoo," Alec requested.

Rafaela had turned from the quarterdeck railing to look at Rais Gilles. "Are you sure that is the *La Victoria*, the *frigata* of Don Rodrigo Alonzo de Mendez?" she asked quietly.

Rais nodded. "I am positive, seño*rita.*"

Rafaela looked at Alec as Alec hung his baldric over his shoulder and thrust his sheathed broadsword into the leather frog at his left side. "You know that he is my fiancé?" she asked.

Alec nodded. "I have known that since we boarded the *Nuestra Señora de la Candelaria.* It was told to me by Don Bartolome Arriola, the commander of the plate ship."

"And you have fought against him?"

Alec thrust his dirk into the frog at his right side. "Twice," he replied noncommittally. "Ye saw the ship of Kate Devon at the rendezvous—the *Kate of Devon*. That was originally Don Mendez's fighting *nao*, the *Invincible*. Kate and I captured her in the Windward Passage." Alec smiled a little wryly. He traced a right forefinger down the twisted scar that marred his left cheek from just beneath his left eye, down the cheek, and into his short, reddish beard. "Your fiancé gave me this during that battle and spoiled my good looks." He grinned. "Aye, he's a bonny fighter, right enough!"

"And Cutlass gave Don Rodrigo his parole because of that," Rais added. "In fact, he virtually paroled him again in the Mona Passage. We could have blown the *La Victoria* out of the water, but Cutlass here would not have it. Don Rodrigo was still full of fight, with his mizzen and main masts down and his decks covered with his dead and wounded. He challenged Cutlass, but Cutlass wanted no more of him." Rais looked toward the longboat that had stopped and was now drifting on the bright sea halfway between the *La Victoria* and the *Adventuress*. "Maybe Cutlass made a mistake that time. We could have sunk him. He had no chance."

Rafaela looked at Alec. "Is that true, Alec?"

Alec was walking toward the quarterdeck ladder. He turned a little. "I do not kill helpless men, señor*ita*," he replied coldly. He turned back and descended the ladder.

"He has great pride," Ynez de Guiterrez murmured. She slanted her eyes at Rafaela. "Too much, perhaps." She smiled a little. "He plays a part—that of wanting to be the gentleman of honor," she added.

Rafaela turned on her friend. "He is *not* playing a part, Ynez! He *is* a gentleman of honor!"

Ynez raised her eyebrows a little. She, like everyone else aboard the *Adventuress*, knew how Rafaela felt about this mad *Escocés*. The forthcoming meeting between Don Rodrigo and Alexander Campbell should be interesting, and perhaps far more interesting if Don Rodrigo ever found out the care Rafaela had taken of the bloody bucca-neer known throughout the Spanish Main as Captain

Cutlass, when he had been close to death in the pavilion of that red-headed *puta* Kate Devon. Too, Ynez and some of the others had seen Rafaela and that man in their secret meetings on the gallery of the great cabin of the *frigata*. Ynez had wondered idly if Rafaela would still have her virginity to bring to her husband on their wedding night.

Alec sat in the sternsheets of the longboat as it was rowed toward the Spanish longboat. Heckart had carefully placed a dozen cutlasses and pistols in the bottom of the craft, close at hand for the crew. One never took chances with Jack Spaniard, even under a flag of truce.

"Oars," Alec commanded.

The longboat drifted fifty feet from the Spanish boat.

"We meet again, Don Rodrigo," Alec greeted the Spaniard.

Don Rodrigo was a handsome man with the proud features of a grandee. "Captain Campbell," he acknowledged. He bowed his head a little. "I tender my thanks for your consideration of the condition of my ship that night in the Mona Passage." It galled the proud Spaniard to admit that, but it was a required courtesy, at least of the moment.

Alec nodded. "Ye are an opponent worthy of the finest steel, sir. I am surprised, however, to see ye are here at Porto Bello."

The Spaniard smiled wryly. "I could hardly have continued on to Spain, sir, with my ship in that condition. However, there was another consideration that brought me back here to recondition my ship." His voice died away.

"And that is?" Alec queried.

"The fact that my fiancée, Señorita Rafaela Maria Espinosa de Vasquez, and other gentlewomen were aboard the *Nuestra Señora de la Candelaria* at the time of her capture. My own ship, and those two others with her, are a squadron that has been raised by the governor-general of Panama for the sole purpose of finding those Spanish gentlewomen to rescue them and bring them back here to Porto Bello." His voice was steady and measured, but Alec could detect a faint desperation in his tone, as though he might be too late.

"Set your mind at rest then, Don Rodrigo. Your fiancée

and the other gentlewomen and their servants are safe aboard my ship," Alec assured the Spaniard.

"And you have brought them here for ransom?" The tone of relief was patently obvious in de Mendez's voice.

Alec nodded. "That is our custom."

"And how much ransom do you request?"

"I think that seventy-five thousand pieces-of-eight for the lot is not beyond reality, sir."

Don Rodrigo showed no emotion on his lean face. "Of course, you realize that I cannot negotiate with you on this matter. I merely represent the naval force of this part of the kingdom of His Most Catholic Majesty Philip of Spain."

Alec studied the Spaniard. "Then perhaps you can take my demand to your superior?"

Even Don Rodrigo had to smile—just a little, but a smile nonetheless. "My immediate superior is Don Esteban de Vargas, commanding officer of this part of the Isthmus of Panama. I am sure you will recognize who he is?"

Alec smiled in return, but a little wryly. "The Steel Fist? Before God, Don Rodrigo, he'd rather give us a broadside than one *escudo* of the king's money."

"That is correct. If there ever was an implacable enemy of your so-called Brethren of the Coast, it is Don Esteban."

"I know him well," Alec said dryly.

The Spaniard studied him. "Is it not true that he captured you some years ago and turned you over to the Inquisition?"

A red haze seemed to pass between Alec Campbell and Don Rodrigo. A burning hatred flared up within Alec's guts. He was a man who could forgive an honorable enemy, but for a man such as Don Esteban de Vargas, he had nothing but the deepest hatred and utter contempt.

"Is that not so?" the Spaniard queried.

Alec could not trust himself to speak. The scars of the steel and fire of the Inquisition were still on his body, and worse still, far worse, they still inflamed his mind at the very thought of what had happened to him and of the good ship-mates he had lost to that same Inquisition. He could still hear their tortured screams from the very next room in which he was being interrogated by the chief inquisitor.

"Yet you escaped, eh?" Don Rodrigo asked. He shook his head. "The only known heretic to have escaped them." He himself hated the Inquisition, but, as it was all-powerful in Mexico and on the Spanish Main, a wise man kept his mouth shut about such matters.

"Five years ago," Alec replied. "I have not forgotten, sir. Not for one waking minute of the day and many hours of the night will I ever forget the inhuman cruelty of your inquisitors."

Don Rodrigo nodded. "I understand," he murmured.

Alec eyed the Spaniard. "Do ye?"

"I think so. We Spaniards have suffered much in turn from your bloodthirsty savages who call themselves Brethren of the Coast. Your L'Ollonois was an inhuman beast, of whom it has been said even his own men could not stand his unspeakable cruelties to his Spanish prisoners. Need I mention Bartolomeo el Portugues, Pierre le Grand, Michel le Basque, Henry Morgan, and the sadistic Jacques Montbars the Exterminator?" Don Rodrigo's cultured voice died away. *"Hostes humani generis,"* he added quietly in Latin.

Alec nodded. "Enemies of the human race," he translated. *"Touché,* Don…"

The Spaniard studied the Scot. "It puzzles me about you, Captain Campbell. You are not like those animals I have spoken about. A gentleman, obviously of good birth, and educated to some extent. Why, that is to say…" His voice died away.

"Go on," Alec urged.

"You could have served with honor and great reward for your country. Why then, this buccaneering, this bloodletting and looting? This capturing of helpless females for purposes of ransom?"

"I am a privateer, sir!"

Don Rodrigo waved a hand. "Licensed piracy. You have aborted that license, such as it is, by consorting with such pirates and buccaneers as Montbars and that red-headed *puta* Kate Devon."

"A means to an end, sir."

"And your country condones this?"

"I have no country, Don Rodrigo." Alec pointed back to

the lovely but deadly-looking *Adventuress.* "She is my country and that is my flag."

"But are you not a Scot?"

"Outlawed."

"English, then?"

Alec shook his head. "Only as a matter of convenience. My people have been fighting against the English since time immemorial."

"Yet you claim to have letters of marque from the English king."

"Again, a means to an end. The English care not who fights for them against ye Spaniards."

The Spaniard's face tightened. *"Corsairos luteranos,"* he muttered. "Heretics. Unbelievers."

"We have no Inquisition," Alec reminded him coldly. "Come, enough of this, Don Rodrigo! Let's do business!"

"As I said before, I cannot negotiate myself. I will take your demand to my superior."

Alec looked beyond the Spaniard to the three powerful *naos.* "How soon can I expect an answer?"

"Within twenty-four hours?"

Alec shook his head. "It must be as soon as possible."

"You do not trust me, Captain Campbell?" Don Rodrigo asked stiffly.

Alec waved a hand. "That is not the point." He indicated the open sea with a flirt of the hand. "Within your twenty-four-hour period of time, there could possibly be four first-class fighting ships in the offing whose captains wanted to use your females for hostages in demanding the surrender of Porto Bello."

Don Rodrigo laughed. "Surely you jest." Alec shook his head. "You know of Kate Devon and her *Kate of Devon.* Jacques Montbars is dead, but his ship, The *Exterminator,* is now under the command of Patrick Quinlan, a skilled sea fighter. Joshua Swan and his *Sea Venture* and Jan Van Schouten and his *Lion* are the other two I have mentioned. Between them, their crews must number over a thousand skilled fighting men. I myself recaptured your female prisoners from them and brought them here as a matter of honor. They cannot be much more than twenty-four hours behind me. I will not expose my ship and crew to their attack. If they appear, I will leave here immediately, and if we have not negotiated for the female prisoners, they will sail with me."

Don Rodrigo smiled a little. He pointed toward the three Spanish ships. "We are not exactly defenseless, sir, as you can see."

"No discredit to ye, sir, but if those four ships appear and your ships attack them, they will be sent to the bottom."

The Spaniard's face tightened.

"And ye will not have your women," Alec added quietly.

"Then I will go ashore at once. There is, however, one minor condition."

Alec nodded.

"I will want at least one of the women to accompany me to show that she is in good condition and has not suffered over much from her captivity."

"Granted," Alec agreed. He studied the Spaniard. "Any one of the women in particular?"

"Señorita Rafaela de Vasquez."

"I thought as much."

Don Rodrigo studied Alec narrowly. "Why so?" he asked suspiciously.

Alec shook his head. "Nothing, sir. Nothing at all. However, I can't grant that request."

The Spaniard placed his hand on the hilt of his fine Toledo blade. "There is a reason?" he demanded.

Alec smiled disarmingly. "Señorita de Vasquez is the daughter of the governor-general of Panama. It might be possible that ye'd keep her safe and sound in Porto Bello and tell me to go hang with the rest of the prisoners."

"Why, damn you!"

Alec raised a restraining finger. "Just a precaution, sir. This is a precarious and dangerous business. One can't take the slightest chance."

Don Rodrigo turned to his coxswain. "Take me to my ship!" he ordered harshly.

"Wait," Alec said. "If ye have the thought of attacking my ship, I can warn ye that I will expose your women to your direct fire. Now, sir, please wait here and I'll have one of your ladies, of good birth, brought to ye. Ye will then take her ashore and return within four hours with the terms of your superiors."

Don Rodrigo nodded shortly. Before God, he hated to do the bidding of this smiling renegade, but he had no choice.

Alec returned to the *Adventuress*. He ascended to the quarterdeck and approached the coterie of Spanish gentlewomen. He told them of Don Rodrigo's terms. "I can let ye select your own representative, ladies," he added gallantly. "With one exception—the Lady Rafaela de Vasquez cannot go."

Her great dark eyes met his. She tried to penetrate those gray orbs of his to sense his intent in this matter, but it was no use.

"I'll go," Ynez de Guiterrez cried.

"You would!" Maria de Cordoba snapped.

Alec grinned as he walked to the weatherside of the quarterdeck. "A bonny gaggle o' lassies," he said aside to Rais Gilles.

Rais studied Alec. "Why not let Rafaela go?"

"She's the daughter of the governor-general of Panama. If they got her ashore, Rais, they might tell us to go to hell with the rest of them."

"Is that the only reason you refused him?"

Alec turned away from him. He looked up toward the maintop. "Keep a good lookout up there, maintop!" he shouted. "If ye spot the tiniest speck of sail, sing out at once, ye understand?"

Rais nodded. He turned to watch the young women. "They've selected Maria de Cordoba, Cutlass."

The smiling young woman was taken to the parley boat of Don Rodrigo and thence to his ship the *La Victoria*.

The *frigata* was then sailed to the harbor mouth, and once the longboat was sent ashore, the *frigata* returned to her station alongside her two consorts.

"They're taking no chances wi' us," Alec murmured.

"Can ye blame them?" Terence Shannon murmured.

Two hours drifted past. The wind had mostly died away, and the sea had calmed to an almost glassy smoothness. The blazing sun burned down upon the sea and the land.

Miles Yeoman raised his telescope. "Small sailing craft leaving the harbor," he said over his shoulder. "A *patache.*"

The *patache* passed the three Spanish ships and headed for the *Adventuress.* She flew a parley flag. As she neared the frigate, a man raised a brass-speaking trumpet. "Captain Campbell, sir! May we come alongside?" It was Don Rodrigo.

Alec beckoned to Ian MacMillan. "Have her covered with one of the swivel guns, Mac."

A gunner uncovered the breech of the small brass gun and removed the breechblock. He quickly loaded the gun and then replaced the breechblock, hammering home the wedges that held it in place. He cast loose the lashings and tilted the gun downward so that it covered the *patache.*

The *patache* dropped her lateen sails when within fifty yards of the frigate. Long sweeps were thrust out through ports in her sides to hold the craft in position close to the frigate.

"Captain Campbell!" Don Rodrigo called out. "My superior grants that the ladies who are your prisoners might have suffered little harm. For this, he thanks you."

Alec waved a hand. "It is nothing, sir."

Don Rodrigo saw Rafaela standing at the lee rail of the quarterdeck. His eyes seemed to cling to her.

"Ye've brought the ransom money?" Alec asked.

"No, I have not, sir."

"Your time is running out, Don Rodrigo. Ye've two mair hours and that is all. We'll set sail the instant the sands run out on the second hour."

Some of the Spanish women began to weep. Others muffled their sobs in their handkerchiefs.

"Can you not give us more time, Captain Campbell?"

Alec shook his head. "I told ye why I could not wait longer."

"If you're afraid of your pursuers catching you here, I can help you repulse them with my ships, sir."

Alec smiled faintly. "A generous offer, Don Rodrigo. But, no, it canna be. If I escaped the battle alive, I would be branded as a mad dog among the Brethren of the Coast. Do ye know what that means? I'll tell ye—my ship and crew would be proscribed by the Brethren. We would be outlaws and fair game for any of them who'd challenge us. Why is it ye must have mair time?"

Don Rodrigo shrugged. "It is not my doing, Captain Campbell."

"They're stalling for time," Rais Gilles muttered out of the side of his mouth.

"Dinna trust them, Cutlass," Ian MacMillan said quietly.

"Take the women and run," Miles Yeoman suggested.

Alec looked at the sailing master. "To where, Miles? The only worth of these women, at least tae us, is for the ransom money. If we leave here, we'll be pursued by our former friends and allies—the Bloody Four. They'll not let up on us, mates. I'll guarantee ye that, at least."

"Captain Campbell!" Don Rodrigo shouted. "I have a suggestion. Come ashore yourself and parley with my superiors."

"And have him end up on a gibbet?" Rais Gilles yelled. "By God, Spaniard, do you think we are fools?"

"Ye'd have the women still aboard," Alec mused. "They'd no harm me in that case."

"But the women must come ashore with you," the Spaniard added. "That is, to make sure they are unharmed."

"That takes care of your ploy," Rais murmured.

"You have my word as a Spanish gentleman and seaman," Don Rodrigo called out.

The officers grinned down at the Spaniard. That is, all of them except Alec. "He can be trusted at least," Alec said, almost as though to himself.

"You're mad!" Rais Gilles accused.

Alec shook his head. "I'll take the women ashore myself. All of them can land save one. That one will be kept in the longboat wi' a pistol at her pretty little head. One wrong move on the part of the Spaniards and she'll die."

"And what if they call your bluff?" Miles Yeoman asked.

Alec smiled. "Not likely, for that particular lady will be the Lady Rafaela de Vasquez."

Rais Gilles grinned. "There's a bit of the demon in you, Cutlass."

"It's how I make my living, Frenchman."

Alec handpicked the crew of the longboat, some of the toughest, most cold-nerved men among his command—Witt, Colman, Moss, Jarman, Devereux, Letcher, Steward, and Merrill. Bosun's Mate Dave Heckart was to coxswain the longboat.

The longboat was lowered into the water, and the women were helped down the Jacob's ladder into it. The masts were raised and the lugsails hoisted. The longboat struck out for the distant shore under the fitful breeze, sailing in concert with the *patache* and under the keen eyes of Don Rodrigo.

They sailed past the *La Victoria* and close by her side. Alec could see the plugged shot holes and the new spars and rigging which had replaced that which the *Adventuress* had blasted from her that dark night in the Mona Passage, now seemingly so long ago.

"Ye know what to do, mates," Alec reminded his crew. "At the first warning, take the longboat frae the harbor wi' a pistol at the head of your hostage. They'll no fire."

Dave Heckart spat over the side. "We hope, sir."

"We'll nae get our *ocho reales* for this lot if we don't take this risk, Davie, lad."

"A chancy business, captain."

Alec looked at him. "Ye chose the life, as did all of us. Why, Davie?"

Heckart scratched in his short beard. "Be damned if I know," he replied. "I had a little bit of trouble at home, you understand?"

Alec grinned. "So say we all, eh, lads?" The reply rang across the water. "Aye, sir!"

"Brave men," Don Rodrigo said to the skipper of the *patache*.

"That is so, sir, but mad, completely mad," the skipper replied.

The ramparts of the Fortresses of San Juan and El

Castillo were lined with soldiers and curious townspeople who had come out to see the accursed *corsairos luteranos* and especially the one known as Captain Cutlass. His fame, or rather notoriety, had long preceded him at Porto Bello, for was it not from this very place he had escaped the sharp metal and burning fire of the Inquisition? No other heretic on the Spanish Main had ever succeeded in such an impossible feat. Some said he had been in league with the devil, and it was not hard to believe when one looked at him, with his long reddish hair, short red beard and that scar that bisected his left cheek. But it was the eyes that almost seemed to brand him as one of the devil's own, for while to the lighter-complected Anglos and northern Europeans the devil was said to have eyes dark like glowing coals, to the darker peoples of Latin origin, it was well known that the devil had curious eyes of light gray, like rime ice. This Captain Cutlass had such eyes, and it was said that it gave one a queer turn to look into them, especially for those enemies who faced him over crossing sword blades.

They dropped the lugsails when the harbor masked the light wind and went in under oars to the quay. A file of large-framed soldiers stood on the quay under the charge of a junior officer. The sun reflected from their polished morion helmets and arms.

"The guard of the governor-general of Panama," Rafaela said.

"Tae greet ye, lassie?" Alec asked. He smiled. He winked at Dave Heckart as she turned eagerly away.

The *patache* came into the harbor under its long sweeps. Don Rodrigo landed on the quay and walked across it. "You can bring your boat alongside, Captain Campbell."

The longboat bumped gently against the stonework of the quay. One after the other the Spanish gentlewomen and the serving wenches were helped from the boat until the only one who was left in the boat was Rafaela de Vasquez. Don Rodrigo walked eagerly forward to help his fiancée from the boat, but Alec Campbell stepped quickly up to the quay and stood in front of the Spaniard.

"What is this?" Don Rodrigo demanded.

"Heckart!" Alec said over a shoulder.

The bosun drew a heavy-barreled pistol and cocked it. He stood close beside Rafaela. His meaning was clear enough to the Spaniard.

"This is not what I expected, sir!" Don Rodrigo snapped.

Alec smiled thinly. "I'll take your word any day, sir, but I have no great love for your superior officer, Don Estebán de Vargas, or Steel Fist, as he is better known to the Brethren of the Coast."

"He is a man of honor, sir!"

"Granted, Don Rodrigo, but ye must realize I will be alone in your city surrounded by hundreds of your people who would gladly kill me for the reward offered five years ago by your same Don de Vargas."

Don Rodrigo shook his head. "That reward was not offered by Don de Vargas, Captain Campbell."

Alec was puzzled. "Then who?" he asked.

"The chief inquisitor."

Despite the blazing sun and the brightness of the day, a cold premonition crept over Alec Campbell. He remembered the man all too well—a dying shell of a being, completely lacking in any warmth or mercy for any other human being, especially those who were heretics, and most especially, *corsairos luteranos.*

Alec looked toward the quayside, now crowded with hundreds of townspeople, seamen from the many ships in the harbor, and soldiers from the garrison. "I thought he would have died by this time," Alec mused to himself. He looked sideways at the Spaniard. "He was a walking death's head when last I saw him."

"It would not matter. The reward still stands—alive or dead. And he *is* alive."

"Where is he now, Don Rodrigo?"

"In Porto Bello."

Alec glanced down into the longboat.

"You are under the protection of a parley flag, sir," Don Rodrigo reminded Alec.

"Do your secular officers have power over the church in the matter of the Inquisition?" Alec asked.

"The governor-general of Panama is here. I am sure he will respect your flag of parley."

Alec smiled wryly. "Certainly, with his daughter in my longboat with a pistol at her pretty head."

"If you knew Don de Vasquez as I do, you would know that his daughter's life would mean nothing if she stood in the way of his honor and duty."

"Then my gesture of holding her hostage means little."

"It means everything to me, Captain Campbell."

Alec looked into the Spaniard's dark eyes. After a moment, he nodded. "Aye, I can see that, Don Rodrigo." Alec turned. "Davie lad, take the longboat out into the middle of the harbor. Do not bring it in to the quayside unless by a direct order from me. If I do not show up within the next hour, ye will return to the ship with your captive. Nor will ye gie her up until I am safe aboard the frigate. Ye ken, Davie?"

Heckart nodded. "I ken, sir." He grinned.

They had escorted the ladies and their servants from the quay. Alec Campell walked side by side with Don Rodrigo to the shore end of the quay. Once he turned and looked out toward the longboat, and then he turned away again and walked with the Spaniard up the long, sunlit street, toward the headquarters of the commanding officer of the city's garrison and defenses, with the soldiers of the governor's guard marching behind them. The crowd parted company in front of Alec and Don Rodrigo while eyeing Captain Cutlass, for had he not escaped from this very city five years past, with the unhealed scars and burns of the Inquisition still on his body? Many had thought he had died in the swamps and jungles beyond the city, victim to his wounds, or fever, or perhaps the many venomous snakes who infested the jungles. Then too, there were the savage Indians, and worse still, the *cimarrones,* half wild Indian and half black escaped slave, with no mercy to Spaniards who fell into their hands. How had he escaped? He had been a thorn in the side of the Spaniards before he had been captured, and after his escape, he had literally become an avenging demon against all Spaniards. But yet he was known to be an honorable and merciful enemy withal.

SIXTEEN

There were three men seated behind the massive table in the low-ceiled, windowless hall of the Fortress of San Juan. They were Don Pedro de Vasquez, governor-general of Panama and father to Rafaela de Vasquez, Don Bartolome de Esquivel, the colonel commanding the *tercio* of Spanish infantry that garrisoned Porto Bello, and Don Estebán de Vargas, better known to his people and his enemies as Steel Fist, who commanded all military and naval forces in that department of the Spanish Main.

Don Pedro de Vasquez was a thin, spare man with a narrow triangular face and melancholy eyes. His hair was thickly streaked with gray, and the color seemed to set the tone for the man's character, which was of a grayness itself. Don Bartolome de Esquivel was a rotund man with a round face and a rather amiable expression which seemed to belie his reputation as a first-class fighting man. Don Estebán de Vargas was a solid chunk of a man with a face seemingly hewed from weathered Spanish oak. His eyes were as dark as ebony and seemed to have as much feeling in them. Don Estebán used his eyes to good effect, while peering from under bushy lowered brows as though to subjugate anyone at whom he might be looking.

Guttering candles set in brass candlesticks were on the table, and in black iron sconces, hung from the stone walls.

The flickering light hardly dispelled the constant gloom in the hall and did little to drive off the deep shadows bordering the pool of candlelight.

Alec Campbell stood before the table with Don Rodrigo one pace behind him and one pace to his right. Behind Alec and guarding the door were two halberdiers of the guard.

Alec had previously known only one of the three men seated behind the table—Don Esteban de Vargas. Don Esteban's hands rested on the table before him—that is, his left hand rested on the table. That was the hand of flesh, bone, blood, and sinew. The right hand was not a human hand at all. The original hand had been lost long ago in combat against the enemies of Spain. Its replacement had been cunningly fashioned by a master metalworker from the finest of Toledo steel in the shape of a closed fist, but the fingers had been articulated in such a manner that Don Esteban could open them against a strong spring action so as to clasp a bladed weapon such as the deadly Spanish *main-gauche* dagger while he wielded his sword or fired a pistol with his left hand. Don Esteban's nature, however, being what it was, he rarely used a dagger in that deadly hand of metal. He preferred to keep it closed into a fist of steel with which to strike out at his enemies or those of his own people who did not obey his orders quickly enough, or who did not please his fancy. It was well known that a number of men had died from blows of that cruel fist.

There seemed to be another person in the hall whose hostile presence was felt by Alec Campell rather than seen. Now and again, he would glance sideways into a far corner of the hall, seeking that alien presence, until at last, an upflaring of the candles in a sudden draft revealed a robed and cowled figure seated behind a small desk. The figure was so blended into the moving shadows actuated by the flickering candles that it was almost impossible to distinguish whether it was a living human being at all rather than one of the mummified padres of long ago whose remains were still cherished by the worshipful living. There was more—a cold hostility that seemed to emanate from the robed one and that was sensed by Alec with that damnable Celtic intuition of his: the second sight, which was at once a blessing and curse, depending upon circumstances.

"It quite impossible to pay you the exorbitant sum of money that you have demanded for the ransom of our womenfolk," Don Pedro repeated. "There are not enough *ocho reales* here in Porto Bello to meet half of that sum. It would take time to get additional monies."

"How long, Don Pedro?" Alec asked. He knew what the answer would be. They were stalling for time, he was sure of that.

The Spaniard shrugged. "I can send a messenger to Panama to request more money."

"That would take days, sir."

The governor-general half smiled. "Waiting need not be unpleasant. We can supply your ship with fresh food and good wines at our expense."

Alec shook his head. "I have already told ye, sir, that it will only be a matter of one day, at most, before the four ships that are pursuing me will arrive here at Porto Bello. I told ye why they wanted the women prisoners."

Don Esteban smiled thinly, a smile only of the facial muscles but not of the eyes and with no warmth within it. "Ah, but *Ingles,*" he murmured, *"we* have the women in *our* hands."

"And I have your word that ye would parley for their ransom. I have allowed them to return here to Porto Bello, in good faith. I hesitate to challenge a gentleman and officer of Spain to uphold his faith and his honor in this matter."

"You speak of honor, *Ingles!"* Don Esteban demanded. He laughed harshly.

"Don Esteban," Don Rodrigo put in, "it was *I* who gave my word of honor in this matter."

Don Esteban stared at the officer as though disbelieving what he had just heard. "Why, damn you, de Mendez," he grated between set teeth, "this is gross insubordination."

Don Pedro raised a conciliatory hand. "Gentlemen, we gain nothing by this display of discourtesy among ourselves and in front of this gentleman who comes to us under a flag of parley."

"Gentleman?" Don Esteban spat out.

Don Pedro turned slowly to look at the tough old soldier. "No matter, Don Esteban, but he is still here under a flag of parley. I must insist that we honor that flag."

"But, we have the women in our hands now! Why must we deal with this *Ingles* pirate?"

"*Escocés,*" Alec corrected Don Esteban.

The soldier struck his steel fist down upon the table. "They are one and the same!"

Alec shook his head. He smiled a little. "Not to *them,* sir. However, that is of no consequence here. I still have Rafaela de Vasquez as my prisoner. I have given orders to my boatswain that until I give him a direct order from the quay-side, he will remain out in your harbor while holding a pistol at the head of Señorita de Vasquez. Further, if I do not show up within an hour of the time I gave him that order, he will take the lady back to my ship, and she will not be released until I myself am safe aboard the frigate."

"Diabolical," Don Bartolome muttered.

The governor-general studied Alec. Don Pedro knew of this man by hearsay and reputation, and that reputation was almost a legend in his own time. He was said to be a man of honor, and yet he was an implacable enemy of Spain.

"One-third of that hour has already passed," Alec reminded the Spaniards. "I can't wait for your messengers to travel to Panama for the purpose of obtaining the rest of the ransom money, nor do I believe ye cannot raise the required sum right here in Porto Bello and within the hour as well."

Don Esteban leaned forward. "You say we lie?" he said in a low voice.

"There are a few plate ships in your harbor, loaded to the marks with treasures for Spain. Surely the required sum can be gotten from those ships, gentlemen."

Don Pedro shook his head. "That treasure is the property of the Spanish Crown, sir."

"Only the Royal Fifth," Alec corrected. "The other four-fifths belongs to investors, merchants, and traders of Spain. Surely the sum I require can be made up from that portion of the treasure, and ye can return it to the rightful owners once ye gather the monies ye claim ye can send for to Panama."

"Impossible!" Don Pedro snapped.

"Then I have no recourse but to return to my ship with your daughter, sir."

"No!" Don Rodrigo cried.

"You forget yourself, sir," Don Pedro admonished the officer.

Don Rodrigo strode forward. "Have you forgotten that Rafaela is my affianced?" he demanded.

"No, and I have not forgotten that she is my daughter and my only child, sir!"

"Then give this man the sum he requests!"

Don Esteban rose slowly from his seat. "Don Rodrigo," he said quietly, "I warn you—return to your position and keep silent."

Don Rodrigo nodded. He knew the voice of absolute authority when he heard it. *No* one ever questioned the orders of Don Estebán de Vargas.

Don Pedro tugged at his sparse gray beard. "It will take time, Captain Campbell. We can't possibly get the remainder of your ransom money within the hour."

"Then I will return to my boat and to my ship and wait until ye do have it," Alec said boldly. He was on chancy ground. He had risked all in coming there and had depended thoroughly on the word of Don Rodrigo as well as holding Rafaela as the last hostage. What was it Don Rodrigo had said when Alec had mentioned the fact that Rafaela would be held as the last hostage with a pistol at her head? "If you knew Don de Vasquez as I do," Don Rodrigo had said, "you would know that his daughter's life would mean nothing if she stood in the way of his honor and duty."

Don Estebán struck his steel fist down on the tabletop. "Wait! *I* am in command here, sirs! No money or treasure can or will be taken from the ships in the harbor to pay this *corsairo luterano!*"

"But I gave my word!" Don Rodrigo cried.

Don Pedro nodded. "As did I, Don Estebán."

The soldier looked at each of them. "I do not recall my agreeing to any of those weakling terms! We are not dealing with a man of honor here, gentlemen. We need not respect any word given to him."

Don Pedro turned in his seat to look at Don Estebán. "But it is my daughter who is still in their hands, sir. This man, in good faith, returned the other women hostages. Surely we must honor our agreement."

Don Estebán shook his head.

"Then I demand that we do so!" Don Pedro snapped.

Don Bartolome, the commander of the garrison, nodded his head. "That is so, Don Estebán. Captain Campbell, despite his piracy, is indeed a man of honor. I..." His voice died away as he saw the look on his commanding officer's hard face.

The steel fist came down once again. "I am in full command here! Don Pedro, you are here on sufferance only. You are out of your jurisdiction and had no right to deal with this man."

"But," Don Pedro protested, "why did you not mention this at the time Don Rodrigo brought us the terms of parley?"

The soldier leaned back in his seat. "This is war. Not a war between nations, in which there may be honor, but a war between Spain and men such as this, this so-called Captain Cutlass, who is nothing but a thief and a murderer, without honor and without shame! An outlaw! A renegade!"

"And an accused heretic," the hollow voice said from the dark corner of the room.

All eyes turned toward the dimly outlined figure of the robed person who now stood upright behind its desk.

It was very quiet in the hall. One of the guards coughed. Then, hardly perceptible sound came to them—as though something was being dragged slowly over the rough flag-stones that formed the floor of the hall. The black-robed figure moved slowly toward the shifting pool of candlelight, planting the right foot forward and then dragging the left foot behind it, as though there was no life in it.

An icy fingertip seemed to trace its way down Alec Campbell's spine. His guts tightened. He remembered all too well the man who had brought him up before the Inquisition five years past. He could recall in faint horror the death's-head mask of a face seemingly worn by the chief inquisitor—Father Gaspar de Humana; the burning eyes that seemed to penetrate into a man's very soul; the withered left foot which the priest dragged behind himself.

"This is not a court of the church," Don Pedro said bravely. It took a brave man to question the edicts of the Inquisition.

There was no answer from the priest. Padre de Humana reached the end of the table and grasped it with his thin, clawlike hands to support himself while he looked steadily at Alec Campbell from within the cowl that overshadowed his gaunt face.

"This man is here under a flag of parley, padre," Don Rodrigo ventured.

"This man is an accused heretic," the priest repeated. "He escaped from the just court of the Congregation of the Holy Office. Heresy is an offense against the State as well as the church. Do you deny that, Don Pedro?"

"I...that is to say..." The governor-general's voice died away. No one, not even the viceroys of both Mexico and Peru, and most certainly not the lower-ranking governor-general of Panama could overrule the chief inquisitor of the Congregation of the Holy Office.

Alec forced himself to look away from the priest. "There is not much time left, gentlemen. I must return to my ship before too long. If ye will, give me that much of the ransom money as ye have, and have the remainder brought out to my ship by Don Rodrigo before the day is out, and Rafaela de Vasquez will be returned to ye as I promised on my word of honor." His voice died away in the faint echoes of the cavernous hall.

No one spoke.

"There is a reward that was offered for this man," Padre Humana said at last. "One thousand *ocho reales,* to be paid to the man or men who returned him to the Congregation of the Holy Office, dead or alive. That reward is yours, Don Rodrigo."

The Spaniard was horrified. "God forbid, Father Humana! I would not betray this man in such a manner!"

"Be careful," the priest warned. "Do you call the offering of such a reward a betrayal of an avowed heretic?"

Even Don Estebán was now concerned. He shook his head slightly at Don Rodrigo.

The priest had not turned from his fixed gazing at Alec Campbell. "Pay no attention to Don Estebán, Don Rodrigo. You must answer my question from your heart as a true son of the Holy Church."

How had he seen Don Esteban's subtle gesture? The eerie thought flashed through Alec's mind. Many thought the chief inquisitor was more than human, sheltering a supernatural spirit in a racked body far less than human itself.

"This man will be held here in the prison of the Holy Office until such time as he may be again brought up for trial," the padre continued in a mechanical-sounding voice.

"But, my daughter is held captive by his men in a boat in our harbor, Father Humana," Don Pedro protested. "If he does not return to that boat within a very short time, my daughter will die at their hands."

The priest shook his head. "She will not die."

"How can you be so sure?" Don Rodrigo demanded. "These are desperate men. This man's orders are obeyed to the letter, and he has such control over them."

"I say again—she will not die," the priest repeated.

"Don Pedro!" Alec cried. "Will ye allow this to happen?"

The governor-general spread out his hand's palms upward. He shook his head and looked away from Alec. Don Esteban looked toward the two guards at the door. He nodded.

Alec whirled. He ripped his broadsword from its sheath and backed away from the approaching guards. They lowered their halberds and looked questioningly not at their commander, Don Pedro, but rather at Padre Humana.

"I want him alive," the priest said.

Alec smiled thinly. "The reward states alive or dead, priest! Ye will not take me alive to that damned dungeon of hell ye held me in before!"

"Get more men, Don Rodrigo," Don Esteban ordered. He stood up and drew his sword with his left hand. The candlelight glittered in wavy patterns on the fine Toledo steel and reflected from the polished steel of his right hand.

Ten more guards entered the room. Some of them carried murderous-looking pikes. It seemed as though a hedgehog of steel surrounded Alec in a half-crescent shape, while behind him was the bare stone wall with no means of escape.

Don Rodrigo looked at Alec. "It would be better for you to lay down your arms, Captain Campbell!" he called out. "You haven't a chance!"

"Only a chance to die," Don Pedro added.

"Rafaela can only be saved by your word," Don Rodrigo added.

"And then I'll die under the fire and sharp steel of your damned Inquisition!" Alec shouted.

But there was something in the tone of Don Rodrigo's voice that touched some perception deep within Alec's mind. Twice in the past, Alec had spared the Spaniard's life. The Spaniard was a man of impeccable honor. If he were in Alec's present position, he would have preferred to die as Alec wanted to die, with reddened blade in hand, safe from the hellish tortures of the Inquisition.

"Believe me," Don Rodrigo said.

He meant somehow to help Alec. It was a thin thread upon which to hang one's life, but there was no alternative. Alec reversed his sword and held it out to Don Rodrigo. The Spaniard came forward and took the proffered weapon. He looked deep into Alec's eyes as though to say: *"Trust me…"*

Alec was stripped of his weapons by Don Rodrigo. They took him from the gloomy hall out into the brilliant sunshine of the street and marched him down to the quayside, followed by a curious, rapidly growing crowd of hundreds of townspeople. Only Don Estebán, Don Bartolome, and Don Rodrigo marched with the party. Don Pedro could not bear to see what might happen to Rafaela if Alec's men obeyed his orders; while Padre Humana was rarely, if ever, seen in public, and never during the daytime, for he was a creature of dim candlelit places where he would question heretics, already partially broken by torture, with a persistence that had no equal. Ultimately, his victims either died under the steel and fire of the tortured or else admitted their heresy, sometimes only to die by cleansing fire in the end.

They stopped at the seaward end of the quay. The longboat floated in the very center of the harbor, surrounded by naval ships, traders, and plate ships. The longboat was the cynosure of all eyes.

"There's Cutlass, Davie," Jeb Jarman said.

The bosun nodded. "Out oars," he commanded. "Give way together."

The longboat moved slowly toward the end of the quay until it was within thirty yards of it. "Oars," Heckart ordered. The dripping blades were raised from the water.

The hour was past. It was obvious that Alec Campbell had been disarmed and was under guard. "What are your orders, sir?" Heckart called out.

"Bring the woman ashore, Heckart!" Alec called back.

"Do you have the ransom money, sir?" Heckart shouted.

Alec shook his head.

"Are you a prisoner?" Heckart asked.

There was no purpose in denying it. "I am," Alec replied.

"Ye know what to do, mates," Alec had reminded his longboat crew on the way into Porto Bello. "At the first warning, take the longboat frae the harbor wi' a pistol at the head of your hostage. They'll no fire."

"What shall I do?" Heckart yelled.

"Bring the woman ashore!" Alec repeated.

Dave Heckart looked down at Rafaela. She was so lovely. He drew his pistol and cocked it. She looked directly into his eyes. He looked about himself. There was to be no help for him in making this decision. He was positive the Spaniards had coerced Captain Cutlass into ordering Rafaela to be brought ashore.

Heckart looked miserably at his commanding officer on the quay. He looked at the hundreds of townspeople lining the quayside. He looked up at the hundreds of Spaniards on the decks of the ships in the harbor and those who lined the frowning ramparts of Fortresses San Juan and El Castillo.

Heckart placed the pistol muzzle against the nape of Rafaela's neck. "Give way together," he ordered in a steady voice. "Hold water starboard; pull hard port; backwater starboard; give way together." The longboat turned slowly around to head for the harbor channel.

The sun reflected from brass swivel guns and falconets on the quarterdecks of the ships on each side of the longboat's course. The muzzles of the guns were depressed to cover the boat. One command would cause those many guns to spit flame, smoke, and sudden death at the longboat's crew.

"We'll never make it, Dave," Tom Colman, the port stroke oar murmured.

"Turn back," Peter Moss, the starboard stroke oar pleaded.

"Heckart!" Alec Campbell's voice rang out across the harbor in a harsh tone of command. "Turn back! Bring the woman ashore!"

Heckart looked back over a shoulder. "I'm only obeying your orders, sir!" he shouted.

A falconet spat flame and smoke. The little ball jetted up a fountain of spray just ahead of the longboat. The shot echo rebounded from the walls of the fortresses and died away.

Alec looked quickly at Don Rodrigo. "My men will be allowed tae leave the harbor once the Señorita Rafaela is brought ashore?"

Don Rodrigo nodded.

"On your word of honor?"

"Of course, Captain Campbell."

Don Esteban said nothing. He rested his left hand on the hilt of his sword. He looked over a shoulder at the sergeant of the file of guards who stood behind him. The sergeant came close to his commanding officer. Don Esteban whispered a few quick words into the sergeant's ear. The sergeant nodded. Don Esteban turned quickly back to face the harbor as Don Rodrigo turned his head to look back at him.

"Bring the lady here, Heckart!" Alec ordered. "Ye will be allowed tae leave once she is safe ashore!"

The bosun shrugged. He had the boat turned. They rowed slowly toward the quay. The boat bumped gently against the stone side of the quay. Heckart gave Rafaela a hand up to the quay. He looked questioningly at Alec Campbell, but there was no response on Alec's face. Heckart noted too that his commanding officer did not bear arms.

"Shove off, Davie lad," Alec ordered. "Get tae hell out of this harbor while the going is good!"

"Wait!" Don Esteban ordered. He turned. "Sergeant!"

The file of guards ran forward and stood along the quayside with their pikes presented toward the heads of the boat crew.

Dave Heckart recocked his pistol. Some of the crew reached down for the cutlasses and pistols that lay at their feet.

"This is betrayal, sir!" Alec snapped at Don Esteban. He looked at Don Rodrigo. "Ye gave me your word, sir!"

The Spaniard's face was set. He looked at his commanding officer. "My word has no value here anymore, it seems, Captain Campbell."

"Order your men out of the boat, sir," Don Esteban demanded. "If not, they'll die in it."

"But why, Don Esteban?" Alec asked. "Your priest has me in his bloody hands once more. My men have nothing to do with that."

"They are heretics, are they not?"

The men in the boat looked sideways out of the corners of their eyes. A cold chill crept through their bodies.

"As such, they must appear for questioning before the Congregation of the Holy Office."

Peter Moss had paled. He looked up at Alec Campbell. "What is that, sir?" he asked.

Alec looked away.

"Captain!" Moss cried.

Don Rodrigo looked at Moss. "Your people call it the Inquisition," he said quietly.

Moss stood up in the boat. He dived over the side of it and struck out for the channel entrance half a mile away.

"Sergeant," Don Esteban said.

The sergeant drew a pistol and cocked it. He rested the barrel across his upraised left forearm and sighted the weapon. The hammer fell. The pistol barked. The slug hit

Peter Moss in the back of the head. He sank at once without a sound, leaving a stain of bright red on the surface of the water.

Don Estebán looked down into the boat. "Get out, *Ingles* scum," he ordered.

Dave Heckart got out of the boat, followed by the rest of the crew. They were marched off the quay. Rafaela turned once to look back at Alec before she was taken from the quay by Don Rodrigo.

Don Estebán eyed Alec. "As an officer, although of doubtful merit, Captain Campbell, I can offer you separate prison accommodations in far better taste than that which your men shall receive. But, in that case, I must have your word of honor that you will not try to escape before your appearance in the court of the Congregation of the Holy Office."

Alec looked steadily at the Spaniard. "Do you know the meaning of a word of honor, sir?" he asked quietly.

The Spaniard's face reddened. His left hand tightened on the pommel of his sword, and he raised his lethal right hand to chest height as though to strike out at Alec. "If the situation here were different, sir, I would make you eat those words or call you out."

Alec smiled. "Please call me out, Don Estebán. The choice of weapons would then be mine, if ye Spaniards adhere to the duelist's code. I'd like nothing better than to spit ye on a yard of my broadsword's steel."

Don Estebán shook his head. "And avoid appearing in the court, sir? No. I am looking forward to that interesting event."

"Have you collected your blood money of one thousand *ocho reales,* Don Estebán? Or should I say your Thirty Pieces of Silver? I am sure Don Rodrigo will never collect it, for he, unlike yourself, *is* a man of honor!"

Don Estebán's face darkened. His eyes seemed like those of a basilisk. He raised his steel fist to strike out at Alec.

"Would ye add the cowardice of striking an unarmed man wi' that devilish hand of yours?" Alec jeered. "Go on, Spaniard! Strike me!"

Don Estebán turned on a heel and strode from the quay.

Don Bartolome wiped the cold sweat from his forehead. "You trifle with death, *Escocés*," he muttered.

Alec smiled thinly. "It is my profession, sir."

"You have made an implacable enemy of him, Captain Campbell."

Alec shook his head. "He is an implacable enemy of *all* my kind, Don Bartolome."

The Spaniard nodded. "And sometimes even of his own kind, sir."

Alec turned and looked out toward the sea. In the far distance he could see the white topsails of his *Adventuress*. "Can ye send word out tae my ship that I will not return immediately, Don Bartolome?"

"Yes," Don Bartolome replied. He was about to add "or ever," but he was too kind a man to do so.

They marched Alec Campbell from the quay and through the gaping crowds to the dungeons of the Fortress of San Juan. He was thrust into a windowless cell far below the ground level with only a tiny barred slit of an opening high above his head. He looked about at his boat's crew, who were seated on the floor with their backs against the weeping stone.

"Be of good cheer, mates," Alec said.

No one answered him.

SEVENTEEN

The water dripped monotonously from the walls of the dungeon. A rat rustled in the moldy straw that served as a bed on the cold flagstone floor. The only light in the cell was from a guttering candle stub stuck to the greasy top of a rickety table. The flickering light played shadow games on the damp walls and outlined the crouched figures of two men who were chained to the wall. The one tiny barred slit of an opening that passed for a window was so high above their heads that it was almost impossible to tell whether or not it was daylight outside. The place was timeless. The cell was like the womb of a woman made of huge blocks of stone, where there was no day or night and no way to tell which hour was passing.

"How long have we been here, captain?" Dave Heckart croaked.

Alec Campbell raised his head from his opened hands. "Two weeks? A month? Two months? Perhaps even a year?"

Heckart nodded. He eased his left arm so that the open, running sore on the wrist under the iron wristlet did not throb with inflammation. He coughed dryly. "We could not have lasted a year," he croaked.

"A month then, Davie, lad?"

"More like it."

They did not look at each other. There was no mirror in the dank, stinking dungeon, but each knew the eyes of the other were mirrors enough. The look of faint horror in them told the tale of their imprisonment, privation, physical torture, and above all, the mental torture inflicted upon them by the inquisitors of the Congregation of Holy Office.

"How many of us are left, Davie?" Alec asked.

The bosun shrugged. His rusted chains rattled as he did so. He cursed softly as the iron wristlet abraded the raw flesh of the running sore. "Peter Moss died in the harbor with a bullet in his head. He was the lucky one. Jim Steward died under the *cordeles*. John Letcher lost his reason under the *garrucha*. Bill Merrill was taken from the prison, and we never saw him again." The bosun's singsong chanting died away.

"Go on," Alec urged. It was a game they played to keep their reason.

"I'm beginning to forget the names."

"Damn it! They were your boat's crew, bosun!"

"Damn it! They were your ship's crew, captain!"

Alec nodded. He reached out a thin hand and rested it on the bowed shoulder of the bosun. "Tom Colman," he prompted.

"He's dying in the next cell. The guard says he was accidentally given too much of the *jarras de agua*, and his stomach burst."

"Jules Devereux."

"A Catholic, at least in his youth. He recanted. They sentenced him to the galleys for five years."

"Jeb Jarman?"

Heckart looked fearfully toward the heavy wooden door of thick oaken planks through which little sound could come. "He's being interrogated this day, or night, whichever it is."

Alec looked at the heaped straw. "Is that someone there asleep, Davie?"

"There is no one there but the rats."

It was very quiet except for the rustling of the huge, plump rats in the straw.

"You left out Dan Witt, bosun," Alec whispered at last.

Heckart shook his head. "I counted all eight of them—

Moss, Steward, Letcher, Merrill, Colman, Devereux, and Jarman."

"That's seven, Davie."

"Eight, damn you!"

"Count again," Alec suggested.

Heckart closed his eyes and counted to himself. He opened his eyes and raised his head. "Seven," he said. "You were right. Dan Witt is missing."

Alec shook his head. "If he is missing, and Jeb Jarman is being interrogated, who's that in the straw, Davie?" His voice rose a pitch. *"Who's being eaten by the rats in the straw!"*

They screamed hoarsely together.

The heavy door swung open, and a guard peered in. "What the hell is the matter with you now?" he asked.

Dave Heckart pointed wordlessly toward the stinking straw.

They took the unconscious Dan Witt from the filthy heap on the floor. Half of his face had been eaten away, and three of the fingers of his right hand had been stripped to the bone. They killed the squealing rats and took the dying man from the cell. There would be other rats, but not Dan Witt back in the cell. The rat number was legion in the dungeons and subcellars of the fortress.

Alec rested his head back against the wet wall. He closed his eyes. The death's head of Padre Gaspar de Humana came slowly into his vision. He saw the burning eyes and heard the dry, rasping voice that had no human qualities in it. Then, the sly, involved questions: *"Do you believe in the Sacrament? Do you believe in the wine and the bread? Were those the true and perfect body and blood of the Savior Christ? Yes or no! What were the beliefs of the family of your father? Of the family of your mother? Tell us which of your companions is an unconfessed heretic."*

On and on, while the awful screams of those being tortured in the room next to the courtroom, rang in the accused's ears.

Alec opened his eyes with a start. The cell was the same as it had been before. Had he been asleep? How long had it been? The candle still guttered on the table. The rats no longer rustled in the straw, but some of their mates would return. Dave Heckart sagged in his chains. His breathing was slow and irregular.

Alec closed his eyes again. He could see the faces of his shipmates, those who had come with him to Porto Bello in the longboat, handpicked men, some of the toughest and most cold-nerved in the crew of the *Adventuress.* Smiling Peter Moss, who had died with a bullet in his head, to be food for the ravenous sharks that infested the Porto Bello harbor. Quiet Jim Steward, a fellow Scot to Alec, who had been subjected to the *cordeles,* wet rawhide cords bound tightly about the skull and allowed to dry, then twisted even tighter with a stick until the eyes bulged out. Big John Letcher, whose powerful frame had literally been pulled apart by the *garrucha,* a pulley arrangement that dislocated the bones. His reason had fled and left him a gibbering wreck of a man. Shrewd Bill Merrill, who had been taken from the cell shortly after they had all been incarcerated in it and had never been seen again. Tom Colman, who had been subjected to the *jarras de agua,* in which long strips of linen were forced down the throat and the contents of many jars of water poured down the strips so that a man would literally drown from the great amounts of fluid taken in. Jules Devereux, a happy-go-lucky Frenchman from Bordeaux, whose recanting had earned him five years in the horrible galleys of the Spanish Mediterranean fleet, a living death. Few men could last as long as five years chained night and day to a galley oar. Dan Witt, who had survived days of horrible torture only to be partially eaten by rats as he lay unconscious from the tortures he had undergone.

Dave Heckart mumbled in his sleep. "Alice," he said clearly.

The bosun had suffered as badly as some of the others in the torture chamber, but he had survived. But, unless he had medical treatment for the running sores on his arms and legs from the abrading effect of the rusted iron that held him chained to the wall, he might lose a limb or two, unless he died from infection.

Alec himself had suffered little in the torture chamber. A few turns of the *cordeles;* a scourging with sharp-pointed steel-wire chains. A rather mild application of the thumbscrews. Perhaps they were saving him? For what? To recant and win a victory for that death's head of a chief inquisitor?

"Never!" Alec shouted aloud.

Dave Heckart raised his head. "Is it time to eat?" he asked hollowly.

"Not yet, Davie."

"Breakfast, lunch, or supper, eh, captain?"

Alec's face cracked into a wry half-smile. "Can ye tell the difference in here, Davie lad?"

Heckart laughed, a dry, snorting sort of a thing, with little or no mirth in it.

The food was always the same—a cup of sour wine and a piece of hard bread fried in honey. It was served three times a day, so that without the light of day or the darkness of night, it was impossible to tell which meal it was at the time. The guards never spoke to the prisoners. If the prisoners were taken from their cells for interrogation, they were led through dark, dripping corridors beneath the great fortress and below sea level to a windowless room where they would be blindfolded and then taken through the streets of the city to the place of interrogation. Thus, being always in darkness or semidarkness, they would never know whether it was day or night. But, knowing Padre de Humana as he did, Alec was sure that his own interrogation, at least, took place always at night.

Hard footsteps sounded in the corridor outside the cell. The door was unlocked and then pushed open on rusted, grating hinges. Jeb Jarman was thrust into the cell and the door was slammed shut behind him.

Alec and Dave looked up at Jeb. He seemed to be all right. No marks of torture were visible on those parts of his body not covered by his rags. Jeb stood there staring at the wall over the heads of his two fellow prisoners.

"Are you all right, Jeb man?" Dave croaked.

"You're here, then?" Jeb queried.

Dave and Alec nodded.

"Light the candle," Jeb said.

It was very quiet in the cell.

"Have you no candle, then?" Jeb asked.

Dave looked at Alec. "The devils," he whispered.

"Damn you, Davie!" Jeb snapped. "Light the bloody candle!"

"It *is* lit, Jeb," Alec said quietly.

"But it's all darkness!" Jeb cried.

"Sweet Jesus," Alec murmured. "They've blinded the poor beggar."

"What's that you say?" Jeb demanded.

"Can you see nothing?" Dave asked.

Jeb shook his head. "Help me," he pleaded.

"Walk forward until you reach us, Jeb," Dave instructed. "We can't reach you now because of the chains."

Jeb shuffled forward. His right foot struck Alec's left ankle. Alec stood up as high as he could and helped the blinded man down beside Dave.

"What did they do to you, Jeb lad?" Dave asked.

"They wanted to know about the captain. They wanted me as a witness against him. They wanted me to say that he had cursed God and had spat upon the altar of the church at Campeche. That he had slain a priest with his own hands because the priest would not tell him where the gold and silver chalices and candlesticks of the church had been hidden. They held a bar of red-hot glowing iron in front of my eyes until, until I…" His voice cracked and died away. He bent his head and covered his face with his thin, dirty hands.

"Go on, Jeb," Dave urged. "Until what?"

"I think I know," Alec put in quietly.

"They took the bar away at last and told me I would be punished no more. I had told them what they wanted to know. But they did not tell me I had been blinded!" His voice rose into a shriek and then cracked. Dave turned to look at Alec. "You know what that means?"

Alec nodded. "The *San Benito* robe and an appointment to the *quemadero* to be burned alive."

"Did ye sign your confession?" Alec asked. Jeb shook his head. He smiled slyly. "I can't write, captain. All I did was make my mark. Is that legal, sir?"

"Ye signed the Articles that way too, Jeb. Ye know that was legal. But, no matter, perhaps one confession such as yours will not matter too much. Custom decrees three such confessions."

"They'll never get one out of me!" Dave Heckart cried.

Jeb turned slowly to look toward the bosun with sightless eyes. "They won't have to, Dave. Before they blinded me, I was shown two other confessions, signed by men of our crew. At least they said they were signed by them."

"Who?" Dave demanded. "I'll break their God damned necks!"

"Too late. Jules Devereux signed such a confession and was sentenced to the galleys instead of wearing the *San Benito* and being burned at the stake in the *quemadero.*"

"But he wasn't even at Campeche!"

Alec nodded. "He joined us three years later." Dave smashed a fist into his other palm so hard that his chains rattled. "This damned court must have some honor! Perhaps the captain can question Devereux's confession."

"Too late," Jeb said quietly. "He has already been taken to a ship in the harbor that will take him to Spain."

"And the other confession?" Alec asked. "Bill Merrill," Jeb replied. It was quiet again.

After a time, Dave spoke out, "And where is Bill Merrill now?"

There was no answer. Bill Merrill had been one of the first of the prisoners to be taken from the cells beneath the fortress. That must have been weeks past. None of the others had ever seen him again.

"Three confessions," Alec murmured at last. "No wonder they went so easy on me during the tortures. All they needed was one more."

"I am sorry, sir!" Jeb Jarman cried.

Alec placed an arm over the bowed shoulders of the blinded man. "No matter, Jeb. They would have gotten me one way or another. I was doomed the day I came back to Porto Bello. That damned devil Humana only wanted to make it legal. Well, legal or illegal, he has won. They pride themselves on the fact that no man has ever escaped the Inquisition and lived to talk about it. I did that very thing. One way or another they had to get me. I was living proof that the Inquisition was not infallible."

"It's possible that you might be sentenced to the galleys, captain," Dave suggested.

Alec shook his head. "No. Humana will want to see me burn. But what of ye men?"

"They told me that I would be sent to the galleys along with Dave here," Jeb replied.

"But, you're blind!"

Jeb shrugged. "Does a man need sight to pull an oar in a galley, sir?"

The guards came while the three prisoners were asleep. They took Jeb Jarman and Dave Heckart with them. Alec knew he would never see them again. He was left alone with his thoughts in the cell.

EIGHTEEN

I t was raining heavily, when at last, they came for Alec Campbell. The water ran in through the barred slit high above his head and flowed down the wall to form a puddle beneath him. He had not been able to move because of his chains. They unlocked him from his chains and stood him up on his feet. He staggered a little as they led him from the cell and along the dim, dripping corridor to the windowless room where he was usually blindfolded before being taken to the courtroom of the Inquisition.

"Is it day or night?" Alec croaked.

The corporal of the guard looked sympathetically at Alec. "Night," he replied. "And after midnight at that."

It was the first time any guard had ever spoken to him in the weeks he had been imprisoned.

"What is it to be tonight?" Alec asked boldly.

The guard shrugged. "Sentencing, I suppose. That is, after you confess fully."

"I heard that they already had the confessions of three of my mates to the effect that I was guilty."

"You know that sonofabitch Padre Humana better than I do, *Ingles.* He feeds his soul on people such as you." The Spaniard studied Alec. "You didn't really do those things at Campeche he has accused you of, did you?"

Alec shook his head.

The corporal nodded. "I thought so. Then why is he so

damned determined to stick you into a *San Benito* and burn you in the *guemadero?*"

Alec looked at the Spaniard. "Because I once escaped from the Inquisition and Padre Humana."

The guard whistled softly. "So that's it!" He shook his head. "You're doomed then, eh?"

Alec nodded.

A guard came in through the outer doorway. His poncho dripped water. "The *carreta* is here, corporal. It's raining like a sonofabitch. Why that bastard priest needs this poor man tonight is beyond me. You won't see Humana out on a night like this."

"It's his black soul, Ramón," the corporal replied.

The guard reached for the blindfold. The corporal shook his head. They led Alec from the guard room out into the street. The driver of the *carreta* was hunched beneath his poncho and wide straw hat. The rain was coming down in leaden-colored sheets. The narrow street was running ankle-deep in rainwater. Not a light was to be seen anywhere.

"It's like driving in a pool of ink," the driver grumbled.

The two guards helped Alec into the back of the cart. The driver touched up his mule with the whip, and the *carreta* rolled slowly forward along the street that led toward the quayside.

Forked lightning cracked across the dark sky. Thunder crashed like the broadside of a ship of the line. The city was illuminated under a ghastly glowing of lightning.

"Jesus bless us!" the corporal exclaimed. He hunched his poncho higher about his neck.

They left the looming shadow of the fortress behind them and rumbled out onto the cobbles of the quayside. The harbor was to the left, and the riding lights of the anchored ships shone mistily through the downpour.

The driver turned the mule to drive up the narrow street that led to the center of the city and the plaza where the *quemadero,* or burning place for heretics condemned by the Inquisition, was situated so that the townspeople would have plenty of room to view the sight and to meditate on their own lack of faith.

The other *carreta* blundered full tilt out of a side street just above the quayside. The driver of the oncoming cart turned his mule at the last possible instant so that the wheels of his vehicle slithered on the wet, greasy cobblestones, and the heavy cart struck full force alongside the cart in which Alec rode.

"What the hell is the matter with you?" the driver of the prison cart shouted. He did not see the dark figure that came from behind him and struck at his head with a long and heavy club. He fell from the seat without a sound.

The two guardsmen struggled to free their swords from beneath their ponchos. One of them went down from a club blow. The other one turned to run. A knife went up to the hilt in his back.

"Quick!" a man shouted in strongly accented Spanish at Alec. "Strip off those God damned rags! Get into the guard's clothing!"

There were three assailants, counting the cart driver. They worked swiftly. When Alec had stripped himself of his rags, the dead guard was stripped and his clothing handed to Alec. Alec's rags were put on the corpse. The corpse was dragged to the edge of the quay and dumped into the harbor. By morning, nothing but the bare bones and a few rags would be left by the ravenous sharks. The cart was led to the quayside and then driven into the water. The mule floundered around pitifully. Two more splashes accounted for the cart driver and the other guard.

"Get into the cart," one of the men said to Alec.

"Where to?" Alec asked. He kept his hand on the guard's sword.

The man grinned. "We don't know. All we know is that we're to drive you to the outskirts of town and leave you there."

"Who paid you to do this?"

The man spat to one side. "You ask a helluva lot of questions for a man who's just been saved from the stake. Now, get to hell into that cart!"

The cart was driven recklessly up the street, bouncing from side to side and bounding over the cobblestones like a small boat in a rough sea. They crossed the wide plaza illuminated by crashing, flashing lightning. There was no one in sight.

The cart was halted at last in the thick, wet darkness far beyond the plaza and near one of the city walls. Alec was dragged from the rear of the cart and set up on his feet. The driver turned the cart and the other two men climbed into the back of it.

One of the men leaned over the rear of the cart. "I'd get rid of those clothes and that sword, mate, if I were you. As far as the Inquisition knows, your cart was accidentally driven into the harbor. The sharks cleaned up the mess, including you."

"Who are you?" Alec demanded.

There was no answer from his saviors. The mule was lashed into a gallop, and the cart plunged and rocked as it was turned back toward the plaza. In a little while, it was gone from sight under the frequent lightning flashes.

Alec looked about himself. The narrow street was lined with great houses whose tall windows were protected by iron gratings. The red-tiled roofs poured sheets of rainwater down into the street. Not a light showed. Not a soul was to be seen.

"Captain Campbell!" a woman called from behind Alec.

Alec whirled and raised the sword.

She stood in a narrow areaway between two of the great houses. "You are safe!" the woman cried. "Thank the good Virgin Mary to whom I prayed for your deliverance!"

Her voice was familiar. "Teresa!" Alec exclaimed.

She came running to him and threw her arms about him. "What have they done to you?" she cried.

He looked about himself. "I'd rather not explain it standing here, my plump pigeon." He grinned weakly.

She led him up the narrow areaway and unlocked a low, narrow door set into a high wall whose top was protected by iron spikes. She led the way into a large patio and locked the door behind them. The house was dark. "Come," Teresa said.

"Wait. Whose house is this?" He was almost sure he knew the answer.

"The house of Don Pedro de Vasquez," Teresa replied. She smiled. "And Señorita Rafaela, of course."

"Don Pedro is here?"

She shook her head. "Don Pedro has returned to Panama."

"Who else is in the house?"

"Just my pet Rafaela."

"No servants?"

"Only myself. Most of them went with Don Pedro. The cook died a week ago of the fever. We have not replaced her."

Lightning exploded across the streaming sky. The tropical rain slashed down violently.

They ran to get under an overhanging roof. Alec coughed hard. A spasm overcame him. He staggered sideways and leaned against the side of the house.

Teresa unlocked a door and helped Alec into a dark passageway. "Wait here," she ordered.

Alec closed his eyes. He still could not believe his miraculous deliverance. It had all happened so swiftly. He opened his eyes. The woman was gone. Could he trust these women even if he had once saved their lives and had brought them home to Porto Bello in safety? Perhaps he should not risk staying there. He opened his eyes and walked back to the outer door. His wrist chains clanked as he felt about for the door handle.

"Alec!" she called.

Alec turned. Rafaela stood at the end of the dark passageway holding a candle. The soft yellowish light shone on the ivory skin of her bared shoulders and glistened from her lustrous dark hair. He could not believe it was she at last. He dropped the sword, clattering to the tiled floor. Alec raised his thin hands to his face and cupped them about it. His shoulders shook.

She ran to him as he fell slowly sideways. The last thing he remembered was the soft pressure of her breasts against his left arm as she raised him to gather him into her arms.

NINETEEN

Alec awoke to the sound of steady rain drumming on the tiled roof. He lay in a great bed. The window shutters of the bedchamber were closed, but he could see faint streaks of gray light through the chinks. The faint and enticing scent of perfume arose from the sheets about him as he moved. The door of a huge wardrobe was partially open, and within it, he could see a row of gowns with tiny little shoes arrayed in a line below the hem of the gowns. A dressing table was crowded with female *impedimenta*.

Alec sat up. He was wearing a man's ruffled nightgown. He got out of bed and padded toward the door. There was a great weakness in his legs. He knew now he could never have made it through the rain-soaked swamps that surrounded Porto Bello. He opened the door and stepped out into a second-story hallway whose one side was open and railed. He looked down into a great room dominated by heavy, dark Spanish colonial furniture.

Rafaela de Vasquez entered the room and crossed it toward the stairway which led up to the second floor.

When Rafaela quietly opened the bedroom door, Alec was seated upright in the bed. His wrists were still chained together. His left hand was beneath the coverlet and grasped a small, silver-hilted dagger he had picked up from the dressing table. His right hand rested on the upper edge of the coverlet.

She smiled. "You're awake at last! We thought you might have left us forever but for your breathing. You slept as one dead throughout last night and almost all of this day. My bed must suit you well, Alec! Sleepyhead!"

Alec nodded. "It's quite a contrast to the moldy straw spread on a stinking wet dungeon floor, lassie, wi' hungry rats for bedfellows."

Rafaela paled. She raised a hand to her full-lipped mouth. There was a look of horror on her lovely face.

"Aye, lassie! The accommodations of your Inquisition are not of the best."

"It is not *my* Inquisition, Alec," she insisted.

"Yet your people allow it!" he cried. "Nine of my shipmates died in that place or were sent tae the galleys!"

Tears glistened in her eyes. She turned her head away.

"Forgive me, lassie," he pleaded. "But for ye and Teresa, I wouldna be here at all, although God alone knows how ye did it."

She came close to the side of the bed and picked up the rusted wrist chain that lay on the coverlet. "How can we get these off?" she asked.

"A guid file or two, and I'll be out of them in an hour. Can ye get me some clothing? Weapons? A guide through the swamps?"

She laughed. "Not so soon! You're in no condition to try to escape from Porto Bello."

"I'd rather try it than be caught here and dragged back tae that hellhole in Fort San Juan!"

Rafaela shook her head. "Teresa went to the market early this morning. They found the cart in the harbor and no trace of any bodies. It is said that you all perished when driven accidentally off the quayside."

"Then I can leave!"

"No! It's not safe as yet. If they suspect anything, they'll keep on searching as long as Padre de Humana has anything to say about it."

Alec nodded. "Ye took a terrible risk, lassie. Who were those men who saved me? Will they talk?"

She shook her head. "They were Flemings, part of the crew of a ship that left for Portugal on the morning tide. It was Teresa who found them. They agreed to save you, for a price, but Teresa, of course, had a great deal to do with it as well." She smiled knowingly. "Besides, they hate the Inquisition and all it stands for."

"Still, it was a dangerous thing to do. Teresa said your father had gone to Panama. Where is Don Rodrigo?"

"At sea, still looking for those ships that were following us here to Porto Bello."

"And my ship as well?"

She shrugged. "I don't know. The *Adventuress* left shortly after you were imprisoned. Rumor has it that she was seen just last week."

"Where?"

"South, along the coast. She was pursued but outran our ships."

Alec smiled. "Easily enough, I'll warrant."

"So, you must remain here in this house until you can regain your strength for your eventual escape."

Alec shook his head. "We can't risk that, lassie. If ye were to be found out…"

She placed a cool little hand against his fevered cheek. "You risked so much for Teresa and me, and we can hardly repay you enough, Alec."

"Would they search this house?"

"It's the house of the governor-general," she reminded him.

"That wouldna stop that human bloodhound Humana."

"Can you get out of the bed for a moment or two?"

He nodded. He thrust his legs out from under the coverlet and stood up. The silver-hilted dagger dropped to the tiled floor.

She looked into his eyes. "Why, Alec?" she asked. "Were you afraid to trust us?"

"A man is not a man wi'out his weapons. Besides, lassie, they'll no take me alive!"

She walked to the wardrobe and pushed aside the perfume-scented gowns. "Look," she said over her shoulder. She pushed down a hook in the back wall of the massive piece of furniture. A panel slid to one side and a cool, damp draft of air played about their features. "This is a passageway down beneath the house," Rafaela explained. "There is a tunnel under the house that leads out beyond the city walls to the jungle. It was built into this house years ago after your Henry Morgan raided and pillaged Porto Bello."

"You're giving away a great secret to another of Henry Morgan's ilk."

She pressed up the hook. The panel slid shut. She turned to look up into his face. "I know you well enough, Alec," she murmured. "You would not betray us."

He bent his head and pressed his dry, cracked lips against her full, moist ones. She turned quickly away. "I'll have Teresa bring you food, Alec." She ran toward the door.

"Wait, Rafaela! I'll need weapons whether I stay here now or escape eventually. Anything! A sword! Dagger! Pistol! Can ye get them for me?"

She smiled a little. "I can and will, Alec." She closed the door behind herself.

Alec walked to the wardrobe. He pushed aside the gowns and pressed down the hook. The panel slid noiselessly open. He went back to the dressing table and lighted a candle. He picked up the little silver-hilted dagger and returned to the wardrobe. Alec held the candle out as he worked his way gingerly down the narrow, steep stairway past the first floor and down beneath the great house. There was a vaulted cellar to one side of a door he opened. He stepped into the cellar and looked back at the door. It was not a door in the true sense of the word, but rather a panel of aged, damp-looking wood similar to panels on either side of it, which reached from one end of the cellar to the other. He returned to the passageway and walked down a farther flight of steps into a vaulted stone tunnel. He held up the candle and peered down the dark and noisome tunnel, which was hardly wide enough for a human being to pass through. Water dripped from the low ceiling. A rat scuttled into the darkness and away from the faint light of the candle.

When Teresa brought up a tray of food and several files

for Alec, he was back in bed, controlling the shivering he had incurred while exploring the passageway and the entrance into the tunnel.

He had finished eating and was industriously filing away at his wrist chains when Rafaela returned to the room burdened with an array of weapons. She proudly placed them on the coverlet at his feet one by one. Alec's great-grandfather's broadsword and dirk. His own pair of all-metal Highland pistols and his four-barreled "murtherer" pistol.

Alec looked up from his weapons. "How did ye come by them? A miracle of your church?"

She shook her head. "Don Rodrigo confiscated them. He left them here when he went back to sea."

He studied her. "But why? Did he want them for himself, or perhaps he thought I might live to use them again? If the latter, the man must be mad, for I will certainly use them against him if the time comes."

"I don't know."

He reached out with his right hand and gripped her left wrist. The wrist chain clinked as he did so. "Tell me," he insisted. "Did Don Rodrigo have anything to do with my escape from the Inquisition?"

"Do you think he would do that?" she cried. "He would endanger his own life if he did so. Do you know the penalty for helping a confessed heretic escape from the Inquisition?"

"I can guess," he replied dryly.

"Burning at the stake, and without the merciful garroting, they sometimes allow the condemned."

Garroting, to be choked to death before the flames seared one's flesh. Alec released Rafaela. He leaned back against his pillows and began filing at his wristband again.

"Do you believe me?" she asked.

He looked up at her. "Yes, Rafaela. But that won't save you from the *quemadero* if you and Teresa alone are responsible for my escape from them."

"They won't find you here! You can always escape through the tunnel and into the jungle."

"I wasn't thinking of my own safety. Even if they caught me here, I would die on my feet with steel in my hands rather than be taken back to the Fortress of San Juan and eventually to the *quemadero*. If that happened, they would surely condemn ye and Teresa to the flames."

She paled a little. "I am not afraid, Alec."

He smiled a little. "I am," he said softly.

She watched him as he completed his filing. He pried the filed-through iron bands from his wrists. Rafaela turned away in horror as she saw the leaking sores that banded his wrists. She sickened as she fled toward the door. "Teresa will bandage them!" she cried.

"I'll need clothing!" he called after her.

When darkness came, the rain had slackened somewhat. Teresa brought up a tray of food and clucked sympathetically about Alec until he had eaten it all. Rafaela had brought some of her father's clothing for Alec, and he insisted on wearing it at once.

"You are not well enough yet!" Teresa snapped.

"Would ye have them catch me here in that damned nightdress, lassie?" he shot back at her. "It's nae dress for a fighting man!"

"Do not the *Escoces* wear such dresses into battle?" she demanded. "Are they not great fighting men?"

"That's a kilt! There's a difference!"

She grinned at him. "You've worn one yourself?"

He nodded and walked right into her sly trap. "As a boy in the Hielands, and later as a soldier. A bonny tartan too, lassie—Campbell of Cawdor, wi' its green and blue and red..."

His voice died away and he looked thoughtfully at his great-grandfather's magnificent sword and dirk.

Teresa came closer to the bed. "And, my bonny *Escocés*, what did you *wear* under that kilt?" She laughed heartily.

Alec looked up quickly. "Shall I show ye, lassie?"

Her face changed. "Now?" she asked.

He leaped from the bed and staggered a little from his weakness. "Aye!" he cried. He reached down for the flounced hem of the nightgown to pull it up and promptly fell forward on his face. Teresa fled, shrieking from the room.

Rafaela collapsed on the bed, overcome with laughter. "You're completely mad!" she cried.

Alec sat up on the floor and decorously pulled his nightgown down about his bare feet. "There's one thing I canna remember," he said thoughtfully.

She sat up and looked down at him. "And what is that, pray, sir?" she asked sweetly.

"When I left the fortress after all that time in that stinking cell, I was as rotten-smelling as the bilge of a ship that has been too long at sea. Now, I see myself here, smelling as sweet as any rose." He looked up at her. "A miracle again, say ye?"

She flushed and turned away from him. "It was Teresa who bathed you."

"Alone?" he asked.

She shook her head. "I helped."

He studied her as she sat on her own great bed. That persistent, recurring memory of her came back to haunt him—the clear ivory skin with the silver chain and crucifix resting in the deep cleavage between her proud, brown-budded breasts. Aye, and those long, slim, lovely legs of hers. She was still wearing the silver chain and crucifix. He could see the silver chain about her shapely neck but not the silver crucifix, no doubt held between her breasts and warmed by them...

She saw the look on his lean face. "You must get back into bed, Alec."

The faint but persistent scent of her perfume came to him. Alec stood up and walked toward her. She sat on the edge of the bed and made no move to avoid him. Something fled through her mind, a haunting, insistent memory that occurred to her again and again—the night she had stood within the shadows of Kate Devon's pavilion at the rendezvous and had watched the naked foreplay between him and Kate Devon until, at last, she had lured him into the pool for the consummate act of fornication.

Kate had placed herself at the edge of the water, and half within it, and half out of it, as Alec completed the sexual act with a heat and vigor that completely belied his weakness from his wounds and the fever that had laid him low.

"Shall I dress now, lassie?" he murmured.

"Before me?" she asked.

"Ye can look away or leave if you've got a mind to."

She turned her head away from him.

He quickly crossed the room and turned the key in the door lock. He blew out all the candles except for a single candle on the dressing table that guttered and flickered within a glass cylinder like a votive light. The shadows moved in swiftly to take over the area of the large room not fitfully illuminated by the candlelight.

"Alec," she murmured. "Let me leave."

He shrugged. "Do what ye will, Rafaela."

"Teresa might return," she suggested.

Alec shook his head. "She knows better."

"She might talk about us being alone together in a locked room."

"Ye know better than that."

It was very quiet except for the light pattering of the rain on the tiled roof just over their heads and the dripping sound of the eaves as the rainwater descended into the garden patio below.

Alec pulled the nightgown over his head. He threw it to one side. Rafaela lay back on the bed and looked up at him. He bent over her and kissed her. Her slim arms rose and were clasped about his neck. He passed a hand along her face and let it caress her smooth throat and then rested lightly on one of her breasts. She turned her head quickly to one side.

Alec kissed the upper curve of her breasts and then her throat. She turned her head to meet his hungry lips and clung to him passionately. He raised his head and looked down at her lovely face and those great eyes of hers. He passed a hand down over her breasts and across her flat belly to the meeting of her thighs.

"Stop," she whispered.

He let his hand linger for a moment longer, pressing gently downward. She raised herself to thrust her loins tentatively against his exploring hand. "The Blessed Virgin, forgive me," she husked.

He sat up beside her. "Shall I stop?" he asked.

She did not answer. She closed her eyes.

"The decision is yours," he said.

She opened her fine eyes. Tears glistened in them. "Is it?" she asked quietly. "Would you stop if I asked you to?"

"Yes," he lied.

* * *

Alec dressed quickly. The clothing was evidently that of Don Pedro and was a rather tight fit through the shoulders. He unsheathed his broadsword and thrust his sheathed dirk under his waistband. He walked to the dressing table and turned to look at her once more. She lay with one arm across her eyes, the other arm outflung and one leg crossed over the other. He could see the dark stain of her virginal blood seeping from beneath her buttocks. Alec blew out the candle. He opened the shutters. The rain had stopped, and a cool draft blew into the warm room.

Alec quietly unlocked the door and stepped out into the hallway. He peered over the railing down into the *sala* below. A single candle guttered on a candlestick set into a wall niche. The room was thick with shadows. The candlelight glistened from the massive polished table and reflected from the crystal chandelier. Nothing moved in that room except the flame of the candle.

He stole down the stairs and paused with his back close to the wall to peer around the corner into the deep entryway into the house. A candle guttered within a red glass, casting a faint and eerie glow about it. Teresa sat nodding in a chair near the door. A large-bored *escopeta* or blunderbuss lay across her plump thighs.

Alec found the wine cabinet. He took several bottles of wine and two glasses and returned to the foot of the staircase. He looked once again at Teresa. She was still asleep. When he started up the stairway, Teresa opened one eye. She smiled.

"It's getting cold in here, Alec," Rafaela said from the darkness of the four-poster bed.

"Just a moment. I have something with which to warm ye," he promised. He closed the shutters and relighted the candle. He turned toward the bed. She was sitting up with the coverlet drawn up under her chin and with her great lovely eyes studying Alec. He placed a wine bottle and the glasses on a bedside table and looked down at her. She turned demurely away from him. He filled two wineglasses and reached out with a hand to cup it under her chin. He turned her head so that she faced him. She averted her eyes. He bent and kissed her lightly.

For a moment, she didn't respond, and then she looked up at him. "What must you think of me?" she whispered.

"Wonderful, lassie," he murmured. "Ye did yourself proud."

"I didn't mean it that way," she said quickly.

"Drink," he suggested.

She held his hand within hers and sucked greedily at the wine so that it ran from the corners of her mouth. She emptied the glass and then lay back against the huge pillow.

Alec sat down on the edge of the bed. "Christ's wounds!" he murmured softly. "After those weeks in hell, it was like a trip to heaven wi' ye. I didn't think I had it in me anymore."

"You certainly did," she said ruefully.

Alec laughed. "We do well together, lassie."

She nodded, a little shyly, but still a little proudly.

They sat quietly for a time, sipping at the good red wine. The rain began again. Rafaela shivered a little.

Alec drew the coverlet tighter up about her. She grasped his hand and pressed it tightly to her breasts while she looked into his eyes. "I'm still cold," she complained.

"You mean?" he asked quietly.

She nodded. "I have a hunger for you, Alec, pet."

He stood up and stripped off his clothing. He placed the naked broadsword on the floor beside the bed.

"We won't need the candlelight this time," she suggested.

"It will burn out soon enough, Rafaela. Besides, I've not seen quite enough of ye. I doubt that I ever will…"

They emptied their wineglasses. Alec refilled them and placed them on the bedside table close at hand. He got into bed with her, and she pressed her cold body tightly against his while she reached down to his crotch. He looked down into her lovely face with its wet, wine-red lips. "So soon?" he murmured.

"When you're ready, sweetness," she said. "I'm nae so strong as I was, lassie."

"Drink more wine. I can wait."

He grinned at her. "Wanton!"

She shook her head. *"Puta!"*

"Whore? Not so!"

In a little while, the wine bottle had been emptied. The candle was flickering out. They lay quietly together, feeling each other's regular breathing. "Alec," she whispered. "Aye."

"Do you love me?"

He could not lie to her. It had always been so easy with other women, so many of them... "Alec?"

"I don't know, Rafaela."

She snuggled close to him. "It doesn't matter now, does it? I've lost my virginity to you. We're lovers now. Perhaps in time we can love each other."

He looked strangely at her. "Ye mean ye don't love me?" he demanded.

She grinned wantonly up at him. "I don't know, Alec, but isn't this a hell of a time to be questioning each other?"

The candle flickered out. There was a strong movement in the great bed. Rafaela gasped suddenly. "Does it hurt, lassie?" Alec asked. "Shall I stop?"

"God yes! God no!" The rain pattered down harder.

TWENTY

Rafaela opened her eyes. Her bedchamber was dark. Faint moonlight showed through the chinks in the closed shutters. She turned her head to look at Alec and then sat bolt upright in the bed. "Alec?" she called into the semidarkness. There was no answer. She thrust her legs out from under the coverlet and felt for her slippers. She stood up, shivering in her nakedness, and drew her filmy night wrap about her. Alec's clothing and weapons were missing from his side of the bed.

Rafaela hurried to the door and unlocked it. She stepped cautiously out into the hallway. The *sala* was dark. A faint aura of candlelight shone through the hallway that led to the front door. Rafaela hurried down the stairs. She had dreaded the coming of this night during the weeks Alec had been hidden in the house. He had been more restless every day. One night, she had awakened to see him standing naked in front of the unshuttered window that looked down upon the garden patio. He had turned slowly when she had asked him what he was doing there.

"The wind and the sea call me away," he had replied quietly. But she had lured him, to her great shame, back to the bed and her arms. That night he had savaged her relentlessly, leaving her spent and weeping, but well satisfied withal...

Ramón, the half-Indian porter, lay asleep on his pallet

which he had placed across the foot of the door. His large-bored *escopeta* lay beside him. Ramón had returned three days past from Panama with a message from Don Pedro that his master would return to Porto Bello within the week, and he had then taken up his customary duties as porter. He knew nothing of Alec's being hidden in the house. At least Teresa *thought* Ramón knew nothing of Alec being there. One could never be quite sure just how much Ramón knew at any time.

Ramón opened his eyes. He had hearing like a jungle cat. He sat up quickly when he saw Rafaela. "What is wrong, mistress?" he asked.

"I thought I heard a strange noise out in the street," she lied.

Ramón stood up. The Indian predominated in his appearance and mannerisms. "You did, mistress, but the sound did not come from this street. Your hearing is as good as mine." He smiled.

"What was the sound?"

"I have heard that sound three nights running. There are patrols in the streets every night now."

"But why?" she asked. A faint feeling of fear ran through her.

Ramón shrugged. "They are the soldiers who act as guards for the Inquisition. They say in the plaza that they are looking for a confessed heretic who escaped from them three weeks past." Ramón's dark eyes studied Rafaela. "An *Ingles*, they say," he added. "A great pirate called Captain Cutlass by his friends and his enemies."

"But what caused that loud noise?" Rafaela asked.

Ramón looked surprised. "The noise was not that loud."

"Damn it! What was it?" she snapped. "They broke into the house of Antonio Carvajal. They say he is a man who would do anything for money. Perhaps they thought he had concealed that escaped heretic for the reward."

"The one thousand *ocho reales?*" she asked quickly.

Ramón shook his head. "Word has been passed around in the plaza that a much greater reward has been offered by this escaped heretic's men, who are said to be lying hidden somewhere along the coast."

"How do you know they broke into the house of Antonio Carvajal, Ramón?"

He smiled. "I was there and saw them, mistress. But I came quickly back here to my post of duty."

She shrugged. "Well, it is no concern of yours, is it?"

Ramón shook his head. "They would not dare to break into the house of Don Pedro, those animals of the Inquisition. I spit upon them!"

"Why?" she asked quietly.

His face was grim. "My mother was Indian and a true Catholic, but she practiced some of the old ways of her people's religion. They suspected her. My father, to save himself, accused her of heresy. They burned her in the *quemadero* when I was only five years old." His voice died away.

"And your father?"

He looked directly into her eyes. "They found him dead in his bed when I was fourteen years old."

"How did he die?"

Ramón shrugged. "My mother's people know many ways to kill a man without wounds, mistress."

"Poison?"

Ramón nodded. "When he died, I fled from the city to live with my mother's people deep in the jungle." His voice died away, but his black eyes remained fixed on Rafaela.

"You must know the jungle well, Ramón," she suggested.

He held out his hands, palms upward. "Like the palms of my hands, mistress."

She turned away. "Guard well, Ramón." She left the entryway.

Ramón watched her leave. He had not been out on the street that night. It had been the night before when the house of Antonio Carvajal had been raided by the guards of the Inquisition, led by that inhuman padre whose face looked like that of a skull covered by tightly drawn parchment from which two burning eyes, like live coals, bored into a man's reason and soul. Ramón knew Padre Gaspar de Humana all too well—it had been that very devil who had sentenced Ramón's mother to the *quemadero*, and that without the merciful garroting. The mistress had heard no sound in the street this night. What had brought her out of her sleep to come downstairs at that hour of the night? Ramón had noticed a great difference in Rafaela since he had come back to Porto Bello. Before this time, she had been a strange mixture of girl and woman, neither one or the other, and yet an intermingled combination of both. Now she was *all* woman, like a girl who had been with a real stud of man for the first time in her life.

Ramón gave Rafaela time to reach her room and then he tiptoed into the *sala* and looked up toward the balcony of the second floor. He heard the clicking of her door lock as she shut the door and then the grating sound of the key being turned in the lock.

Ramón heard someone moving quietly behind him. He whirled, drawing his knife as he did so.

"What are you doing away from your post of duty, you halfbreed dog?" Teresa demanded angrily.

Ramón smiled a little. "I thought I heard a noise coming from upstairs, Teresa."

"You heard nothing!" she snapped.

He shook his head. "I had better look," he suggested.

"There is nothing, you idiot!"

The candlelight behind her outlined her plump body and thick legs through the thin material of her nightdress. Mother of God, Ramón thought, to have such a one in bed, with her great belly and heavy tits to lie upon…

"What are you looking at?" Teresa demanded.

Ramón smiled a little. "There is so much to see. Well, I'd better look upstairs now." He turned away from her.

"Wait!" Teresa cried.

Ramón turned back toward her. "It is my duty," he said stiffly.

Teresa smiled. "It's late, Ramón. We should all be in bed."

"Whose bed?" Ramón asked with a grin.

Teresa coyly turned her head to one side. "Well, I'm not real sleepy."

Ramón looked back toward the second floor of the house. He knew damned well there must be someone up there with Rafaela. She had been with a man of late. His instinct told him that.

Teresa came up close behind him. "It's cold here, Ramón," she murmured.

Teresa had never paid much attention to Ramón. "That damned dirty halfbreed," was her usual description of him. He knew well enough Teresa was a lusty woman. He had heard stories from the other men servants and also rumors in the plaza.

Ramón turned to find her almost upon him. There was a curious intermingling aura of cheap perfume and sour sweat about her.

"Ramón," she whispered softly.

"Get to my pallet," he ordered.

"*There?* Are you mad?" she demanded.

"It is my post of duty," he answered loftily. "I can't leave it."

Teresa shrugged. She had diverted the dirty halfbreed from poking his nose upstairs. Well, he wouldn't last long. She'd see to that. That skinny frame of his couldn't have much vitality in it, at least in fornication, such as Teresa was able to give out to any man who thought he had the stamina to keep up with her. She smiled secretly to herself.

Teresa waddled to the pallet. She wrinkled her nose as she looked down upon it. She turned her head a little. "Well, Ramón, must I wait all night?"

He was on her like a night-hunting jaguar. He flung her face downward on the pallet and then lifted her by the sides of her plump hips so that she rose to her knees. He flipped her nightdress up over her broad back to free her rump for action. Before she had a chance to cry out, he had rammed himself full bore into her and was pumping back and forth like an aroused stallion so hard that her head struck the wall. She braced her hands against the wall. It was all she could do to hold herself there, or the halfbreed stallion would have rammed a hole in the plaster with her head.

"Mother of God!" she gasped. "Take it easy!"

He dug his broken-nailed fingers into her rounded hips and worked ever harder until she began to quiver in a semi-hysterical sort of ecstasy. Her orgasm was such that she almost fainted. Ramón laughed softly. He withdrew himself from her and wiped the sweat from his forehead. Teresa rolled over on her back and lay there, unashamed to the candlelight that revealed her sweat-dewed body, her great rolls of flesh, and the thick mat of hair at the junction of her thighs and body.

Ramón tiptoed through the house. He took a bottle of wine from a cabinet and pulled the cork out with his strong white teeth. He spat the cork out and drained half the bottle with his corded throat working convulsively. He sat down in one of the great chairs until the bottle was almost empty.

Teresa finally rolled over onto her belly. She pushed herself up from the floor and held her hands flat against the wall, gathering strength to get to her room.

"Wait, *puta*," Ramón murmured from the doorway.

She turned and looked at him. Her sweating face paled.

He grinned loosely. "Get down on your knees," he ordered.

She shook her head. "You've had enough," she protested.

"You, maybe, but not me. Now, get down on your knees!"

She did as she was bid. She watched him with frightened fascination as he stalked toward her, unbuttoning his trousers. He pulled out his organ. Her face blanched. My God, had he put that thing in *her?*

"What do you want now?" she cried.

He grinned. "Guess…"

"Not tonight!"

"Keep your big mouth open," he commanded.

She opened her mouth, and he promptly filled it to the full. "Get busy, fat one," he ordered.

When he was ready again, he threw her back on the pallet. He dropped atop her and forced his way in between her plump, sweating thighs. This time, she received him and gave as good as she got until they exploded together, and he rolled sideways from her and lay panting irregularly beside her. She closed her eyes and threw a plump arm over them.

After a time, the candle guttered out.

Teresa opened her eyes. She could hear his soft, regular

breathing beside her. Slowly, oh so very slowly, she rolled off the pallet and forced herself up on her hands and knees. No man, even her second husband, Manuel the muleteer, had ever serviced her like that. She had had enough to last for a month at least. She tried to get up on her feet, but the effort was too much for her. Finally, she made it, rested a hand against the wall and took one step back toward the interior of the house.

"Where are you going, fat one?" Ramón asked quietly out of the darkness.

She stopped. Cold sweat bathed her forehead. The man was a devil.

"Get back here," he commanded her.

She knew better than to resist. God knew what he'd do to her next if she resisted him.

"Get down here, Teresa."

She got down on the sweat-soaked pallet.

"On your hands and knees," he said.

"Not again!" she cried.

Ramón nodded. He got up on his knees beside her and passed an exploring hand under her massive, pendulous breasts while, with the other hand, he massaged her crotch.

"Please, Ramón," she pleaded. "I am sore. I ache."

"You?" He laughed softly.

"You will not do it again?"

"That depends, fat one."

"Upon what?"

"Is there someone hiding in this house?"

She stiffened. "What are you talking about?"

"You know."

It was very quiet. A cool draft crept through the chink where the large double doors came together and played over their sweating bodies.

He rammed his hand up into her sore crotch. She winced in pain. "Tell me," he insisted, "or..."

"I know nothing."

He pinched one of her large nipples. "Talk!" he snapped.

Oh, the pain of it! Oh, the shame of it! To give herself to this inhuman stud to protect her mistress' lover!

He reached down for his knife and placed the tip of it against her rounded belly. "Go on," he ordered.

"You'll let me go then?"

"Of course!"

"Yes, there is a man hidden in the house."

"The escaped heretic Captain Cutlass?"

She shook her head. The knife tip drew blood. "For the love of God!" she cried hysterically. "Yes! Yes! Yes!"

"He's in her room?"

"That is where he hides," she admitted.

"And in her bed as well?"

"I don't know."

"You lie! He is said to be a stud. I'll swear she is a real woman now and no longer a virgin."

Teresa nodded. She looked sideways and up into his shadowy face. "What will you do?" she asked.

"I haven't made up my mind yet. There is a reward of one thousand *ocho reales* for him."

"You'd take the money of the Inquisition?" she demanded hotly.

"Money is money," he said dryly.

"His men have offered much more than that for his return."

"How much?"

"Two thousand *ocho reales*, it is said."

Ramón whistled softly. "You are sure of this?"

"It is so."

Ramón threw his knife to one side. "It makes a man think," he murmured, almost as though to himself.

Teresa tried to get up, but a firm hand pressed her back down so that she again rested on her hands and plump knees. She slid her eyes sideways to look at him. She was deathly afraid of this strange man.

Faint gray dawn light came through the door chink.

Ramón stood up and stretched himself.

"You said you'd let me go," Teresa said.

"In time, fat one."

"Oh, my god! Not again!" she cried.

Her head was slammed hard against the wall as he

mounted her with the drive and virility of a breeding stallion.

* * *

Rafaela raised her head from the pillow. Faint gray dawn light showed through the chinks of the shutters. She heard the panel in the back of the wardrobe slide softly back. Her gowns rustled as they were pushed aside. She saw the dim, shadowy figure of a man dressed in funereal black step out into the room. He reached back between some of the gowns and pressed the hook that closed the panel.

"Alec?" she queried.

Alec turned. "The same," he said in a dispirited tone.

"Where have you been?"

He walked across the room and lighted a candle. As he turned, she saw that he was plastered in mud and slime from his feet up to his midthighs. He had left a trail of muddy footprints across the thick rug in the center of the hardwood floor. There was mud on his face and his hands.

"You tried the jungle," she said quietly.

Alec nodded. He reached for a wine bottle and drank deeply from it. He wiped his mouth with the back of a muddy hand and seemed to be looking right through her to a vista of his beloved sea with his ship riding upon it.

"You didn't tell me, Alec."

"Aye, lassie. I couldna bear to say goodbye."

"You damned liar!"

He smiled crookedly. "Ye think ye know me so well, lassie. Not so."

"No one knows you! Your own mother never knew you!"

He shrugged. "'Strewth," he murmured.

She didn't want to tell him. Oh God, she didn't want to let him know that the Inquisition guards suspected that he had not died in the harbor the rainy dark night he had escaped from his guards and into the sanctuary of her home and bed.

Alec came close to the bed and looked down at her. Her lustrous dark hair was spread over the pillow, and her great, lovely eyes studied him soberly. "Ye knew this couldna last, Rafaela. I must return to my ship and my men."

"And your trade?" she sneered. "My profession," he corrected her stiffly. Alec filled a wineglass for her and sat down on the bed, heedless of the mud stains he placed upon the coverlet. She sat up, and the coverlet fell from her to reveal her bare, full breasts. She took the wineglass from his hand and drank it greedily. She handed it back to him, and he refilled it.

Alec studied her. "What is it ye are holding back from me?"

"Nothing, Alec."

He shook his head. "Ye may not know me, lassie, but I know ye. What is it that's bothering ye?"

"The Inquisition guards are searching the city every night now, trying to find you. They do not believe you died in the harbor."

"Sweet Jesus!" He jumped to his feet and looked toward the door.

"It's locked, Alec. This is the house of Don Pedro. They wouldn't dare enter here without permission."

He looked down at her and shook his head. "Not so. Those human bloodhounds can go anywhere that devil Humana sends them. I'll have to leave now, Rafaela."

"You don't know the jungle!" she cried.

"I'd rather die in that stinking morass than to wait here for them to come for me."

Quick tears sprang into her eyes. She turned her head away from him. "Please stay a little longer," she pleaded. Alec shrugged. He stripped himself of his soaked clothing. He drank deeply from the wine bottle. He withdrew his broadsword from its sheath and placed it on the floor close to the bed as he did every night. He placed his three pistols and dirk on the bedside table.

Alec slowly pulled the coverlet from her lovely nakedness. She lay there like a luscious seed in a great pod. She shivered a little in the cool air.

"Ye'll be warm soon enough, lassie," he promised her.

Alec lay down beside her and gathered her into his arms.

She rested her head on his chest and sobbed softly. He patted her head. "There, there, lassie," he soothed her.

They lay there together while the dawn light grew.

"You'll stay awhile longer, then?" she asked.

Alec nodded. "Of course."

She opened herself to him as he kissed her. It was a lovely and gentle thing, on this cold gray morning, almost like a considerate bridegroom with a child bride. They both knew this would probably be their last time together, but neither one of them spoke about it. *Remember this well,* Rafaela thought, *I'll never forget this,* passed through Alec's mind.

There was mingled sadness and joy in the act. At last, she fell trustingly asleep in his arms. He lay there for a long time looking upward with eyes that did not really see the ornate cover of the four-poster bed. Instead, he saw a sparkling blue sea with white swirls of foam and a lovely frigate under full sail.

TWENTY-ONE

Alec Campbell stood at one of the windows in Rafaela's bedchamber that overlooked the garden patio. The soft dusk light had already begun to form shadows within the patio. It was Sunday. Hours earlier, Rafaela had gone to the church accompanied by Teresa. She had not wanted to go, but her absence might be noted by the religious-minded busybodies of Porto Bello. She had insisted that Alec not attempt the jungle again unless she could find a guide for him. Alec had waited as she had requested him to do. He had no great desire to enter that green hell beyond the city walls again unless he did have a guide. Still, where would she find such a guide? Few if any of the Spaniards in the city knew the jungle. The Indians in the jungles and the *cimarrones,* the savage product of runaway male Black slaves and Indian women, hated the Spaniards with a venom almost beyond belief. Rafaela could hardly contact any of them to guide Alec through the jungle to the sea coast many leagues to the south. The only Indians and *cimarrones* to be found in the city would be prisoners, and most of those captured were summarily executed.

Alec lifted a wine bottle to his lips. It was almost empty. He looked about the big room. The pleasant, sensual memories of his short span of time there with Rafaela had already begun to fade in his mind, to be overwhelmed by an intense desire to leave this self-imposed prison. It had always been so with him; the land and the life of the people who lived there, particularly those people of the cities, had always been against his very nature. He was a creature of the wild and misty hills of his native Scotland and of the wild and restless sea. No one had ever been able to hold him back for very long when the call of the sea came to him.

"The call of the sea is the greatest love song the world has ever known," the quiet voice seemed to say from behind Alec.

Alec whirled, dropping his right hand to his dirk.

There was no one there.

It was not the first time he had heard such words, and always there had been no one there to say them.

Alec raised the wine bottle. It was empty. He looked out into the patio. The dusk had faded almost imperceptibly into night.

Alec gently unlocked the door. He eased out into the hallway. The house was in complete darkness. He knew Teresa had gone with Rafaela, but Ramón, the porter, was usually somewhere around the house.

Alec worked his way quietly down the stairs to the ground floor. It was deathly quiet. He padded through the ground-floor rooms. There was no one in any of them. He returned to the *sala* and opened the wine cabinet. He took a bottle of fine Madeira from it and pulled out the cork with his teeth. He upended the bottle and drank deeply. He lowered the bottle and wiped his mouth with the back of a hand.

There was a subtle, brooding uneasiness in the darkened house. It was almost as though some unseen evil creatures were watching him thoughtfully from shadowed corners. It seemed as though someone or something slowly traced a line down his back with the tip of an icicle. Damn that Celtic imagination of his!

Alec raised the bottle. He suddenly put it down and turned to look through the darkened entryway toward the large double doors that opened to the street. He tip-toed to the doorway and placed an ear hard against one of the doors. At that instant, a key inserted from the outside turned in the lock.

Alec whirled. He ran into the *sala* and up the stairs. The

doors swung open and crashed against their stone stops. A flood of torchlight flowed into the entryway and partway into the *sala*. Alec dropped flat on his face at the top of the stairs and bellied his way toward Rafaela's room.

"Show us the woman Rafaela's room, you halfbreed bastard!" a hoarse voice shouted.

They tramped into the *sala*. A man was hurled to the floor and was booted freely about the ribs. It was Ramón, the porter. Blood trickled from his mouth and nostrils. There were six armed men standing about the prostrate porter— Inquisition guards.

"Upstairs," Ramón gasped.

"Show us the way!"

Alec stood up. He was still in shadows. He drew his broadsword with his right hand and his dirk with his left hand. He wanted no pistol shots to alert whoever might be outside in the street.

Ramón came slowly up the stairs, prodded by the point of a sword. He turned to progress along the hallway and then he saw a dark shadowy figure quickly enter Rafaela's room. Ramón stumbled and went down on one knee. He grunted in savage pain as the flat of the sword struck him full force across the shoulders.

Alec left the bedchamber door unlocked. There was nothing that belonged to him lying about the chamber. All his possessions were on his body, just his clothing and weapons. He ran quickly across the room to the wardrobe and reached inside to press down the hook. He heard harsh voices in the hallway outside of the bedchamber door. He squirmed in through the fragrant-smelling gowns and through the open panel. He slid it shut behind himself just as the bedchamber door was booted open.

Alec felt his way slowly down the dark narrow passageway to the cellar. He entered the vaulted chamber and felt his way across it to the doorway at the foot of the stairs that led up to the ground-floor kitchen. He eased open the door and passed into the kitchen and from there into the hallway that led to the front of the house.

The front doors had been left ajar. Alec peered out into the darkened street. The street was empty. He closed the doors and locked them and took the key with him. He stole into the *sala* and looked up toward Rafaela's bedchamber. The sound of harsh voices and the crashing of furniture and the wanton breaking of glass came to him.

Alec worked his way quickly up the stairway with bared blades in his hands.

Sergeant Alejandro Calva lifted the coverlet and sheets from Rafaela's bed with the blade of his sword. He sniffed the faint scent of her perfume and grinned loosely. He looked back at Ramón, who was standing with his back to the wall while Corporal Enrique Chavez held his sword point at Ramón's throat, while pushing up his chin with the blade.

"So, the little *puta* had a heretic in her bed with her all these weeks, eh, bastard?" the sergeant asked.

"I know nothing of that!" Ramón gasped.

Sergeant Calva grinned again. "That fat pig Teresa told us it was so. Of course, we had to put a touch of fire to the bottoms of her flat feet before she'd talk. We could get nothing out of Rafaela, the *puta*, no matter what we tried with her."

A Highland fury came charging into the room. *"Cru-achan!"* he yelled. One sword thrust pierced the back of the guard nearest him. Alec leaped over the falling body and thrust deep into the guts of another guard, withdrew and slashed sideways with a Highland drawing stroke that opened the third guard's face from temple to chin point. He shrieked once and died with a dirk thrust clear up under his ribs into his heart.

Corporal Chavez whirled with outthrust sword. Ramón brought his clenched hands down in a smashing blow to the nape of Chavez's neck. Ramón closed in on another guard before the man had wits and reaction enough to half draw his sword. Ramón kicked him in the groin, and as his head came down involuntarily, Ramón raised a knee up under his face to drive his head backward. Ramón jerked the man's sword the rest of the way from its sheath and sank it into his belly.

Sergeant Calva backed away from Alec, watching him warily, while his sword point described a small circle out in front of him. His five men had died so fast, Calva still found it hard to believe.

Ramón turned toward the sergeant with bloodied blade advanced.

"No," Alec said quietly. "He's mine."

"He tortured Teresa, my woman!" Ramón shouted.

"He slandered the name of Rafaela," Alec countered. "Stand back, or by God I'll cut ye down out of the way!"

Calva grinned. He was the best guards swordsman in Porto Bello. "Come on, heretic," he invited.

The attack came so fast and with such controlled ferocity that Calva was caught unawares. A sword point pierced his left wrist and he dropped his dagger. He counterthrust with his sword and had it twisted out of his grip so that it flew across the room and clattered against the wall.

"Mercy, for God's sake," Calva pleaded. He died with the words hardly out of his mouth.

Alec turned to Ramón. "Where have they taken Rafaela and Teresa?"

"To the Fort of San Juan."

"Get some weapons. Follow me!"

Ramón stared at the mad *Escocés*. *"There?"* he asked incredulously.

"Get moving!"

Ramón took his courage in his hands. "You'll die. We'll both die. The streets are full of soldiers. There are patrols with bloodhounds outside the walls trying to find your trail. It will only be a matter of time before they come here looking for this dog of a sergeant and his men."

The blind fury faded slowly from Alec's mind.

"Get out of here while you can," Ramón said.

"Do you know the way through the jungle to the coast south of here?"

Ramón smiled. "Like the palms of my hands, *Escocés.*"

A thudding sound emanated from downstairs. Alec ran to the door and looked over the railing. The front door was being battered in. Alec turned back into the room and locked the door.

Alec turned on a heel. "Arm yourself! Follow me!"

Alec reached in between some gowns and pressed the

hook down. The panel slid open. Alec jerked his head at Ramón. "Get in there," he ordered.

Ramón grinned. "I had heard there was such a secret way but never knew where it was. They never told me."

"For good reason, porter."

Ramón looked back over a shoulder. "Why?" he asked.

"Betrayal. *Vámonos!*"

Alec stepped into the wardrobe and then turned his head to look back into the bedchamber. He did not see the sprawled and bloody corpses of the guards but rather a lovely young woman, with a gown that bared her ivory shoulders, and whose great dark eyes looked at him in a way no other woman' had ever done.

He closed the wardrobe door and stepped through the panel. He slid the panel closed behind himself and heard the catch click.

"It's dark as Hades down there," Ramón murmured.

"There are candles in the cellar vault. Get moving!"

They worked their way slowly down the narrow staircase until they reached the bottom of it. Alec opened the panel into the cellar. They could hear thudding footsteps on the floor above their heads. They snatched up candles and a lantern and whatever food they could find. Alec found a container of black powder, some flints, and bullets of a caliber that would fit his pistols. Ramón picked up a short-barreled caliver with its powder and bullet flask and some lengths of slow match.

Footsteps sounded on the kitchen floor above their heads. Alec shoved Ramón through the panel opening and jumped in behind him just as someone opened the door at the top of the stairway to the kitchen.

Alec led Ramón through the darkness to the vaulted tunnel. He lighted a small candle lantern he had picked up. They heard no sound in the tunnel other than the steady, insistent dripping of water.

"You've been down here before, eh?" Ramón asked.

Alec nodded. "A few times," he admitted.

"Where does it lead?"

"Under the city wall to the jungle beyond."

"Let's hope a patrol with bloodhounds is not waiting for us."

Alec looked sideways at the halfbreed. "They'll no stand in my way."

Ramón nodded. "I can see that, *Escocés.*"

Alec led the way into the depths of the tunnel. The floor slanted down and soon they were wading calf-deep in stagnant water. The air became foul and the candle flickered feebly within the lantern.

Ramón began gasping for air. "I can't go on," he said.

"Stay here then, damn you!" Alec snapped. "It's only a little way further."

Alec stopped. He blew out the candle. He drew one of his pistols and held it in his left hand while he held his broadsword in his right hand. "Load that caliver," he whispered over a shoulder. "If we're seen, there will be no going back. It's either the freedom of the jungle for us, or death. We have no other choices."

The halfbreed loaded the big-bored musket. The sound of the charge and bullet being tamped home sounded inordinately loud in the tunnel. Then it was deathly quiet again.

"Ready?" Alec whispered.

"Go on," Ramón replied.

"Hold on to my belt."

Slowly, foot by foot, they worked their way through the stygian blackness of the tunnel.

"Wait," Alec hissed.

In a moment Ramón felt a draft of cooler air playing about himself.

"Quiet," Alec whispered.

Alec pushed back the thick vegetation that shrouded the narrow mouth of the tunnel. He scrambled up a short, steep slope and turned to help Ramón up beside him.

Ramón looked about himself. He ducked involuntarily as he saw the ramparted city walls looming up in the darkness two hundred yards behind them. It was hard for him to realize they had passed under those massive walls.

Alec grinned. "So far so good, eh, Ramón?"

Ramón nodded.

It was rather quiet except for the subdued sounds of the

nocturnal life of the jungle letting itself be known by buzzings, hummings, clickings, and soft, muted calls that suddenly died away.

Ramón quickly stood up. He turned his head from one side to the other.

"What is it?" Alec whispered.

Ramón shook his head.

Minutes dragged slowly past.

"Listen," Ramón said softly.

Faintly, from somewhere to their right and seemingly from along the base of the city walls, came the mournful baying of bloodhounds.

"Christ's wounds!" Alec gasped. He turned to run into thicker cover.

"Wait!" Ramón snapped. "Don't run like that ever in the jungle. Take your time. Follow me."

"How long will it take to reach the coast?" Alec asked.

"Where?" Ramón queried.

"Near Isla de las Mulatas."

"Five days at least through the jungle."

"Can we do it in three days?"

Ramón looked back at Alec. "I can, *Escocés*. Can you?"

Alec nodded. "Try me, Ramón."

"Why Isla de las Mulatas?"

"There is a rendezvous there."

"How many ships and men?"

"Enough, Ramón, enough…"

Ramón shrugged. "We can cut in toward the coast in two days and get a pirogue from my people. You can sail it then to where you want to go."

Alec nodded. He followed the halfbreed on through the dark jungle. There would be a moon later on that evening. Somewhere behind them bloodhounds bayed. They sounded closer this time.

Ramón looked back at Alec. "They have our trail, *Escocés*. We'll have to move faster."

"Go on!"

"It will be dangerous."

Alec grinned at him. "What isn't around here?"

The halfbreed lengthened his stride. They splashed

through water and cut their way through matted vegetation with their swords. The sweat streamed from their bodies and stung the many cuts and insect bites that had begun to affect them.

The new moon rose and bathed the jungle in a pale, soft light.

Alec looked up at the sweat-soaked back of Ramón as the guide led the way at a fast pace across a wide savannah that was inches deep in water. What had been his real role in the devious drama which had been played out there in Porto Bello that Sunday? Who had betrayed Rafaela and Teresa? Who else could have known that Alec Campbell had been hiding in the bedchamber of Rafaela de Vasquez all those weeks?

TWENTY-TWO

T he frigate *Adventuress* lay anchored fore and aft in a cove on the Isla de las Mulatas. Her starboard batteries covered the entrance to the cove. Four tall ships cruised slowly back and forth off the island, waiting for the frigate to make her break for freedom. Joshua Swan, Jan Van Schouten, Patrick Quinlan, and Kate Devon had finally tracked down the *Adventuress*.

An Indian *pirogue* fitted with a ragged scrap of sail had come from the Panama coast that day. The lookouts on the four buccaneer ships had scanned the tiny craft with their telescopes, then had reported to the deck of their respective ships that the two occupants of the *pirogue* were nothing but Indians and a wild enough looking pair at that.

The *pirogue* dipped deeply as it sailed through the reef channel to enter the calm waters of the cove within musket shot of the *Adventuress*. The ragged sail was dropped and the two Indians began to paddle toward the frigate.

"What do you want?" Rais Gilles shouted in Spanish.

One of the Indians stood up. "A clean change of clothing, a decent meal, a good bottle of wine, and command of my ship again, in the order named, Frenchman!"

"By God!" Rais shouted. "It's Cutlass!"

The cove rang and echoed with the cheers of the officers and crew of the *Adventuress* as Alec Campbell came alongside her. He was barefooted, and his filthy clothing was in rags. A dirty cloth was bound about his long hair. The instant he set foot on the deck of the ship he was surrounded by his excited crew.

Rais Gilles shook his head. "I can't believe it. How in God's name did you escape from the Inquisition this time?"

Alec shrugged carelessly. "I did it once before, ye ken. So, I had the practice. The second time it was somewhat easier."

"You're lying, Cutlass! Dave Heckart told us what you went through in Porto Bello."

"Heckart? Where did ye see him? The last I heard of him, he had been sentenced to the galleys."

Heckart pushed his way through the men crowded about Alec. "I was, captain, but thank God the *Adventuress* met the ship I was on off the coast and captured her. Devereux and Jarman were with me, and there were thirty other prisoners aboard who are now members of the *Adventuress'* crew."

"And we took forty thousand pieces-of-eight from the same ship," Miles Yeoman put in.

"Can I borrow two thousand of those *ocho reales* against our next venture?" Alec asked. "After all, ye did offer that sum as a reward for the man who saved me from the Inquisition." Alec jerked a thumb at Ramón. "He stands there," he added.

Ian MacMillan eyed the savage-looking Ramón. "We could drop him over the side at sea," he suggested out of the side of his mouth, "and save our two thousand."

Alec shook his head. "I gave him my word. Besides, we may have further need for him, if ye agree to my plan for a new venture."

Miles Yeoman opened a bottle of Canary when all the officers had assembled in the great cabin. They chatted idly with Alec as he bathed in a tub and then dressed himself in fresh clothing. They noted the fresh scars of the recent lashing he had sustained on his back.

Alec dropped into his customary chair at the head of the table. "What think ye of taking Porto Bello?" he asked casually.

For a moment, no one spoke and then Rais Gilles broke the silence: "I've always thought of you as being a little mad,

Cutlass. Now, I am sure the Inquisition has completed that task."

"It can't be done by sea," Ian MacMillan added. "We've not got the weight of a cannon to beat those fortresses into submission, even if we had the help of those four ships lying off the island waiting for us to sail forth."

Terence Shannon nodded. "And, if we did get past the fortresses, our losses would likely be too great for us to carry the city."

"Not to mention the great damage the ships would suffer and possibly the loss of some of them," Miles Yeoman put in.

Alec looked about at his officers. "I did not mean by sea, mates," he said quietly.

"By land, then? Impossible!" Rais Gilles cried.

"Henry Morgan did it," Alec reminded the Frenchman.

"But he had guides through the swamps. You know they're impassable except to the local Indians."

Alec nodded. "Exactly! Ramón, the halfbreed Ian wanted to drop over the side, is such a guide."

Ian MacMillan leaned forward. "So, we have a guide. But at what cost to march through those stinking swamps? We'd have to leave men aboard the *Adventuress* tae take care of her. We'd have but a handful of men left by the time we reached Porto Bello."

"True," Alec agreed, "but, we've four fine fightin' ships lying just off this island, crammed tae the marks wi' the best fighting men in the New World. Wi' them, we could carry the city."

Rais studied Alec. "I'm right. They did drive you mad at last."

"Listen to me!" Alec cried. "I escaped from the city by a secret way, unknown to the Spaniards themselves, with the exception of Don Pedro de Vasquez and his daughter. Ramón now knows it too, for we escaped from the city by means of that way. If we can reach the city by land, I can lead a few men into the city and open a gate for the rest of ye."

"There's a catch, Cutlass," Terence Shannon said.

"We've not been too friendly with our friends off the island. Who's to convince *them* that they'd gain by joining us?"

"That's my job, Terry," Alec replied. "After stickin' your sword into Kate Devon's arm and disabling her ship? After taking the Spanish women back to Porto Bello and losing them without a *centavo* of ransom money?"

"She's only one of four captains. If Quinlan, Van Schouten, and Swan listen to my proposition, Katie will have to go along. Further, if her crew learns she has refused to join up with us to take Porto Bello, ye know what will happen to her."

"Still," Miles Yeoman said thoughtfully, "if they do agree to join us, they'll outnumber us about five to one. Betrayal could be an easy course for them."

Alec shrugged. "Two men know the way into the city without being seen, Ramon and me. They'd hardly betray us *before* they reached Porto Bello, and once the whole command is within the gates, the immense loot to be taken in the city will blind them to anything else."

Rais nodded. "It's a risk, but it could be well worth it."

Alec stood up and looked about the table at the others. "Well?" he asked. "Are there any of ye others who are against this venture?"

No one spoke. Terence Shannon reached out a long arm to the sideboard. "Then we'd better drink on it, mates," he said with a grin.

The longboat of the *Adventuress* footed along with a fine breeze filling her lugsails. A white parley flag snapped at the small jackstaff in her bows.

Roche Brasiliano lowered his telescope. "It's Cutlass, captain," he said over a shoulder.

Kate Devon's eyes widened. "Impossible! We heard he was in the hands of the Inquisition."

"See for yourself, then," Roche offered. He handed Kate the telescope.

Kate focused the telescope on the sternsheets of the longboat. She drew in a sharp breath. The familiar figure of Alec Campbell seemed to swim into view in the lens. There was no mistaking Cutlass—the plumed hat, the shining metal pistols hanging from his baldric, the big nose and scarred face.

Kate whirled. She pulled out the breechblock of a falconet swivel gun. "Get me powder, ball, and a slow match!" she shouted. "I'll put a three-pound ball into his damned Scots belly!"

A gunner's mate came running with the cannonball, a powder charge, and a length of burning slow match. Kate shoved the ball into the breech chamber and followed it with the powder charge. She reset the breechblock and hammered home the wedges.

"Wait, captain," Roche said.

Kate turned on him in a fury. "You hate his guts as much as I do, you damned mustee!" she snapped.

"What the hell is the matter with you?" Roche demanded. "He's probably got a damned good reason for risking his neck by coming out here flying that parley flag."

"I don't trust him! I'll never trust him again!"

Kate poured priming powder into the touchhole and reached for the burning slow match. She applied it to the touchhole. Roche Brasiliano instantly shoved the barrel of the swivel gun upward just as it spat flame and smoke. A ghostly plume of spray arose far astern of the longboat.

Kate turned on Roche. She dropped a hand to one of her pistols, but the mustee was too fast for her. He gripped her wrists. "You damned bitch!" he hissed.

"He's mine! Not yours! Let him come aboard and I'll caponize him before I kill him!"

Alec whistled softly as the cannonball hummed over the longboat. "Come about, Heckart! That was likely just a warning shot."

Wally Dahlman trimmed the foresheet. "We won't outrun the next one, sir."

"Cutlass, you Scots bastard!" Kate shrieked. "Come back and fight like a man! You yellow-bellied bastard son of a diseased halfbreed whore! I'll slit your gizzard! I'll…" Her voice was suddenly cut off as though someone had clamped a hand over her foul mouth.

"Captain Campbell!" Roche Brasiliano shouted through

a speaking trumpet. "Come alongside, sir! There'll be no more trouble for you, I guarantee that!"

"I will on one condition, Brasiliano! Signal to the other captains to meet me aboard your ship!"

"For what purpose, you Scots Judas?" Kate roared.

"A business proposition, Katie!" Alec replied. "A plan I have that can make all of us rich as Croesus!"

"I've heard that from you before, Cutlass!"

"All right then, lassie! I'll sail over tae the others and forget about ye!"

"You'll get a three-pound ball up your ass if you do!"

Alec grinned. "What have ye got to lose? Ye're gaining nothing by pleasure cruising around these waters."

"What's this proposition of yours?"

"To take Porto Bello, Katie!"

"I'll give you a count of ten to get out of range of this falconet, you damned Judas!"

"Time to say farewell," Dave Heckart murmured.

Alec sat down in the sternsheets. "Come about, Davie."

"So she'll get a better shot?" the bosun asked wryly.

Alec shook his head. "Look," he said. He pointed toward the *Kate of Devon. A* string of signal flags was creeping up the mizzen halyard. "She's calling on the others for a parley."

An hour later Alec Campbell held the attention of Joshua Swan, Jan Van Schouten, Patrick Quinlan, and Kate Devon in the familiar great cabin of the *Kate of Devon.* "The combined force for the landing party should be about five hundred men. We've got to leave enough men aboard the ships to handle them and fight them if Jack Spaniard comes upon them off Porto Bello. Don Rodrigo de Mendez is said to have gone to Havana with his squadron, but we have no assurance of that. The present garrison of Porto Bello, outside of the fortress troops, is about a *tercio* of infantry. A *tercio* usually numbers about five hundred men, but fever cuts down that number, at least in Porto Bello. Even so, there should be about three hundred and fifty of them left after a year's service in Porto Bello and in the swamps around the city. Counting other troops in the city, guards, and so forth, there should be about five hundred fighting men to defend the city."

"Militia!" Josh Swan scoffed.

Alec shook his head. "Regulars."

"How do you plan to get past the city walls?" Jan Van Schouten asked. "We've not got enough men for a frontal assault."

"Ye can leave that up to me, Jan. If my plan works, ye can all walk into the city through one of the gateways."

Pat Quinlan studied Alec. "And we're supposed to go ahead on your say-so that you can do that for us?"

"That's about the size of it," Alec admitted.

"It's a helluva risk," Quinlan said.

Alec smiled. "What isn't in this profession of ours? Besides, think of the rewards. By God, I think we could all retire on what we can loot in Porto Bello."

"I've heard you promise that before," Kate said dryly.

Alec shrugged. "There's a nae need for any of ye to go, if ye lack the heart for it. After all, it is work for *men*…"

"Damn you!" Kate snapped.

Alec grinned at her. "Temper, temper, lassie." He looked about the table. "Will ye vote on it now?"

Jan Van Schouten nodded. "Count me in," he said.

"I'll go," Josh Swan said.

Pat Quinlan nodded. "I'm for it."

They all looked at Kate Devon.

Kate drained her wineglass. "I want until dawn tomorrow."

Alec shook his head. "By dawn tomorrow we should be closing the land."

"I'm not convinced yet!" she snapped.

"We can always go on without ye," Josh Swan threatened.

She sniffed. "Go on! You need my men to take the city and my ship to take them off when the venture is completed."

"She's got us there," Quinlan admitted.

Jan Van Schouten stood up. He was no fool. Kate's ploy was obvious. She wanted time alone with Cutlass. "I'll get back to my ship, mates. There's much to be done."

"Aye," Pat Quinlan agreed.

Josh Swan nodded. "Ye'll signal us either way, then?" he asked.

"Before dawn light," Kate replied.

The door closed behind the last of them.

Kate lighted a candle. "You sly sonofabitch," she murmured. "How did you manage to get around those three sharks? They swore they'd kill you on sight."

Alec shrugged. "So did ye, Katie," he reminded her.

"I could have sunk you with that falconet."

Alec shook his head. "Ye could have, but ye didn't. Ye never could and ye never will."

She studied him in the growing candlelight. "Aye," she agreed. "But you had no right to disable my ship."

"Wrong, lassie. At that time ye would have killed me and sunk my ship. Ye were mad with hate and jealousy then."

She narrowed those lovely green eyes of hers. "Hate? Yes! Jealousy? Hell, no!"

Alec shrugged. "Perhaps I *was* mistaken."

"You speak now of that Spanish milksop? That muling, puking, baby girl? That helpless bit of virgin fluff?"

Alec had an instant recollection of being in the great bed of Rafaela's bedchamber.

Kate refilled the wineglasses. "No matter, Cutlass. Let's do business. You claim we can make our fortunes there in Porto Bello?"

"Aye, Katie. No question about it."

"You think I should throw in with the rest of you?"

Alec eyed her. "Ye always intended to, didn't ye?" he asked quietly.

She looked away from him. "Of course."

"Well, ye've made a wise decision for a woman. Ye can stay safe aboard this ship while the rest of us will wade waist-deep through stinking mud, harassed by every stinging, biting, and sucking kind of beasties the devil thought up to plague all mankind."

Kate shook her head. "No, Alec, for I'm going with you on this land venture."

He stared at her. "Are ye mad? Tis nae place for a woman!"

"Alec, if I sign the Articles for this venture, that means I have committed my ship and my command to it. Shall I sit safe aboard the *Kate of Devon* while the rest of you attack Porto Bello and maybe make off with all the loot?"

"I'll look after your, interests, lassie."

She shook her head. "I have every right to go."

"That is true, as a ship's commander, but think of the risks, Katie."

"I have, Alec. Have you?"

"What do ye mean?"

She leaned forward. "You're in excellent condition for a man who spent weeks in an Inquisition dungeon. You could not have left Porto Bello directly from that dungeon. Somewhere you gained strength to attempt the jungle."

Alec nodded. "That's so, Kate."

"Why don't you tell me the real reason for your returning there, against all the risks you've plainly laid out for me?"

Alec drained his wineglass. He reached for the wine bottle. "The place is like an open-air gold mine, Kate. There is enough loot in Porto Bello to make us rich for the rest of our lives. I..." His voice died away as he saw the look in her eyes. "Ye know, don't ye?" he asked quietly.

"Do you love her that much, Alec?"

He could not look at her. "I don't know, Kate."

"But, you must go back there on a desperate venture to find out. Is that it?"

"She saved my life. I owe her that much. Besides, she is in the hands of the Inquisition now, for aiding me."

"What will happen to her?"

"She will be brought to trial on that charge."

"And if she is proven guilty?"

He looked up at her. "She will be, have no fear of that. There is a man there, nay, a devil, who will see to that. She will be forced to wear the *San Benito* and will be condemned to the *quemadero*."

"The burning place..."

Alec nodded. "She will not escape that, Kate."

"And to save her, you'll risk five hundred men."

Alec shrugged. "They will go of their own free will. The reward will be well worth it."

"By God, but you're the sly one!" she cried.

He grinned at her. "Well, lassie, ye need not gang along."

She shook her red head. "Someone must back you up, Cutlass. It's up to me."

"Even after ye know why I'm truly going back there?"

She stood up. She nodded.

"But why, Katie?" he asked curiously.

"Man, man, there are times when I think you are the wisest of men, and other times, like now, when I think your brains have been addled by smelling too much gunpowder smoke!"

He looked up at her. "And which of the twa spirits struggling within me, lassie, do ye like the best?"

She rounded the table and bent close to him. "Dinna ye ken, ye muckle geit, ye?" she aped his broad Scots accent.

Alec drew her down to him. She slid her arms about his neck as she sat in his lap. She kissed him softly, working her luscious mouth against his. She drew back her head. "I'm glad ye stayed aboard," she murmured.

"I'll be gone before the dawn light," he reminded her.

Kate stood up. She walked into her sleeping cabin. She lighted a candle. When he entered the room, she lay nude on her bed with an arm across her eyes. He could see the puckered bullet hole in her left shoulder and the healing scar on her right bicep, two manmade blemishes on an otherwise perfect skin.

Alec stripped to the skin. He stood there for a time, feeling the cool breeze against his body. No matter how hard he tried, he could not get the mental vision of Rafaela out of his mind.

Kate lifted her arm. She looked up at Alec. "Blow out that damned candle, my Scots stud, and get down here on top of me, and let's to business on a matter that has been lacking these long weeks!" she cried.

Alec took her into his arms. This time, there was no mad lusting, no fierce and almost insensate ravaging of each other, but rather a gentle idyll which, when it was over, was a new and never-to-be-forgotten experience in their tempestuous on-again, off-again relationship.

Alec woke up in the dark of night. He could hear the woman breathing gently beside him. Sleep was strong within him. He leaned close to her warm softness. *"Rafaela,"* he murmured. Then he remembered where he was. He got up quickly and dressed, then left the cabin.

TWENTY-THREE

The daylight was almost gone. The last of the sunset still tinted the western sky and reflected from the many pools of water on the wide savannah. The thick, matted jungle that surrounded the savannah was strangely quiet. The mournful baying of bloodhounds suddenly broke the silence.

Ramón turned his head to look at Alec Campbell. "It must be a patrol from Porto Bello, *Escocés*. They're headed this way. They must be trailing someone."

A man broke out of the swamp tangle on the far side of the savannah. He staggered in his stride as he splashed through the many pools of rainwater. Once, he looked back over a shoulder as the bloodhounds bayed again. He ran directly toward where Alec, Ramón, and Tattoo lay hidden just within the edge of the jungle.

Five hundred men and one woman were slowly moving through the great morass behind Alec and his companions, after five arduous days' march from the Gulf of Darien.

Alec had planned to lead them to Porto Bello that evening before the full moon rose.

Ten Spaniards appeared on the far side of the savannah. Their three bloodhounds bayed in unison, along with the triumphant shouting of the Spaniards as they caught sight of the fugitive.

"Let the fugitive pass by," Alec ordered. "Tattoo, run ye

back to the company and bring up enough men to handle these eager Spaniards."

Tattoo vanished into the forest. A moment later, the escapee crashed into the cover of the trees and passed Alex and Ramón. Ramón thrust out a foot, and as the fugitive fell, Alec struck him behind the ear with the butt of one of his pistols. Tattoo reappeared, followed by a dozen men.

Alec held out a warning hand toward his men. "Let them pass and then move in behind them. No shooting. No quarter."

Alec drew his broadsword as Tattoo drew his cutlass. Steel scraped thinly as cutlasses were drawn from their scabbards.

The bloodhounds crashed into the leafy tangle, followed by the panting Spaniards. It was all over in a few minutes. The only sounds to be heard were the dull thudding and clashing of the cutlass blades, an occasional gasp from one of the Spaniards, and one yelp from a hound.

"Strip off their uniforms, helmets, and weapons," Alec ordered. "We'll need them to enter the city."

The fugitive sat up and gingerly felt the lump behind his left ear. "Don't you recognize me, Captain Campbell?" he asked.

Alec wiped the mud from the man's face. "By God! Billy Merrill! I thought the Inquisition had done for ye!"

Merrill grinned. "I'm here," he said simply.

"How did ye survive?"

"I told them I had been a Catholic and was repentant. They sentenced me to wear the *San Benito* for five years while working as a scullion in the monastery at Porto Bello. The monks hated the Inquisition. They took good care of me, but I couldn't see staying in Porto Bello for five long years. So, I ran away."

Josh Swan, Jan Van Schouten, Kate Devon, Patrick Quinlan, Rais Gilles, and Roche Brasiliano came through the tangle and grouped themselves about Alec and Merrill. Kate Devon stood a little way behind the others with her back against a tree. She was soaked to the waist in swamp filth. Her face was streaked with mud, and she was close to exhaustion. During the past two days, she had been carried through the morass by some of her men.

"Do the Spaniards suspect an attack on the city?" Josh Swan asked Merrill. "How many men do they have in the garrison? Are there any fighting ships in the harbor?"

Merrill nodded. "There have been rumors of an attack, but only by sea. Your ships were seen in the Gulf of Darien by a Spanish scouting *patache*. Some of the bigger guns in the land defenses have been moved to the harbor area. Some of the relief troops from Havana arrived two days ago. The rest of them are supposed to arrive within the week."

"Has the relieved garrison left the city?" Alec asked.

Merrill shook his head. "Not yet. They will likely stay there until the rest of the relief arrives."

"How many men in the city garrison now?" asked RaisGilles.

"About eight hundred and fifty, but there are more troops in the fortresses."

"How many men are due from Havana?" Jan Van Schouten queried.

"A *tercio* of infantry, say about five hundred men, sir."

Kate Devon passed a hand across her eyes. "If all this be true," she said wearily. "We'll be facing about a thousand or more Spanish troops within the city and the forts, with another five hundred due in from Havana."

Pat Quinlan nodded. "This venture is hopeless, mates."

"Damn it!" Alec snapped. "We've got the advantage of complete surprise. We've time yet before the rest of the relief troops get there."

"There are strong patrols in the streets every night now," Billy Merrill said quietly. "There are double sentries on the walls, and the gate guards have been doubled. A patrol is sent out of the city at dusk and returns there at dawn. It was that patrol that pursued me. The Spaniards have stationed strong units of infantry here and there in the city so that they can be rushed to any point of attack."

"Which means they might still suspect an attack by land," Quinlan suggested. "It isn't as though it wasn't done before now. Henry Morgan and Jack Coxon both took Porto Bello by land, but it's never been done by sea. The

Spaniards are not stupid enough to forget that fact. They may be looking to the sea, but they're keeping an eye on the jungle as well."

It was quiet in the jungle except for the slogging, squashing, and splashing footsteps of the tired men as they moved up through the swamp to reach the savannah.

"Maybe we'd better retreat while we can," Pat Quinlan said at last.

Foremost in the minds of every one of them was the stinking muddy hell of the past five days as the command moved slowly through the thick and pathless mangrove swamps with each man heavily laden with his provisions, weapons, powder, and ball, while many of them carried heavy sacks of grenades on their backs. The swamps were infested with all sorts of stinging, biting, and sucking insect life. Each man marched along with his own personal cloud of flies, gnats, and mosquitoes about his head, whose stings were like the stabs of red-hot needles. Leeches continually clung to their legs while sucking their blood. Chiggers burrowed under their toenails, then swelled and burst to spread infection. Their flesh had been lacerated by thorned growths and saw-edged grasses, and the resultant flow of blood had brought myriads of insects to thrive upon the feast. Poisonous snakes had accounted for a number of men. Long-tusked wild boars, startled in their accustomed solitude, had charged the marching men and had killed and wounded some of them before they had been shot or cut down. Jaguars had been seen trailing the column to pick up those who had fallen out from sickness or exhaustion. Above all, they had suffered from the humid tropical heat bearing down upon them so that the heavy air was difficult to breathe. Daily downpours of torrential warm rain had added to the enervating heat and had raised the water level of the swamps so that, at times, it was almost impossible to distinguish between land and water.

The faintest of dusk light remained. The entire body of raiders now stood ankle-deep in the water of the semi-flooded savannah, looking at their commanders, who stood apart from them, holding a low-voiced council of war.

There was no need to tell the men that all was not well; they had sensed it as soon as they had emerged from the swamp.

Alec looked about at the muddy, dispirited faces of the other officers. "We haven't much time," he reminded them. "What's it to be? To attack Porto Bello, or crawl back through the swamps with our tails between our legs?"

"I'll not go back, Cutlass," Kate Devon said quietly. "Nothing, not even death itself can make me go back through that stinking hell."

Jan Van Schouten smiled wryly. "I'd rather die in the streets of Porto Bello than run from the Spaniards."

Josh Swan nodded. "Ye can count on me, Cutlass."

"Who's to tell them?" Pat Quinlan asked. He gestured toward the waiting men.

Alec plucked a leech from his left calf and hurled it back toward the swamp. "If I am to tell them, I must tell them the truth. There can be no going back once we cross the savannah."

None of the others spoke.

Alec nodded. "So be it." He stepped apart from the others and faced the command. "Mates!" he called out. "We've just received the good news that the garrison of Porto Bello has been doubled and that more reinforcements can be expected within the coming week. If that happens, we'll be outnumbered at least two or three to one. We commanders have decided to press the attack on the city. If any of ye would return to your ships, he can do so without fear of reprisal from the company."

"The damned fool!" Roche Brasiliano growled.

"He knows what he's doing," Rais Gilles said.

"If any man feels he wants to return, he can step out of the ranks right now," Alec continued.

The men looked at each other out of the corners of their eyes. They shuffled their feet. Some of them looked over their shoulders at the brooding darkness of the swamps. None of them stepped forward.

Alec held up an arm for attention. "Henry Morgan took eight hundred thousand pieces-of-eight from Porto Bello. Jack Coxon took at least half that sum on his raid. There is still plenty more where that came from, plus other treasures.

Porto Bello is therefore a bank upon which we can make a great draft, lads, at the points of our cutlasses and the muzzles of our firearms. All it will take is a little guts, and we've got more than our share of that!"

It was quiet again except for the persistent humming of the mosquitoes. There seemed to be a hesitant, waiting tension among the men.

Alec drew his famed Highland broadsword. He flourished it over his head. "If our number is small, our hearts are great! And, the fewer persons we are, the more union and better shares we shall have of the spoil!"

A rippling murmur passed through the close-packed ranks of the buccaneers.

"The Scot has done it," Josh Swan said.

"Trust him," Jan Van Schouten added.

"Even if he leads us all to our deaths," Pat Quinlan put in dryly.

"He's the best among us!" Kate Devon cried.

Alec turned. "Ramón! Lead the way!" He followed the guide across the savannah, and he did not look back to see if he were being followed by the others.

The noise of a thousand feet splashing through water and mud drowned out any other sounds as the command followed behind Captain Cutlass for the assault on Porto Bello—the Treasure House of the Spanish Main.

TWENTY-FOUR

Alec Campbell slid back the panel in the cellar of the de Vasquez house. He stepped into the cellar, followed by the men of the *Adventuress'* crew who had volunteered to accompany him into the city, along with Tattoo and Ramón. The rest of the company of buccaneers waited near the mouth of the tunnel out beyond the city walls.

Alec stole up the cellar stairs to the door that opened into the kitchen. He eased open the door. There was no one in the kitchen. Alec crossed the room to the door which opened into a hallway. Faint light shone at the far end of the hallway. Alec felt his way along the dark hall until he could see into the *sala* at the end of it. Teresa sat at the table with a bottle of wine in front of her. As Alec watched, she upended the bottle and drank deeply from it with her throat working convulsively. She lowered the bottle and then stared incredulously at the man wearing the red and yellow uniform of a Spanish soldier who stood at the opposite side of the table.

"Don't cry out, Teresa," Alec warned. "It's me, Alec Campbell. Is there anyone else in the house?"

Teresa shook her head. "I am alone."

"Is Don Pedro in the city?"

"He's in the plaza. He's been there much of the day."

"Why?" Alec asked.

"The *quemadero*," Teresa replied simply.

"Is it because of Rafaela?" he asked quietly.

Teresa nodded. "She has already been sentenced and will be burned."

"How soon?"

"The bells of the church will toll just before she is committed to the flames."

Alec ran to the front door. He opened it and stepped out into the narrow street. A strong patrol of soldiers had just passed. The street was filled with many people hurrying toward the plaza to view the burning. There would be no surprise attack of the buccaneers through the tunnel and the house of Don Pedro. The risks would be too great.

Alec ran back into the house. "Heckart!" he shouted.

Dave Heckart and the others crowded into the *sala* where Teresa still sat with her wine bottle. She bolted from the room when she saw the fierce-looking faces staring at her from beneath the brims of the morion helmets. Ramón called after her, but she did not turn.

Alec took a bottle of wine from a cabinet and handed it to Heckart. "Drink quickly! Pass it along! The streets are filled with people going to the plaza, and there are street patrols just as Merrill said there would be. We've no chance of getting the whole command through the city without the garrison being warned, and we'd be cut to pieces before we had a chance. Ramón, get ye back to the command! Lead them to the nearest city gate, the one that is to the west of this house. *Vámonos!*"

The wine bottle went from hand to hand and ended up empty in the fireplace. "What's for us, captain?" Heckart asked.

Alec smiled faintly. "Tae get through the streets to the gate and get it open for the lads. We may be able to get past the Spanish patrols. We can't afford to be stopped. If we are stopped, and are forced to fight, *whoever survives must get tae the gate.*" Alec looked at Tattoo. "Get ye back tae the others, Tattoo. Ye'd be a dead giveaway for us, and even a Spanish uniform such as we are all wearing would never disguise that black face of yours."

"No, master!" Tattoo cried.

"Get ye gone!" Alec snapped.

Tattoo left the room. The others heard the cellar door close with a bang as the disgruntled black left the kitchen.

"Hang those sacks of grenades over your shoulders," Alec told Dave Heckart and Wally Dahlman, "and let's hope the Spaniards don't notice them."

Alec opened the front door and stepped out into the street. There were only a few people left in the street, and they were beyond the house, hurrying toward the plaza. Alec looked the other way. A party of monks was moving slowly toward him, evidently on their way to the *quemadero*.

"Quick!" Alec said over his shoulder. "Form in twos out here in the street!"

When the men had formed themselves into twos, Alec thrust out his right arm in the direction of the street that led to the closest gateway. *"Adelante!"* he commanded. They marched steadily behind him as he led the way.

As the column of slowly walking monks passed the deep doorway of the de Vasquez house, a dark figure moved out of the doorway just behind the last monk. Tattoo hooked an arm about the throat of the monk and quickly dragged him back into the house. He stripped the frightened monk of his cowled robe and then put it on himself. He raised the cowl to cover his head and pulled it forward on each side to conceal his face.

"Jesus bless me!" the monk cried. "What are you, man or demon from hell?"

Tattoo grinned. He thrust his face close to that of the Spaniard. "Debbil," he hissed. "You leave this house, I kill you on sight. You understand?"

The monk slumped into a senseless heap on the floor. Tattoo stepped over him and quickly left the house. He ran swiftly to catch up with the rear of the column of monks and took the place of the monk whose robe he had confiscated. When the monks turned into a street that led toward the plaza, Tattoo kept on walking in the direction where Alec Campbell and his men had gone.

The Spanish patrol turned a street corner a block ahead of Alec Campbell and his companions. A lantern hung from a pike point. The steady thudding of marching feet echoed from the high fronts of the houses on either side of the street.

"I'll try to bluff our way past them, lads," Alec said back over a shoulder. "If I don't succeed, the watchword is '*Cruachan!*'"

"Halt!" the sergeant leading the Spanish patrol commanded. His men came to a halt and grounded their pikes. "What unit, corporal?" the sergeant asked Alec.

Alec took a chance. The uniforms his men wore and those worn by the Spaniards had different-colored facings, indicating they belonged to different regiments. It was obvious that the Spaniards were of the relief unit that had just come to Porto Bello. "Second Company, that of Captain Diaz," Alec replied easily.

"Where are you coming from?" the sergeant asked.

"We were patrolling beyond the walls. We pursued a fugitive from the Inquisition. We caught him. We didn't bother to bring him back." Alec grinned.

The sergeant eyed the dark stains of mud on the uniforms. "Christ's Blood! You must have had a hard time of it in the swamps."

Alec nodded. "It's no fiesta."

The sergeant studied Alec. "You're light for a Spaniard, corporal," he said a little suspiciously. "You've got an accent, too."

Alec smiled. "My mother was a Fleming. She married a sergeant of artillery in the Low Countries. I'm the result."

The sergeant nodded. "Well, pass on then."

The two patrols passed each other. The last pike-man turned to look curiously after Alec, and as he did so, his pike struck the helmet from Wally Dahlman's head. Dahlman turned in a fury. "Watch what the hell you're doing, you clumsy bastard!" Dahlman roared in good King's English.

There was no time to waste. *"Cruachan!"* Alec shouted as he drew his broadsword.

The quiet of the street was broken only by the clashing of weapons, the harsh breathing of the combatants, and the thud of falling bodies until, at last, Alec and the surviving seven of his men stood looking down at the bodies of the dead. Garvey, Pyle, and Powers had been lost, a cheap enough price, but one the little party could ill afford.

"Take the pikes!" Alec ordered. "Fall in! Forward! At the double!"

They neared a side street that led into the plaza, which was a full city block away. The murmuring of the large crowd in the plaza came to them as Alec halted his command. Then suddenly, a bell tolled from the great church tower that dominated the plaza.

"There's not much time, captain," Dave Heckart ventured. "If the dead lying back there in the street are found…"

The bell tolled again.

Alec turned. "Davie, lad," he said quietly, "ye must make it tae the gate and open it for the others."

"What about you, sir?"

"The woman who saved my life from the Inquisition is about to be burned to death in yon plaza. I've got tae go tae her."

"You won't have a chance!"

"That may be, but I must go. Ye understand?"

"Not alone, then! The rest of us will go with you!"

Alec shook his head. "Ye'll need every man ye have left."

Big Wally Dahlman came forward. He patted the heavy sack of grenades he had carried all the way from the Gulf of Darien. "You'll need a grenadier to back you up, captain."

The bell tolled.

Alec nodded. "All right, Dahlman. Heckart, get tae the gate. Godspeed tae ye all!"

Alec and Dahlman trotted to the junction of the street and the plaza. The light from many torches and bonfires flickered against the fronts of the many buildings that surrounded the plaza. There was a solid mass of people between the four sides of the great opening in the center of the city. A platform had been erected at the foot of the wide steps that led up to the huge double doors of the church. The platform was filled with officials, both of the church and of the secular body of Porto Bello. A ring of Spanish pikemen held back the crowd from an open space before the platform. Combustible materials had been piled high in the open space. Within the open area were prisoners of the Inquisition wearing the hideous *San Benito*, a garment of coarse-red material emblazoned with a yellow St. Andrew's Cross on the back. The plaza was very quiet except for the mournful tolling of the bell and the faint murmuring voices of the densely packed people.

Alec climbed up into the back of a *carreta* so that he might look over the heads of the crowd. Don Estebán de Vargas, Steel Fist, was on the platform of the officials. Seated beside him was Don Pedro de Vasquez, the father of Rafaela. A black-robed man sat on a chair that was slightly higher than those of the other officials. Although Alec could not see his face because of the cowl that shadowed it, he had no doubt as to who the man was—Chief Inquisitor Padre Gaspar de Humana, of the Congregation of the Holy Office.

Then Alec saw Rafaela. She was garbed in a *San Benito* that was far too large for her. Her long disheveled hair hung partway in front of her pale face. Her slender wrists had been bound in front of her.

Alec dropped to the ground. "Dahlman," he said, "we've got to move fast. Rafaela is standing in front of that platform over there."

"Surrounded by fifty Spanish pikemen."

A cowled monk came toward them from the side street. As he neared them, he raised his head and pulled back his cowl a little, so that they might see his face.

"Damn you, Tattoo!" Alec snapped. "I told ye to get to hell out of the city to join the others!"

The black shook his head. "Where you go, I go, master."

"Well, anyway, that makes three of us now," Dahlman said dryly. "That should be enough to carry off any plan you might have in the way of taking the woman right out from under the noses of fifty Spanish soldiers."

Alec gripped Tattoo by an arm. "Get to the church. When the time comes, ye must help me get the woman inside of it! *Vámonos!*"

"For sanctuary? Here in Porto Bello?" Dahlman asked in

disbelief. "The Inquisition doesn't recognize sanctuary here, or anywhere else for that matter."

"I know. But the doors of the church are thick and strong. If we can get Rafaela into the church, we may be able to stand off the Spaniards until the rest of the lads get intae the city."

"You're mad, sir, begging your pardon. Is it asking too much to inquire if you have a plan of action?"

"There are no soldiers behind the platform of the officials. Now, if twa madmen, disguised as Spanish soliders wi' a grenade in one hand and a lighted slow match in the other, were tae get onto that platform, do ye think they might cow those officials and the soldiers long enough tae take the woman and get her into yon church before the Spaniards could get up enough courage tae stop them?"

Wally shrugged. "It's worth a try, captain." He rolled his eyes upward.

They worked their way around the rear of the crowd to the open space between the rear of the platform and the front of the church. They ducked under the platform. Dahlman struck flint and steel and lighted two lengths of slow match. He took six grenades from the sack and gave three to Alec. They each stuffed two grenades within their doublets and kept the third one in their hands. Dahlman slung the grenade sack over a shoulder. He nodded to Alec.

Alec got out from under the platform and calmly ascended the short flight of steps up to the top of it. He held the grenade and slow match in front of himself.

"Gentlemen, please do not make any threatening moves toward me and my mate here, or make any outcry. Some of you know me well. I will not hesitate to light this grenade. There is enough power within it to kill or wound the lot of you."

"What do you want, *Escocés?*" Don Esteban demanded harshly.

"I want Rafaela de Vasquez freed, and a written pardon for her."

Padre de Humana rose partway from his chair. He fixed his burning eyes on Alec's eyes as though to dominate him.

"Impossible!" he snapped. "The woman is a condemned heretic!"

A flicker of hope had shown in the sad eyes of Don Pedro until he had realized the utter futility of what Alec had demanded.

"I'll have you cut down!" Don Esteban shouted.

Alec smiled faintly. "Keep your voice down, Don Esteban. Ye are not on the parade ground now, sir. Or is it you want to die suddenly, blown to bloody bits, without the final rites of absolution?"

Don Bartolome de Esquivel, commander of the garrison of Porto Bello, squirmed in his seat. He kept his widened eyes fixed on the deadly-looking grenade in Alec's hand. "He's got a good point there, Don Esteban," he began. "I really think..." His voice died away as he saw the look in Don Esteban's eyes.

"There is not much time left," Alec warned them.

"Put down the grenade," Don Esteban suggested in a controlled voice. "Then we can talk business. I give you my word as a soldier of Spain that we will fairly consider your proposition."

Alec shook his head. "It is not a proposition, sir. It is a demand."

"We refuse that damned demand!" Don Esteban shouted.

Alec looked back over a shoulder into the taut face of Wally Dahlman. "Are ye ready, lad?" he asked.

"The match burns well, sir."

Sweat had begun to trickle down the face of Don Esteban. His eyes moved about as he sought desperately for a solution to the dangerous dilemma with which they all were faced.

"How far can they get, Esteban?" Don Bartolome asked out of the side of his mouth. "For the love of God, let him have the woman before he blows us all to hell!"

Don Esteban got slowly to his feet. "Captain de Anza!" he called out to the commander of the pikemen. "Release the prisoner Rafaela de Vasquez to this man! Allow them to leave the *quemadero!*"

Alec smiled. *"Gracias, mil gracias,* Don Esteban!"

Rafaela looked up at Alec as he cut the bonds about the wrists. Her eyes widened, and she slumped into his arms in a dead faint. Alec lifted her over his left shoulder and drew his broadsword. He looked back at Dahlman and nodded.

"For God's sake, Captain Cutlass!" one of the twelve prisoners of the Inquisition who had been condemned that day to the galleys called out. "We are all good Englishmen here! Let us go with you! We'll fight to the death with our bare hands rather than submit to being sent to the galleys."

"Cut them loose," Alec ordered the Spanish officer. "Ye men, take weapons from the Spaniards. Move fast! Follow us tae the church!"

Tattoo stood at the top of the steps in front of the church. He still wore his monk's gown, but now he flourished his cutlass. The huge double doors of the church stood open behind him. "The church is empty, master!" he shouted. "I drove everyone out!"

Alec carried Rafaela into the church. A moment later, the entryway to the nave was crowded with the released prisoners who now bore the arms they had taken from the Spaniards. Tattoo and Dahlman slammed shut the heavy, bolt-studded doors and dropped the bar across the supports.

"Close and bar the other doors!" Alec ordered. "Dahlman! Take a few men with you and get up into the belfry! Tattoo, see to it that the other doors are guarded!"

Don Estebán de Vargas was beside himself. "Get reinforcements!" he shouted. "Get a piece of light artillery to blow in those church doors! I want every available man in the garrison here within ten minutes!"

Alec had placed Rafaela in a pew. He pushed the sweat-damp hair back from her pale face. "Get water, someone!" he said.

"There's none but in the holy-water font, sir," a man reported.

"That should do the trick then, eh, mate? At least for a Catholic."

Alec bathed her face and wet her lips. She opened her eyes and saw the high roof of the nave above her. She looked at Alec. "Where are we?" she murmured. "Have we died and gone to Heaven?"

Alec smiled. "Not yet, lassie. But we keep trying. Ye are safe, at least for the time being."

"Sanctuary?" she whispered.

Alec shook his head. "Ye know there is no sanctuary from the Inquisition."

"How did you get back to Porto Bello?"

Alec shrugged. "Ye might say it was God's will," he answered dryly.

"Isn't it?"

"¿Quién sabe? I will not question it. All I know now is that I am here and that ye are safe with me."

The first stroke of a battering ram struck one of the front doors of the church. The heavy, thudding sound echoed hollowly through the nave.

TWENTY-FIVE

Five hundred desperate men lay to their arms in the darkness of the jungle within eyeshot of the walls of Porto Bello. They could hear the slow and measured tolling of a bell from within the city. A faint trace of the coming moon pewter-tinted the eastern sky.

"They've failed," Joshua Swan muttered. "They've had time enough to reach the gate by now, if they haven't been cut down."

"Aye," Jan Van Schouten agreed.

Patrick Quinlan nodded. "That's likely a warning bell we're hearing. The Spaniards may already know we're out here. If they come out from the city with their entire infantry force and field artillery, it'll be the end of us."

"Damn you all!" Kate Devon snapped. "Give Cutlass a little more time!"

"This is a hell of a place to get caught by the Spaniards," Josh Swan argued. "We've no retreat other than that damned swamp we came through."

"If Cutlass is still alive, would you leave him alone in there?" Rais Gilles demanded. "He's depending on us."

Swan spat to one side. "And we're depending on him. To hell with Cutlass! I'm thinking of my own ass now and that of my lads. This was a damn-fool venture in the first place!"

Jan Van Schouten spoke out: "We haven't a chance now, unless we pull out of here right away."

"You yellow bellies!" Kate Devon raged. "Will you not stand by the Articles we signed with Cutlass?"

"Where is Cutlass now?" Swan sneered. "That damned Scots braggart claimed he'd have the gate opened so that we could walk into yon city like a stroll in the park. *No!* He's failed! The venture is a failure. I don't know about the rest of ye, but I'm pulling out of here before the moon rises and lights up the countryside to allow the Spaniards to make a partridge shoot out of us."

"Aye!" Jan Van Schouten cried.

"I'm with you both," Pat Quinlan said.

Kate Devon drew two pistols, one to a hand, and full-cocked them. She pointed one at Joshua Swan and the other at Jan Van Schouten. "Cover Quinlan, Rais," she ordered. She smiled a little. "Now, gentlemen, stand fast, or I'll put a ball between your eyes faster than you can spit."

"You're outnumbered, Kate," Josh Swan said coolly. He looked beyond her. "Between the three of us, we have three hundred men waiting for orders from us."

Kate smiled again. "Can your three hundred reach you before you're dead, Swan? Besides, maybe your men won't want to run away the way you do for fear of a few Spaniards."

It was quiet except for the constant humming of the mosquitoes and the measured tolling of the bell within the city.

"Henry Morgan took eight hundred thousand *ocho reales* out of Porto Bello," Kate reminded them. "He didn't have many more men than we have now, and none braver."

"Or more desperate," Rais Gilles added.

"Listen!" Ian MacMillan said.

The bell had stopped tolling. A moment later a distant explosion coupled with a faint crackling of gunfire sounded from within the city.

"Cutlass!" Kate Devon cried.

"He's been discovered," Josh Swan said. "I knew it!"

Kate Devon turned on Swan. "Stand fast, you beggar!" she snapped. "If that *is* Cutlass fighting for his life in there, he needs our help."

"This is hopeless!" Pat Quinlan argued. "Let's get to hell out of here!"

Kate looked through the dim, tangled aisles of the jungle where five hundred men lay silently listening to the talk between their commanders. "Listen, mates!" she shouted. "That's Captain Cutlass in that damned city, fighting his way to the gate to let you all in! Will you lie there like pigs in a wallow while a brave man loses his life for your sakes?"

"She's as mad as Cutlass," Roche Brasiliano muttered. He rested a hand on the butt of one of his pistols.

"Don't move, mustee," Terence Shannon said from just behind Brasiliano, "or I'll put a scalpel clean through your back into your black heart!"

Kate thrust one of her pistols into her belt and drew her sword. "Come on, you dirty, misbegotten slobs!" she shouted. She ran toward the city gate.

In a moment, every man in the forest was on his feet, caught up by the spirit of Kate Devon and the thought of the thousands of *ocho reales* Henry Morgan had taken from Porto Bello with only a handful more men than was numbered in their own ranks.

Dave Heckart, Jack Jamison, and Phil LaCroix were fighting for their lives within thirty yards of the city gate. The gate guards had already killed Dan Brown and Ben Lewis. The church bell had stopped tolling. The sound of an explosion from the direction of the plaza carried through the city streets. The gate guards were cautious. Five of their comrades lay dead or wounded on the bloody cobblestones, for the *corsairos luteranos* fought like demons.

Dave Heckart knew there was little chance of cutting their way through the Spaniards to reach the city gate. A sack of grenades lay at his feet. A length of burning slow match was in his left hand. The Spaniards fell back from a determined rush by the three buccaneers. Heckart ignited a grenade and lofted it over the heads of the Spaniards. He and his two mates dropped to the cobblestones. The grenade exploded. Cast-iron fragments tore into the backs of the Spaniards. The buccaneers were up on their feet in an instant to close with the dazed guards. Cutlasses rose and fell. Pistols cracked.

Heckart broke through the ranks of the Spaniards and slammed full tilt into the bolt-studded wooden gate. He looked back over a shoulder. LaCroix had gone down from a pike thrust. Jamison's broken left arm hung dangling at his side. He wielded his cutlass with his right hand, but the end was near.

Dave Heckart knew he alone could never lift the heavy wooden gate bar from its iron brackets. There could be no help from anyone. Jamison was almost helpless and could last only a few more minutes at the most. The measured thudding of many booted feet sounded on the cobblestones, and a body of Spanish pikemen rounded the next corner and double-timed toward the gate.

Dave turned. He lifted the heavy sack of grenades and hung it on one of the gate-bar supports, leaving the top of the sack open. He ignited a grenade and dropped it into the sack and then jumped sideways to stand behind the heavy buttress that supported the side of the gateway. Jamison went down from a pike thrust. The Spanish reinforcements were closing in.

A thin thread of smoke arose from the grenade sack. Dave drew his cutlass and cocked a pistol. A shattering explosion erupted from the sack of grenades. The blast and hundreds of iron fragments blew right into the faces of the approaching Spaniards. Thick, stinking smoke filled the narrow street. The heavy gate bar fell in two pieces from the gate supports. Not a Spaniard was left on his feet.

Dave Heckart, half deafened by the explosion and almost blinded from the dense, swirling smoke, grasped a huge iron ring on one of the half doors of the gate and dragged on it with all his strength. The door creaked and groaned as it opened inch by inch and then foot by foot, until Dave could stagger through the gateway.

Kate Devon was still leading the desperate charge of five hundred men toward the city gate. She was within a hundred yards of the gate when a violent, shattering explosion occurred just inside the gateway. Flames and smoke erupted above the city wall.

"The Spaniards are opening fire with artillery!" Pat Quinlan yelled. "They'll mow us down like a field of wheat!"

"You damned fool!" Kate yelled back. "That explosion was *inside* the gate! Are you not still alive? Can you see any dead or wounded? Come on, God damn you!"

One of the huge gate doors creaked inward. A lone man staggered out into the open and stared almost uncomprehendingly at the mass of yelling buccaneers nearing the gateway.

Roche Brasiliano raised a pistol and aimed it at the lone man standing just outside the gate. Rais Gilles knocked the pistol upward just as it was fired. "Damn you, Brasiliano!" he roared. "That's one of our brave lads—Davie Heckart!"

A great grin cracked the smoke-blackened face of Dave Heckart. "Cutlass is fighting for his life in the plaza, mates!" he shouted. "Follow me!" He promptly fell forward on his face.

One of the thick double doors of the church cracked with the sound of an arquebus shot as the ram broke through it. Alec Campbell loaded the last of his bullets and primed his pistols. He looked sideways at Tattoo. "Can ye get out of the church somehow, Tattoo?" he asked. "Someone will have to reach the lads outside the city walls. We can't last much longer."

Tattoo nodded. He ran through the nave toward the altar. The sacristy was to the right of the altar, and there was a barred door that opened into an arcaded cloister behind the church.

A grenade exploded just outside the front door. Stinking smoke leaked through the crack in the door. The thudding of the ram was halted. Already, many Spaniards lay dead or wounded, clustered on the broad steps and pavement in front of the church. An arquebus was fired through a great crack in one of the doors. It spat flame and smoke. One of the prisoners released by Alec fell dead beside him.

Wally Dahlman came down from the church tower. "We're down to but five grenades, captain," he reported. "We're out of bullets. Two of my men have been killed by arquebus fire and another one is dying. The plaza is filling with hundreds of soldiers. There's no sign of our men anywhere."

Alec wiped the sweat from his smoke-blackened face. He looked about himself at the taut faces of his men. Rafaela stared uncomprehendingly at Alec. This mad heretic, whom she had once thought she loved, had defiled the house of God with his killing.

The ram smashed into the door. Splinters flew into the entryway of the nave. Bullets hummed through the cracks in the doors and ricocheted from the walls. Those men who were still on their feet gathered about Alec Campbell. Their faces were grim. They would not be taken alive, for they knew if that happened, they would be sentenced to the *quemadero* rather than the galleys—if they survived the final attack of the Spaniards on the church once the doors were battered in.

The ram broke completely through one of the doors. Alec presented both of his Highland pistols and fired just over the top of the ram. Men screamed as his bullets struck home.

"We're out of bullets!" a man cried to Alec.

Alec looked across the entryway. The slotted poorbox rested there on a wooden pedestal. Alec crossed to it in five quick strides. He whipped out his broadsword and brought the blade down in a shattering blow on top of the box. Wood splintered, and the box fell to the floor. Gold and silver coins clinked on the paved floor.

Alec whirled. "There's your bullets, lads! Hammer them into shape wi' your pistol butts and send them back tae the Spaniards!"

"Sacrilege!" Rafaela shrieked. "Is nothing sacred to you, heretic?"

Alec shook his head. "'Tis not sacrilege, lassie! Maybe those coins will save our lives and yours as well!"

Alec followed Dahlman up the steep and narrow tower stairs to the belfry. A bullet smacked into one of the bells. Another bullet hummed just past Alec's ear.

Alec looked down into the plaza. "Sweet Jesus!" he exclaimed.

The plaza was packed with troops. Artillerymen were

manhandling a small field piece into position at point-blank range from the church doors. Wherever Alec looked, he saw more troops pouring into the plaza from the side streets. The strident notes of a bugle rang clearly from one of the harbor forts.

Bullets struck the tower or the heavy bells. The thudding of the ram sounded again as the Spaniards redoubled their efforts to smash in the church doors.

Dahlman lighted the fuze of a grenade with a slow match. He handed the smoking globe to Alec. "Your turn," he said with a wide grin.

Alec dropped the grenade down atop the sweating Spaniards who were working the heavy ram. The grenade exploded, scattering pieces of cast iron and leaden pellets among the Spaniards. Men were hurled backward from the explosion. They fell down the wide, blood-spattered stairs. Those who were still alive or only slightly wounded panicked and fled from the front of the church.

Don Esteban de Vargas, Steel Fist, was a paragon of strength and courage in the attack on the besieged church, but he had forgotten one paramount factor—surely Captain Cutlass had not entered Porto Bello with only a few men to rescue Rafaela de Vasquez? The *Escocis* was a madman, that was true enough, but he was also a skilled and daring soldier. Don Bartolome de Esquivel, commander of the garrison of Porto Bello, had realized that fact. While Don Esteban focused his full attention on the tempest in a teacup going on in the plaza, Don Bartolome left the plaza and hurried down toward the harbor, pushing his way past oncoming soldiers. Surely the *corsairos luteranos* would attack by sea, and here was Don Esteban, in his infinite madness, stripping most of the city's garrison to join in his insane attack on the church to capture a handful of heretics who would be dead within a few hours in any case. Don Bartolome would hold those troops who still remained in the harbor defenses to their appointed posts of duty, and as long as Don Esteban, in his madness, persisted in attacking the church, he, Don Bartolome, would be credited with saving Porto Bello in case the buccaneers attacked by sea.

Don Bartolome was secretly congratulating himself as

he rounded the corner of a street that led to the harbor past the northern city gate. His eyes opened wide. "Mother of God!" he gasped. Those were to be the last words he would utter in his life. Kate Devon's sword point passed just above the rim of Don Bartolome's cuirass and penetrated his throat. Kate hardly paused in her stride as she withdrew the blade. A mass of running buccaneers trod the body of Don Bartolome down into a reddened pulp of blood and flesh between the big cobblestones.

Kate Devon held up an arm to halt the onrush of the buccaneers from the street into the plaza. She whistled softly as she saw the massed Spanish soldiery with their backs toward her. Their attention was completely riveted on the siege of the church.

"What now, Kate?" Josh Swan asked. "If we rush them, we've hardly enough strength to take them all. We'd likely have heavy losses, and there are plenty more Spaniards elsewhere in the city."

Kate nodded. She looked over a shoulder at the men packed from one side of the street to the other. They were waiting for her next command, as though she had been accepted temporarily as their leader despite her sex and lack of experience in land fighting.

Tattoo came from beneath a shadowed arcade. He was wearing the monk's robe. He threw back the cowl and grinned at Kate.

"You black bastard!" Kate cried sharply. "Have you deserted your master? If so!" She raised her sword.

Tattoo shook his head. "My master still fights in church, Captain. The Spaniards will soon break in. He sent me for help."

"How did you get out of the church?"

"Through the back, wearing this robe." Tattoo grinned. "It was easy. No one back there but one fat Spaniard. He didn't see me until too late."

"Can you get some of us into the church without being seen?" Rais Gilles asked quickly.

Tattoo nodded. "Easy. No one back there but one dead Spaniard."

Kate looked at Rais. "What do you think, Rais?"

"It's our chance to rescue Cutlass."

The Spaniards were falling back from the church. They spread to either side to leave a wide V-shaped opening among themselves at the apex of which was the field-artillery cannon, which was aimed directly at the church doors.

"They'll blow that door down in a matter of minutes," Rais warned Kate.

Kate turned. "I want fifty volunteers to enter the rear of the church with me and hold it while the rest of the command attacks the Spaniards. It will be hot and desperate work, lads, but the altar will be covered with crosses, candlesticks, and chalices of pure gold and silver. They will be yours for the taking. Who's for it, mates? Who'll follow Kate Devon?"

Every man of the one hundred in the *Adventuress* contingent pressed forward. "I'll go! Take me! I'm for it, Katie!" they cried.

Kate turned to Rais Gilles. "I'll lead them. You take command of my men and the remainder of yours."

"What of me?" Roche Brasiliano demanded hotly. "I'm next in rank to you, Kate!"

"I'll need you to back me, Roche," Kate replied.

Josh Swan looked at the main body of buccaneers. "As soon as they leave, we'll rush the fieldpiece and turn it on the Spaniards. Quinlan, take half your crew and cover the street opening into the plaza from our rear. Van Schouten, ye'll join me in the attack on the rear of the Spaniards."

"Lead on, Tattoo!" Kate shouted.

They followed the black through a side street to skirt around the plaza. Now and again, a Spaniard would flee at their approach, but a fast pistol shot from Kate or Roche dropped him in his tracks.

Tattoo paused at a door that led into the cloister garden and then eased it open. He stole into the dark garden, still unlighted from the rising moon. He stepped over the body of the fat Spaniard he had killed during his escape from the church. The garden was deserted. Tattoo turned and whistled softly. Kate and Roche came through the doorway, followed by the men of the *Adventuress*.

The front doors of the church were masses of great splinters. A cannonball passed through the splinters, scattering them like chaff, and was deflected downward to strike the pavement within the nave. The ball rebounded and struck off the head of a man who stood near Rafaela. The head fell in front of her and spun about like a top, scattering blood across the pavement and against the *San Benito* robe she wore. Rafaela screamed and screamed again.

Alec waved his men back from their posts on each side of the shattered doors. "Stand back, lads!" he shouted. "A few more shots like that, and the doors will come off their hinges! Stand ye back and wait for their rush! There's no retreat, ye ken! We stand firm, or we die here this night!"

A cannonball smashed through a door, and it sagged back, held in place only by its massive lower hinge. Wood splinters flew through the smoky air and skewered two men. Rafaela ran shrieking into the baptistry. Bullets poured through the great holes in the shattered doors. A grenade exploded just outside of the doors, and some of the fragments sang through the air just over Alec's head. It must be one of the last of Dahlman's grenades.

Alec fired the last two bullets from his Highland pistols. He thrust the smoking pistols under his belt and then drew his broadsword. As he did so, the cannon outside blasted flame and smoke. The ball passed through a hole that had already been made and struck the high altar, smashing through it to the rear wall of the sanctuary. Chalices, candlesticks and candles, crosses, and other sacred items were scattered throughout the sanctuary. A fire started in one of the thick altar hangings.

The next cannonball blasted the sagging door from its one remaining hinge. It fell with a crash to the floor of the entryway. A triumphant shout rose from outside as the Spaniards, led by none other than Don Estebán himself, charged toward the doorway.

Alec fell back with his few remaining men. He gripped Rafaela by an arm and half led and half dragged her back with him. He thrust her behind one of the pillars of the nave and drew his last-resort firearm, his four-barreled "murtherer."

The Spaniards poured through the shattered doorway. They did not fire. This was the time for the cold steel of sword and pike. They slowed down and marched relentlessly toward the handful of smoke-blackened men who waited for them halfway down the nave.

Kate Devon and Roche Brasiliano led their men into the smoke-filled sanctuary. They were dim and shadowy figures just behind the few men who stood facing the Spaniards in a last-resort stand.

"Charge them!" Don Esteban roared. *"Adelante! Adelante!"*

Kate Devon brushed past Alec Campbell. "Get to hell out of the way, you Scots bastard!" she shouted. "Let the rest of us draw some Spanish blood for a change!" The men of the *Adventuress* closed in tightly behind Kate and Roche Brasiliano as the two of them met the charge of the Spaniards with a countercharge.

The nave rang with the clashing of steel. Firearms popped. Smoke swirled throughout the nave. Men went down, and their places were instantly taken by others. There was no quarter given from either side. If a man was wounded and went down, he was instantly killed. Don Esteban was a fighting fury, slashing and thrusting with his sword or parrying thrusts and slashes with his steel fist. A pistol ball thudded against his helmet. The shock of it caused him to stagger backward.

"Surrender, Don Esteban!" Alec shouted across the nave.

"Shit!" Don Esteban roared back.

A Spaniard thrust his pike at Alec. Alec parried the thrust and sank his sword tip into the Spaniard's throat. When he looked for Don Esteban, he saw him being helped through the doorway of the church while the last of his men retreated stubbornly, holding back the yelling buccaneers.

Alec jumped back into the baptistry to avoid a sword thrust. He parried the blade and retreated as two Spaniards came through the doorway after him. There was an intense flurry of flashing, blood-reddened blades, and when the melee was over, the two Spaniards lay dead on the floor of the room. Alec splashed water from the baptismal font over his heated face and grinned at Rafaela.

Rafaela crouched in a corner of the room. "Mother of God!" she cried. "You *like* this bloody slaughter!"

Alec grinned again. "It's no a slaughter yet, lassie! We're giving as good as we're taking!" He charged back into the nave.

The Spanish artillerymen had been reloading their piece when the buccaneers, charging from behind them, hurled their grenades. The deadly missiles exploded among the Spaniards about the gun and those who had packed together in front of the church. Before the Spaniards could recover from the surprise, the buccaneers were on them with flashing cutlasses and cracking pistols.

Ian MacMillan, master gunner of the *Adventuress*, took charge of the captured cannon. He ordered it to be double-shotted and turned to cover the main street which led from the plaza to the waterfront. The street was packed from wall to wall with Spanish pikemen driving back Pat Quinlan's fifty men.

Ian MacMillan cupped his hands about his mouth. "Quinlan!" he roared. "Fall back! Scatter to the sides!" The instant the buccaneers scattered, the big Scot fired the cannon. Two cannonballs traveling, one just behind the other, smashed into the Spaniards still packed in the street. Before the stricken Spaniards could reorganize themselves, two more cannonballs ripped through their shaken ranks with devastating effect. They dropped back from the deadly fire and then fled in panic. The cannon blasted flame and smoke once more and sent two deadly bowling balls skipping along the pavement into the backs of the stampeding Spaniards.

The impetus of the buccaneer charge in the plaza had scattered the Spaniards crowded in front of the church. Many of them died there or retreated down side streets pursued by the yelling buccaneers. Dense powder smoke drifted about the plaza and the streets, and under its cover, some of the Spaniards managed to retreat along a street that led to Fortress San Juan. They carried with them a cursing, fuming Don Estebán, who, had they allowed him, would have returned single-handed to the plaza to fight to the death. There was another personage with them—Padre de

Humana—but they had no trouble with him wanting to stay in the plaza and fight. The chief inquisitor knew well enough that if Alec Campbell found him, he would receive no mercy from the mad *Escocés*.

Don Esteban took command once again when he was within the walls of the fortress. He strode back and forth behind the landward battlements, shouting his orders: "Have the garrison of El Castillo brought here! Leave only enough men there to hold the gate against the heretics! Some of you officers who have been sitting on your fat arses behind these walls while the fighting has been going on, get out into the streets and rally any men you can find! Get them back here on the double! I want one officer-courier to get out of the city and ride to Panama for every man he can get! If the reinforcements I have requested are already on the road, I want them force-marched here! They must not follow the Panama Road directly to the city, but rather they should march first to the Chagres River and then turn toward the city! If these damned heretics should take it in their heads to retreat that way, they'll have a bloody surprise in store for them! You artillerymen! Get your heaviest guns moved back from the seaward wall to the landward wall! We'll blow those damned heretics to pieces!"

By the time the moon rose, the center of the city, that area around the plaza, was fully in the hands of the buccaneers. Groups of them ranged through the streets, killing every Spanish soldier they could find. The frightened citizenry were rounded up and herded into the plaza. The night was alive with the shouting of the buccaneers, the screaming of the Spanish women who were tracked down or dragged from their hiding places, the cracking of pistols, and the sound of doors being smashed in.

The interior of the church was a bloody shambles. It reeked of blood, powder smoke, spilled sacramental wine, and smoke from the burnt altar hangings. When the fighting had been finished within the church, the buccaneers had gathered up the gold and silver ornaments and sacred objects. Some of the men had found a store of sacramental wine within the sacristy and had gulped it down. They ranged through the nave, hacking off the arms of the religious statues with their blood-stained cutlasses. Pistols cracked as potshots were taken at the desecrated statues.

Alec Campbell wiped the blood from his sword and dirk on the doublet of a dead Spaniard. He grinned at Kate Devon. "Ye and the lads were not a moment too soon, lassie."

Kate grinned back. She handed a bottle of sacramental wine to Alec. "You have the devil's own luck, Cutlass."

Rafaela leaned against a side of the baptistry doorway. She was dazed and uncomprehending as she looked down at her blood-soaked garment.

"There's your Spanish tidbit," Kate said. She jerked a thumb at Rafaela. Her great emerald eyes studied Alec.

"Aye," Alec agreed quietly, "although I don't think the lass is in the same world wi' us now."

A drunken member of Josh Swan's crew staggered through the doorway of the church. He saw Rafaela and then swayed toward her. "Come on, lass!" he roared. "Gie us a kiss." He plucked at her robe. "What delights do ye have under there, eh?"

Alec walked up behind the drunk. "She's not for ye, lad," he said quietly.

The man whirled and drew a knife. Alec hit him in the belly and then on the jaw to drop him unconscious to the floor.

Kate drank from the wine bottle. "What can you expect?" she asked. "Five days in that stinking morass. We've likely lost a quarter of our force in dead and wounded. You can't hold them in check now. This will be a night of hell for every living Spaniard in Porto Bello."

The chief officers gathered together in the house of the alcalde. Pat Quinlan was already half drunk. Jan Van Schouten had taken a sword stroke across his scalp and now wore a bloody bandage about his head. Josh Swan had his left arm in a sling to support his forearm, which had been broken by a bullet. Kate Devon was dead weary from the five day' march to the city and the desperate fighting therein. Roche Brasiliano was in his element. The blood lust had not dissipated from his dark eyes. Rais Gilles, as always, was cool and collected.

"This situation will not do," Alec said. "The men are getting out of control. The Spaniards still outnumber us in the city and are not defeated yet. We've lost a lot of men. The rest of them are into the liquor and after the Spanish women."

"What the hell can you expect?" Roche Brasiliano demanded. "They've got a right to it!"

Alec shook his head. "Not as long as all of us are bound by the Articles. This is not the time to lose all discipline. Not when the Spaniards are sober and still in strength. Further, Don Rodrigo de Mendez is due here almost any day with reinforcements for the garrison."

"What do we care?" Pat Quinlan put in. "We can hold this city against an army!"

"With the harbor fortresses still in the hands of the Spaniards? Control of the fortresses gives them control of the harbor. Control of the harbor will allow Don Rodrigo to enter it with his ships and his men."

"The Spaniards will waste no time in sending to Panama for reinforcements," Rais Gilles added.

"How the hell do you know that?" Josh Swan demanded.

"Don Estebán de Vargas is still in command of the Spaniards. It would be the first thing he would do."

Alec nodded. "Chances are, reinforcements might be on the way already. Remember that Billy Merrill warned us that the Spaniards seemed to suspect an attack."

"Aye," Josh Swan agreed, "but he also said they suspected an attack by *sea*. Did he not also say the Spaniards had moved some of the heavy guns from the land defenses to the harbor area?"

Alec banged a fist on the table. "Dammit, Josh! Don Esteban is too good a soldier to take such a chance as that! Until we know for sure he has not sent for reinforcements from Panama, we must act as though he has!"

"If that is so," Rais put in, "we'd be caught with our bollacks in the pincers between the Spaniards here in Porto Bello and those marching from Panama."

"Shit!" Swan barked. "It's a guessing game ye're playing!"

"We can't take chances!" Alec snapped.

"What do you want us to do, Cutlass?" Kate asked.

"Strip the city of as much loot as we can within the next forty-eight hours and then get to hell out of here. Our ships should be sailing westerly by now. They could be off the mouth of the Chagres in forty-eight hours. We can march west from here wi' our loot and get picked up by the ships before the Spaniards are organized to attack us."

Pat Quinlan stared at Alec. "Are ye mad? We can't possibly get all the hidden loot wrung out of these damned stubborn Spaniards in that short a time! Besides, the men are bone-weary from marching and fighting. They've a right to some pleasure."

"What the hell good is all that loot going to do ye if the Spaniards trap us here in Porto Bello?" Alec snapped. "Ye can't spend it in the grave, Quinlan, if the Spaniards allow ye the luxury of a grave!"

"Are ye still in command then? What right have ye to tell us what to do? We agreed that ye'd be in command only until the city was taken! Well, the city *has* been taken! Your only command now is your own crew!"

Alec looked about at the other officers. "Is that the decision of all of ye?" he asked quietly. "I care not for full command, but I do care about being trapped here by the Spaniards, for, by God, that might very well happen as sure are ye are sitting here now, mates."

"We'll risk it, eh, mates?" Josh Swan asked.

All of them nodded their heads except Kate Devon and Rais Gilles.

"It's greed that's going to hold ye here, and it's greed that will lead ye tae your deaths," Alec warned them.

Roche Brasiliano smiled. "It's not the loot he was after, mates. He was after that bit of Spanish fluff Rafaela de Vasquez. What the hell does he care about us now that we took the city for him, just so he saved her futile arse from the flames? That's the real reason he's pulling out as soon as he can."

Kate Devon slapped a hand down on the table. "You haven't heard from me yet!" she cried. "Cutlass is right! I'm taking my crew along with him. All the pieces-of-eight in

Porto Bello will do you no good if Jack Spaniard shows up sober during the night and cuts your drunken throats!"

Josh Swan looked speculatively at Roche Brasiliano. "Do ye go along wi' that, Brasiliano?"

The mustee shook his head. "I'll stay on with the crew of the *Kate of Devon*. She's no longer fit to command."

Kate jumped to her feet. "Who says that? You alone? What about the crew? It's share and share alike on this venture, mustee! My crew will be putting their lives on the line every minute they stay over Cutlass' forty-eight-hour limit!"

Roche looked up at her. "Go ask your crew, Kate. Do you think you can stop them now?"

Josh Swan nodded. "Are ye siding wi' Cutlass only to win him back from the Spanish woman, Katie? Or, do ye want to stand by us to garner enough spoils to make ye rich for the rest of your natural life?"

Kate looked from one to the other of those who were against her. Their feelings were quite apparent in their scornful expressions. "I'll do what I damned well please!" she cried defiantly.

Jan Van Schouten shook his head. "That's not an answer, Katie."

Kate wanted to side with Alec even though she knew she'd never get enough loot to satisfy herself within the two-day period he had suggested. Then, too, Alec Campbell had that eerie second sight of his, a faculty with which he had always been able to forecast the probabilities in their dangerous profession. If Alec predicted a situation, as he had done this evening, odds were that he was right. Kate had seen him make such predictions in previous perilous situations, and *he had always been right.*

"After all," Pat Quinlan sneered, "she's only a woman under those men's clothes she wears. Why should we wait for this English whore to make her decision? We'll *tell* her what to do, mates."

Kate dropped a hand to the hilt of her sword. "Will you do the talking then, you Irish bastard?" she yelled. "Is it you who'll make up my mind for me? I'll..." Her voice died away as she saw the looks on the men's faces.

"Ye've lost control, lassie," Alec said out of the side of his mouth as he led Kate from the table toward the door. "Forget about them. Let Brasiliano have your men and come wi' me and my lads. If we can get out of Porto Bello with a whole skin and some of the loot, ye've still got your own ship waiting for ye off the coast, lassie."

Kate stamped through the doorway. "Go to hell, Cutlass!" she flung back over a shoulder.

Josh Swan laughed. "And all because she has a soft spot in that red head of hers for ye, Cutlass. She's thrown everything away just to side with ye."

None of them knew Kate better than Alec did, of course, but then none of them had been with Kate and Alec in the great cabin of her ship, seemingly so long ago, when he had foretold her possible future: "But ye, once your days on The Account are over, what will happen to ye? Ye'll maybe end up as a drunken, broken-down old whore in some stinking tavern in Port Royal, pissing under the table and crying in her cups about the great old days when she was known as Mad Kate Devon, the Scourge of the Spanish Main." None of the others could possibly know the great melancholia that haunted Kate Devon and belied her arrogant, swashbuckling manner as she tried to play a man's part in a purely man's world—the Spanish Main.

Alec walked out into the plaza. The area was littered with the dead, the dying, and the wounded. The pyre of the *quemadero* was on fire, and the flaring, flickering light reflected from the pools of blood dotting the pavement. Drunken buccaneers laden with loot staggered out of the great houses and dumped it on the growing piles in the center of the plaza. Casks of wine and other spirits had been placed atop tables and hauled out of the houses. Men crowded around the tables, drinking their fill from cups and goblets of pure gold and silver. The sounds of breaking wood, smashing glass, and an occasional pistol shot came from the buildings surrounding the plaza.

Rais Grilles, Ian MacMillan, and Terence Shannon joined Alec in the plaza. "This is a time when the discipline of our men will stand the acid test, mates," Alec said. "We're on our own again, and within the next forty-eight hours, we've got to gather our share of the loot and keep it tae ourselves. See if ye can round up as many men as possible. Bring them here. I'll have tae make the greatest speech in my life, ye ken, tae keep them from the liquor after what they've been through."

The moon was flooding the plaza with light when the men of the *Adventuress* gathered about Alec Campbell and their other officers. Most of them had been drinking, but none of them seemed drunk, not yet in any case. There were only sixty of them out of the original one hundred men who had marched to Porto Bello from the Gulf of Darien.

"What are the losses, Rais?" Alec asked.

"Nineteen wounded, of which five are serious or mortal. Nine dead. Twelve missing, but some of those may turn up yet."

Alec shook his head. "Still, it is better than I expected." He stepped up on a carriage block. "Ye lads of the *Adventuress!* Ye've done a fine job in the taking of Porto Bello, and ye will reap your rewards for that, but there are some things I must warn ye about. The situation here is a dangerous one. We hold only the city. The Spaniards are still in possession of the forts. A squadron of their fighting ships carrying reinforcements for the garrison here is due almost any day. There's a possibility that Spanish troops might be sent from Panama to this place. I have just had a meeting with the other captains, in which I suggested we take no more than forty-eight hours to strip Porto Bello of her riches and then get the hell out of here and back to our ships. None of them agreed, with the exception of Kate Devon, and she has been deposed by Roche Brasiliano. So, we are a separate command again. I have told them we would leave here within the forty-eight-hour limit, but that is only my decision. We are still bound by the Articles. If any of ye, or all of ye, do not agree with my decision, ye need not leave Porto Bello wi' me."

"And what if we don't?" Big Harry Armitage asked.

Alec shrugged. "Look about ye, Harry. Do ye think yon drunken fools could hold back triple their numbers of sober Spanish soldiers? Even if we stayed, our numbers would make little difference. There will be no quarter from the Spaniards after what we have done here in Porto Bello."

"But what about our share of the loot, captain?" Ralph Burdick asked. "We've come through hell to get here and have lost quite a few of the lads in the taking of the place."

Alec nodded. "I know this is askin' ye a hell of a lot, lads, but if ye can stay reasonably sober within the next forty-eight hours to collect enough loot to make the time worthwhile, I'll guarantee ye that I'll have Port Royal turned over tae ye once we get there, for your evil pleasures," Alec grinned.

"Can we talk this over?" Rob Johnson asked.

Alec waved a hand. "As ye will, lads."

A gun thundered from the direction of Fortress San Juan. Something hummed over the roofs of the houses between the fortress and the plaza. The cannonball struck the facade of a large house and rebounded to skip along the pavement and pass into a group of prisoners, scattering them in a bloody heap on the pavement. A moment later, another cannonball struck the bell tower of the church and exploded, scattering cast-iron fragments far and wide.

"There's your answer, mates!" Ralph Burdick shouted. "Jack Spaniard has made up our minds for us! I vote we agree to follow Captain Cutlass!"

The third cannonball smashed through the door of Don Estebán de Vargas' fine house and exploded within the *sala.* Wall hangings and the carpeting were set on fire. Almost simultaneously, a cannonball struck the ammunition chest of the abandoned Spanish fieldpiece. The chest blew up with a thunderous report and scattered burning fragments of wood throughout the plaza. One of the fragments set fire to a load of straw piled high in a *carreta.* The evening wind wafted, burning straw about and started a score of fires. A thickening smoke pall began to rise above the plaza. The black smoke stood out clearly in the bright moonlight, visible for many miles.

The men of the *Adventuress* had fled from the plaza and into a side street at right angles to the line of fire from the fortress. If there had been some doubt in their minds about the wisdom of Captain Cutlass' decision to leave Porto Bello within forty-eight hours, it had vanished with the appearance of the first cannonball in the plaza.

"Mates," Alec said, "we're on our own now. I want our wounded taken to the house of Don Pedro de Vasquez. Heckart, see to it that Don Pedro and his daughter get there. We'll take no other hostages. Mister Gilles will divide ye up intae strong parties for the looting. Bring the loot to the house. Take only jewelry, coins, and ornaments of gold and silver, as well as precious stones. In short, anything high in value and small in size. Remember, anything we collect, we've got to carry with us when we leave the city. Work fast and well. If ye have any trouble wi' the other crews, ye know what to do. I want a lookout sent down tae the harbor area to keep watch for Spanish ships. Tattoo will scout out on the Panama Road tae keep an eye out for approaching Spaniards."

"Is that all, Cutlass?" Rais Gilles asked.

"Find Kate Devon, and bring her tae me at the house."

Another cannonball crashed into the plaza.

"There's your starting signal, lads!" Alec cried. "Gang tae it!"

TWENTY-SIX

T he ship *Exterminator* was off the wind. She drifted aimlessly through the darkness before the rising of the moon. The sails slatted and the blocks clashed together as the ship veered back and forth. There was no one at the helm. She had been abandoned two days past by the other ships of the buccaneer squadron. Yellow Jack had struck the crew of the *Exterminator* with unusual virulence. The *vomito negro* had passed through the entire ship's company in three days. Only a few men were still alive on her decks. Their pitiful cries for help from the other ships had gone unheeded. No man in his right mind tarried long in the company of other men who burned with fever and vomited black. The *Exterminator* was now a death ship.

Once upwind and out of sight of the *Exterminator,* the other ships—Alec Campbell's *Adventuress,* Joshua Swan's *Sea Venture,* Jan Van Schouten's *Lion,* and Kate Devon's *Kate of Devon* had wasted precious little time in getting as far away from each other as they could to avoid possible contagion. One took no chances whatsoever with Yellow Jack.

Dick Walker, in command of *Sea Venture,* had turned in too close to the dangerous coast, and had not shortened sail after dark, a usual precautionary measure in those waters studded with reefs, shoals, and submerged rock formations. The lookouts did not see the telltale swirling of phosphorescence on the water which indicated an obstruction just under the surface. The *Sea Venture* was a fast and powerful ship. That night, she was carrying her courses, topsails, and topgallant sails, with a strong offshore breeze to fill them to tautness. She drove onto a spike of rock which ripped through her underwater planking like a hot knife through butter. She took thousands of gallons of water into her hull and began to list heavily to starboard. The guns of the port-side main- and gun-deck batteries began to break loose from their breechings. They cascaded down the tilted decks and crashed against the guns of the starboard batteries. The added weight of the heavy guns forced the ship over on her beam ends. In a matter of minutes, she went down. The sharks came swiftly in through the darkened waters.

The *Kate of Devon* had been steered on a course, north by northeast. She was bound for Port Royal, Jamaica, and to hell with having anything more to do with such ventures as she had just deserted.

Jan Van Schouten's *Lion* had been sailing at a distance from the *Adventuress*, and upwind. The crew had lost sight of the frigate after nightfall, but they had intended to sail with her to the rendezvous off the mouth of the Chagres to pick up the land force, *if* they reached there. The moonlight faintly tinted the eastern sky and then touched the topsails of the *Lion*.

"Sail ho!" shouted the maintop lookout of the Spanish *frigata La Victoria*.

Don Rodrigo de Mendez had been pacing the quarterdeck of his ship since dusk, hoping to see the distant, faint lights of Porto Bello. "Where away?" he called out.

"Two points off the port bow, sir!"

"Can you make her out?"

"A large ship, sir."

"Is she alone?"

"I can't see any other ships, sir!"

Don Rodrigo cupped his hands about his mouth. "Captain Morelos! Clear for action!"

A shielded lantern was used to signal "Prepare for Action!" to the other two ships of Don Rodrigo's squadron. One took no chances at any time in these dangerous waters.

The maintop lookout of the *Lion* stared at the faint

whiteness of topsails in the dimness ahead of the ship. "Sail ho!" he shouted.

"Where away?" the officer of the deck cried.

"Almost dead ahead, sir!"

"It must be the *Adventuress.*"

When the moon rose, it was too late for the *Lion* to avoid the oncoming Spanish squadron. Before she could get her guns into action, she was struck by a deadly broadside from the *La Victoria* which cleared her main deck. When each of the Spanish ships had poured their broadsides into the *Lion,* she was a stricken ship and a dismasted hulk, with a list to starboard and down by the head. Blood trickled from her scuppers. No one moved on her decks.

"Burn her, Captain Morelos," Don Rodrigo ordered.

Flaming spike-shot arched between the two ships. A score of little fires started on the *Lion.* By the time the Spanish squadron was three miles nearer the coast, the *Lion* blew up and sank hissing beneath the waves.

Don Rodrigo leveled his telescope on the pillar of smoke rising high above Porto Bello. "No question about it, Carlos, the city is on fire."

"Do you think the city has been taken, sir?"

"The presence of that *corsair luterano* ship we just sank may indicate that it *has* been taken."

"But that is hardly possible, sir!"

"There were said to be five of their ships in these waters. We have seen only one. Could it not be possible that those other four ships are in the harbor at Porto Bello?"

"But how could they get past the fortresses?"

"It is not impossible. These *corsairos luteranos* fight like devils. They may have taken the fortresses. We can't risk sailing there to find out, Carlos."

"But what can we do?"

"Steer for the old harbor at Nombre de Dios. Signal to the other ships. We'll land the soldiers there, and they can march to Porto Bello, while we return here off the city to see what can be done."

The gun flashes and faint thunder of gunfire came across the sea to the *Adventuress.* The shapes of four tall ships were illuminated by the gunfire.

Miles Yeoman lowered his telescope. "Without doubt, Spaniards attacking the *Lion,*" he said quietly.

Boatswain Pieter Heydt nodded. "We saw no other ship but the *Lion* at dusk."

Later, as the *Adventuress* closed in on the coast, a great explosion erupted, and the thundering shock of it carried across the sea. The brilliant illumination revealed the three Spanish ships standing in toward Porto Bello. A towering pillar of smoke was rising above the city.

"God help the lads," Miles murmured. "They may have failed to take the city. I always felt they were too few in numbers."

"What can we do to help them, sir?" Pieter Heydt asked.

"My orders were to take the ship to the rendezvous at the mouth of the Chagres River and wait there for three days for our men or a message from Captain Campbell. We can't risk the ship by sailing toward Porto Bello."

"I can take a pinnace back along the coast once we are at the Chagres, sir."

Miles nodded. "Good thinking, but it will be *I* who will take the pinnace back toward Porto Bello."

"But what of the ship? Can we risk losing her?"

"She'll be in your excellent hands, Pieter. There's no better seaman on the Spanish Main than you."

"But what if you don't return?"

Miles shrugged. "Then the ship is yours. I will not leave this coast until I know the fate of Captain Cutlass and the lads."

The *Adventuress* sailed on toward the mouth of the Chagres.

TWENTY-SEVEN

I t was late in the day at Porto Bello. The usual afternoon rain was overdue. It had been a day of intolerable heat and sinister silence since the bloody fighting and wild debaucheries of the night before. The sun-soaked plaza was still littered with corpses, already blackened and swollen from the great heat. The windless air was thick with the stench of decomposition mingled with the acrid odor of burnt gunpowder and charred wood. Dead-drunk buccaneers lay unconscious in the side streets or in the buildings, sometimes cheek-by-jowl with the dead. Lone looters or small groups of them prowled in and out of the despoiled houses, hunting for hidden stores of treasure. Alec Campbell and Kate Devon sat at the massive polished table in the *sala* of Don Pedro de Vasquez's house. The candlelight glistened on the heaps of gold coins, gold and silver ornaments, sacred vessels, and jewelry piled on the tabletop. There was more loot on the floor—kegs of wedge-shaped silver ingots packed like cuts of a pie, piles of expensive clothing, weapons ornamented with gold and silver inlays, mirrors framed in gold and silver, cases of fine wines, and kegs of the best brandy.

Rais Gilles and Jan MacMillan came into the *sala*. They dropped into chairs, and each of them reached for a brandy bottle. They were bone-weary, for they had been up all that night supervising the looting. They drank convulsively and then placed the bottles back on the table. "Mother's milk," Ian MacMillan said. Rais nodded. "The very soul of life," he added.

"Well, Rais?" Alec asked. "Your report?"

Rais Gilles leaned forward. "Josh Swan, Jan Van Schouten, Pat Quinlan, and Roche Brasiliano have their loot piled in a house just off the plaza. Most of their men are dead drunk or asleep. Even if they wanted to pull out of Porto Bello now, they'd never get their men to move. I've had twenty mules with panniers rounded up to transport our loot, as you ordered."

"Any report from the Panama Road?"

Rais shrugged. "Not yet."

"Mac?" Alec asked.

"The Spaniards abandoned El Castillo sometime last night. There's only a corporal's guard in charge of it now. The rest of the garrison, mostly artillerymen, reinforced the garrison at Fortress San Juan. That Spanish squadron of three ships seen off the port last night sailed up the coast and hasn't been seen since. It must have been the squadron of Don Rodrigo."

Alec nodded. "No question about it. Loaded with the rest of the relief garrison for Porto Bello."

"Maybe they sailed for Cartagena," Ian suggested hopefully.

"More likely Nombre de Dios."

"The town there is covered by jungle," Rais said. "The place was abandoned almost eighty years ago. There's nothing but a landing place there now, and none too good at that."

"Nothing but a landing place there now," Alec repeated sarcastically. "Ten miles from Porto Bello! Less than three hours' march through the jungle! Perhaps five hundred Spanish Regulars landed there sometime this morning."

"And certainly sober," Ian MacMillan added dryly.

"Still, they wouldn't approach Porto Bello by daylight for fear of ambush," Alec mused. "If they do attack, it will probably be sometime tonight, between dusk and the rising of the moon."

Rais nodded. "And the best force we can number is

about seventy men, and some of them wounded at that. We couldn't defend one wall with that number of men, much less the whole damned city, with perhaps another three hundred Spaniards sitting in Fortress San Juan who could hit us in the back. Still, if we had a few more men we could risk moving out toward Nombre de Dios to ambush the Spaniards."

"And leave all our loot?" Ian demanded.

Rais shrugged. "We couldn't take it with us. If they attack while we're still here, we'll lose the loot and our lives as well. By God, Cutlass, if those damned fools had listened to you last night, we could have enough men to strip the city of loot and get out of here in plenty of time."

"If you marched out to meet these Spaniards who are supposed to be marching here from Nombre de Dios and left the loot behind," Kate put in, "those Spaniards in San Juan would be out into the streets and manning the walls against our return, *if* we did return."

Tattoo suddenly appeared in the *sala*, by way of the kitchen and the tunnel that led beyond the city walls. His legs were plastered to the thighs with stinking mud. Sweat glistened on his muscular body. He was breathing hard. "Master!" he cried. "There are many Spaniards marching here from the Chagres River!"

"Christ's wounds!" Alec jumped to his feet. "How many of them? How close are they?"

"Three or four hundred, mebbe more. They stopped in the jungle two miles from here, like mebbe waiting for someone, mebbe more soldiers."

"Or dusk," Rais added.

"Send a man to alert Swan and the others," Alec ordered. "Get our men together, load the mules with the wounded and the loot."

Ian MacMillan stared at Alec. "Are ye mad, Cutlass? We can't get through the swamps with the mules if we start back for the Gulf of Darien. We can't get past the Spaniards between here and the Chagres."

"And we can't stay *here*, Mac!" Alec snapped.

"Then what the hell are we going to do?" Rais shouted. "We're in a bloody trap now, Cutlass!"

Alec smiled. "I can see ye never learned the wonderful game of chess, ye two. Have ye never heard of the term castling in the game? I'll tell ye—that is when ye place your king behind a line of three pawns, wi' a rook or castle, if ye will, standing at his side tae protect him against attack."

"What the hell are you talking about?" Kate demanded.

"The Spaniards abandoned El Castillo last night. It is held by a handful of men. It is on the far side of the harbor from Fortress San Juan, on a long sand spit that thrusts itself into the ocean like a stiff cock, with the fortress on the tip of it. If we can take El Castillo, we've got enough men tae man the guns. We can hold off a thousand Spaniards in there, mates!"

"My God!" Rais cried. He rolled his eyes upward. "The man is truly mad!"

Kate Devon nodded. "I've known it all along," she added dryly.

Ian MacMillan studied Alec. "And what happens then, Cutlass? We could be besieged in that fortress until we starve or surrender."

Alec half smiled. "It's better than sitting on our asses here in the city waiting for Jack Spaniard to come and get us."

"It's madness, as they say!"

Alec looked from one to the other of them. "Have any of ye a better plan?" he asked quietly.

There was no answer.

Rais drank from a brandy bottle. He put it down and wiped his mouth. "I needed that. Cutlass, how do you propose taking El Castillo? We've but seventy men. We'd stand out on that sand spit like Skittles on a bowling green."

Rain suddenly pounded down on the city. It hammered on the tiled roofs like a devil's tattoo.

Alec rolled his eyes upward. "There's your answer, Rais. It will soon be dark as well. We can use the darkness and the rain as cover. Any other questions, mates?"

No one spoke.

Alec drank from a brandy bottle and threw the empty bottle into the fireplace. "Then what the bloody hell are ye standin' around looking at *me* for? Do I have tae do *all* your thinking for ye? Ye've got your orders! *Vámonos! Vámonos!*"

"What about me, Alec?" Kate asked quietly after the others had left the *sala*.

"Are ye sober enough tae do a man's work this night?" he asked coldly.

"You can be damned hard on a person, Alec. Am I no longer of any use to you?"

Alec shrugged. "Ye've no men tae back ye. I could use those men of yours now, if Brasiliano hadn't taken them away from ye. You're all alone now, lassie."

"By God! I helped you take Porto Bello! I saved your skin in that church, didn't I?"

Alec nodded. "That ye did, and ye did well. But this is a different jig we're dancing tae now. I've little time to stand here talking to ye while ye're feeling sorry for yourself. Find something tae do!"

Alec walked toward the foot of the staircase that led up to the second floor and the bedchamber he remembered so well. Rafaela was up there now, under guard.

"Is it the Spanish tidbit you're after again?" Kate jeered. "Will you never learn about women?"

Alec turned slowly. "What the hell do ye mean?" he demanded.

Kate laughed. "She's all through with you, Cutlass. Haven't you noticed the way she looks at you now? If you haven't noticed that, you're a bigger fool than I thought you were. It's a look of sheer horror."

"I saved her life. Why should she look upon me with horror?"

"You can't stand that, can you? It pricks that damned Scots pride of yours. Imagine the thought that *any* woman could look upon the great Scots stud Captain Cutlass with horror!"

Alec was puzzled. "But why? I only came to Porto Bello to repay her for what she did for me."

"Is that the truth, Alec? My God, what a price you paid, but then it wasn't *your* life that was lost. Did you tally up the price? At least one hundred and fifty men dead or wounded on our side. Perhaps five hundred Spaniards dead in the streets. Do you understand now?" Alec shook his head.

She came slowly toward him. Her eyes were bright from the brandy she had been drinking. "Then you *are* thick-headed, pet. Rafaela saved you from the Inquisition and kept you hidden here in her house and her bed until you were able to escape from Porto Bello. She was the one who showed you the secret way to escape from the city—the secret way by which you reentered the city so that the rest of us scum could take it without storming it. Don't you see? She betrayed her own people for the love of you—a man without a conscience and a heretic to boot!"

Alec swung hard at Kate. His open hand cracked like a pistol shot against her face. She staggered and struck her side against the table. She bent over from the stunning shock and the pain and then slowly straightened up. There was a triumphant look in her great green eyes that watched him ascend the stairs to go to Rafaela.

Rafaela was alone in her bedchamber. She lay upon the bed with her right forearm across her eyes. She did not move her arm when Alec came into the room.

Alec stood beside the bed. "Rafaela," he said quietly. "What is it you want of me, Alec?" she asked. "My jewels? My body?"

"I have come to get you. We are leaving this house within the hour."

She moved her arm and looked up at him. "You're leaving Porto Bello?"

Alec smiled a little. "Not exactly. But we must get out of the city."

"Because you've looted it to the bare walls? Because you are avoiding the stench of the bodies you've left in the plaza and the streets?"

Alec shook his head. "There are soldiers marching on the city. I don't have enough men to stop them from retaking the city."

She sat up. "Where is all your bravado now?" she demanded. "That bravado you love to display while killing men?"

"That bravado and killing skill saved your virginity for you once. It saved you from the *quemadero.*"

"And you took my virginity from me here in this very bed!"

"Did I indeed? It was not a struggle, as I recall."

"Damn you! Don't remind me of that!"

Alec shrugged. "Rafaela. Will you come with me? There is not much time."

She stood up and walked away from him. "Why should I go with you? You'll not escape from my people this time. It's hopeless."

"If I do not escape, Rafaela, I will die before I am captured."

"Bravado again!" she flung back over a shoulder. She turned to face him. "Supposing I did go with you? What would be my fate? I can tell you! I'd either die beside you rather than be taken by my own people, whom I betrayed, or if you did manage to escape with that devil's luck of yours, what would happen to me?"

Alec was puzzled. Damn women anyhow! "Why, I'd take you to Port Royal with me, or to Tortuga. Perhaps even to France! I've got enough riches now! I..." His voice died away as he realized what he had just said.

The look of scorn on her face made him turn aside. "I meant I had other wealth, Rafaela," he added quickly. "I no longer need to go privateering."

"Licensed piracy," she jeered.

"You'll stay here, then?" he asked. "You know what will happen to you if your people retake the city. You'll be taken by the Inquisition again, and this time you'll not be saved."

"It matters not to me."

"It does to me!"

She studied him for a moment. "Does it, Alexander? Truly?"

He moved toward her. She made no effort to avoid him. He took her in his arms and bent her backward to kiss her with a fever and a passion that had never failed to arouse her. This time, there was no response. She remained limp in his arms, waiting solely for him to release her. At last, he stepped back from her. He knew he had lost her. Kate Devon had been right.

"You had better leave," she warned him. "Wherever it is you are going, you must not tarry too long here in Porto Bello."

Alec nodded. "What will you do?" he asked.

"I'm not sure, Alec. I can't stay here in Porto Bello."

"Where can you go?"

She shrugged. "I have relatives in Lima. One of my aunts is a mother superior in a convent there. I once thought of joining her there in the convent."

"Yes! A sanctuary, is it? Good!" he cried.

She looked steadily at him. "Not for sanctuary, Alec."

"Before God," he said quietly. "You mean…"

Rafaela nodded. "I must serve my religion and my people the best way I can for what I have done."

A quick vision came to him—those full, brown-budded breasts and those long, shapely legs of hers; the incredible ivory-hued skin so transparent that the intricate network of tiny blue veins could easily be seen.

She smiled a little. "There is no going back for us, Alexander. You understand, don't you?"

"I'm not sure."

She smiled. "You will someday."

He drove the gathering thought of great loss from his mind. "But if you stay here in the city and your people take over again, you'll be doomed if that bloodhound Padre de Humana has his way. Look! I'll send your father to ye. Leave here by means of the tunnel. There are Spanish troops a few miles from here between Porto Bello and the Chagres. They know nothing of your sentencing by the Inquisition. Your father is the governor-general of Panama. They will pass you without question through their lines and help you to Panama. Once there, take ship as soon as you can for Peru, where you should be safe with your aunt in the convent."

She smiled again. "Always the man of action."

"You'll go then?"

"Yes."

He strode to her and took her in his arms. He kissed her,

and this time she responded, almost eagerly, but then he released her and strode to the doorway.

Alec turned as he opened the door. She stood there beside her bed, looking at him. She was no longer the girl-woman whom he had made love to many times in that very chamber. She was a mature woman now and forever. It was a moment neither of them would ever forget.

Alec smiled his crooked smile. *"Vaya con Dios,* Rafaela," he murmured. He closed the door behind himself.

Rafaela heard the rapid tattoo of his footsteps in the hall and his strident voice shouting out orders. Slow tears trickled from her eyes.

The rain slashed down in a torrential downpour, pounding on the tile roof and drowning out any other sounds.

Twenty-Eight

T he rain was falling in a thick veil mingled with the indeterminate light of the dusk. The streets of Porto Bello ran ankle-deep in water. Alec Campbell and Tattoo stood in a doorway facing the long stone quay. The rest of the *Adventuress* company, along with the mule train, waited around the street corner. None of the buccaneers from the other companies had agreed to join the men of the *Adventuress* in the taking of El Castillo. They had been blinded by gold and liquor to any thought of the possibility that the Spaniards might be marching on Porto Bello.

The walls of Fortress San Juan were barely discernible through the downpour. The quay was deserted. El Castillo, isolated on the long sand spit on the west side of the harbor, was not visible at all. A rakish-looking fifty-foot *patache* was moored to the quayside directly opposite the doorway in which Alec and Tattoo stood.

Two dim figures crossed the quayside and stepped softly down onto the deck of the *patache*. Alec softly slid back the lid of the cabin scuttle. He wrinkled his big nose at the uprush of warm, fetid air from within the cabin. He eased himself down the short flight of steps. The cabin was dark. He waited a few minutes listening for any sounds of occupancy; then he felt his way about it until he found flint and steel. He struck a light. The cabin was empty.

"Tattoo," Alec called softly. "Check the hold for any Spaniards."

Alec returned to the deck. He found several small grapnel anchors and some coils of good line. The craft was equipped with long sweep oars. She mounted two *versos,* wrought-iron breech-loading cannon that could throw a three-pound ball. The *patache* would serve Alec's purpose well.

"No one else aboard, master," Tattoo reported.

Alec crossed the quayside to the side street where his men waited. "The *patache* is ours," he reported to Rais Gilles and Ian MacMillan.

"Can she take us all to sea?" Ian asked hopefully.

Alec shook his head. "With a Spanish squadron possibly waiting offshore? Besides, she'd be greatly overloaded even if we could avoid the Spaniards. Let's get on with the plan, else we'll have the Spaniards coming up behind us with blood in their eyes."

Ten men followed Alec back to the *patache.* She was cast loose and rowed by means of the great sweeps out into the harbor. They passed close to anchored ships, but no one was seen on their decks in the torrential downpour. Alec steered toward the westerly side of the long harbor where El Castillo was hidden by the rain and the gathering darkness.

Rais Gilles sent out an advance of twenty men led by Ian MacMillan. They moved swiftly and unseen along the quay front toward the base of the sand spit upon which El Castillo was sited. Rais Gilles followed them with the remainder of the men and the twenty-mule train. A rear guard of ten men waited in the side street to give the main party a chance to reach the sand spit.

"There it looms!" Rob Johnson called back from the bow of the slowly moving *patache.*

The walls of El Castillo showed dimly through the rain.

The *patache* bumped gently against the sea wall of the fortress. Grapnels were flung upward and lodged in embrasures. Alec and Tattoo climbed up quickly to the battlements and went over them to the walkway. A row of heavy cannons was ranked on either hand. Alec and Tattoo separated and catfooted to look for sentries along the wall. There were none.

One man remained aboard the *patache* while the rest of the party climbed to the top of the wall. In twenty minutes, the fortress was completely taken over, and the small guard had been locked up. Tattoo was sent to contact the advance guard of the main party. Soon, the twenty mules were led through the gateway, followed by the rear guard. The gates were closed and barred. The *patache* was moved around the outer side of the fortress and moored on the western side of it between the walls and the great salt marshes that stretched almost to the mouth of the Chagres River. The mast was unstepped and laid on the deck. The sails were spread over the deck and covered with rushes from the salt marsh.

The rain stopped. An hour later, the moon appeared. El Castillo seemed exactly as it had been before the rain and the dusk had blotted it out of sight, even to the sentries leisurely pacing behind the battlements.

Lieutenant Ricardo Espejo, the officer-courier sent out from Fortress San Juan by Don Esteban de Vargas, had contacted the Panama force east of the Chagres River. On his return toward Porto Bello, he had met the advance party of the force landed at Nombre de Dios by Don Rodrigo. Lieutenant Espejo reentered the city under cover of darkness and rain with an officer from each of the relief columns. They noted that the buccaneers had set no guards on the walls, nor were there any apparent in the rainswept streets or plaza.

Don Esteban had personally supervised the removal of his heaviest guns, two massive 42-pounders, from the seawall of the fortress to the landward wall, covering the center of the city. Upon the return of Lieutenant Espejo with the two officers of the relief forces, Don Esteban had immediately worked out a plan for a three-pronged, coordinated attack upon the center of the city, after a preliminary bombardment of the buccaneer-occupied plaza area by his heavy guns. The surprise should be complete. Meanwhile, he had sent the fastest small craft in the harbor out to contact Don Rodrigo de Mendez, commander of the three-ship naval squadron, with orders to bring his ships into the harbor at

Porto Bello as soon as possible, so that his seamen could be added to the force by which Don Estebán meant to crush the lives out of the accursed Lutheran thieves and heretics. It would be a victory that would resound throughout the Spanish Main and put the fear of God and Spanish might into the pestilent buccaneers who infested and polluted it with their presence.

"There is one man I want alive, gentlemen," Don Estebán had said at the conclusion of his orders. "Captain Cutlass!"

Padre de Humana had agreed with Don Estebán. "The man is not human but a demon," he had said in his dry, thin voice. "He must be exorcised by the Congregation of the Holy Office and then condemned to the *quemadero* along with his paramour—Rafaela de Vasquez."

Captain Juan de Narvaez, of the Panama force, had opened his mouth to tell Don Estebán and Padre de Humana that he himself had seen Don Pedro de Vasquez, governor-general of Panama, and his lovely daughter Rafaela that very evening while approaching Porto Bello, and he had helped speed them on their way to the relief force, with his instructions to send them on to Panama. It had been Lieutenant de Espejo, a longtime friend of his, who had shaken his head out of sight of both Don Estebán and Padre de Humana. Later Espejo had quickly explained to de Narvaez why he thought Don Pedro and Rafaela had fled the city. Neither Espejo or de Narvaez had any great love or even liking for Don Estebán and none at all for Padre de Humana, whom they considered in the same light he himself had considered this so-called Captain Cutlass, that is, as a demon straight from hell, despite his religious facade.

The moonlight shone on the wet roofs of Porto Bello and reflected from the pools of rainwater on the streets and plaza of the city. The buccaneer leaders, Joshua Swan, Jan Van Schouten, Patrick Quinlan, and Roche Brasiliano were in a heated, drunken argument in a large house on the plaza. Josh Swan and Jan Van Schouten had begun to be concerned about the warning Alec Campbell had sent to them. Pat Quinlan was far too drunk to make any sense. Roche Brasiliano had been waiting to see which way the wind blew. He had managed to collect a small fortune in jewelry which he had secreted away from the communal loot of the company. His only concern now was to get himself alone out of Porto Bello in the safest and most expeditious way.

Josh Swan finally staggered to his feet. "Mates!" he shouted above the squabbling. "The rain has stopped, and the moon is up. The way is not clear toward the Chagres and our ships, but if we march out now and hit the Spaniards when they least expect it, we can win through to the ships wi' our loot."

"That is madness," Roche Brasiliano argued. "We've hardly enough men, and sober ones at that, to get through the Spaniards."

"Ye forget we've got Cutlass and his men," Swan reminded him. "He's had his lads rounding up cargo mules. We can load our loot onto those mules as well as his. It's all company property, isn't it? He's got to abide by the Articles. Even if we can't load all of it on his damned mules, we can claim our shares on whatever is loaded on them."

Pat Quinlan dubiously shook his head. "Ye don't know Cutlass," he warned. "He'll never let ye get away with it."

"No matter," Jan Van Schouten said. "It's our lives that may be at stake. None of us have the skill in fighting Jack Spaniard on land that Cutlass has. If it hadn't been for him, we'd not have taken Porto Bello in the first place. Aye, he's shrewd, that one, and if anyone can save our porridge for us this night, it will be Cutlass." He nodded in solemn agreement with himself. Then he smiled a crooked smile. "Besides," he added, "once we get past the Spaniards with twenty mule loads of loot, we'll still outnumber Cutlass and his men."

Josh Swan grinned his death's-head smile. "Aye, Jan," he agreed, "and there's his fine ship, the *Adventuress,* waiting for him off the Chagres. If Cutlass doesn't survive the fighting to reach the Chagres, his ship is ours, according to the rules of the Brethren of the Coast."

Jan Van Schouten got unsteadily to his feet. "We've got to move fast, mates. I vote we get at it right away."

Roche Brasiliano nodded. "I'll round up my lads and

lead to the house where Cutlass has his headquarters." He left the house and rounded a corner, intent on heading for his secret cache of loot.

"I don't trust that damned mustee," Josh Swan growled.

"Trust him long enough to get out of here," Jan Van Schouten suggested. "Once we reach the Chagres, we'll have no further use for him either."

Josh Swan grinned. "Ye've a thinkin' head on your shoulders, Van." He looked down with speculation on Pat Quinlan, whose head had fallen forward to hit the table. "We won't have to bother wi' this one now. We'll draft his men into our companies and take over the *Exterminator* once we reach the Chagres, eh?"

"A toast to that, Josh!" Jan Van Schouten cried heartily.

They raised their glasses and grinned at each other. Somewhere toward the waterfront, a heavy cannon roared. Seconds later, a massive 42-pound cannonball came directly through the doorway behind Josh Swan and Jan Van Schouten. It cut the two of them in half and neatly struck off Pat Quinlan's head, leaving his body still seated at the table.

At the sound of the first cannon shot, the relief forces marched through gateways and converged on the center of the city, fanning out so that strong units covered each of the streets that reached out from the plaza like the strands of a spider's web. Those buccaneers who were sober enough had fled from the plaza area, leaving behind many of their dead, dying, and wounded mates. They ran directly into the Spanish units, and without their firing a shot or striking out with a cutlass, every last one of them was shot or cut down.

The bombardment stopped on schedule. Gunpowder smoke swirled throughout the plaza and the side streets. The only sounds to be heard were the steady thudding of booted feet on the wet cobblestones and the clashing of arms as the Spaniards took complete control of Porto Bello.

Ramón had been sleeping with a drunken Teresa in Rafaela de Vasquez's fine bed. He raised his head as he heard the distant sound of cannonading. He crawled over Teresa's naked, sweating body and dressed quickly. He looked back at her once to make sure she was still asleep.

Ramón had no intention of taking her with him when he left Porto Bello forever.

Ramón stepped out into the hallway and looked down into the *sala*. A man had just entered the house. Ramón lay down on the floor and watched him through the space between two uprights. The intruder struck a light. He placed a sack on the table and emptied it. Ramón whistled softly. The candlelight shone on a heap of fine jewelry that could be worth a small fortune. Now and then, the man would glance toward the entryway of the house. Ramón recognized him. It was Roche Brasiliano, the big mustee mate of Kate Devon.

Ramón softly descended the staircase with a cocked pistol in his right hand and a dagger in his left hand. He paused at the foot of the stairs.

Roche Brasiliano whirled. He dropped his hand to a pistol butt and then slowly removed the hand as he saw the weapons in the halfbreed's hand. He recognized the man.

"What's going on out there?" Ramón asked.

"The guns of Fortress San Juan are bombarding the plaza."

"Why?"

Roche shrugged. "There is a rumor that the Spaniards are approaching Porto Bello."

Ramón nodded. "Cutlass was right, then."

"Where has he gone?"

"Who knows? If he has gone west of the city, he'll run into the Spaniards, but Cutlass is too smart for that."

"Where else could he have gone?"

Ramón shook his head. "He's like the devil, that one. They'll never kill him. No matter. What are you doing here?"

"I had hoped to find Cutlass here and go with him."

Ramón's eyes wandered a little. He studied the heap of fine jewelry on the table. Ramón had planned to secrete the loot Cutlass and the others had left behind, to return some day when it was safer and regain it. That, of course, would be extremely hazardous.

"Did Cutlass leave here by the tunnel?" Roche asked.

"With twenty mule loads of loot?" Ramón grinned. "It's almost too narrow for a man to get through."

"You know where it is?"

"Of course!"

"You'll show me?"

Ramón shrugged. "At a price, friend."

"What price?"

"Say a half of that heap of jewelry."

"Damn you! No!"

Ramón smiled. "One can but try. A quarter then?"

"All right," Roche growled.

The cannonading had stopped.

"Follow me," Ramón said. He took the candle and led the way toward the kitchen and then down the stairs into the cellar. He waited for Roche at the bottom of the stairs. "Over there," Ramón said, as he pointed toward a dark corner of the cellar behind the piled-up casks and barrels. He placed the candle on top of a barrel.

"Show me," Roche said.

"There's no time, friend. The Spaniards will likely be in the streets by now. I'll take my quarter of the jewels now."

"Hold out your hands," Roche said. He poured about a quarter of the sack's contents into the cupped hands of the eager Ramón. His knife blade was thrust under the outthrust hands and into Ramón's belly. As the halfbreed fell, the withdrawn knife struck him in the side of the throat and was ripped sideways.

Roche picked up the pieces of jewelry. He poured them back into the sack and grinned. He took the candle and felt his way back behind the casks and barrels. There was nothing there but a stone wall draped with spider webs and shiny with moisture.

The mustee raged around the cellar, battering at the walls and wooden paneling with his fists. He stood there sweating and trembling. He heard the sound of heavy foot-steps on the floor above the cellar. When the Spaniards found him hours later he was crouching in the darkness behind the casks and barrels with his sack of jewelry held closely against his chest. There was no comprehension in his eyes as they dragged him up the stairs and finished him off in the street.

By the light of dawn, Porto Bello did not have a living buccaneer within its walls. The bodies of the dead, including those left after the buccaneer attack, both Spaniard and buccaneer, were loaded on carts and carried beyond the city walls and dumped in a great pyre downwind from the city. None of the bodies had been identified as being that of Alec Campbell.

Don Estebán de Vargas raged in his headquarters at Fortress San Juan. He smashed his steel fist down repeatedly on the top of the table before him. "Look again, God dammit!" he roared. "He cannot have escaped! One escape from us was too much! This is the third time he has done so!"

"We have searched the city from one end to the other, sir," Captain de Narvaez explained. "Not one hiding place has been overlooked."

"Perhaps he escaped through the jungle?"

The officer shook his head. "There was no chance of that, sir. He would have had to stay on the trails either east or west of the city. He could not have passed us on those trails as we approached the city."

"What about the swamps?" Padre de Humana suggested. "That was how they got to Porto Bello."

"With twenty mule loads of loot?" Don Estebán said dryly.

"Perhaps they escaped by sea," Lieutenant Espejo said.

Don Estebán nodded. "That is possible. They could have managed it during the rainstorm and the darkness. A *patache* has been reported as missing. They are fine seamen," he admitted grudgingly. "Still, the vessel would have been greatly overloaded with all those men and loot."

"And twenty mules?" Captain de Narvaez asked.

A lieutenant of artillery came into the headquarters. "Sir," he reported. "The squadron of Don Rodrigo is just off the harbor. They waited for daylight before attempting the channel."

Don Estebán nodded. "There's your answer, Lieutenant

Espejo," he said. "The heretics could not have gotten past Don Rodrigo. Perhaps he has them aboard."

When the *frigata La Victoria* dropped anchor in the harbor, Don Rodrigo de Mendez reported at once to Don Esteban. He had not seen any small craft at sea other than the one that had been sent with orders for him to report to Porto Bello. "There's no chance any such *patache* could have gotten past me, Don Esteban," he added.

At sunrise, the flag of Spain was raised to the top of the flagstaff of El Castillo with a spirited accompaniment of trumpets and drums. The sun flashed from the polished helmets of the guard that had been left in charge of the fortress. There was evidently no slackness in the little command at the fortress.

The frigate *Adventuress* was heaved off the mouth of the Chagres. Now and again, the bright morning sun flashed from polished metal on the shore. The distant thunder of cannon had rumbled down the coast from Porto Bello the night before.

Miles Yeoman lowered his telescope. "Spaniards," he said. "The damned fools don't realize the sun is shining on their helmets."

Pieter Heydt nodded. "Aye, sir, but we *know* they are there. If our lads have left Porto Bello and are marching here to the rendezvous with us, will *they* know the Spaniards are waiting for them in the jungle?"

Miles Yeoman looked toward the east. "By God, Pieter," he said quietly, "I do not know what to do. This waiting and wondering is murderous." He snapped the telescope shut. "I can take it no longer! Have the pinnace lowered into the water. I'll risk sailing her close along the shore toward Porto Bello. Perhaps I can see the lads on the beach if they have left the city."

"There are Spanish naval ships near Porto Bello," the boatswain warned.

"I'll keep in the shoal water. Out of musket shot from the shore and cannon fire from the sea. The Spaniards will not risk a fine ship in shoal water to take naught but a pinnace."

Pieter grinned. "Especially one that is flying Spanish colors, eh, sir?"

The big pinnace was lowered into the water. Miles Yeoman and five men sailed her toward the east and distant Porto Bello.

Pieter Heydt bowed his head in prayer. "God help all the lads," he said softly.

TWENTY-NINE

Alec Campbell studied the distant ramparts of Fortress San Juan through a telescope. He had been studying the streets of the city and the ships in the harbor for over an hour. The late afternoon sun was low in the west. Hundreds of seamen armed to the teeth had been taken from the three naval ships in the harbor to join the soldiers in the town. He turned the powerful glass toward the sea. There were no ships in sight except for a tiny craft inching its way from the west and close inshore just beyond the coastal rollers and within the dangerous shoals that studded the coast line for hundreds of miles. He could just make out the red and yellow flag of imperial Spain snapping at her jackstaff.

"It's only a matter of time before they send the garrison back to this fortress," Rais Gilles said from behind Alec.

"If we try to hold them back, Cutlass," Ian MacMillan added, "the Spaniards will know we're here, and if we know Don Estebán, he won't rest until he's blown this fortress down stone by stone to get at us. Ye used the chess term castling tae describe the move into El Castillo. How would a chess master defeat one who has castled?"

Alec turned and leaned his back against the battlements. "He'd use his most powerful pieces on an open board, Mac. His queen and rooks, if he still has them, to force a checkmate."

"And our opponent has his queen and rooks," Rais Gilles said dryly. "The heavy guns of Fortress San Juan and his three naval ships lying there in the harbor within easy cannon shot of us."

"What would a player do when his castle defense is broken?" asked Terence Shannon.

Alec shrugged. "Defend his king with his most powerful pieces and try to check or checkmate his opponent's king."

"And if he has no powerful pieces left?" Ian MacMillan asked.

"Stalemate," Alec replied quietly.

"Which is it to be, Cutlass?" Rais asked. Alec looked along the row of heavy guns which peered through their embrasures out toward the harbor. "Don Estebán moved his heaviest artillery pieces from the sea wall to the land wall. He has not moved them back as yet. How heavy would you say they were, Mac?"

"The biggest should be 42-pounders," Ian replied. "I would say all he has covering the sea approaches would be perhaps a 32-pounder, some 24-pounders, and maybe some 18-pounders."

Alec looked along the line of guns again. "And what have we here?"

"One 42-pounder, the rest are 18-pounders."

"Is there a hot-shot furnace?"

"Aye, there is, Cutlass."

Alec grinned. "Stoke it up, then, Mac. Heat up plenty of shot."

"The smoke will be seen by the Spaniards," Rais objected. "They'll know something is wrong."

Alec nodded. "But by that time, we'll be making our move."

The hot-shot furnace was lighted and stoked. The smoke rose above the battlements of El Castillo and stained the sky. When the fire had begun to burn down into a thick bed of embers, the 42-pound and 18-pound solid shot were placed on top of the embers and another roaring fire built up about them.

The gunner's mates prepared the guns for action. Powder charges were brought up from the magazine. Boxes of spike-shot were placed beside the guns and their shanks wrapped in tar-soaked rope. All the time this preparation was going on, a close watch was kept on Fortress San Juan and the naval ships in the harbor. Curious seamen lined the railings of the ships in the harbor to watch the thick smoke rising from El Castillo. Soldiers at Fortress San Juan watched from the battlements.

Don Esteban was summoned by the officer of the guard. He came up to the battlements and was handed a powerful telescope. He studied the distant fortress across the harbor.

"Is it possible that the place might be on fire, sir?" Captain de Narvaez suggested.

"We would have been notified by now, captain."

"Shall I make an inspection?"

Don Esteban nodded. "And take a company or two with you, de Narvaez."

The captain was puzzled. "You don't think?" His voice trailed off.

"The heretic Campbell could not have vanished into thin air, Captain de Narvaez," Don Esteban said dryly.

Don Rodrigo de Mendez came up to the battlements. "I request permission to return my men to my ships, sir. They are no longer needed ashore. There are hardly enough men left on my ships to handle them in case of emergency."

"Do so," Don Esteban said. He looked at Don Rodrigo. "What do you think, Don Rodrigo? Is it possible that devil of an *Escocés* has taken over El Castillo?"

And has he taken Rafaela de Vargas in there with him? The thought was that of Don Rodrigo. No trace of Rafaela and her father had been found in Porto Bello, either among the living or the dead.

Padre de Humana had been standing at the battlements gazing intently at distant El Castillo as though he would bore a hole through its walls with his burning eyes. He looked sideways at Don Rodrigo. "You did not answer Don Esteban's question, sir," he said.

Don Rodrigo hated the cleric with a passion he dared not show by word or deed. He knew well enough that if Rafaela de Vargas were found in Porto Bello, she would not escape the *quemadero* this time. Was it possible that

Captain Cutlass *was* in El Castillo and *that Rafaela de Vargas was with him?* Teresa, Rafaela's serving woman, had confessed to the Inquisition that her mistress had indeed saved the *Escoces* from the Inquisition, had hidden him in her house for many weeks, and then had been instrumental in helping him to escape from Porto Bello. "Don Rodrigo?" Don Estebán asked sharply. Don Rodrigo looked quickly at his commanding officer. "It is possible, sir. In that case, I'd like to command the troops that are sent there to investigate."

"That is not your duty, sir!" Don Estebán snapped. "Your duty is with your ships!"

"But, sir..." Don Rodrigo's voice died away. He could not make it apparent that he wanted to find Rafaela de Vargas at any cost, perhaps even of his duty, and if Alec Campbell did indeed have Rafaela with him, perhaps it was for the best. It would be far better for her to die in El Castillo than to be turned over to the Inquisition. Don Rodrigo could not bear to think of the latter prospect.

"De Narvaez!" Don Estebán said. "Get over to El Castillo! Take a battalion with you! Don Rodrigo! Get your men back aboard your ships! Prepare your ships for action against El Castillo if necessary! Lieutenant Espejo! See to it that the heavy guns on the landward wall are returned to their original positions! *Vámonos! Vámonos!*"

A battalion of musketeers was formed on the quayside under the command of Captain de Narvaez and then marched toward El Castillo. The seamen of the naval squadron were assembled in the plaza preparatory to returning to their ships. Artillerymen and engineers made their preparations to move the massive 42-pounder guns from the landward side of Fortress San Juan to the seaward side, where they could, if necessary, cover El Castillo. Meanwhile, the column of smoke rose higher and thicker above El Castillo.

Rais Gilles studied the small craft flying the Spanish flag that was tacking back and forth in the shoal water beyond the salt marshes. Rais was getting concerned. A detail of men had been unloading the mule panniers of treasure which they took up to the battlements overlooking the concealed *patache.* Rope ladders and slings had been prepared so that the treasure could be lowered to the *patache.*

"Fisherman, do you think, sir?" Dave Heckart asked Rais.

"Flying Spanish colors? Hardly."

"Guarda-costa, then?"

"She's small for that, but it's possible. If they have a good glass aboard her, they could see us loading the treasure into the *patache.* That could create quite a situation, eh, Heckart?"

Heckart looked toward the sun. "It will be dusk before long. I could take a few men out there and check that craft out."

"A risky business, bosun."

The boatswain nodded. "Aye, but if by the devil's own luck we could escape from here with the *patache,* she'd be down to her gunwales what with the weight of treasure and all the men aboard her. That's a good-sized craft out there. We could use it."

"I'll take it on myself to let you go," Rais said.

Alec Campbell leaned over the railing above the court-yard where the hot-shot furnace was located. "How do they look, Mac?" he called down.

The big Scot looked up. "They're beginning to glow, Cutlass."

"How much longer?"

Ian shrugged. "Twenty more minutes should do the trick."

Alec shook his head. "Ten minutes, no more. Spanish infantry are at the foot of the spit. Seamen are being ferried out tae the ships. Jack Spaniard suspects something."

Alec turned back to the battlements. "Ready, Dahlman?" he asked.

Dahlman nodded his head. "Four of the 18-pounders will fire hot-shot. Four others will fire burning spike-shot. I've checked the range to a gnat's hair, sir. Just give us the word!"

Captain de Narvaez was a brave but cautious soldier. He halted his battalion just out of good musket range from the fortress. Everything looked in order. Sentries in the red and yellow uniforms of Spain paced back and forth on the battlements. The flag of Spain ruffled in the rising breeze from the land. Still, there was that damnable column of smoke rising from within the fortress.

Captain de Narvaez looked back at his command. "Are any of you familiar with the fortress?" he asked. Sergeant Carlos Vaca stepped forward.

"I am, sir."

"What would that smoke be? From the cooking ovens?"

The sergeant shook his head. "The chimneys from them are on the far side of the fortress just behind the sea wall, sir."

"Where could that smoke be coming from?"

"Only one place, my captain—the hot-shot furnace." De Narvaez was startled.

"But why? On a day as hot as hell's hinges?" His voice died away. "Mother of God!" he cried. He looked toward the harbor, crowded with shipping, merchant vessels, and naval craft alike. He looked again at the fortress. He looked down at the soft-surfaced road under his feet. The surface was pocked with many footprints and hundreds of hoof prints, each print with its own individual puddle of rainwater from the storm of the night before. He looked again at the fortress. A horrible thought flashed through his mind.

One of the massive 42-pounder guns on the harbor side of El Castillo blasted flame and smoke. A ponderous cherry red cannonball flew toward the shipping in the harbor. The ball struck squarely amidships on the *La Victoria*, the *frigata* commanded by Don Rodrigo de Mendez. A moment later there was a rippling discharge of gunfire from a row of 18-pounder guns aligned on the battlements of El Castillo. Glowing red cannonballs and flaming spike-shot arched out across the darkening harbor toward the three naval ships.

Two 18-pounders, one on each side of the gateway of El Castillo, roared. The projectiles struck deep into the massed ranks of the battalion of musketeers, scattering them right and left.

"Stand fast!" Captain de Narvaez shouted. It was a foolish command. No battalion of infantry in the world could stand fast on that open sand spit under point-blank range from two cannons.

The guns were fired again. The cannonballs slammed into the backs of the fleeing musketeers and smashed them to pieces. By the time the Spaniards reached the end of the sand spit, a quarter of their number lay dead, dying, or wounded on the sands, and among them was Captain de Narvaez, who was missing both his legs.

Gunner's Mate Dahlman ranged back and forth behind his charges as the heavy guns were sponged, charged, and shotted. They bellowed constantly and slammed back in their carriages. Smoke was rising from the hulls of the three naval ships.

Ian MacMillan lowered his telescope with which he had been studying the distant battlements of Fortress San Juan through the rising smoke. "Elevate the 42-pounder and take the fortress under fire, Dahlman," he ordered. "They're beginning to man the guns over there for counter-fire. Keep up the fire on the ships."

The Spaniards were trying to get up sail on the harbor shipping, but even as they hoisted the sails, some of them were already in flames. Burning pieces of canvas floated about on the rising breeze and alighted on other ships.

There was no cessation of the gunfire from El Castillo. Forty-two-pound cannonballs arched through the air and passed beyond the burning ships to slam into the battlements of Fortress San Juan. Guns were upset. Crews were smashed into fragments. A powder store blew up and set fire to other powder stores arranged on the battlements. Within fifteen minutes, the battlements were untenable.

The harbor was thickly shrouded with powder smoke through which the incessant gun flashes from El Castillo forked like heat lightning. Flames were now soaring up from the *La Victoria*. The Spanish gunners on the ships were afraid to bring powder charges up from the magazines for fear they'd be set off by the growing fires. Not one cannon shot was gotten off by the three naval ships.

Rais Gilles appeared through the smoke wreathing the battlements of El Castillo. "Sir," he reported, "the treasure is loaded. We can evacuate as soon as you're ready."

Alec nodded. "Well done." He grinned. "We may not have checkmated Jack Spaniard as yet, Frenchman, but we've damned well checked him!"

"We're out of hot-shot, sir," Ian MacMillan reported.

"Spike all the guns except those that are still firing, Mac. Rais, I want every man not working the guns to get into the *patache*. Raise the mast. Hoist the sails. Ye ken?"

Rais nodded. "I ken," he said drolly.

Kate Devon came through the battle smoke to Alec. "That small Spanish craft is nearing the west side of the fortress, sir. Shall I take it under fire?"

Alec shook his head. "It may be Davie Heckart and his lads. Make sure of it, Captain Devon."

"Aye, aye, sir!" Kate replied smartly.

"Guns are all spiked, sir," Ian MacMillan called out.

The Spanish shipping was thickly shrouded in smoke through which the myriad fires showed like rubies strewn on gray-black velvet. Dusk light was settling in on Porto Bello.

The crepitation of the hammering guns shook the pavement under Alec's feet. He looked once more toward the burning ships of Don Rodrigo's squadron. A few scattered raindrops began to fall.

Kate Devon came running to Alec. "You were right, Cutlass! The small craft was the pinnace from the *Adventuress!* Miles Yeoman has brought her in close under the fortress walls and is taking some of the men aboard her."

The fire of the eight 18-pounders died out. Only the Huge 42-pounder roared at intervals, still slamming her shot through the thick smoke.

"Ian!" Alec cried.

"Aye, sir!"

"Spike all the guns except the 42-pounder! Send your gunners tae the small boats! Load the 42-pounder with one last shot!"

In a little while, only Alec, Ian MacMillan, and Wally Dahlman were left on the battlements of El Castillo. The two gunners grinned at Alec with their smoke-blackened faces.

Alec grinned back. "Fire your last shot, Dahlman."

The gunner's mate shook his head. "The honor is only yours, sir." He handed the burning slow match to Alec.

Alec looked toward Porto Bello, now covered with a pall of gunpowder smoke mingled with the smoke from the burning ships. For a fleeting moment he thought of Rafaela, and then he applied the slow match to the touchhole of the great cannon.

The rain began to patter steadily down on El Castillo, and then the deluge came, pouring down in solid-looking sheets from the lowering skies.

The dawn light tinted the eastern sky. When the sun rose, the light struck the topgallant sails of the frigate *Adventuress*. The coast of Panama was a dim line far astern from which a pall of thick smoke seemed to be sprouting.

"Mister Yeoman!" Alec Campbell called out. "Set your course nor'-nor'east for Port Royal, sir!"

"Aye, aye, sir!"

Rais Gilles looked at Alec. "I'd never have believed you'd get us out of Porto Bello with a whole skin, Cutlass."

Alec shrugged. "'Twas easy, Rais. A knowledge of chess and of good men is all it takes in such situations."

They grinned at each other.

"Can ye take this watch?" Alec asked.

Rais nodded. "With pleasure. I couldn't sleep now, in any case."

"Easy enough, Frenchman, just set your mind on it."

Alec walked to the break of the quarterdeck. Kate Devon was waiting for him in his bed in the great cabin.

"Cutlass!" Rais called out

Alec turned. "Aye, Rais?"

"Can *you* sleep now?" Rais asked.

Alec studied the Frenchman for a moment. "Aye, I can, if need be," he replied.

"I thought so."

Alec turned and descended the ladder to the main deck. He looked back at Rais and grinned. *"Cruachan!"* he shouted, and then he vanished below.

A Look at: Calgaich the Swordsman

The heroic journey of a Barbarian turned Gladiator...

Son of a barbarian chieftain and a Roman noblewoman, Calgaich mac Lellan is exiled from his beloved country after slaying his cousin in a sword duel over the beautiful but vain Morar, "The Golden One." When his father is betrayed into the hands of the Romans by the one closest to him, Calgaich vows to overthrow his treacherous uncle and to take his rightful place as chief of the Novantae.

The gods do not mean to let you return home.

Recalling the prophecy of Cairenn, the bewitching slave woman, Calgaich is captured and condemned to the arena in Rome, from which few gladiators emerge alive. Will Calgaich have the strength to claim something once thought impossible for a man of his background and upbringing?

"A powerful dramatic story." **—Dana Fuller Ross, bestselling author of the Wagons West series**

AVAILABLE NOW

ABOUT THE AUTHOR

Gordon D. Shirreffs published more than 80 western novels, 20 of them juvenile books, and John Wayne bought his book title, Rio Bravo, during the 1950s for a motion picture, which Shirreffs said constituted *"the most money I ever earned for two words."* Four of his novels were adapted to motion pictures, and he wrote a Playhouse 90 and the Boots and Saddles TV series pilot in 1957.

A former pulp magazine writer, he survived the transition to western novels without undue trauma, earning the admiration of his peers along the way. The novelist saw life a bit cynically from the edge of his funny bone and described himself as looking like a slightly parboiled owl. Despite his multifarious quips, he was dead serious about the writing profession.

Gordon D. Shirreffs was the 1995 recipient of the Owen Wister Award, given by the Western Writers of America for "a living individual who has made an outstanding contribution to the American West."

He passed in 1996.